THE IRON HORSE

Derby Day at Epsom Downs. A multitude of people crowd to watch the races: dukes and dustmen, bishops and beggars, privileged ladies and prostitutes. It is a hotbed for crime and crooks of all kinds. With the nation a-flutter in the run up to this national event, a disembodied head is discovered on a passenger train at Crewe, the first in a murky course of events that takes in murder, fraud and race-fixing. Detective Inspector Robert Colbeck and his assistant are assigned to the case, and are forced to ask themselves, just how much is someone prepared to hazard to win?

THE IRON HORSE

THE IRON HORSE

by

Edward Marston

Magna Large Print Books
Long Preston, North Yorkshire,
BD23 4ND, England.

British Library Cataloguing in Publication Data.

Marston, Edward
    The iron horse.

    A catalogue record of this book is
    available from the British Library

    ISBN   978-0-7505-2750-7

First published in Great Britain in 2007 by Allison & Busby Ltd.

Published in Large Print 2008 by arrangement with
Allison & Busby Ltd.

Magna Large Print is an imprint of Library Magna Books Ltd.

Printed and bound in Great Britain by
T.J. (International) Ltd., Cornwall, PL28 8RW

CHAPTER ONE

1854

The accident could have happened to anyone but it was much more likely to befall Reginald Hibbert. He had, after all, a tradition to maintain. Hibbert was not so much clumsy as unlucky. Whenever there was an opportunity to stub his toe, or tear his clothing on a protruding nail or bruise himself by walking into an unexpected obstruction, he would somehow always manage to take it. His devoted wife, Molly, had lost count of the number of times he had returned from work with a black eye, a decided limp or a jacket unwittingly ripped open. Life with Reginald Hibbert meant that there was a constant demand on her sympathy.

'Be careful, Reg!' she cried.

But her warning came too late. He had already tripped over the step by the back door and pitched helplessly forward on to the hard stone floor of the scullery. The tin bath he had been carrying hit the slab with a loud clang then bounced out of his grasp. Hibbert landed heavily on his left hand before rolling over. His wife bent over him.

'Are you hurt?' she asked solicitously.

'No, no,' he replied bravely. 'I'm fine, Molly.'

'You always forget that step.'

'I just didn't see it with the bath in my hands.'

'You should have let me bring it in.'

7

'It's my job now,' he said seriously. 'A woman in your condition must be spared any lifting. You must learn to take it easy.'

'How can I take it easy on washing day?' she said, clicking her tongue. 'Besides, the baby is not due for months and months. Now, come on – get up off that floor.'

When she grabbed his left hand to pull him up, he let out a yelp of pain and snatched it swiftly away. Rubbing his wrist gingerly, he got to his feet and almost fell over the tin bath. His wife quickly retrieved it and put it on the table. She studied him with a love that was tempered by mild irritation.

'I wish you didn't keep doing that sort of thing, Reg.'

'What sort of thing?'

'Hurting yourself all the time.'

Hibbert grinned amiably. 'I'm a big boy. Nothing hurts me.'

But he was clearly in pain and winced as his left hand brushed the sink. His wife took charge at once. Leading him into the next room, she made him sit down so that she could examine the injury, doing so with great tenderness. They were in their little red-brick terraced house in Crewe. Cramped, cluttered and featureless, it had two small rooms and a scullery. A bare wooden staircase led up to two bedrooms, one at the front and the other at the back. The privy was at the end of the tiny but well-tended garden.

To a married couple in their late twenties, however, it was a paradise after years of sharing an even smaller house in Stoke-on-Trent with

Molly's intrusive parents. The Hibbert household had only one major defect. It bristled with possibilities of incurring minor accidents and he had explored them all.

His wife scrutinised the injured wrist.

'I think you may have broken it, Reg,' she said with concern.

He gave a boastful laugh. 'I don't break that easy.'

'You ought to see a doctor.'

He shook his head. 'I can't afford to, Molly. With a baby on the way, we need to save every penny that we can.'

'Then stay off work for a day or two.'

'And lose my pay? No chance of that.'

'At least ask Mr Fagge to put you on light duties.'

'Douglas Fagge does *nobody* any favours,' said Hibbert grimly as an image of the head porter came into his mind. 'He's a slave driver. If I showed even the slightest sign of weakness, he'd be down on me like a ton of bricks.'

'Then let me come to the station with you. I'll speak to him.'

'Oh, no! That wouldn't do at all.'

'You need to rest that hand, Reg.'

'I need to do my job properly,' he said, rising to his feet and easing her away. 'Think how it would look. If my wife came and asked for special treatment for me, I'd be a laughing stock.'

As it was, Hibbert was often the butt of his colleagues' jokes and he did not wish to offer them more ammunition. He was a short, thin individual with a shock of red hair and a bushy moustache

9

that acted as the focal point in a freckled face. The fact that his pretty wife was both taller and older than him caused much amusement at the railway station and he wanted to protect her from the routine mockery that he endured. Though she was still in the early stages of pregnancy, he was afraid that someone would guess their little secret, exposing him to endless ribald comments. Whatever happened, he resolved, his wife must be kept away from his place of work.

'That wrist needs seeing to,' she urged.

'I sprained it, Molly, that's all.'

'At least let me put a bandage around it.'

'No need,' he said, bending forward to give her a farewell kiss. 'It feels better already. In any case, I have to be off straightaway. Now remember what I said – if that washing is too much for you, leave it until I come home.'

'I can manage,' she said, touched by his consideration. 'Forget the washing. I'm more worried about that poor wrist of yours.'

'There's nothing wrong with it, I tell you.'

By way of demonstration, he clapped his hands several times together then held up both palms, beaming as he did so. It was only when he had left the house that the agony showed in his face.

Until the arrival of the railway in 1837, Crewe had been a sleepy hamlet in the heart of the Cheshire countryside. Three separate railway companies then moved in and Crewe became the connecting point for their respective lines. The Grand Junction Railway, the largest of the companies, soon bought large tracts of land around Crewe and moved its locomotive and carriage works there. It also built two hundred houses for the employees it attracted to the area. When the GJR was absorbed into the London and North West Railway in 1846, the latter markedly increased the number of dwellings and added churches, chapels, schools, shops, public houses and all the amenities needed by a growing community.

An archetypal railway town had been created.

Reginald Hibbert had been delighted to move there with his wife. He loved the fact that he worked at the hub of the LNWR. Passenger and freight trains came in and out from all directions. The variety was unlimited. No two days were the same. There was always something new, exciting and unscheduled. As a porter, he gave directions to board trains, stowed luggage on the roofs of departing carriages and unloaded it on arrival before carrying it out to waiting cabs and horse-drawn omnibuses. Dealing with the public was what he enjoyed most. His wage might not be high but it was regular and he gained immense satisfaction from his work.

As he approached the station that morning, he gazed at it with pride. Four years earlier, the LNWR had replaced the original building with a larger and much more ornate one. In Hibbert's eyes, it still had an air of newness about it and he always felt a slight thrill as he went through its doors. He was content with his lot, asking nothing more of life than to be doing a valuable job at an important junction on the railway network. Hibbert entered the station with a spring in his step. In spraining his wrist at home, he had already had

11

his daily accident. That, he hoped, absolved him from any further mishaps.

There was, of course, still the wrath of his boss to be faced.

'Hibbert!'

'Good morning, Mr Fagge.'

'You're two minutes late.'

'I'm sorry, sir. I was held up by–'

'Spare me your excuses,' snapped Douglas Fagge, interrupting him with a dismissive wave of his hand. 'I've heard them all before. You're working on Platform Two.'

'Yes, Mr Fagge.'

'Well, don't stand there, man. Get across there quickly. The next train is due in five minutes.'

'Three, actually,' corrected Hibbert, who knew the timetable by heart. 'It's the through train to Carlisle.'

'That's immaterial,' said Fagge testily. 'I'm talking about the Birmingham train that terminates here in...' He consulted his watch. '...in less than five minutes. All available porters must be on duty.'

'Of course, Mr Fagge.'

'One small plea.'

'Yes, sir?'

'Try to have a day without any little accidents.'

There was a withering scorn in the head porter's voice. Fagge was a tall, wiry man with all the attributes of a martinet. He subjected Hibbert to verbal persecution but the latter had learnt to live with the discomfort. He saw it as a small price to pay for the privilege of working at Crewe Station. As he made his way to Platform Two, he was

12

relieved that Fagge had not noticed the handkerchief that he had tied around his left wrist.
Had he been forced to admit suffering yet another
domestic mishap, Hibbert would have provoked
more ridicule from the head porter.

It was a busy morning. Passenger trains came
and went. Goods trains thundered past in both
directions on the through lines in the middle.
Traffic was relentless and Reginald Hibbert was
kept on his toes along with the other porters.
Working with his usual enthusiasm, he tried to
ignore the twinges in his left wrist. By the afternoon, he had forgotten all about his injury. Hibbert was emboldened to handle even the heaviest
luggage without trepidation. His overconfidence
was to prove fatal.

Another train steamed into the station in a riot
of noise, vibration and pungent smoke. As soon
as the passengers had alighted, Hibbert climbed
on to the roof of one of the carriages and began
to pass down the luggage to another porter.
Stacked on the platform, it was singled out by its
owners before being carried away for them.
Hibbert had no problems until he tried to handle
a large leather trunk. Having manoeuvred it to
the edge of the roof, he attempted to lift it in one
fluent move but his left wrist suddenly gave way
and he let go of the trunk with a cry of anguish.

It plummeted through the air and the porter
waiting to take it from him had the presence of
mind to step back smartly out of the way. The
trunk hit a lady's hatbox with such force that it
broke the strap attached to its lid. A small crowd
of passengers stood beside the piles of luggage

13

and a collective gasp of horror went up. As the lid of the hatbox flipped open, its contents were tipped roughly out. Reginald Hibbert could not believe his eyes.

Rolling around below him on the platform was a human head.

CHAPTER TWO

Seated at the desk in his office, Detective Inspector Robert Colbeck was writing a report on his latest case. Details of a brutal murder in Seven Dials were somehow robbed of their full horror by his elegant hand but they remained fresh and disturbing in his mind. He was nearing the end of his work when the door suddenly opened and Superintendent Edward Tallis burst in without bothering to knock.

'Stop whatever you're doing, Inspector,' he ordered.

Colbeck looked up. 'Is there a problem, sir?'

'There's *always* a problem at Scotland Yard. Problems arrive on my desk by the dozen every day. Policing a city like London is one long, continuous problem that defies solution.'

'I think you're being unduly pessimistic, Superintendent.'

'Be that as it may, I've a new assignment for you.'

'Here in London?'

'No,' said Tallis. 'In Crewe.'

'That means a railway crime,' said Colbeck with interest, getting to his feet. 'Have the LNWR been in touch with you?'

'They requested you by name.'

'I'm flattered.'

'This is no time to preen yourself,' warned

Tallis. 'The London and North West Railway want immediate action. A severed head was found in a hatbox that was unloaded at Crewe station this afternoon.'

'Male or female?'

'What does it matter? A head is a head.'

'Do you have any more details, sir?'

'None beyond the few that were sent by electric telegraph.'

Colbeck opened a drawer in his desk. 'I'll set off at once,' he said, taking out a copy of *Bradshaw's Guide*. 'Let's find a train that will get me there fast.'

'You'll take Sergeant Leeming with you.'

'Victor will not be happy about that.'

'His job is to obey orders.'

'And he always does so,' said Colbeck, running his finger down a list of departure times. 'Since we won't get to Crewe until well into the evening, it means that we'll have to stay the night. Victor hates to be away from his wife and children.'

Tallis raised a contemptuous eyebrow. 'You know my view of families,' he said. 'They cease to exist when a major crime has been committed. Detection takes precedence over *everything*. It's the main reason that I never married.'

Colbeck could think of other reasons why the superintendent had not succumbed to holy matrimony, chief among them being the brusque, authoritarian manner that would have little appeal to a member of the opposite sex. Tallis was a solid man in his fifties with grey hair and a neat moustache. Though he had left the army many years ago, he still looked as if he were on the parade ground. He respected Colbeck for his skill as a detective but he could never bring himself to like the undisputed dandy of Scotland Yard. There was a permanent unresolved tension between the two men.

Having selected a train, Colbeck closed his *Bradshaw* and put it back in the desk drawer. He gave his superior a token smile.

'Your devotion to duty is an inspiration to us all,' he said without a trace of irony, 'but some of us need more than the relentless pursuit of the criminal fraternity to get true fulfilment from life. Victor Leeming is a case in point.'

'A wife and children are unnecessary handicaps.'

'That's a matter of opinion, Superintendent.'

'Mine is based on experience.'

'Mine is tempered by a recognition of basic human needs,' said Colbeck suavely. 'A police force is not a monastic order, sir. I refuse to believe that celibacy in our ranks is to be encouraged.'

'I'm well aware of your eccentric views, Inspector,' said Tallis with exasperation, 'and I'd be grateful if you kept them to yourself. What time is your train?'

'In just under an hour.'

'Then find Sergeant Leeming and get over to Euston Station.'

'At once, sir.'

'And don't presume to rest on your laurels.'

'I'd never dare to do that.'

'This is an entirely new case.'

Colbeck knew what he meant. It was not the first time that the inspector had answered the call

17

of the London and North West Railway. When a mail train was robbed on its way to Birmingham, a succession of other serious crimes had been committed in its wake. Because of the way he had brought the investigation to a satisfactory conclusion, Robert Colbeck had earned the gratitude of the LNWR as well as that of the Post Office and the Royal Mint. Newspapers had unanimously christened him the Railway Detective. It was an honour that he cherished but it also placed a heavy and often uncomfortable burden of expectation on his shoulders.

'Are you sure you've picked the fastest train?' asked Tallis.

'I couldn't have chosen a better one, sir.'

'What do you mean?'

'The engine driver is a good friend of mine.'

Caleb Andrews was a short, thin, sinewy man of middle years with the energy of someone half his age. Though he had spent his entire working life on the railway, he had lost none of his boyish enthusiasm for his job. Having begun as a cleaner, he had eventually become a fireman before reaching the pinnacle of his profession as an engine driver. Andrews considered himself to be one of the aristocrats of the railway world and expected deference from those in lowlier positions. He was on the footplate of his locomotive, checking that everything was in order for departure, when two familiar figures came along the platform to see him.

'Hello, Mr Andrews,' said Robert Colbeck.

'Ah!' exclaimed the driver, turning to look at

them. 'I had a feeling that I might be seeing you on my train, Inspector.'

'You remember Sergeant Leeming, don't you?'

'Of course.'

Andrews and Leeming exchanged a friendly nod.

'We need to get to Crewe as fast as possible,' said Colbeck.

'Then you've come to the right man.'

'You sound as if you expected us,' said Victor Leeming.

'I did, Sergeant. When a man's head is found inside a hatbox at a railway station, the people they'll always send for are you and Inspector Colbeck.'

'A *man's* head, did you say?'

'You already know more than us,' noted Colbeck.

'That's the rumour, anyway,' said Andrews, scratching his fringe beard. 'Messages keep coming in from Crewe. According to the station-master, it was the head of a young man. It was discovered by accident.'

'What else can you tell us?'

'Nothing, Inspector.'

'Then take us to the scene of the crime.'

'But not too fast,' pleaded Leeming with a grimace. 'Trains always make me feel sick.'

'Not the way that I drive,' boasted Andrews, adjusting his cap. He beamed at Colbeck. 'Well, what a piece of news to tell Maddy! I'm helping the Railway Detective to solve a crime.'

'It won't be the first time,' said Colbeck with a smile.

19

Caleb Andrews had been the driver of the mail train that had been robbed a few years earlier, and he had received such serious injuries during the incident that it was doubtful if he would survive. In the event, he had made a complete recovery, thanks to his remarkable resilience and to the way that his daughter, Madeleine, had nursed him back to full health. During the course of his investigation, Colbeck and Madeleine had been drawn together in a friendship that had slowly matured into something much deeper.

'I knew that you'd probably be driving this train,' said Colbeck. 'Madeleine always tells me what your shift patterns are.'

Andrews grinned. 'It feels as if I'm on duty twenty-fours a day.'

'Just like us,' said Leeming gloomily.

'Climb aboard, Sergeant. We're due off in a couple of minutes.'

'Is there any way to reduce the dreadful noise and rattle?'

'Yes,' said Andrews. 'Travel by coach.'

'At a conservative estimate,' observed Colbeck, 'it would take us all of sixteen hours to get to Crewe by coach. The train will get us there in just over four hours.'

'Four hours of complete misery,' Leeming groaned.

'You'll learn to love the railway one day, Victor.'

Leeming rolled his eyes. He was a stocky man in his thirties, slightly older than the inspector but having none of Colbeck's sharp intelligence or social graces. In contrast to his handsome superior, the sergeant was also spectacularly ugly with a face that seemed to have been uniquely designed for villainy rather than crime prevention.

'Let's find a carriage, Victor,' advised Colbeck.

'If we must,' sighed Leeming.

'When you catch the person who was travelling with that hatbox,' said Andrews sternly, 'hand him over to us.'

'Why?' asked Colbeck.

The engine driver cackled. 'That severed head had no valid ticket for the journey,' he said. 'We take fare-dodging very seriously.'

On that macabre note, they set off for Crewe.

It was a warm May evening but Reginald Hibbert was still shivering. Since the accident with the hatbox, he had been relieved of his duties and kept in the stationmaster's office. When a local policeman interviewed him, the hapless porter was made to feel obscurely responsible for the fact that a severed head had been travelling by train. Dismissal from his job was the very least that he expected. The worst of it was that his wife would be at home, wondering where he was and why he had not returned at the end of his shift. She would grow increasingly worried about her husband. He feared that Molly might in due course come to the station in search of him and thereby witness his disgrace.

'When can I go home?' he asked tentatively.

'Not until the detectives arrive from Scotland Yard,' said Douglas Fagge with a meaningful tap on the nose. 'They'll need to speak to you. We can't have you disappearing.'

'I'd only be gone ten minutes, Mr Fagge.'

'How do we know that you'd come back?'

'Because I'd give you my word.'

'And I know you'd keep it,' said Percy Reade, the stationmaster, adopting a gentler tone. 'I trust you implicitly, Reg, but I still think it better that you stay here until they arrive.'

Hibbert quivered. 'Am I in trouble, Mr Reade?'

'Yes!' affirmed Fagge, folding his arms.

'No,' countered the stationmaster. 'Accidents will happen.'

'Especially when Hibbert is around.'

'You're too harsh on him, Douglas.'

'And you're too lenient.'

Percy Reade was a mild-mannered little man in his forties with a huge walrus moustache concealing much of his face. Conscientious and highly efficient, he treated the staff with a paternal care in the belief that it was the way to get the best out of them. Fagge, on the other hand, favoured a more tyrannical approach. Left to him, flogging would have been meted out to anyone who failed to do his job properly and Fagge would happily have wielded the cat o' nine tails himself. Hibbert was relieved that the stationmaster was there. His kindly presence was an antidote to the venom of the head porter.

The distant sound of an approaching train made all three men turn their heads to the window. Reade consulted his watch and gave a nod of satisfaction at the train's punctuality. Fagge's hope was that it would bring the detectives from Scotland Yard and allow him to play a decisive part in a murder investigation. As the train thundered into the station and slowly ground to a halt amid

22

a symphony of hissing and juddering, all that Hibbert could think about were his anxious wife, the threat of unemployment and his rumbling stomach. It was several hours since he had last eaten.

After stopping at major stations on the way, the train had finally arrived at Crewe. Robert Colbeck and Victor Leeming were aboard and the stationmaster went out to greet them. When he brought the visitors back to his office, Reade introduced them to Hibbert and to Fagge. At a glance, Colbeck could see that the porter was trembling and that his superior was revelling in the man's discomfort.

'This is the miscreant,' declared Fagge, pointing at Hibbert. 'He dropped a trunk on to that hatbox.'

'How do you know?' asked Colbeck.

'He admits it.'

'But did you actually *see* the incident, Mr Fagge?'

'No – I was on another platform.'

'Then we have no further use for you. Goodbye.'

'But I have to be here,' blustered Fagge. 'I'm the head porter.'

'We're only interested in the porter with the head,' said Leeming, unable to stop himself from blurting out his joke. He was immediately contrite. 'I'm sorry, Inspector. I meant no disrespect to the dead.'

'I'm sure that you didn't, Victor,' said Colbeck easily, turning to the stationmaster. 'Mr Reade, I assume that you reported the grim discovery to the local police.'

23

'Yes, Inspector,' said Reade. 'Constable Hubble-day was summoned at once. He took statements from several witnesses.'

'Then I'll want to hear what else he did.' Colbeck swung round to confront Fagge. 'How far away is the police station?'

'Not far,' said the head porter.

'In that case, perhaps you'll be good enough to show Sergeant Leeming the way and introduce him when you get there.' He ushered both men to the door. 'You know what to ask, Victor.'

'Yes, Inspector.'

'Leave your bag here.'

Putting his valise down beside Colbeck's, the sergeant led the reluctant Fagge out and the door was closed behind them. Colbeck could sense the air of relief in the office. Hibbert was clearly afraid of his hectoring boss and Reade unwilling to challenge him. Now that Fagge had gone, both of them had relaxed.

'Right,' said Colbeck, removing his top hat and placing it on the desk, 'let's get down to business, shall we, gentlemen? Before you tell me how the severed head was found, perhaps you'd be good enough to show it to me.'

'Of course,' said Reade. Crossing to a cup-board, he took out a bunch of keys and inserted one of them into the lock. 'I had to hide it away in here. When it was standing on the floor, people kept peering in at it through the window. It was so ghoulish.' Unlocking the door, he opened it and lifted the hatbox out. 'Here we are, In-spector.'

Hibbert flinched at the sight but Colbeck was

fascinated. The leather hatbox was large, beautifully made and very expensive. Tied to the handle was a ticket that told him Euston was the point of departure. The name on the ticket, written in a spidery hand, was Mr D Key. Capital letters had been used for the destination – CREWE.

Since the strap had been broken, Colbeck simply had to pull back the lid to expose the occupant of the hatbox. It was the head of a young man and dark bruising on the forehead suggested that he had been beaten before being killed. Extracting a large handkerchief from his pocket, Colbeck used it to encircle the back of the head so that he could lift it gently out.

Reginald Hibbert emitted a gasp of alarm as it came into view once again. The open eyes seemed to be staring accusingly at him. He stepped back guiltily and collided with a chair, almost knocking it to the floor. Percy Reade admired the detective's coolness. Simply carrying the hatbox had induced feelings of nausea in the stationmaster and he could not possibly have handled its contents with his bare hands. Colbeck seemed to have no qualms. He was examining the head from all angles as if it were a bronze bust of a Roman emperor rather than part of a human being.

'You've obviously done this before,' remarked Reade.

'Not at all,' said Colbeck, coming to the end of his scrutiny. 'As a matter of fact, this is my first severed head. I am, however, all too accustomed to looking at dead bodies, many of them, alas, hideously mutilated.'

'What happens next, Inspector?'

'We'll do all we can to unite this fellow with his torso.'

'How on earth can you do that when you have no clues?'

'We have two important ones right here,' said Colbeck, lowering the head carefully back into its box. 'We know from the ticket that this began its journey at Euston station and we may be able to find the porter who loaded it on to the train. Failing that, we'll begin our enquiries in Jermyn Street.'

'Why there?'

'Clearly, you didn't study the inside of the hat-box. The name of a milliner is sewn into the silk padding on the underside of the lid.' He pointed to the gold thread. 'I should imagine he will be very upset to learn to what use the box has been put.' He closed the lid. 'Now, Mr Hibbert,' he said, straightening up, 'we come to you.'

'I didn't *mean* to do it, Inspector,' said the porter defensively.

'Dropping a trunk on to a hatbox is not a criminal offence.'

'Mr Fagge said that I ought to be arrested.'

'Well, Mr Fagge is not here any longer so why don't you tell me, in your own words, exactly what happened?'

Hibbert was reassured by Colbeck's friendly tone and courteous manner. Clearing his throat, the porter licked his lips.

'It all began this morning, when I sprained my wrist...'

It was a slow, long-winded account filled with much extraneous detail but the others heard him out in silence.

While he was speaking, his essential character was laid bare and Colbeck saw that the porter was a decent, honest, hard-working young man in terror of losing a job that was a labour of love to him. The inspector was surprised to hear that he had been kept at the station beyond the time when his shift ended and guessed that the wife about whom Hibbert had spoken so fondly would be very distressed at her husband's lateness. When the narrative at last came to an end, Colbeck's first concern was for Molly Hibbert.

'Did you not think to send your wife a message?' he asked.

'Mr Fagge refused to let me, Inspector.'

'That was very high-handed of him. He had no right to deny you and should have been overruled by the stationmaster.'

'I tried to put myself in Mrs Hibbert's position,' said Reade, attempting to justify his actions. 'I felt that she would be very upset if she had a note from Reg to say that he was being held here, pending the arrival of detectives from Scotland Yard.'

'Why not simply tell her that her husband was working overtime?' said Colbeck reasonably. 'That would at least have given her peace of mind.'

'That never occurred to me, Inspector. To tell you the truth, this incident with the hatbox left me rather jangled. It's not the sort of thing that happens every day – thank God!'

'It must have caused a great stir.'

'It did,' confirmed Hibbert. 'There were dozens of people on the platform. They all gathered round for a goggle at the head.'

'That was unfortunate,' said Colbeck. 'In the confusion, the person who would have reclaimed that hatbox slipped away. I don't suppose you recall any other luggage for a Mr Key?'

'I never look at the names, Inspector – only the destination. If it says "Crewe" on the ticket, I unload it here.'

'In that case, he may have reclaimed any other items with which he was travelling and beat a hasty retreat. A severed head is hardly something that anyone would willingly admit to owning.'

'It gives me the creeps just to look at that hatbox.'

'Then you don't have to suffer any more,' decided Colbeck, taking pity on him. 'Your statement was very thorough and I'm sure it will be corroborated by the many that Constable Hubbleday took. We'll be staying the night in Crewe so, if I need to speak to you again, I know where to find you.'

'Off you go,' said Reade. 'Molly will be missing you.'

Hibbert was overjoyed. 'Thank you, Inspector,' he said, grinning inanely. 'Thank you, Mr Reade. Does that mean I'm in the clear?'

'As far as I'm concerned, that's always been the case.'

'Mr Fagge said there'd be repercussions.'

'Then he was wildly misinformed,' said Colbeck.

He opened the door to let Hibbert out, only to find a buxom young woman bearing down on them. Molly Hibbert had the look of a wife who has just been told that her husband is in grave

28

danger. She flung herself at him and held him tight.

'What's going on, Reg?' she demanded.

'Nothing, my love,' he replied. 'I was just coming home.'

'I met Mr Fagge on the way here. He said you were being questioned by a detective from London and that you ought to face charges for what you did.'

'On the contrary, Mrs Hibbert,' said Colbeck politely. 'The only thing your husband will get from me is praise. My name is Inspector Robert Colbeck, by the way, and I'm here because a severed head was found in a hatbox that arrived at this station. Your husband not only showed bravery in coming to work with an injured wrist that must have given him constant pain. He inadvertently rendered us a great service. But for him,' he went on, patting Hibbert on the shoulder, 'a heinous crime would have gone unnoticed and therefore unpunished.'

'That's true,' said Reade, feeling obliged to make a comment 'In a sense, Reg is something of a hero.'

'Am I?' Hibbert was baffled by the news.

'He's always a hero to me,' said Molly, clutching his arm.

'Take him home, Mrs Hibbert,' suggested Colbeck. 'And if you happen to pass Mr Fagge on the way, please warn him that I shall need to speak to him about the unnecessary cruelty he displayed towards your husband. If anyone is due a reprimand, it's Mr Fagge.'

Hibbert had never laughed so triumphantly in

all his life.

Victor Leeming was deeply unhappy. It was bad enough to be exiled for a night from the marital bed but he had additional causes for complaint. The first had come in the burly shape of Constable Royston Hubbleday, a good-hearted but ponderous individual who had insisted on reading out every statement he had taken relating to the discovery at the railway station, however repetitive, hysterical or contradictory they happened to be. Leeming's second grievance was that he had to share an airless room with Robert Colbeck at a public house. Situated near the station, it was called *The Rocket* and its inn sign sported a painting of Stephenson's famous locomotive. To a man who loathed railways as much as the sergeant, it was an ordeal to stay the night in a place that celebrated them.

His major source of unease, however, was only feet away. For reasons the sergeant did not understand, Colbeck had placed the hatbox between the two beds so that each of them would be sleeping cheek by jowl with incontrovertible evidence of foul play. Leeming was by no means squeamish but the proximity of the severed head unnerved him. Yet it seemed to have no effect on the inspector. When they retired to their beds for the night, Leeming voiced his thoughts.

'Why would anyone do it?' he wondered.

'Do what?'

'Carry a human head in a hatbox.'

'I can think of a number of reasons,' said Colbeck.

'Such as?'

'It could be a trophy, something which sig-nalled a victory.'

'Who would want to keep such a grisly item as that?'

'There's no accounting for taste, Victor.'

'What else could it be?'

'A gift.'

Leeming started. 'A weird sort of gift, if you ask me.'

'I agree but we may be dealing with a weird mind. Don't forget that case we had last year. A young woman was dismembered and pieces of her body were returned one by one to the bereaved family.'

'I remember it only too well, Inspector. The killer worked at Smithfield – a butcher in every sense.' He glanced down at the hatbox. 'Do you have a theory about this crime, sir?'

'One is slowly forming in my brain, Victor.'

'Well?'

'I fancy that it's a warning,' said Colbeck. 'Look how far it's travelled. Would somebody bring it all that way without a specific purpose? My belief is that it was going to be delivered to someone by way of a dire warning. Think what an appalling shock it would have given as the lid was opened.'

'I'm scared stiff when the lid is *closed*.'

'Only because you know what's inside the box.'

'The one consolation is that we'll soon catch the villain.'

'I wish that I shared your confidence.'

'You must do, sir,' argued Leeming. 'The man was kind enough to put his name on the ticket –

31

Mr D Key. What does that initial stand for, I wonder – David, Donald, Derek perhaps? We had a census only three years ago so his name will be somewhere in the list of London residents. All we have to do is to work our way through them.'

'That would be a complete waste of time.'

'Why?'

'Because we have no proof that the person we want lives in London. All we know for certain is that the train was boarded there. As for the name, I'll wager every penny I have that it's a false one. Who would be stupid enough to attach his real name to a hatbox that contained a human head? Besides,' Colbeck added, 'the person who brought it to Crewe might have nothing what-soever to do with the murder. He might simply have been a delivery boy.'

'It's not a job I'd have taken on,' confessed Leeming with a shudder. 'Nothing on God's earth would have persuaded me to get on a train with something like that.'

'You'll be doing so tomorrow, Victor.'

'That's different, sir. Now it can be classed as evidence.'

'Vital evidence – that's why we mustn't let it out of our sight.'

'Does it *have* to spend the night with us?'

'Most certainly.'

'Why not leave it at the railway station?'

'Because the man who lost the hatbox might well try to retrieve it,' Colbeck pointed out. 'We can't allow that, can we? Imagine what Super-intendent Tallis would say if something as im-portant as this was stolen from under our noses.'

'Do you really think that someone will come back for it?'

'It's highly likely.'

'Then shouldn't a watch be kept on the station-master's office?'

'Of course. I took the precaution of speaking to Constable Hubbleday on the matter and he agreed to patrol the area throughout the night. There's no point in our losing sleep when we have a uniformed policeman at our disposal, is there?' He leant over to give the hatbox a companionable pat. 'This chap is perfectly safe with us,' he went on before reaching up to turn off the gaslight. 'Good night, Victor – and sweet dreams.'

Sergeant Leeming gurgled into his pillow.

It was well past midnight before Constable Royston Hubbleday began to tire. Eager to impress a detective from Scotland Yard, he had been delighted when Colbeck asked him to keep a close eye on the railway station that night. Hubbleday was a hefty young man with a fondness for action and a desire to move to a large city where he might find plenty of it. Nothing appealed to him more than the notion of joining the Metropolitan Police Force and, if he could make a significant arrest while assisting two members of it, he felt that it would help him to fulfil his ambition.

The night was humid, the sky dark and Crewe passenger station was no more than a shadowy outline. Having circled it time and again, he paused to remove his top hat so that he could wipe the back of his hand across his sweaty brow. It was a grave mistake. Before he could replace his hat, something struck him hard on the back of his head and sent him sprawling forward into oblivion. After checking that the policeman was unconscious, his attacker stepped over the body and trotted off in the direction of the station-master's office.

When he reached the door, he used a powerful shoulder to smash it open then stepped inside. Having studied the office earlier through the window, he knew where to find the oil lamp and lit it at once, moving it so that it illumined the large cupboard in the corner. Pulling a knife from inside his jacket, he inserted it in the gap beside the lock and jiggled it violently until the door suddenly flipped open. It took him a split-second to realise that the item he was after was no longer there. He thrust the knife angrily back into its sheath.

'Damnation!' he swore.

Then he ran off swiftly into the darkness.

CHAPTER THREE

Ever since the death of her mother, Madeleine Andrews had looked after her father and willingly taken on the roles of housekeeper, cook, nurse, maidservant and companion. She was an intelligent woman in her twenties, vigorous, decisive and self-possessed, with attractive features framed by auburn hair parted in the middle. In spite of her domestic commitments, Madeleine had taken the trouble to educate herself way beyond what might be expected of an engine driver's daughter and to develop her artistic talent. In a busy life, she had somehow managed to strike a good balance between her household duties and her leisure pursuits.

Working the late shift, Caleb Andrews had not returned home to the modest house in Camden until after his daughter had gone to bed the previous night. Unable to pass on his news, therefore, he was keen to do so when a new day dawned. As he came downstairs, there was a jauntiness in his gait and a twinkle in his eye. He went into the back room to find Madeleine ladling porridge into two bowls.

'Breakfast is ready,' she said.

'Thank you, Maddy – you spoil me, you know.'

'That's what I'm here for, Father.'

'I don't think I could manage without you,' he said, taking a seat at the table. 'Though I suppose that I'll have to sooner or later.'

'Now, don't play that little game,' she warned.

He feigned innocence. 'What game?'

'You know quite well. Robert and I are close friends but I won't be teased on that account. Eat your breakfast.'

'I'm not teasing anybody. It's a father's duty to safeguard his daughter and to make sure that nobody takes advantage of her. I have your best interests at heart, Maddy.' He gave a sly grin. 'I also have a surprise for you.'

She sat opposite him. 'I don't like surprises this early in the morning,' she said briskly. 'Save it until later.'

'You'd never forgive me if I did.'

'Why not?'

'It concerns Inspector Colbeck.'

'Robert?' Her face ignited with pleasure. 'What about him?'

He shrugged. 'I'll tell you after breakfast.'

'Tell me *now*.'

'You said that you'd rather wait.'

'Father!'

'And it's not that important,' he said dismissively.

'You're teasing me again,' she told him, 'and I don't like it. Remember who got up early this morning in order to make your breakfast. You ought to show some gratitude.'

'I always do, Maddy.'

'Then stop annoying me.'

He gave another shrug. 'Is that what I'm doing?'

'What do you want to tell me about Robert?'

'Only that I drove the train that took him to his latest case,' said Andrews, thrusting out his chest. 'I helped in the investigation.'

'Investigation?'

'It will be in all the newspapers.'

'What will?'

'A hatbox was unloaded at Crewe Station yesterday afternoon.'

'Nothing unusual in that.'

'Yes, there was – it had a man's head inside it.'

'Goodness!' she exclaimed, bring both hands up to her face. 'You mean that someone had been ... beheaded? That's grotesque.'

Andrews told her all that he knew about the incident, omitting some of the more lurid details he had picked up but giving the impression that he was an essential part of the investigative team. What Madeleine really wanted to hear about was Robert Colbeck and she pressed for more information.

'Did he find any clues to the crime?' she asked.

'I don't know, Maddy. There was no time to speak to him after we reached Crewe. I had to drive a train back to London. But I daresay he'll call here at some point to ask my advice,' he added airily. 'After so many years with the LNWR, I can tell him all he needs to know about the transport of luggage.'

'There's nothing you can teach Robert about railways. He has a real passion for them.'

He chuckled. 'It's not the only thing he has a passion for.'

'Being able to travel around the country by train,' she said, ignoring her father's innuendo,

37

'has made his job so much easier. That's why he relishes any crime that's connected to the railways.'

'There's far too much of it, Maddy.'

'There's too much crime everywhere.'

'If railways aren't safe, people won't travel on them.'

'People like Robert *make* them safe,' she said proudly. 'Did he come back to London on your train last night?'

'No, they stayed the night in Crewe – all three of them.'

'All three?'

'Yes,' he said cheerfully. 'Inspector Colbeck, Sergeant Leeming and that absent-minded fellow who mislaid his body somewhere.'

'Father!' Madeleine was shocked. 'It's cruel to make a joke out of something like that. The man has a family somewhere. They'll be distraught when they learn what's happened to him. How can you be so callous about it? This is an appalling crime.'

'I know, Maddy,' he said penitently. 'You're right. Please forgive me.' Andrews rallied immediately. 'But there's one consolation.'

'Is there?'

'The Railway Detective is in charge of the case.'

As soon as he got back to Scotland Yard that morning, Robert Colbeck went to the superintendent's office to deliver a verbal report of the visit to Crewe. Wreathed in cigar smoke, Edward Tallis listened intently, irritated that he was unable to find fault with the inspector's methods

38

or his thoroughness. Colbeck's account was crisp, comprehensive and lucid. Tallis invented a reason to offer some criticism.

'The station should have been guarded by more men,' he said.

'Constable Hubbleday volunteered for night duty, sir.'

'Two other officers should have been there with him. In your place, I'd have added Sergeant Leeming as well.'

'Four people would have frightened away the intruder,' argued Colbeck, 'whereas he might have been tempted to make his move if he saw only one person on patrol. That, indeed, proved to be the case. I'm sorry that the constable was attacked in the process. Fortunately, he seems to have recovered well. And the main thing is that the thief left the station empty-handed.'

'It was sensible of you to take the severed head with you.'

'Victor didn't think so.'

'Where is it now?'

'Being examined at the morgue by an expert.'

'And where is the sergeant?'

'I told him to wait there in case the doctor was able to glean any information that might be of use to us. It would, for instance, be interesting to hear his opinion on exactly how the head was separated from the body. When he has the report, Victor will return here.'

It was not strictly correct. Since the sergeant had been parted from his wife overnight, Colbeck had shown his usual compassion and allowed him to go home as soon as they reached Euston, instructing him to call at the morgue for the report on his way back to work. Tallis would not have approved.

'No luck at Euston, then?' asked the superintendent.

'None whatsoever,' replied Colbeck. 'We spoke to all the porters who helped to load that particular train but not one of them recalled a hatbox or the person carrying it. They stow so much luggage aboard in the course of an average morning that it's impossible to remember individual items.' He raised the hatbox. 'It was only by complete chance that we learnt what was in this.'

'Let me take a look at it,' said Tallis.

Putting his cigar down in the tray, he stood up and took the hatbox from Colbeck. Noting the broken strap and the dent in the shiny leather where it had been struck by the heavy trunk, Tallis opened it slowly, as if still expecting to find a severed head inside. As it was, he was still surprised by what he saw. A pleasing aroma drifted into his nostrils and countered the smell of tobacco smoke.

'Herbs,' explained Colbeck. 'The interior of the box was scented and, as you see, packed with wool.'

'What was the purpose of that?'

'It was not for the comfort of its occupant, sir, that much is certain. My guess is that the wool was used to prevent the head from rolling around and the herbs were there to kill any unpleasant odour. The care taken also suggests that the hatbox was going on a lengthy journey which may not have ended at Crewe.'

'But that's where it was unloaded.'

'It's the hub of the LNWR. Trains go off in all directions. The passenger carrying that hatbox might have been travelling on to another destination.'

Tallis lowered the lid. 'How do you intend to find him?'

'By starting with the hatmaker, sir,' said Colbeck. 'What you failed to notice was that his name is on the underside of the lid.'

'I assumed that it would be,' claimed the superintendent gruffly. 'It's standard practice in the trade.'

Colbeck was amused. 'I didn't know that you were so well informed about the running of ladies' hat shops,' he said wryly. 'They are the last places in London where I'd expect to find you.'

'This is no time for drollery, Inspector.'

'I was merely making an observation, sir.'

'One that's entirely uncalled for,' said Tallis.

'Yes, sir.'

Tallis looked at the ticket attached to the hatbox. 'Mr D Key. I don't suppose that particular key will open any doors for us. It's sure to be a false name.'

'Elijah Swinnerton, however, is certainly not.'

'Who the devil is he?'

'The milliner,' said Colbeck with a disarming smile. 'The one whose name you rightly assumed would be inside the hatbox.'

Tallis bristled. 'Do I detect a note of sarcasm?'

'Mistakenly, sir.'

'I'll brook no mockery, Inspector.'

'None is intended,' said Colbeck, stretching out

his hands. 'If I may have the box back, Super-intendent, then I propose to go and meet Elijah Swinnerton right now. I have every confidence that he'll be able to point us in the right direction.'

Jermyn Street had been a fashionable address ever since the reign of Charles II when it was first built and when it numbered luminaries such as the future Duke of Marlborough among its residents. It still boasted many fine houses but had also acquired a reputation for its hotels and its many shops. Gentlemen's outfitters had started to appear alongside specialist shirtmakers, shoe-makers and hatters. The bow-fronted establish-ment owned by Elijah Swinnerton was the only one that sold quality millinery and its popularity among wealthy ladies had grown steadily during the five years of its existence.

Though the staff was entirely female, it was presided over by Swinnerton himself, a vigilant man who watched his employees with care and reserved for himself the privilege of serving any titled customers. Tall, slim, beak-nosed, dark-haired, of middle height and years, Swinnerton was immaculately attired in a frock coat and striped trousers with a red cravat bursting out from under his chin like a giant rose. Seasoned in all the arts of flattery, he was much liked by his customers for his fastidiousness, his delicate hand gestures and his confiding manner. Most men felt less at ease in his presence, finding him altogether too foppish to suit their taste.

It was very busy in the shop that day and every member of staff was serving an individual cus-

tomer. Elijah Swinnerton adopted a purely super-
visory role until a tall, well-favoured, elegant man
came through the door, carrying a hatbox. Struck
by his appearance, the owner ran an appreciative
eye over him before crossing to greet him.

'Good day to you, good sir,' he said, glancing at
the hatbox. 'I hope that you're not here to return
one of our hats.'

'Am I speaking to Mr Swinnerton?' asked
Colbeck.

'The very same.'

'Then perhaps I could have a word with you in
private, sir.'

'To what does it pertain?'

'I'll tell you when we're alone, Mr Swinnerton.'

'And who might you be, may I ask?'

'Inspector Robert Colbeck from Scotland
Yard.'

Swinnerton's unctuous smile vanished immediately and he looked round nervously, hoping that
nobody else had heard the name. A visit from a
detective was unlikely to bring good news and he
did not want his clientele upset by any bad
tidings. Escorting his visitor to a storeroom at the
back of the premises, he closed the door firmly
behind them. Alone with the man in a confined
space, Colbeck caught a faint whiff of perfume.
One shelf was lined with hatboxes very much like
the one that he had brought. He held it up.

'Do you recognise this, Mr Swinnerton?'

'Of course,' replied the other. 'It was sold here.'

'Does everyone buy a leather box with their
hat?'

'By no means, Inspector – most of the ladies

43

with whom we deal already have a travelling hatbox. They take home what they purchase in a cardboard box with my name exquisitely emblazoned on its top.'

'Buying something like this, then,' said Colbeck, indicating the hatbox, 'is the exception rather than the rule.'

'That's correct.'

'So there's a good chance that you might remember to whom this particular item was sold?'

'It's not a question of chance, Inspector,' said Swinnerton, adjusting his cravat. 'I keep a careful record of each sale. That record, of course, is highly confidential. Before I could even begin to think of providing you with a name, I'd need to know how Scotland Yard came by the item in the first place.'

'That's your right, sir, and I'm happy to oblige you. When this hatbox was damaged on Crewe railway station, a human head was found inside it.'

'Oh, my God!' cried the other, shying away as if Colbeck had just produced a severed head from the box like a conjuror extracting a rabbit. 'Please don't tell me that the silk lining was soaked in blood.'

'It was not, sir. Whoever put the head in here took great care not to soil it in any way. It was even filled with aromatic herbs.'

'A head in a hatbox – what a gruesome thought!'

'I need to find the person who put it there, Mr Swinnerton.'

'You may rely on my complete cooperation.'

'Then tell me who bought this from you,' said

Colbeck. 'That will at least give me a starting point.'

'Excuse me for one moment, Inspector,' said the other, opening the door. 'The record book is kept in the shop.'

'I apologise for coming at such an awkward time.'

'Business always picks up when the Derby is in the offing. Every lady wants to look her best on Epsom Downs. It's been like this for several days now.'

Swinnerton went out and closed the door behind him, leaving Colbeck to take a closer look at the storeroom. As well as the row of leather hatboxes, there were a number of brightly coloured cardboard ones with the name of the milliner painted boldly on the lid. Evidently, it was a thriving enterprise with a constant demand for the hats that Swinnerton designed and sold. Catering for the upper echelons of society, the shop clearly fulfilled its requirements. When he returned with his ledger, the first thing that Swinnerton did was to lift up the hatbox so that he could look at the number on the back. He then referred to his record book, flipping over the pages until he came to the one he sought.

'Here we are,' he said, tapping the name with a long finger. 'The hat and hatbox were sold two months ago. As a matter of fact, I handled the sale myself. Certain customers expect my individual attention, you know, so I have to oblige them. Yes, I remember the hat clearly – a little too flamboyant for most ladies but she carried it off well. It was almost as if it were made for her, Inspector.'

'Made for whom?'

'His wife,' replied Swinnerton. 'He came in with her and waited patiently while she tried on almost everything in the shop. That's the hatbox he bought, no question of it. Though I can't believe for a moment that he would have been responsible for putting a man's head in it. That's unthinkable. He would never dream of such a thing.'

'How do you know?'

'I'm an astute judge of character, Inspector. One has to be in this trade. Dealing with the public sharpens one's instincts.'

'What did your instincts tell you about this gentleman?'

'He's a pillar of society – decent, upright, wholly incorruptible.'

'May I know his name, please?'

'Lord Hendry.'

'Thank you, Mr Swinnerton.'

'Shall I furnish you with his address?'

'There's no need,' said Colbeck, picking up the hatbox. 'I think I know exactly where to find Lord Hendry.'

Hands on hips, Lord George Hendry stood back to admire the painting that had just been hung over the marble fireplace. Every detail intrigued him, every nuance of colour was a delight. He was a stout, distinguished-looking man of medium height with a fleshy, rubicund face that looked much older than his fifty years and large, blue eyes that had a zestful glint. He was still gazing at the portrait when his wife came into the library, leaning heavily on her walking stick.

'Aren't you tempting Providence somewhat?' she enquired.

He turned round. 'Providence?'

'I would have thought it much safer to hang the painting *after* Odysseus had won the Derby, not before the race had even taken place. What happens if your horse loses?'

'Out of the question, my dear.'

'You've said that on many previous occasions.'

'Yes,' he admitted, 'and my confidence has often proved to be without foundation. Not this time, Caroline. I have the best trainer and the best jockey. More to the point,' he went on, indicating the racehorse in the oil painting, 'I have the finest three-year old ever to enter the race. Look at a true thoroughbred, my dear, look at that conformation, look at that imperious quality the artist has caught so brilliantly. Every bookmaker in London has made Odysseus the favourite. I account him a certainty.'

'Then I hope, for your sake, that he is, George,' she said, coming forward to take a closer look at the animal. 'It's a superb piece of work – quite inspiring, in its own way.'

Lady Caroline Hendry did not share her husband's passion for the Turf but she tolerated all of his sporting interests. If a painting had to be given pride of place in the library, she would rather it be of a champion racehorse than of one of the battle-scarred pugilists whom he chose to patronise. She was a short, full-bodied woman with a beauty that had slowly given way to a startling pallor savagely criss-crossed by age. Rheumatism and its attendant pain had put many of the lines in her face and hampered her movement. It did not, however, diminish her spirit or her Christian impulse.

'Did you speak with the archdeacon?' asked her husband.

'I've just returned from the meeting.'

'Well?'

'He agreed that the charity was eminently worthwhile.'

'You have to draw the line somewhere, my dear. You already give to far too many people. Why add to the burden?'

'I only give to the deserving poor, George,' she said.

'But how do you *know* they are deserving?'

'I take the archdeacon's advice.'

'Not in every instance,' he recalled. 'He had severe reservations about your donation to the lunatic asylum.'

'I visited the place – he did not. The conditions there are quite revolting. I simply had to do what I could for those benighted souls.'

He forced a smile. 'As always, my dear, you were right.'

Lady Hendry was a woman of independent means. Her private wealth had been an agreeable irrelevance when her husband had first met and fallen in love with her. He had been ensnared by her beauty, grace and sophistication. The fact that she took an interest in various charitable institutions only added to her appeal. Now, however, it was different. Lord Hendry strongly resented the recipients of his wife's benevolence. On those occasions when he had heavy gambling debts to settle, he would have liked to turn to her for help but felt unable to do so. Someone who owned a splendid mansion at the heart of a large estate in Surrey could hardly claim to be one of the deserving poor.

'How much do you propose to give this time?' he asked.

'Five hundred pounds.'

He felt a pang of envy, thinking of how he could spend that amount of money. The familiar bitterness rose up within him but he concealed it behind another bland smile.

'You could donate even more than that, Caroline.'

'We felt that was the appropriate amount.'

'There's a very simple way to increase it.'

'Is there?'

'Of course,' he said, turning back to the painting. 'Invest the money in Odysseus and let him double or treble it. I own the horse so you'll be supporting the family into the bargain. After all,' he went on with a chortle, 'charity begins at home. Even the archdeacon would accept that, I dare venture.'

Victor Leeming was more lugubrious than ever. The past twenty-four hours had been something of a nightmare. Forced to endure a long train journey, he had spent an uncomfortable night in the company of a severed head before having to suffer another four hours or more on the railway. Though he was allowed a brief respite to see his wife and children, all the pleasure from the encounter had been dissipated by his visit to the

49

morgue where he had had to listen to details of the decapitation that had made his stomach heave. No sooner had he taken the medical report back to Scotland Yard than he was grabbed by Robert Colbeck and taken off to another railway station. As the train rumbled south with ear-splitting assurance, Leeming retreated into a moody silence.

Colbeck had no difficulty in reading his mind.

'You'll thank me for bringing you on this trip, Victor.'

'I doubt it, sir.'

'You are about to meet an interesting gentlemen.'

'What is interesting about buying your wife a hat?'

'You obviously don't know who Lord George Hendry is.'

'I rarely rub shoulders with the aristocracy.'

'You might enjoy doing so on this occasion.'

'Why?'

'Lord Hendry is a devotee of the Turf.'

'So are thousands of other people, Inspector.'

'Very few of them own racehorses,' said Colbeck. 'Lord Hendry has a whole string of them. One horse is due to run in the Derby.'

'Really?' Leeming's curiosity made his face glow. 'It's the only race I always place a bet on.'

'Have you ever picked a winner?'

'Not so far – I was born unlucky.'

'Judgement is just as important as luck, Victor. The more you know about a particular horse, the better able you are to assess its chances of success. If you simply pick a name out of a newspaper, then you are making a blind choice.'

'Do you think Lord Hendry will give us any advice?'

'I'm sure that he will.'

'Then I must ask a favour,' said Leeming.

'Favour?'

'Could you please let me get the information about the Derby from Lord Hendry *before* you arrest him?'

'I've no intention of making an arrest.'

'But the severed head was in his wife's hatbox.'

'That doesn't mean he or she are guilty of putting it there. Neither are possible suspects, in my view. Who would be rash enough to place a head in a hatbox that they must have known could be traced to the person who sold it to them in the first place? My guess is that Lord and Lady Hendry are victims of this crime rather than the perpetrators. Our visit to Reigate is only the first stop on what may turn out to be a very long journey.'

Leeming shuddered. 'Does it all have to be by train?'

'Unless you can provide us with a magic carpet.'

They were travelling on the London, Brighton and South Coast Railway, a network that enjoyed a virtual monopoly in the area that it covered. Colbeck was impressed with their carriage but less impressed by the engine driver, who seemed unable to bring the train to a halt at the various stations without jolting the passengers from their seats. When they eventually alighted at Reigate, the detectives needed a cab to take them out to the

Hendry estate. Leeming was contented at last.

'This is more like it,' he observed, settling back.

'You were born in the wrong age, Victor. The future will be forged by railway engineers, not by those who design coach and cab.'

'That's a pity in my opinion.'

'Lord Hendry would beg to differ.'

'Why – is he another train fancier like you?'

'No,' said Colbeck, 'but I'm sure he's a practical man. When you move thoroughbred horses between racecourses, you have to do so with great care. If Lord Hendry wanted to enter one of his horses in some of the major meetings in Yorkshire, it would take him at least two weeks to get it there by road. In a train, horses can be carried from one end of the country to another in a matter of hours.'

'Then they have my sympathy.'

'You're a Luddite, fighting a losing battle against the inevitable.'

'And I'll go on fighting,' Leeming resolved.

'What presents did your children have for Christmas?'

'Not very many on my wage, sir.'

'You gave them lots of things. I remember you telling me about them. And what was it that they liked best? Of all the gifts, which was the most popular?' Leeming looked shifty. 'Come on, admit it – what did your children get most plea-sure from last Christmas?'

'Something that you kindly bought for them.'

'And what was that, Victor?'

Leeming spoke through gritted teeth. 'A toy train.'

'I rest my case,' said Colbeck with a smile.

Lord Hendry was surprised to hear that two detectives had travelled down from Scotland Yard to see him and he had them shown into the library for the interview. After introductions had been made, they all sat down. Victor Leeming was mesmerised by the painting of Odysseus over the mantelpiece but Colbeck was more interested in the library itself. Lord Hendry had catholic tastes. Greek and Latin texts nestled beside novels by Richardson, Fielding and Smollett. Gibbon's *The History of the Decline and Fall of the Roman Empire* occupied a whole shelf in its handsome calf-bound volumes. Books of sporting prints abounded and there were learned works devoted to almost every subject under the sun.

'You're a reading man, I see,' said Colbeck with approval.

'When I have the time, Inspector,' replied Lord Hendry.

'What do you think of our present-day novelists?'

'I'm bound to say that I've little enthusiasm for them. Dickens is too earnest and Mrs Gaskell too dreary. Why will they persist in writing about what they view as the downtrodden classes? Novels should be about people who *matter*. However,' he continued, 'I refuse to believe that you and Sergeant Leeming came all the way here in order simply to discuss my literary interests.'

'Quite so, Lord Hendry,' said Colbeck. 'My superintendent would never have condoned that. We're here in connection with a distressing incident that occurred yesterday at Crewe.'

He gave a brief description of what had happened and explained that they had traced the hatbox to him. Seeing indignation show in the man's face, Colbeck assured him that he was not a suspect in the case. He failed to mollify Lord Hendry.

'Swinnerton had no right to give you my name,' he said sharply.

'He had no choice, Lord Hendry. This is a criminal investigation. Withholding evidence would have made him liable to arrest.'

'Breaking a confidence like this also renders him liable to the harshest reproach, Inspector, and I shall deliver it. Elijah Swinnerton will get no more business from me, I promise you that.'

'All that concerns me is one particular hatbox.'

'It concerns me as well,' said the other. 'That hatbox was stolen from a hotel where my wife and I stayed earlier this year. We went to the races in Newmarket.'

'Is that where the hotel was?'

'No, Inspector – it was in Cambridge.'

'Which hotel would that be?'

'That's of no consequence.'

'Have you any idea who took the hatbox?' asked Leeming, finally tearing his eyes from the painting and feeling that he should make a contribution. 'Did you report the theft to the police, Lord Hendry?'

'No, Sergeant.'

'Why not?'

'Because I chose not to, man. It was only a hatbox. Fortunately, there was no hat inside it so

I did not feel that it justified a hue and cry. To be honest, I'd forgotten the whole business.'

'What about your wife?' said Colbeck.

'What about her?'

'Well, she must have been upset by the theft. What did she do when she first discovered it?'

'Let's keep her out of this, shall we?' said Lord Hendry quietly. 'My wife is not in the best of health. Losing that hatbox was a shock to her at the time. If she heard what became of it, it would cause her a lot of unnecessary distress. I'd rather she was not brought into this at all. I'm sure that I can count on your discretion, Inspector.'

'Yes, my lord.'

'And while we're on the subject, I'd be very grateful if my name could be kept out of any newspaper reports. It would not only trouble my wife deeply, it would cause a lot of distraction for me. With the Derby in the offing, I need to concentrate all my energies on the race. I could never do that with reporters snapping at my heels.'

'We'll keep them well away from you.'

'Especially if you give us any advice about the Derby,' said Leeming with a hopeful smile. 'You must have a good idea who the serious contenders are.'

'The only serious contender,' declared Lord Hendry with a gesture in the direction of the fireplace, 'is the horse in that painting. I commissioned it by way of celebration of his victory. There's the winner, Sergeant – Odysseus.'

'Thank you, my lord.'

'There are other horses in the race,' Colbeck reminded them.

'None that can touch Odysseus,' insisted Lord Hendry.

'What about Merry Legs?'

'An overrated filly.'

'Hamilton Fido is a shrewd judge of horses.'

'I question that.'

'Mr Fido did win the Derby once before, Lord Hendry.'

The older man appraised him. 'You seem to know a lot about the Turf, Inspector,' he said. 'Are you a confirmed racegoer?'

'My job gives me little opportunity to be one,' said Colbeck sadly, 'but I do read the racing pages and I like an occasional wager. From what I hear, this year's Derby will be a three-horse race.'

'With Odysseus being the winner,' said Leeming.

'We shall see, Victor. I fancy that Merry Legs, owned by Hamilton Fido, will not be easily beaten.'

'Yes, she will,' said Lord Hendry firmly.

'How can you be so sure?'

'That's my business, Inspector.'

'What about Limerick Lad? He, too, will pose a challenge.'

'If that's what you feel, put your money on the horse.'

'I think I'll bet on Odysseus,' said Leeming.

Colbeck was circumspect. 'And I'll make up my mind nearer the time of the race,' he decided. Reaching into his pocket, he took out a piece of cartridge paper and unfolded it. 'This is an artist's impression of the young man whose head was discovered in the hatbox. It's a rough approximation of what he must have looked like. I wonder if you might recognise him.'

'Let me see.' Lord Hendry took the drawing from Colbeck and studied it for a full minute before shaking his head. 'No, Inspector,' he said at length. 'I'm sorry but I can't help you.' He returned the paper. 'Have you any idea at all who he might be?'

'Not yet, my lord, but we will do before too long. Apart from anything else, someone is likely to report him missing.' After folding the paper, Colbeck slipped it back into his pocket. 'Well, thank you for seeing us,' he said. 'We won't trouble you any further.' Leeming's attention had drifted back to the painting of the horse. 'It's time to go, Victor. Bid farewell to Odysseus.'

Prodded out of his reverie, the sergeant thanked Lord Hendry profusely before following Colbeck out. The cab was waiting for them outside the house and they clambered in. Colbeck was pensive but his companion was overcome with envy. As they drew away, the sergeant looked back over his shoulder.

'What a wonderful existence!' announced Leeming. 'To live in a mansion like that and to own racehorses – it's my notion of paradise. Lord Hendry was such an impressive gentleman in every way.'

'Yes,' agreed Colbeck. 'A pity that he felt the need to lie to us.'

'He struck me as an honest, straightforward man.'

'You may revise that opinion when you go to Cambridge.'

Leeming spluttered. 'Cambridge?'

'I want you to find the hotel where Lord Hendry stayed.'

'Why?'

'Two reasons, Victor. I'd like to know how and when that hatbox was stolen. And I'd like you to get a good description of the woman posing as Lady Hendry.'

'But she *was* Lady Hendry. You heard what he said, sir.'

'What I heard was a man being evasive,' said Colbeck. 'If he really had been there with his wife, he'd have volunteered the name of the hotel instead of refusing to give it. And if he was going to the races in Newmarket, why not stay there instead of Cambridge?'

'Perhaps the accommodation is better in Cambridge.'

'It's not the accommodation that interests me but the person with whom he was sharing it, the person for whom he bought that hat in Jermyn Street. Since we can't get her name from Lord Hendry, we'll have to find it by other means.'

Leeming sighed. 'Do I have to take a train to Cambridge?'

'Go on horseback, if you prefer. Emulate a king.'

'What king?'

'Charles II,' said Colbeck. 'He used to ride all the way to Newmarket to see the races then ride back to London again. That's upwards of eighty miles in the saddle. Do you think you could manage that in a day, Victor?'

'I'll go by rail,' conceded Leeming. 'And I hope

you're wrong about Lord Hendry. He spoke so caringly about his wife that it never crossed my mind he might have a mistress.'

'You're too trusting, Victor.'

'What other lies did he tell us?'

'Wait and see.'

'Am I to go to Cambridge on my own, sir?'

'Yes.'

'Then how do I find the hotel where Lord Hendry stayed?'

'By using your intelligence,' said Colbeck. 'Cambridge is a charming city but it won't have many hotels where a member of the aristocracy would deign to stay. Eliminate them one by one.'

'What about you, Inspector?'

'Oh, have no fear. I'll be on my travels as well – if I can persuade the superintendent to let me go there, that is.'

'Go where?'

'Ireland.'

CHAPTER FOUR

Superintendent Edward Tallis was pushed to the verge of apoplexy.

'Ireland?' he said. 'You want to go to *Ireland?*'

'With your permission, sir,' said Robert Colbeck.

'Denied.'

'I haven't given you my reasons yet.'

'Save your breath, Inspector.'

'I'm not making this request lightly, sir.'

'And I'm not turning it down lightly,' said Tallis, glaring at him. 'Here you are, in the middle of a murder investigation, and you come up with some hare-brained scheme about crossing the Irish Sea.'

'That's where the answer may lie, Super-intendent.'

'Poppycock! When a severed head is found in Crewe and when the hatbox in which it was being transported was bought in London by someone who lives near Reigate, then I'd say we were dealing with an exclusively English murder.'

'That's one way of looking at it,' said Colbeck.

'It's the *only* way of looking at it, Inspector.'

Arms folded, Tallis sat back heavily in his chair. They were in his office at Scotland Yard and he was not in an accommodating mood. If Colbeck had suggested sailing to America, he could not have met with a more resounding rebuff. It was time to delve into the murky reservoir of their past disagreements.

'Do you happen to recall a murder that took place aboard a train in Twyford a couple of years ago?' asked Colbeck.

'Vividly.'

'Then you may also recall how obstructive you were when I argued that the only way to solve a crime that took place in Berkshire was to travel to Ashford in Kent.'

'I was not obstructive,' said Tallis indignantly. 'I was simply being cautious. When further evidence emerged, I saw the virtue of sending you to Kent.'

'Where two separate murders were successfully solved.'

'We can both take credit from that, Inspector.'

'Let's move on to the Sankey Viaduct, if we may,' said Colbeck smoothly. 'When a man was hurled over the viaduct from a moving train, you thought I was mad to insist that my investigations should begin in France.'

'It seemed a lunatic course of action at the time.'

'What was the result, sir?'

'The killer was eventually tracked down and caught.'

'You did everything in your power to stop me from sailing to France,' said Colbeck. 'The only way I finally wrung a concession out of you was by threatening to resign from the Detective Department.'

Tallis's face darkened. 'Where is all this leading?'

'To the present situation – it's comparable to the two cases I've just mentioned. When you trust my judgement, I secure arrests. When you block my initiatives, guilty men go free.'

'The cases bear no resemblance to each other,' Tallis said, waving a hand. 'The murder victim at the Sankey Viaduct was a Parisian. There was a reasonable argument for moving the inquiry to France. As for the other victim, he was so closely linked to an execution at Maidstone Prison that I encouraged you to go to Kent.'

Colbeck's memories were very different. In both instances, Tallis had hampered him at every stage of the investigation and only the inspector's single-mindedness had enabled him to solve the respective crimes. The superintendent had deliberately rewritten history.

'We have no proof whatsoever,' Tallis continued, 'that the murder victim discovered at Crewe has any discernible link with Ireland. You might just as well charge off to the Hebrides.'

'I'd not find many racehorses there, sir.'

'What?'

'This crime is somehow connected to the Turf,' said Colbeck with obviously conviction. 'I feel it in my bones, Superintendent.'

'Sciatica.'

'It's no accident that the hatbox in question was one purchased by Lord Hendry. He owns the favourite for the Derby.'

'That information is irrelevant. I'm not a betting man.'

'It might advantage you to take an interest in this year's race, sir. Three horses stand out from the listed starters – Odysseus, Merry Legs and – the one that fascinates me – Limerick Lad, an Irish horse.'

'I abhor gambling in all its forms,' said Tallis coldly, 'and that's not the only thing I have against the Derby. It's a magnet for every criminal within a hundred miles. Year after year, pickpockets, prostitutes, fraudsters, ruffians and villains of every kind flock to Epsom Downs in search of rich pickings. Only a veritable army of policemen could keep them under control and we do not, alas, have such an army at our disposal. Don't mention the Derby to me, Inspector,' he went on, curling his lip. 'If it was left to me, I'd cancel the whole disgraceful event.'

'You'd cancel most things that people enjoy, sir.'

'Large crowds mean constant crime.'

'Abide by that argument and you'd stop every circus, fair and public celebration in London – not to mention royal processions.'

'You're being facetious.'

'I'm questioning your prejudice against racing.'

'I have no prejudice – I just oppose it whole-heartedly.'

'Then I beg you to assign this case to someone else,' said Colbeck abruptly. 'Find someone who doesn't have wild impulses like mine. Someone who believes that the crime has nothing what-soever to do with the forthcoming Derby and who would therefore never imagine in a million years that a severed head found in Cheshire might be destined for Brian Dowd in Ireland.'

'Who?'

'Brian Dowd is the owner of Limerick Lad, sir. Unlike the vast majority of owners – Lord Hendry among them – he is also the horse's trainer. However,' he went on, getting to his feet, 'none of this is germane to the investigation. The person who replaces me will conduct his enquiries exclusively on English soil.'

Edward Tallis glowered at him. Resisting the temptation to reach for a cigar, he weighed up the implications of what Colbeck had said. To replace the inspector would be as rash as it was foolish. Nobody commanded the respect of the London and North West Railway in the way that Colbeck did. He was revered and his knowledge of railway lore was unmatched. But that did not make him infallible. Colbeck had made mistakes in the past and Tallis was convinced that he was making the biggest of all now. He flung out a challenge.

'Give me one good reason why I should send you to Ireland.'

'Look at my copy of *Bradshaw*,' suggested Colbeck.

'Why?'

'You'd see the choice of trains confronting the person who travelled with that stolen hatbox. One destination would catch your eye, sir – Holyhead. Fifteen minutes after leaving the train at Crewe, the man could have caught another to North Wales.'

'This is idle supposition.'

'Humour me, Superintendent.'

'I've made that mistake before.'

'Let me go to Ireland.'

'It's an unwarranted use of police money.'

'Then I'll pay for the trip myself,' said Colbeck earnestly. 'As long as you reimburse me when you discover that idle supposition can sometimes produce benefits.'

'Not in this case,' Tallis promised, asserting his authority. 'Sound, solid, unrelenting detective work is the only way to achieve a good result and it must be done here in England where the crime occurred.' When Colbeck tried to speak, he was silenced with a peremptory gesture. 'I'll hear no more, Inspector. Get out there and find me a killer – and don't you dare mention Ireland to me again.'

There was a tap on the door. In response to a barked command from the superintendent, a young detective constable came in with a letter. After giving Colbeck a deferential smile, the newcomer handed the letter to Tallis.

'This came from the coroner, sir,' he said. 'Marked urgent.'

'Thank you.'

While the messenger went out, Tallis tore open the letter and took out the missive. His eyes widened with interest.

'A headless body was hauled out of the Thames this morning,' he explained, still reading it. 'From its condition, it appears that it was in the water for a couple of days at least. Although it was hideously bloated, the coroner is certain that the body and the severed head belong to the same person.'

'May I hazard a guess, Superintendent?' asked Colbeck.

'If you must.'

'Is the man's height given?'

'Yes, it is.'

'Then I guarantee that he'll be no taller than five feet.'

Tallis blinked. 'How did you know that?'

'I suspect that he might be a jockey.'

'His height is approximately four foot ten.'

After studying the letter again, Tallis put it aside and reached for a cigar. Deep in thought, he did not light it but rolled it slowly between his palms. He was reluctant to change his mind at the best of times, particularly where Robert Colbeck was involved, but he came to see that he had no choice. His voice dripped with rancour.

'You did say you'd pay your own fare to Ireland, didn't you?'

Colbeck beamed. 'There and back, Super-intendent.'

'I'm still not persuaded, however,' warned Tallis.

'Then I'd better find the evidence that will bring you around to my point of view. Thank you, superintendent,' he went on, moving happily to the door. 'You won't regret this decision.'

'I wasn't aware that I'd made one,' grumbled the other.

Then he lit his cigar and puffed on it with a vengeance.

Victor Leeming surprised himself. For the first time in his life, he almost enjoyed a train journey. Though he was travelling away from London, he had the comfort of knowing that he would be able to return to his family that night and shake off the memory of his two unsought trips on the railway.

Cambridge was within comparatively easy reach of the capital and he realised how beautiful the scenery was on the way there. As the train maintained a steady speed through open country, Leeming observed how effortlessly it overtook coaches and carts rumbling along roads that, from time to time, ran parallel with the line. By the time he reached his destination, he was compelled to admit that the railway did, after all, have its advantages.

Renowned for its university, Cambridge was also a thriving market town that brought people in from a wide area. While students inhabited the cloistered calm of the colleges or sought more boisterous pleasures on the playing fields, the narrow streets were thronged with local residents, visitors and the occasional beggar soliciting money from both. Having no inclination in that direction himself, Leeming had always been daunted by Cambridge's reputation for scholarship. In reality, it was not at all intimidating. To his relief, he found it a warm, welcoming, friendly place filled with what he deemed were refreshingly ordinary people.

Cambridge was small enough to explore on foot and replete with such wonderful medieval architecture that even the sergeant stopped to gape from time to time. There were a number of hotels but, as Colbeck had predicted, not all of them would have attracted someone like Lord Hendry, especially if he was there with someone other than his wife. Comfort and discretion would be the qualities he would expect from his accommodation. It took Leeming less than half an hour to find the establishment. After three failed attempts, he finally located the hotel he was after, a half-timbered building from the late Elizabethan period with a recently painted exterior and a sagging charm. Situated in a quiet street, the Angel Hotel offered a compound of luxury, tradition and quality service

When he asked to see the manager, Leeming was taken to a low-ceilinged room that served as an office and obliged Neville Hindmarsh to duck as he rose to his feet behind his desk. Had the sergeant not already have removed his top hat, it would have been scythed from his head by one of the solid oak beams. Unsettled by a visit from a Scotland Yard detective, the manager waved him anxiously to a seat before resuming his own.

'What brings you all the way from London?' he inquired.

'We're involved in an investigation, sir,' replied Leeming, 'and the name of this hotel cropped up in the course of it.'

'And what exactly are you investigating?'

'A murder.'

Hindmarsh gulped. He was an exceptionally tall man in his forties, lean, long-faced and with a studious air. He looked less like the manager of a hotel than the Fellow of a nearby college who had wandered absent-mindedly into the building after mistaking it for the Senior Common Room. When the sergeant explained that he wanted to know more detail about the theft of a hatbox, Hindmarsh blushed as if being accused of the crime himself. He needed a moment to compose himself.

'I think you've been misinformed, Sergeant,' he said.

'Really?'

'No hatbox – or any other item, for that matter – was stolen from this hotel. We pride ourselves on the security we offer our guests. It's a major reason why many of them return to us again and again.'

Leeming was puzzled. 'Nothing was stolen?'

'If it had been, it would have been reported to the police.'

'Lord Hendry assured us that the theft occurred here and he would surely know. You do recall the recent visit he and his wife made here?'

'Very clearly.'

'Then why does his version of events differ from yours?'

'I can't answer that,' said Hindmarsh nervously. 'What I can tell you categorically is that the hatbox was not taken on these premises. I distinctly remember seeing Lady Hendry depart with it.'

'Oh?'

'I was standing by the door to bid her farewell when the porter carried it out to the cab. Lady Hendry arrived with one hatbox and left with it. I'd take my Bible oath on that.'

'I can't believe that her husband deliberately misled us.'

'I'm sure it was an honest mistake,' said Hindmarsh, groping for an explanation. 'Perhaps the item was stolen at the railway station. Unfortunately, we've had luggage taken from there before. When he mentioned this hotel, Lord Hendry could have been hazarding a guess. After all, he

69

was not here at the time.'

'That's odd,' said Leeming. 'Where else would he be?'

'At the races in Newmarket.'

'What about Lady Hendry?'

'She remained here for a while then left to catch an afternoon train. Lady Hendry had all of the luggage she had brought.'

'How long did they stay at the Angel?'

'They booked in for three nights, Sergeant Leeming. In the event, they only stayed for one.'

'Why was that, sir?'

'Not because of any shortcomings on our part,' said Hindmarsh quickly. 'Lady Hendry's sudden departure was quite unexpected. When her husband got back from Newmarket, he was astonished that she was not here. After paying the bill, he left immediately.'

'Did you find that behaviour rather strange?'

'It's not for me to say, Sergeant.'

'Have Lord and Lady Hendry ever stayed here before?'

'Yes,' said Hindmarsh. 'On two previous occasions.'

'When there were races at Newmarket?'

'Precisely.'

'Did his wife accompany Lord Hendry to the races?'

'No, sergeant – Lady Hendry always remained at the hotel.'

'Does she have no interest in the Turf?'

'Who knows, sir?'

'You must have speculated on the reason.'

'When guests book a room here,' said Hindmarsh tactfully, 'they can come and go as they wish. I do not keep an eye on them or pry into their private lives.'

Leeming was not hindered by any restraints. He was employed to pry. There was one obvious reason why the woman posing as Lady Hendry did not go to Newmarket. Lord Hendry was a familiar figure at any racecourse. Had he been seen flaunting his mistress, word would certainly have trickled back to his wife. Colbeck's theory about the Lady Hendry with the hatbox had now turned into hard fact. The sergeant took out his notebook then licked the end of his pencil.

'I need your assistance, Mr Hindmarsh,' he said with what he hoped was a disarming smile, 'and I don't think you'll be breaking a confidence in giving it to me.'

The manager was suspicious. 'What kind of assistance?'

'I want you to describe Lady Hendry to me.'

When he finished work that evening, Caleb Andrews paid his customary visit to a tavern frequented by railwaymen. He enjoyed an hour's badinage with friends, a couple of pints of beer and, by dint of winning two games of dominoes, he did not even have to pay for the alcohol. As he sauntered home towards Camden, therefore, he was cheerful and the mood continued when he reached his house and found that Madeleine had supper waiting for him.

'You're back early for a change,' she observed, giving him a token kiss of welcome. 'Did you have a good day?'

71

'Yes, Maddy – I've been to Crewe and back again.'

'You must know every inch of that line.'

'I could drive it in my sleep.'

'Well, I hope I'm not a passenger when you do it.' They shared a laugh and sat down at the table. 'And thank you for coming back while I'm still up. It makes a big difference.'

'I stopped playing dominoes while I was still winning.'

'We could have a game afterwards, if you like.'

'Oh, no,' said Andrews, raising both hands as if to ward her off. 'You have the luck of the devil whenever we play a game together. Cards, dominoes, draughts – it's always the same. You manage to beat me every time somehow.'

Madeleine grinned. 'I had an excellent teacher.'

'It was a mistake to teach you at all.' He forked some food into his mouth. 'What have you been doing all day, Maddy?'

'Working and reading.'

'Have you started your latest painting yet?'

'I've done a pen-and-ink sketch, that's all.'

'Will I be in this one?'

'No, Father – just the locomotive.'

'It has to have a driver,' he complained.

'Figures are my weak spot. I try to leave them out.'

He munched disconsolately. 'What have you been reading?'

'All sorts of interesting things,' she said chirpily. 'Robert lent me some books. He has hundreds of them in his library.'

'I'm glad you mentioned Inspector Colbeck,'

he said, swallowing a piece of bread and washing it down with a sip of tea. 'Next time he gets in touch, tell him I need to speak to him.'

'What about?'

'That severed head, of course. I've been thinking about it a lot and I've got an idea of what might have happened.'

'Why not leave the detection to Robert?'

'He's always grateful for help from the public.'

'Only if it's useful to him.'

'Well, this will be, Maddy,' he argued. 'I've worked it out, see? It was a crime of passion. A married woman who lives in Crewe betrayed her husband with a young man from London. The husband was so angry that he took his wife's hatbox to London – I may even have been driving the train that took him there – and killed the lover before cutting his head off. Then he took it back to Crewe to give to his wife.'

Madeleine grimaced. 'That's a horrible story!'

'It could also be a true one.'

'I doubt that very much, Father.'

'Let the Inspector be the judge of that.'

'He already has been.'

'I know I'm right, Maddy. I've solved the crime for him.'

'If that were the case,' she said, 'Robert would be grateful. But he has his own notions about the murder. To start with, that hatbox was not going to Crewe at all.'

'It had to be – that's where it was unloaded.'

'Only so that it could be transferred to another train.'

'You know nothing,' he said, irritated at the way

she dismissed his idea. 'I've put a lot of thought into this. It was a crime of passion.'

'Robert has discovered who owned that hatbox.'

'An unfaithful wife in Crewe.'

'Someone who lives in Surrey,' she explained. 'He gave me no details but he's picked up clues that are sending him off in another direction altogether.'

Andrews was hurt. 'You've *discussed* the case with him?'

'Not exactly.'

'Why didn't you keep him here until I came back? You know how keen I am to help, Maddy. I'm a bit of a detective myself.'

'Robert didn't call here,' she said, 'but he sent me a short note to say that he'd be away for a few days and would speak to me when he came back.'

'Where has he gone – back to Crewe?'

'Yes, Father.'

He clapped his hands. 'I knew it!'

'But only to change trains, I'm afraid,' Madeleine went on. 'He was planning to spend the night at Holyhead before catching the morning tide tomorrow.'

He was startled. 'Where, in God's name, is the man going?'

'Ireland.'

Robert Colbeck's passionate interest in railways was not only based on the fact that they could get him from one place to another quicker than any other means of transport. They also gave him a privileged view of town and country that he

74

would never have got from a coach, and he always saw something new to admire even on lines he had used many times. After leaving Euston on the LNWR, he changed trains at Crewe, had a few cheering words with Reginald Hibbert, now restored to his job as a porter at the station, then went along the North Wales coast by courtesy of the Chester and Holyhead Railway, a line built specifically to carry the Irish mail. Some of the panoramas that unfolded before him were stunning – dramatic seascapes, sweeping bays, craggy headland, sandy beaches and long, scenic stretches of unspoilt countryside. The train hugged the coast until it reached Bangor where it gave Colbeck an experience he had been looking forward to since the moment of his departure.

He had read a great deal about the Britannia Tubular Bridge over the Menai Straits and recognised it as one of the most significant advances in railway engineering. With only existing rock for intermediate support, the bridge had to span a gap of over 450 feet that could not be traversed by suspension techniques used elsewhere. Five years in construction, the Britannia Bridge comprised two very stiff rectangular wrought-iron tubes with cellular tops and bottoms to increase rigidity. With a novel application of beam action, the tubes were made to act as continuous girders over five spans. When it was finally opened in 1850, the bridge was daring, innovative and an instant success.

Colbeck was unable to appreciate its finer points as he crossed the bridge but he felt an excitement as they entered the tube and liked the way that the clamour of the train was suddenly amplified. By the time he reached Holyhead, he had travelled 84 miles on the CHR and had relished every moment of it. Having obtained the monopoly to carry mail by land, the company had hoped to extend this to sea and had secured the powers to own and operate steamships. To their utter dismay, however, the CHR failed to win the contract for taking the mail across the Irish Sea.

When he sailed on the following morning, therefore, Colbeck did so on a vessel owned by the City of Dublin Steam Packet Company. The first thing he noticed was that far more passengers poured off the incoming steamer than actually went aboard. Emigration from Ireland had reached its peak in the previous decade when a succession of disastrous harvests had driven hundreds of thousands out of their native land. Though the process had slowed markedly, it still continued as whole families left the poverty and hunger of Ireland in the hope of finding a better life in England or beyond its shores.

The sea was choppy and the crossing uncomfortable. Gulls accompanied them all the way and kept up a mocking chorus as they dived and wheeled incessantly around the vessel. Colbeck was glad when they eventually entered the relative calm of the harbour and when he was able to step on to dry land again. He would have been interested to travel on an Irish railway but it was not possible. The place he was visiting was not accessible by rail and was, in any case, only a twenty-minute ride by cab from Dublin.

Though vast numbers had fled Ireland, not all

of those who remained lived in the squalor and penury that had driven the others away. The capital city was full of beautiful Georgian properties and fine civic buildings and there was ample evidence of prosperity at every turn. Ireland had its fair share of wealthy men and, judging by the mansion in which he lived, Brian Dowd was one of them. Set in a hundred acres of parkland, the house was an impressive piece of Regency architecture that stood four-square on a plateau and commanded inspiring views on every side. At its rear was the extensive stable block that Colbeck had come to visit.

He had no difficulty picking out Brian Dowd. Standing in the middle of the yard, the racehorse owner and trainer was a bull-necked man in his fifties with a solid frame and a gnarled face. He wore an old jacket, mud-spattered trousers and a bowler hat. Yelling orders to all and sundry, he had a natural authority that gained him unquestioning obedience. Colbeck ran an eye along the stalls and guessed that at least thirty racehorses were kept there. He walked across to Dowd and introduced himself. The Irishman laughed affably.

'Have you come to arrest me, then, Inspector?' he taunted. 'Since when has there been a law against breeding a Derby winner?'

'It doesn't exist, Mr Dowd. Over the years, Parliament has put many absurd pieces of legislation in the statute book but it's far too fond of racing even to contemplate such a ridiculous law as that.' He shook hands with Dowd and felt the strength of his grip. 'No, I come on a different errand.'

'Pleasant or unpleasant?'

'Unpleasant, I fear.'

'Then let's discuss this over a drink.'

He led Colbeck to an office at the edge of the stable block and took him in. Horses dominated the little room. Every wall was covered with paintings of them and their smell pervaded the whole place. Equine memorabilia covered the desk. While his visitor removed his top hat and looked around, Dowd produced a bottle of whiskey and two glasses from a cupboard. He poured the liquid out generously.

'Irish whiskey,' he said bluntly. 'Never touch any other.'

'That suits me, Mr Dowd,' said Colbeck, taking a glass from him with a nod of gratitude. 'We had a rough crossing. I need something to settle my stomach.' He sampled his drink. 'Excellent.'

'You'll not find better in the whole of the Emerald Isle.'

'It was worth the long journey just to taste this.'

'You're a good liar.'

Colbeck smiled. 'Part of my stock-in-trade.'

'Sit yourself down, Inspector.'

'Thank you.'

Putting his hat aside, Colbeck lowered himself into a chair and Dowd perched on the edge of his desk. As they sipped their drinks, each weighed the other man up. The Irishman had a friendly grin but his gaze was shrewd and calculating. Nobody as elegant and as quintessentially urban as Colbeck had ever been in the office before and he looked distinctly incongruous. That did not disturb the visitor in any way. He was relaxed and self-assured. Dowd had another sip of whiskey and savoured its taste before speaking.

'So what's this all about, Inspector Colbeck?' he asked.

'A murder, sir.'

'Murder? I don't like the sound of that.'

'I'm hoping that you may be able to help me solve the crime.'

'I'd gladly do so, my friend, but I don't rightly see how. I'm no policeman. This murder happened in England, I take it.'

'Yes, sir.'

'And who was the victim?'

'We're not certain,' said Colbeck, putting his glass on the desk so that he could take a sheet of paper from his pocket. 'I got an artist to draw a rough portrait of the young man.' He unfolded the paper and handed it over. 'I came here in search of his identity.'

Eyes gleaming and brow corrugated, Brian Dowd looked at the drawing with great concentration. He took a long time to reach a decision and even then he qualified it.

'I could be wrong, mind you,' he cautioned.

'But you think you recognise him?'

'I might do. It's like the lad in one way, then again it isn't.'

'Make allowances for the fact that the face was distorted in death,' said Colbeck. 'When the artist drew this, by the way, he only had the head to work from. The body was hauled out of the Thames long after he'd finished.'

Dowd was aghast. 'The lad was *beheaded*?'

'Yes, sir.'

'Dear God!' exclaimed the other. 'What monster did that?'

Colbeck explained the circumstances in which the head had been found and how the hatbox had been linked to Lord Hendry. The more the inspector spoke, the more convinced Dowd became that he knew the deceased. Folding the paper, he gave it back.

'His name is John Feeny.'

'Are you sure?' pressed Colbeck.

'Pretty sure – he used to work for me.'

'As a jockey?'

'No, Inspector,' replied Dowd, 'it was as a groom. That was the reason we fell out. John thought he had the makings of a jockey. I told him straight that he wasn't good enough.'

'What did he do?'

'What any lad with real mettle would've done – he went off in search of a job at another stables. He'd no family here to turn to so he sailed off to try his luck in England.'

'Did you keep in touch with him?'

'I'd no reason to, Inspector. One of my other lads did, though. John Feeny couldn't read or write but he got someone to send a letter or two on his behalf. Things were tough at first but he found a job in the end. He even boasted he'd soon be a jockey.'

'That will never happen now,' said Colbeck sadly.

'No – and it's a crying shame.' He smacked his thigh. 'Jesus, I feel so guilty! I wish I'd kept him here and given him a chance in the saddle. But,' he added with a deep sigh, 'it wouldn't have been fair to other lads with more talent as riders. John

Feeny was never strong enough or ruthless enough to make a living as a jockey.'

'Could I speak to the person who kept in touch with him?'

'Of course – his name is Jerry Doyle.'

'Did he tell you which stables Feeny was working at?'

'He did, Inspector – I had a vested interest in knowing.'

'Did they happen to belong to Lord Hendry?' When the Irishman shook his head, Colbeck was disappointed. 'I obviously made the wrong assumption.'

'In the world of racing,' said Dowd sagely before gulping down more whiskey, 'you should never make assumptions of any kind. It's far too dangerous, Inspector.'

'I can see that.'

'It was a big decision for someone like John to go to England but the lad seemed to have fallen on his feet.'

'For whom was he working?'

'Hamilton Fido.'

'The bookmaker?'

'There's only one Mr Fido in this game,' said Dowd bitterly, 'and that's one too many in my book. The man is as slippery as an eel and as vicious as a polecat. He gives racing a bad name. He ought to be drummed out of it in disgrace.'

'You and he are clearly not on the best of terms.'

'We're not on any kind of terms, Inspector.'

'Mr Fido has a horse running in the Derby – Merry Legs.'

81

'She'll be left standing by Limerick Lad.'

'Odysseus is the favourite.'

'Not from where I stand,' asserted Dowd, 'and I've spent my whole life around racehorses. I've seen both Odysseus and Merry Legs at their best. Neither of them cause me any worry.'

'Let's go back to John Feeny,' said Colbeck, reclaiming his glass from the desk. 'I believe that severed head was destined to come here. It could have been sent to you as a warning.'

'I agree, Inspector.'

'Someone is trying to frighten you off.'

'It was a message for me,' said Dowd grimly, 'no question about that. Because he used to work here at one time, John Feeny was suspected of being a spy. Someone thought he'd been planted in the stables so that he could feed back information to me about a leading Derby contender. Since I was seen as the villain, they tried to send a piece of the lad back here to give me a scare.'

'That means Hamilton Fido is somehow involved.'

'He's your killer, Inspector. He's such a cruel bastard that he'd enjoy cutting off someone's head. Go back and arrest him.'

'It may not be as simple as that, Mr Dowd,' said Colbeck. 'From what I've heard of Mr Fido, he's devious and manipulative. He'd get someone else to do his dirty work for him and make sure that he kept his hands clean. In any case, we've no proof that he's in any way connected to the crime. But let me return to this charge of spying,' he continued. 'When a major race is coming up, there must be a lot of that sort of thing going on.'

'We all like to know as much as we can about the competition.'

'How would you find out about Merry Legs and Odysseus?'

'Not by putting a lad like that in someone's stables,' retorted Dowd. 'I didn't send him off to his death, Inspector, so don't look to accuse me. I told you what happened. John Feeny left of his own accord. I wished him well before he went and gave him twice what I owed him. You can ask Jerry Doyle – or anyone else, for that matter.'

'I take your word for it, sir.'

'The man you're after is Hamilton Fido.'

'I'll speak with him at the earliest opportunity,' said Colbeck, taking a longer sip of his whiskey. 'If he's capable of murder, he'll clearly stop at nothing to win the Derby.'

'Nothing at all.'

'I hope you've taken extra precautions to protect Limerick Lad.'

'Don't trouble yourself on that score.'

'Mr Fido – or your other rivals – might have someone watching these stables and biding their time until they can strike.'

'We took that into account, Inspector Colbeck.'

'What do you mean?'

'As I told you,' said Dowd, looking him in the eye, 'racing has been my life. There's not a dirty trick or a clever ruse I haven't seen ten times over. On the night before a big race, I've often slept on the straw beside one of my horses with a loaded shotgun. Nobody has ever managed to cause serious injury to one of my animals.'

'They killed one of your former grooms.'

'John Feeny was an innocent victim – God save his soul!'

'How can you be sure they won't strike at Limerick Lad next?' said Colbeck. 'You've a long journey ahead of you. There'll be plenty of opportunities to attack him on the way. When do you leave?'

'Tomorrow.'

'I'll be happy to come with you to act as a guard.'

'Kind of you to offer, Inspector,' said Dowd, 'but it won't be necessary. We'll travel on our own, if you don't mind. And don't worry about my horse. It's quite impossible for anyone to get at Limerick Lad on the way to England.'

'Not if someone is desperate enough.'

'That'd make no difference.'

'Have you forgotten what happened to John Feeny?'

'No, I haven't,' said Dowd soulfully, 'and I'll do everything in my power to help you catch his killer. It's the least I can do for the boy. But I still have no concerns about Limerick Lad.'

'Why not?'

'For reasons of safety, he was taken to England days ago. Until the Derby, he's being kept in a secret location.' Dowd grinned broadly. 'I wouldn't tell my own mother where we've got him hidden.'

CHAPTER FIVE

When he eventually returned to London, it was too late for Victor Leeming to report to the superintendent so he was glad to postpone that unappealing duty until the following day. There was a further delay. Edward Tallis spent all morning at a meeting with the commissioner. It was not until early afternoon that Leeming was able to speak to the superintendent. He approached the office with trepidation. Robert Colbeck enjoyed sparring with Tallis and welcomed their encounters. Leeming viewed them as nerve-racking ordeals. With the inspector beside him, he could put on a brave face at such interviews. When he had to confront the superintendent alone and unaided, he quailed inwardly.

Plucking up his courage, the sergeant knocked on the door. The invitation for him to enter was an angry bellow. Superintendent Tallis, it appeared, was not at his most docile. Leeming went in.

'I've been waiting for you,' said Tallis irritably. 'What kept you?'

'Nothing ... that is ... I mean ... well, you see...'

'Spare me your excuses, sergeant. I know from past experience that they'll be embarrassingly weak. What do you have to report?'

'I went to Cambridge yesterday,' said Leeming.

'That much I know. Tell me something I don't know.'

'It's a very pleasant place, Superintendent.'

'I don't want a guided tour of the town,' snapped Tallis. 'I want to hear what evidence you managed to gather.'

'Ah, yes.'

'Take a seat while you give it.'

Leeming sat down. 'Thank you, sir.'

Consulting his notebook throughout, he gave a halting account of his visit to the Angel Hotel and explained that the hatbox had not been stolen from there. When Leeming passed on a description of the woman who had stayed in Cambridge with Lord Hendry, the superintendent's eyebrows went up and down like a pair of dancing caterpillars. A note of moral outrage came into his voice.

'That does not sound like his lawful wife.'

'She was so much younger than him, sir,' said Leeming. 'The inspector was certain that the real Lady Hendry had not been at that hotel. He sensed it from the start.'

'Let's forget Inspector Colbeck for a moment, shall we?' said Tallis with a sniff. 'All that interests me at this juncture is what you found out about that hatbox.'

'It must have been stolen elsewhere.'

'Then why did Lord Hendry lie about it?'

'I intend to ask him that very question, sir.'

'No, no – don't do that. We don't want Lord Hendry to know that we've found him out. That will only throw him on the defensive. Also, of course,' he went on, stroking his moustache, 'the fact that he and a certain person spent the night together may have nothing whatsoever to do with the crime we are investigating.'

'Inspector Colbeck felt that it did.'

'I told you to keep him out of this.'

'But he's usually right about such things, sir.'

'We have to tread very carefully,' insisted Tallis, thinking it through. 'Lord Hendry has misled two officers of the law and I deprecate that but it is not, at this stage, an offence that renders him liable to arrest. It may well be that this so-called "Lady Hendry" *told* him that the hatbox was stolen from that hotel. What she said to him was thus passed on to you in good faith. Conceivably, he may be the victim of her deception.'

'His wife is the real victim here,' noted Leeming.

Tallis nodded. 'One of the many perils of marriage.'

'It has its compensations, sir.'

'How can you compensate for adultery?'

'That's not what I meant, Superintendent. Because one man goes astray, it doesn't mean that marriage itself is at fault. There's nothing so wonderful as being joined together in holy matrimony. Family life is a joy to me.'

'We are not talking about you, Leeming.'

'You seemed to be criticising the whole idea of marriage.'

'I was,' said Tallis vehemently, 'and I'll continue to do so. Lord Hendry's case is only one of thousands. All over London, husbands and wives readily forget the vows they took so solemnly at the altar. If adultery were made the crime that it should be, every gaol in the country would be bursting at the seams.'

'For every bad marriage, there are dozens of

good ones.'

'How do you know?'

'It stands to reason, sir.'

'Then why do we have to deal with so much domestic strife? Policemen in some parts of the city seem to spend half their time stopping married couples from trying to kill each other. Wives have been bludgeoned to death. Husbands have been poisoned. Unwanted children have had their throats cut.'

'We only get to see the worst cases, Superintendent.'

'They show the defects of the institution of marriage.'

Victor Leeming bit back what he was going to say. Arguing with the superintendent was never advisable. He decided that it was better to weather the storm of Tallis's vituperation in silence. The tirade against holy matrimony went on for a few minutes then came to an abrupt stop.

'Where were we?' demanded Tallis.

'You thought Lord Hendry might be the victim of deception, sir.'

'It's a possibility we have to consider.'

'What we need to find out is who that other Lady Hendry was.'

'I doubt very much if he would volunteer the information.'

'Since the hatbox belonged to her,' said Leeming, 'it may even be that she was a party to the conspiracy to murder. She only *pretended* that the item was stolen.'

'That would implicate Lord Hendry as well.'

'Not necessarily, sir.'

'You met him – what manner of man was he?'

'Exactly what you'd expect of a lord, sir,' recalled Leeming, pulling at an ear lobe. 'He was dignified, well spoken and a bit too haughty for my liking. He seemed honest enough to me until Inspector Colbeck pointed out something I'd missed. Lord Hendry was a proper gentleman.' He became confidential. 'And the best thing about the visit was that he told us who'd win the Derby. I know where to put my money now.'

Tallis scowled. 'You intend to place a bet, Sergeant?'

'Just a small amount, sir.'

'I don't care if it's only a brass farthing. Gambling is sinful. Think what a bad example you're setting.'

'Everyone bets on the Derby.'

'I don't and nor should you.'

'Why not, Superintendent?'

'Because it only encourages crime,' said Tallis. 'Bookmakers are, by definition, thoroughgoing villains. They rig the betting so that they can never lose and they exploit gullible fools like you. They're a despicable breed who should be hung in chains and left to rot.'

Leeming was roused. 'Betting is harmless fun, sir.'

'It's a foul disease.'

'People are entitled to dream.'

'Not if their dreams have a selfish foundation. That's what gambling is about, sergeant – investing little money in the hope of making a large amount. Work!' declared the superintendent, pounding his desk with a fist. 'That's the only decent way to acquire money.'

'But when people *have* worked,' said Leeming, stung by the blanket condemnation of gambling, 'they're entitled to spend it how they wish. Betting on the Derby is a tradition.'

'A very bad tradition.'

'Wanting to win is a normal human urge, sir.'

'But commonsense tells you that the overwhelming majority of people will lose. All that gambling does is to fill up debtors' prisons. In the case of the Derby, it's part of the whole ugly panoply of crime.'

'What's criminal about putting a few shillings on a horse?'

'You're helping to fund a national scandal,' said Tallis, raising his voice and gesticulating as he warmed to his theme. 'What are the constituent elements of the Derby? I'll tell you, Sergeant. Violence, theft, deceit, drunkenness, gluttony, gambling and sexual licence – all played out against a background of loud music, bawling crowds and a loss of inhibition that would make any true Christian weep.'

'I like to think *I'm* a true Christian,' said Leeming meekly.

'Then why do you condone this annual saturnalia?'

'All I want to do is to put money on Odysseus.'

'Off-course betting was banned last year. Surely, you're not intending to go to Epsom for the express purpose of being tricked by a bookmaker?' He saw Leeming shrink back in his chair. 'I hope you're not thinking of flouting the law by indulging in *illegal* betting.'

90

'It would never cross mind, sir,' said Leeming hastily, wishing that he had held his peace. He sought a means of escape. 'Thank you, Superintendent – you've talked me out of it.'

'At least, some good may have come out of this conversation.'

'Yes, sir.'

'Let's put the Derby from our minds, shall we?'

'But this murder is connected to the race.'

'Inspector Colbeck is the only person who thinks that.'

'I agree with him,' said the sergeant loyally. 'There's a huge amount of money at stake, sir. Whenever that happens, you'll always have corruption of some sort or other.'

'That's exactly what I've been saying.'

'The inspector wouldn't have gone to Ireland on a whim.'

'I reserve my judgement on that particular venture,' said Tallis coolly. 'I still fear that it may have been a wild goose. While we're waiting for Inspector Colbeck to return from his unnecessary visit to Ireland, exercise your mind with this question – what is the name of the bogus Lady Hendry?'

Lord Hendry was not known for his patience. He was accustomed to getting what he wanted when he needed it. Waiting quietly was an alien concept to him. Instead of relaxing in a chair, he paced the room like a caged animal, checked his watch every few minutes and kept pulling back the curtain to look out into the street below. The time arranged for the meeting came and went. Half an hour soon scudded past. His impatience gave way to a cold anger that was, in turn, replaced by a burning desire for revenge. When he saw that it was an hour past the appointed time, he could stand the suspense no longer. Snatching up his hat, he moved towards the door. Before he reached it, however, someone tapped on the other side.

Torn between rage and hope, he flung open the door.

She had come at last.

'Where on earth have you *been?*' he demanded.

'I was unavoidably detained.'

'By whom?'

'If you'll let me in,' she said with an appeasing smile, 'then I might be able to explain.' He stepped aside so that she could enter the room then shut the door. 'First of all, let me apologise.'

'You're an hour late, Kitty!'

'Be grateful that I came at all. When I got your letter, my first instinct was to burn it along with all the others. It was only after calm reflection that I felt you deserved the right to see me.'

'I told you how important it was.'

'Important to you, George,' she said with mock sweetness, 'but not quite so important to me, I suspect. Before we go any further, let me make one thing crystal clear. If the purpose of this meeting is to make overtures to me, then I may as well leave immediately. After what happened between us, I could never countenance a return to our earlier situation.'

Kitty Lavender glanced around the room with mingled distaste and nostalgia. They were in the London hotel where their romance had first started and it aroused mixed emotions in her.

She was a graceful woman in her twenties with a startling beauty that was enhanced by exquisite clothing. Her blonde ringlets hung around the flower-trimmed edges of a poke bonnet. Kitty Lavender had the bearing and assurance of an aristocrat even though she had been born much lower down the social scale. In spite of himself, Lord Hendry felt the pull of an old affection.

'You look positively divine,' he said, appraising her with a smile.

She stiffened. 'I need no compliments,' she said frostily.

'At least, take a seat while you're here.'

'I'll not be staying.'

'Doesn't this room bring back memories?'

'Ones that I'd prefer to forget.'

'Have it your way,' he said, reverting to a subdued fury. 'I asked you here for one reason only. What happened to that hatbox I bought you in Jermyn Street?'

'Hatbox!' she echoed with a splutter. 'You brought me all the way here to talk about a hatbox?'

'Yes, I did – and you won't leave until I know the truth.'

Kitty bridled. 'You can't keep me against my will.'

'I'll do as I wish.'

'Stand aside,' she ordered as he put his back against the door. 'If you don't do so at once, I shall call for help.'

'Answer my question, Kitty – or would you rather have it put to you by the police? I've already had them banging on my door.'

93

'The police?'

'Two detectives from Scotland Yard.'

She was mystified. 'And they asked you about my hatbox?'

'It's taken on a gruesome significance,' he told her. 'It was found at Crewe railway station with a severed head inside it.'

She opened her mouth to emit a silent scream of horror then she slumped on to a chair. Seeing her distress, he tried to put a consoling hand on her shoulder but she waved him away. Kitty Lavender pulled out a delicate lace handkerchief and dabbed at her eyes. It was some time before she was able to collect herself.

'Can this be true, George?' she asked.

'Unfortunately, it can.'

'But how did they know it was *my* hatbox?'

'The milliner's name was inside. Inspector Colbeck visited him and discovered who purchased it. That brought the inspector to me.'

'What did you tell him?'

'The same as I told that posturing ninny Elijah Swinnerton – that I was buying the hat and hatbox for my wife. To get rid of him, I said that it had been stolen from that hotel in Cambridge.'

'Supposing that he checks your story?'

'There's no chance of that,' he said confidently. 'Besides, I made sure that I didn't give him the name of the hotel. But the fact remains that your hatbox was responsible for the police visit. It was highly disturbing, Kitty. Had I not been there, Caroline might have spoken to them and discovered what I had been doing in Jermyn Street. That would have been a catastrophe.'

'It's your own fault for buying gifts for another woman.'

'You *wanted* that hat.'

'I did – it was perfect for me.'

'At the time, I was happy to get it for you. Now, however,' he went on, 'I wish I'd never gone anywhere near that confounded shop.'

'Near the shop – or near to me?'

Their eyes locked and he felt a surge of affection. Though they had parted acrimoniously, he had not forgotten the intimacies he had once shared with her in that very room. He tried to read her thoughts but could no longer do so. Uncertain whether she was teasing him or flirting with him, he dared to believe that it might be the latter. Out of the corner of his eye, he could see the bed in which they had spent their first night together.

'I never regretted being near to you, Kitty.'

'That's not what you said the last time we met.'

'I was provoked, as you well know.'

'So was I, George.'

She held his gaze a little longer then stood up to walk past him. Whatever lingering fondness he felt for her, it was not requited. All that Kitty could think about was the hatbox.

'You were not so far from the truth,' she said.

'What do you mean?'

'As it happens, the hatbox *was* stolen from a hotel but it was not the one where we stayed in Cambridge.'

'Which hotel was it?' he asked.

'That's of no concern to you.'

'It's of *every* concern, Kitty. A hatbox that I bought as a present is at the centre of a murder

investigation. I want to know exactly what happened to it.'

'So do I, George.'

'What was the name of the hotel?'

'I'm not telling you.'

'And I suppose you won't tell me the name of
the man who took you there either, will you?' he
said nastily. 'What did *he* have to buy you to win
your favours?'

She struck a pose. 'I'm saying nothing.'

'Was the hotel in London?'

'Nothing whatsoever.'

'Oh, no,' he gasped as realisation hit him with
the force of a blow. 'Please don't tell me that it
was here – in *our* hotel. Even you would never
sink that low, Kitty.'

'I must be on my way.'

'Then it *was* here.'

'It was a mistake to meet you again. I should
have had the sense to foresee that.' She moved
away. 'Goodbye, George.'

'But the conversation is not over yet.'

'Yes, it is – for good.'

'There are still things to discuss.'

'Not any more.'

'You haven't explained why you were so late.'

'No,' she said with utter disdain. 'I haven't,
have I?'

With a tinkle of laughter, Kitty Lavender went
out of the room and left the door wide open.
Lord Hendry was mortified.

Madeleine Andrews had had a full day. After doing
her domestic chores, she had visited the market to

buy food then spent several hours on her painting of a Crampton locomotive. It was only when light began to fade in the early evening that she put her easel aside. After cooking herself a meal, she gave herself the pleasure of starting a new book. Borrowed from Robert Colbeck, it had been warmly recommended by him. As she settled down beside the lamp, it occurred to her that she was probably the only woman in London who was reading John Francis's *History of the English Railway; Its Social Relations and Revelations (1820–45)*.

The writing was lively and the material absorbing to someone with her abiding interest in the subject. Madeleine became so immersed in the book that she did not hear a cab approaching in the street outside or even the sound of the front door opening. Caleb Andrews came into the house with a knowing grin on his face.

'Hello, Maddy,' he said.

'Oh!' she cried, looking up in surprise. 'I didn't expect you for hours yet, Father.'

'Does that mean there's no supper yet?'

'I can soon make some.'

'Stay here and entertain our visitor.'

'What visitor?'

'This stray gentlemen I picked up in Crewe.'

He stood aside so that Robert Colbeck could come into the house. Doffing his top hat, the detective gave Madeleine a polite bow.

'I hope I'm not interrupting anything,' he said.

'No, no,' she told him, leaping to her feet and putting the book aside. She straightened her dress. 'I was reading.'

'That book on railways, is it?' asked Andrews

scornfully. 'Why bother with that when you only have to ask me? I can tell you more about railways than John Francis will ever know.'

'Your father's train brought me back to London,' said Colbeck.

'I wish I'd known that you were coming,' said Madeleine.

'I did promise to call in when I returned from Ireland.'

'How was it?'

'Invite him to sit down,' said Andrews, nudging her, 'and make him feel welcome. I need to have a wash. That's one thing your book won't say about work on the railway – how dirty you get.'

Whisking off his cap, he went out to the kitchen and closed the door firmly behind him. Colbeck stepped forward to give Madeleine a proper greeting, taking both hands and kissing her on the lips.

'I missed you,' she said.

'I wish I could have taken you with me.'

'Was the journey worthwhile?'

'Extremely worthwhile,' he replied. 'I know the identity of the murder victim now and I got some more insights into the ramifications of the racing world.'

'Do you have a suspect?'

'A possible one.'

'Who is he?'

He was cautious. 'Let me speak to the gentleman first. He may well turn out to be wrongly accused. In my experience, we rarely find our perpetrators this easily. I fancy that I have a long way to go in the investigation yet.'

'But you still think the murder may be linked to the Derby?'

'There's no doubt about it.'

'Why?'

'The victim was a groom. He worked at the stables where one of the fancied runners in the race is kept.'

Madeleine smiled. 'I've always wanted to go to the Derby,' she said wistfully. 'Father keeps telling me that it's no place for a young lady to go on her own but it sounds so exciting.'

'Highly exciting and unique.'

'You've been?'

'A number of times,' he told her. 'But don't give up hope, Madeleine. You may get to see the race one day.' He squeezed her shoulders tenderly. 'There's something I wanted to say before your father comes back in.'

'Oh, he'll stay in the kitchen for a while. Father can be tactful when he wants to be. Has he told you about his theory yet?'

'He did nothing else on the cab ride from Euston. According to Mr Andrews, instead of rushing off to Ireland, I should be searching for a wayward lady in Crewe who had a dalliance with the murder victim. It seems that the killer was a jealous husband. Your father has obviously devoted time to thinking about the case,' said Colbeck tolerantly, 'even though he's not in possession of the salient facts.'

'What did you want to say to me?'

'Only that you look as lovely as ever.'

She laughed. 'In this old dress – stop lying to me.'

'It's not the dress that matters, it's the young lady inside it.'

'You pay me the sweetest compliments.'

'Thank you.' He became serious. 'I need to ask you a favour, Madeleine. Unbeknown to the superintendent, you've been able to help me a couple of times in the past. If Mr Tallis ever found out, he'd probably have me boiled in oil but I'll take that risk. Could I impose on you to assist me again, please?'

'Of course, Robert – it's no imposition.'

'It may not be necessary but I'd like to have you in reserve.'

'Why?'

'Why else? There's a lady in the case.'

'Ah, I see. You want to set a thief to catch a thief.'

'Not exactly,' he said. 'This particular lady may turn out to be a hapless victim but she does hold critical information. I need to get it from her and that may involve you.'

'I'll do anything you ask me, Robert.'

He smiled roguishly. 'You might care to re-phrase that,' he said. 'It puts you in a position of great vulnerability.'

'I trust you completely.'

'Then I'll do nothing to break that trust.'

'Who is this lady?'

'That's the problem – I don't have her name yet.'

'But you think she's involved in some way?'

'Oh, yes,' he said. 'I need to ask her about a missing hatbox.'

If he had not become a bookmaker, Hamilton

Fido could easily have pursued a career on the stage. Tall, slim and lithe, he had an actor's good looks, mellifluous voice and sheer presence. In his black frock coat and fawn trousers, he was an arresting figure with his mane of black wavy hair almost brushing his shoulders. Still in his thirties, Fido was so astute, well informed and ruthless that he had become one of the most successful bookmakers in London. His office was in an upstairs room in the tavern where he sometimes staged exhibition bouts with promising young boxers. In the courtyard at the rear of the building, illegal cock fights and dogfights were also arranged for those who liked to mix blood with their betting.

Hamilton Fido was seated at his desk, poring over a copy of the *Sporting Times*, when the door suddenly opened. Panting slightly, Kitty Lavender stood in the doorway with her hands on her hips. Fido did not even bother to look up.

'Go away, whoever you are,' he ordered. 'I'm too busy.'

'You're not too busy to see *me*, Hamilton.' She slammed the door for effect. 'I need to talk to you.'

'Kitty!' he exclaimed, going across to embrace her. 'What are you doing here?'

'Let go of me,' she said, turning her face away when he tried to kiss her. 'It's not that sort of visit.'

He released her and stepped back. 'What's the matter?'

'That's what I've come to tell you.'

'Can I offer you a drink?'

'No, I just want you to listen to me.'

101

'I'll do that all day and all night,' said Fido, leering politely at her. 'Especially all night.' He conducted her to a chair and sat beside her. 'You look distressed, my darling. Has anything happened?'

'Do you remember that stolen hatbox?'

'The one that was taken from that hotel?'

'Yes, Hamilton.'

'Forget all about it,' he advised. 'I know it was a shock at the time but I forced the management to pay for a new one. When a theft occurs on their premises, they must take responsibility.'

'That's not the point.'

'If you're still upset, I'll buy you another one – two, if you wish.'

'You're not listening to me,' she complained.

He took her hand. 'I won't let anything trouble you,' he said, placing a gentle kiss on it. 'You're mine now and I'll look after you.'

'My hatbox has been found, Hamilton.'

'What?'

'By the police.'

His smile vanished instantly and he let go of her hand. Recovering quickly, he gave her a reassuring pat on the arm. 'That's wonderful news,' he said. 'Where was it found?'

'At the railway station in Crewe.'

'Crewe – now that rings a bell.'

'Apparently, it had a man's head in it.'

Kitty's face crumpled at the memory. When he reached out to embrace her, she went willingly into his arms. She held her tight for a few moments then drew back so that he could look her in the face.

'You obviously don't read the newspapers, my

darling. There was an item days ago about a severed head being discovered in Crewe. It never crossed my mind that it was found in *your* hatbox.'

'Well, it was.'

'How do you know?'

'Let's just say that I was reliably informed.'

'Have the police been in touch with you?'

'No,' she replied, 'and there's no reason why they should. They won't be able to connect me with the hatbox.'

'Then what are you worrying about?'

'You, Hamilton – don't you see the implications?'

'All I can see is that my little darling has been badly shaken and that my job is to soothe her. You must have had a terrible jolt when you heard the news.'

'It made me feel sick, Hamilton.'

'Try to put the whole thing behind you. It's the best way.'

'How can I?' she asked in despair. 'This affects both of us. It was quite deliberate.'

'What was?'

'The theft of that hatbox – somebody stole it on purpose. That means somebody *knew* we were staying at that hotel. We must have been watched, Hamilton. That terrifies me.'

'I told nobody where we were going – neither did you.'

'One of us must have been followed.'

'In that case,' he said with a flash of anger, 'you're right to be alarmed. I won't stand for it, Kitty. I'm bound to make enemies in my profession but I didn't think any of them would go this

103

far. The murder victim must be linked to me in some way. This is an attack on me and the worst of it is that you were involved.'

'I'm frightened,' she confessed. 'I keep looking over my shoulder in case someone is following me.'

'We can soon solve that problem, Kitty. I'll have one of my men act as your bodyguard. Nobody will dare to come anywhere near you.'

'What about you?'

'I can look after myself,' he said, flicking his coat open to show her the pearl-handled pistol he kept in a leather holster. 'There are too many bad losers about these days. I have to protect myself.'

'I keep thinking about that severed head.'

'Somebody will pay for that, mark my words!'

'I didn't believe that anyone could do such a thing,' she said. 'Who do you think the victim could be, Hamilton?'

'I intend to find out straight away. I didn't get where I am today without knowing who and when to bribe. I have two or three policemen in my pocket, Kitty. It's time they earned their money,' he said harshly. 'I'll have that name before the day is out.'

'John Feeny?' said Victor Leeming. 'Who was he, Inspector?'

'An Irish lad with ambitions to be a jockey.'

'Poor devil!'

'He came to England to better himself,' said Colbeck sadly, 'and fell foul of someone. Brian Dowd spoke well of him. Feeny had a real love of horses and he worked hard for low pay.'

'I can sympathise with that,' muttered the sergeant.

'What have you been doing while I was gone, Victor?'

'Trying to keep out of the superintendent's way.'

Colbeck grinned. 'I enjoy playing that game as well,' he said. 'Did you learn anything useful in Cambridge?'

'I think so, sir.'

It was early morning and they were in an office at Scotland Yard. Leeming gave him a brief account of his visit to the Angel Hotel and passed on the description of Lady Hendry that he had drawn out of the manager. Colbeck was interested to hear that the hatbox had not been stolen on the occasion of the couple's visit to Cambridge.

'I've proved that it was not Lord Hendry's wife,' said Leeming.

'That was my feeling from the outset.'

'I mean, I've got evidence right here, Inspector.' He pointed to a pile of newspapers on the desk. 'Lord Hendry has a busy social life. I wondered if he'd ever been featured in *London Illustrated News*. So I went through all these back copies.'

'Very commendable, Victor.'

'I found two drawings of him, both quite accurate. I recognised him immediately.' He sifted through the papers. 'One showed him at the races in Newmarket but this one,' he went on, picking up a copy, 'was more interesting. It shows his wife as well.'

Robert Colbeck took the newspaper from him and studied the illustration. The caption told him that he was looking at the wedding of Lord

Hendry's daughter but it was not the bride who caught his eye. It was Lady Caroline Hendry, standing beside her husband, who held his attention. In age, height and in every other way, she differed sharply from the description of the woman who had accompanied Lord Hendry to the Angel Hotel in Cambridge.

'It says in the article,' Leeming pointed out, 'that Lady Hendry devotes all her time to charity.'

'I don't think even she would be charitable enough to lend her husband to another woman.' Colbeck put the newspaper down. 'If the artist is to be trusted, they have a beautiful daughter.'

'What would *she* think if she knew the truth about her father?'

'I hope that she never does, Victor.'

'Will we have to speak to Lord Hendry again?'

'I'm sure that we will,' said Colbeck. 'Before that, however, I'll have to give my report to the superintendent. Did he say anything about my visit to Ireland?'

'He felt it was a complete waste of time.'

Colbeck laughed. He went out, walked along the corridor and knocked on a door. The booming voice of Edward Tallis invited him in.

'The prodigal returns,' said the superintendent sardonically as his visitor entered. 'When did you get back?'

'Last evening, sir.'

'Then why didn't you come here? You know how late I work.'

'I had some calls to make.'

'Nothing should have taken precedence over me, Inspector.'

'I felt that it did,' Colbeck took the drawing from his pocket and unfolded it before putting it in front of Tallis. 'His name is John Feeny,' he explained. 'His parents died years ago. His only living relative was the uncle with whom he'd been staying while he was in England. As next of kin, the uncle deserved to be told of his nephew's death at the earliest opportunity.'

'How did you get this uncle's address?'

'From a young man called Jerry Doyle, sir – Feeny was a good friend of his. They kept in touch.'

Tallis indicated the drawing. 'Who identified this?'

'Brian Dowd, sir – John Feeny used to work for him as a groom.'

'What was Feeny doing in England?'

'Trying to become a jockey,' said Colbeck. 'But I couldn't rely wholly on Mr Dowd's identification. It was, after all, only based on a rough drawing of the deceased. When I got back to London, therefore, I took John Feeny's uncle to the morgue where he was shown his nephew's head. It shook him badly but we have what we needed – a positive identification from a family member.'

'Good,' said Tallis grudgingly. 'We now have a head, a body and a name – a degree of progress at last. What else did you learn in Ireland?'

Colbeck had carefully planned what he was going to say so that his report was concise yet filled with all the relevant detail. While in Ireland, he had been shown around the stables and talked at length about Limerick Lad's chances in the Derby.

'His trainer thinks he's a certain winner,' he said.

'I hope you're not suggesting that I place a bet on the Irish horse, Inspector. Gambling is hateful to me. I had to talk Sergeant Leeming out of falling under its wicked spell.'

'My major concern is to ensure that it's a fair race, sir.'

'Mine is to solve a murder.'

'The two things go together,' Colbeck reasoned. 'That severed head was destined for Brian Dowd as a warning of how desperate one of his rivals is to prevent Limerick Lad from winning.'

'Then you must arrest the man immediately,' said Tallis.

'Who?'

'Hamilton Fido, of course – his guilt is undeniable.'

'I think he's entitled to a presumption of innocence before we accuse him of the crime. Mr Dowd may have pointed the finger at him but we have to bear in mind that the two of them are sworn enemies. The villain may be someone else entirely.'

'What conceivable motive could he have?'

'The most obvious one, Superintendent,' said Colbeck, 'and that's financial gain. If someone has bet heavily on one horse, the best way to protect his investment is to impede any other runner who's likely to be a serious contender.'

'You told me that the Derby was a three-horse race.'

'That's the received wisdom, sir, but one should never rule out the possibility that an

108

outsider could win. It's happened in the past. It only needs the favoured horses to have an off day, or for their jockeys to make bad tactical mistakes. Look at the evidence we've collected so far, sir,' said Colbeck. 'A severed head is found in a hatbox belonging to the mistress of the man who owns the Derby favourite, Odysseus. The head was destined for Brian Dowd, owner and trainer of another fancied runner, Limerick Lad. The murder victim worked at stables owned by Hamilton Fido, whose filly, Merry Legs, also features well in the betting. The three most dangerous horses have been singled out.'

'What do you conclude, Inspector?'

'That we may have seen the opening moves in a campaign to set the respective owners at each other's throats. If they feel they've been abused, they'll seek retribution. No quarter will be given. It's possible that of the three horses – Odysseus, Merry Legs and Limerick Lad – one or two might not even make the starting post at Epsom.'

'Do you predict more skulduggery?' asked Tallis.

'No, sir,' replied Colbeck calmly. 'I don't predict it – I guarantee it. In my considered opinion, the worst is yet to come.'

Hidden in the trees, he kept the stables under surveillance all morning and bided his time. From his elevated position, he had a good view of the yard through his telescope. When the colt appeared, he recognised Odysseus immediately and knew that his moment was at hand. The travelling box was hauled into the yard by a cart drawn by a pair of matching grey dray-horses. It was time for him to move. Mounting his horse, he rode off until he reached the steepest part of the incline. Then he tethered his horse behind some thick bushes and took up his position. Five minutes later, the travelling box was pulled out of the stables to begin the long, slow climb up the hill.

The man was taking no chances. In case he was seen, he was wearing a wide-brimmed hat pulled down low over his forehead and a scarf that covered the lower half of his face. His clothing was nondescript. Even close friends would not have been able to identify him. He remained concealed in the undergrowth until he could hear the clatter of hooves and the rattle of the cart and the travelling box getting closer and closer.

When the vehicles finally drew level with him, he acted swiftly. Leaping out of his hiding place, he ran to the coupling pin that held the cart and travelling box together. He grabbed it, yanked it out and flung it into the long grass. The vehicles parted dramatically. As the cart was driven forward, the travelling box rolled crazily backward down the hill, swaying from side to side and gathering speed all the time. Reaching a bend, it left the road altogether and spun wildly out of control until it turned over with a sickening crash.

The man did not linger. His mission had been completed. Before the driver of the cart even realised what had happened, the man was already back in the saddle, riding off to report the good news.

CHAPTER SIX

Victor Leeming was relieved to be going on a journey that did not involve a railway. Instead, he and Robert Colbeck sat side by side in a hansom cab as it picked its way through a labyrinth of streets in east London. There was something about the gentle swaying of the vehicle that the sergeant found reassuring. It was like being rocked in a giant cradle with the rhythmical trot of the horse providing a soothing lullaby. Even when they turned down a narrow lane, bouncing and sliding over a cobbled surface, Leeming felt snug and unthreatened.

'This is better than hurtling along in a train,' he opined.

'It's an agreeable alternative on a short journey,' said Colbeck, 'but I'd hate to have gone all the way to Anglesey by cab. Horses and railways are not mutually exclusive, Victor. They're complementary.'

'Give me horses every time, sir.'

'You'll have a wide choice of those today.'

'Will I?'

'Yes,' said Colbeck. 'We're going to see a bookmaker. He'll offer you whole cavalry regiments. Horses are Hamilton Fido's business. Judging by the success he's had, I'd say that he was an expert.'

'Does he know who's going to win the Derby?'

'I'm sure that he'll tell us.'

'Why does such a rich man live in one of the poorest districts of London?' asked Leeming. 'Since the weaving industry fell on hard times, Bethnal Green is starting to look like a grave-yard.'

'Mr Fido only works here, Victor. His house is in a far more salubrious part of the city. Some of his more questionable activities would not be allowed there whereas they suit the character of Bethnal Green perfectly.'

'Milling and cock-fighting, you mean?'

'It's not only boxers and birds who entertain the crowds here,' said Colbeck. 'Hamilton Fido will arrange any contest in which blood can be drawn and on which bets can be laid.'

'Why has he never been arrested?'

'That, I suspect, will become obvious when we meet him.'

The cab eventually came to a halt outside the Green Dragon, a large, rambling, double-fronted tavern built with an eye to Gothic extravagance but now badly besmirched. As he alighted and paid the driver, Colbeck glanced around him. Signs of extreme poverty were unmistakable. Small, dark, mean, neglected houses and tene-ments were clustered together in the filthy street. Emaciated and unwashed children in tattered clothes were playing games. Old people sat on stools outside their dwellings and looked on with vacant stares. Filling the air with their strident cries, street vendors sold wares from their hand-carts. Dogs and cats had ear-splitting disputes over territory. Hulking men with darting eyes sauntered past. There was a hint of danger in the air.

Victor Leeming was troubled by the stink from the accumulated litter and open drains. He wrinkled his nose in disgust. Within seconds, he and Colbeck were approached by a couple of ancient beggars with threadbare suits, battered hats and ingratiating smiles. From other denizens of the area the visitors collected only hostile stares and muttered curses. They went into the tavern and found it full of rowdy patrons. In the boisterous atmosphere, Colbeck had to raise his voice to be heard by the barman. In answer to the inspector's enquiry, they were directed upstairs.

Hamilton Fido's office occupied the front room on the first floor. What surprised them as they were invited in was how little of the hubbub below rose up through the floorboards. A thick oriental carpet helped to insulate the room against the noise from the bar. The office walls were adorned with sporting prints and every shelf was covered with silver cups and other trophies. Yet there was no sense of clutter. Everything was neatly in place. Hamilton Fido was clearly a man who valued order.

He rose swiftly from his seat as the introductions were made.

'How fortunate!' he exclaimed, beaming at Colbeck. 'I've always wanted to meet the famous Railway Detective.'

'And I've always wanted to meet the infamous bookmaker,' Colbeck returned pleasantly. 'You have a spacious and well-appointed office, Mr Fido. It's the last thing one might expect to find

113

in a place like Bethnal Green.'

'I was born and brought up here,' explained Fido, looking fondly through the window. 'My father was a weaver – his loom took up most of the space on the ground floor. When he was too ill to work, we had no money coming in. When he recovered his health, the trade had declined and he could find no employment. Life was a daily struggle for us and, from an early age, I had to learn how to survive. Though I say so myself, I became very adept at survival.' He held the lapels of his frock coat. 'What you see before you is a self-educated man who was fortunate enough to make good. Most people in my position turn their backs on their humble origins but I rejoice in mine.'

'That's creditable, sir,' said Leeming.

'Bethnal Green folk are the salt of the earth. When I bought this tavern and set up my business here, I wanted to put something back into the district. But I forget my manners,' he said, indicating the chairs. 'Do make yourselves comfortable, gentlemen.'

The detectives sat down and Fido lowered himself into a seat opposite them. Like Colbeck, the bookmaker was impeccably dressed but he had a flamboyance that the inspector lacked. Gold rings shone on both hands and an ornate gold pin anchored his cravat. He produced a ready smile for the detectives.

'What brought you here was that hatbox, I presume,' he said helpfully. 'There's no need to tell me the name of the unfortunate young man whose head was found inside it. He was John Feeny.'

Colbeck was taken aback. 'May I ask how you

114

come to know?'

'The fact was important to me.'

'But the name of the deceased has not yet been released.'

'It was released to *me*, Inspector,' said Fido complacently. 'In my walk of life, accurate information is vital so I employ every means of acquiring it.'

'Even to the extent of bribing a police officer?'

Fido held up both hands in a comic gesture of surrender. 'Inspector, *please* – I would never dare to do that.'

'Then how did you find out?' asked Leeming.

'Not because I put the head in the hatbox, Sergeant.'

'Then how, sir?'

'An anonymous letter was slipped under my door,' said Fido glibly. 'It claimed that the dead man was John Feeny, a lad who used to work as a groom at my stables. Is that correct?'

'It is, Mr Fido,' conceded Leeming.

'Of course, I never met him. My trainer employs several grooms. He's always had a free hand in his choice of lads. Until this morning, I had no idea that someone called John Feeny even existed.'

'And when you did discover his existence,' said Colbeck, 'and learnt of his bizarre murder, how did you react?'

'With pity and apprehension,' said Fido.

'Apprehension?'

'Feeny was Irish. According to my anonymous informant, he once worked at the stables owned by Brian Dowd. I was horrified.'

'Why?'

'Mr Dowd and I have exchanged hot words,' said Fido sourly, 'on and off the racecourse. He's totally unscrupulous. All that the public sees is the endless stream of success that he's enjoyed. What's hidden from them is the deep-dyed villainy behind that success.'

'You sound as if you're accusing Brian Dowd,' said Colbeck.

'He deliberately infiltrated my stables.'

'Is that what you believe, sir?'

'It's obvious, Inspector,' argued Fido. 'My filly, Merry Legs, has an excellent chance of winning the Derby. John Feeny was sent over to England to make sure that Merry Legs did not even run in the race.'

'Then it would have been in your interests to stop him.'

'I'd never have employed him in the first place.'

'Why did your trainer take the lad on?'

'I mean to ask him that selfsame question when I meet him later today. Who killed John Feeny, I'm unable to tell you, but the person who dispatched him to England to spy on my filly was Brian Dowd.'

'Could it be that someone at the stables took the law into his own hands?' wondered Colbeck. 'When he suspected that the lad had been deliberately planted on them, he struck back.'

Fido was fuming. 'I do not employ killers, Inspector.'

'How do you know?' said Leeming. 'Until today, you didn't even know that John Feeny worked at your stables.'

'Do you have any proof that that is where he was murdered?'

'No, sir.'

'Or any evidence to connect the crime to me?'

'None at all, Mr Fido.'

'Then I'll trouble you not to make any unfounded allegations. Instead of badgering me about this murder, you should be chasing that crooked Irishman, Brian Dowd.'

'I've already spoken with Mr Dowd,' said Colbeck.

'You *have?*' said Fido. 'I didn't realise that he was in this country yet.'

'I went to Dublin to see him. What your anonymous informant failed to tell you was that the severed head was destined for Ireland. It was Mr Dowd who identified a rough portrait of the deceased and thus enabled us to move this investigation on to another stage.'

'Don't believe a word that liar told you!' snarled Fido.

'He said much the same about you, sir.'

'Dowd set out to disable Merry Legs in some way.'

'That's pure supposition,' said Colbeck. 'According to Mr Dowd, the reason that Feeny left Ireland was that there were no prospects of his becoming a jockey there. That must have rankled with the lad. Why should he help a man who told him frankly that he had no future in the saddle?'

Hamilton Fido took a moment to absorb what he had been told. His face remained impassive but his mind was racing. He seized on one piece of information.

117

'What makes you think the severed head was destined for Brian Dowd?' he asked. 'It was found in Crewe.'

'Inspector Colbeck looked closely at the railway timetables,' said Leeming. 'Not long after that hatbox arrived in Crewe, there was a connecting train to Holyhead.'

Colbeck took over. 'There was also the fact that Limerick Lad posed a serious challenge to your filly and to Lord Hendry's Odysseus. Since I was certain that the crime was linked to the Derby,' he went on, 'I deduced that Mr Dowd was the most likely recipient of that ghastly present in the hatbox. He agreed with me.'

'On what grounds?' said Fido.

'The false assumption already made by you, sir – namely, that Feeny was paid to report on the progress of Merry Legs and was thus seen as an enemy in the camp. The killer's motive was revenge.'

'You're being fanciful, Inspector Colbeck.'

'I am merely telling you how it looks to me.'

'You made the mistake of listening to Brian Dowd.'

'I'm giving you the chance to set the record straight.'

'Then let me deny categorically that neither I – nor anyone in my employ – was involved in this murder. If that's what Dowd is claiming, I'll sue the bastard for slander.'

'Some of the things *you've* said about Mr Dowd could be considered slanderous,' noted Colbeck. 'They are also very unhelpful. A shouting match between the pair of you will achieve nothing beyond giving you both a sore throat.'

'Keep him away from me – that's all I ask.'

The conversation had reached a natural end. Before he could stop himself, Leeming blurted out the question that had been on the tip of his tongue since they had entered the room. 'Which horse will win the Derby, sir?'

'The first past the winning post,' replied Fido.

'Will that be Odysseus, Merry Legs or Limerick Lad?'

'Odysseus has to be favourite, Sergeant.'

'But you want your own horse to win.'

'I hope and pray that she does,' said Fido guardedly. 'But I draw back from overrating her chances. All I will say is that Merry Legs has a wonderful opportunity to beat the field.'

'That's not what tradition tells us,' said Colbeck knowledgeably. 'The only filly to win the Derby was Eleanor in 1801. Before and since that year, colts have always taken the honours. Why should it be any different this year?'

'Speaking as a bookmaker, I'd say that Merry Legs was an unlikely winner even though, as a filly, she'll have a slight weight advantage. Speaking as an owner, however,' Fido continued, 'I'm ruled by my heart rather than my head.'

'Does that mean you'll be betting on Merry Legs?' said Leeming.

'The odds I'm setting are well advertised. Odysseus is 5–2; Limerick Lad is 4–1; and Merry Legs is 8–1. But there are eighteen other runners in the race. One of them might surprise us all.'

'Bookmakers are rarely surprised,' observed Colbeck.

Fido smiled. 'We know how to cover every eventuality.'

'Even an attack on your own horse?'

'Merry Legs is under armed guard day and night, Inspector.'

'I'm glad to hear it. Interested as I am in the race, my prime concern will always be the murder of John Feeny. All that you and Brian Dowd have done so far is to speak disparagingly of each other. Answer me this, Mr Fido,' said Colbeck. 'It occurs to me that the death of the groom might simply be a device to turn you and Mr Dowd into a pair of fighting cocks, trying to tear each other to bits. Who would profit most from that?'

'One name leaps out of the pack immediately,' said Fido.

'And who is that, sir?'

'Lord Hendry.'

'I had hoped to speak to Inspector Colbeck,' said Lord Hendry as he was shown into the super-intendent's office. 'I know that he's in charge of this case.'

'Colbeck is answerable to me,' said Tallis, staying on his feet as he waved his guest to a chair. 'I control the investigation from here.'

'Then I bring my complaint to you.'

'Your complaint, Lord Hendry?'

'Yes, Superintendent – if the blame lies with you.'

'What exactly is the nature of your grievance?'

'I deplore your methods,' said Lord Hendry, tapping the floor hard with his silver-topped cane. 'It was quite unnecessary for two detectives to come all the way to my house for the sole purpose of asking about a hatbox that was stolen from my wife.'

'How else could the information have been obtained?'

'By letter, Mr Tallis – I'm a prompt correspondent.'

'Inspector Colbeck was anxious to meet you in person.'

'Then he could have done so at my club,' said Lord Hendry testily. 'I'm there on a regular basis. It's unsettling when two of your men bang on my front door. What are my servants to think? That their master is under suspicion for some dastardly crime? This whole business could have been handled more discreetly.'

'We wanted an immediate answer, Lord Hendry.'

'Damn it, man – you offended me, don't you see that?'

Tallis met his gaze without flinching. In view of what his detectives had found out, he was glad that they had visited Lord Hendry at his home. He certainly felt no need to apologise. There was a lengthy and uncomfortable pause. Lord Hendry finally broke the silence when he took a handkerchief from his sleeve and held it to his mouth as he sneezed.

'God bless you!' said Tallis.

'I'm still waiting for your comment.'

'I've none to make, Lord Hendry.'

'Won't you admit you were wrong to send your men to my house?' demanded the other, slipping the handkerchief back into his sleeve. 'Or do I have to take my complaint to the commissioner?'

'I'd advise against that.'

'Why?'

'Because the commissioner has been made fully aware of the details of this case,' said Tallis, tired of being glared at. 'Like me, he knows that you lied to my detectives when they called on you. And, like me, he knows that the lady for whom you bought a hat and hatbox in Jermyn Street was not, in fact, Lady Hendry.'

'How dare you, sir!' yelled Lord Hendry, getting to his feet and frothing with rage. 'That's a monstrous allegation and I insist on a retraction.'

'Insist all you will,' said Tallis. 'But before you issue any more denials, I should tell you that Sergeant Leeming visited the Angel Hotel in Cambridge recently. He not only discovered that you and a certain young lady had stayed there on more than one occasion, he learnt that the hatbox was *not* stolen from the hotel. Why did you tell my officers that it had been, Lord Hendry?'

'This is insufferable!' howled the other. 'Is a peer of the realm to be allowed no private life? Since when has it been the function of detectives to pry into the personal affairs of a man who has committed no crime whatsoever?'

'Your private life has a bearing on a brutal murder.'

'I'll not be *watched*, Superintendent,' warned Lord Hendry. 'I'll not be treated like the basest scoundrel in London.'

'You've been treated with the respect you deserve,' said Tallis levelly. 'Inspector Colbeck believed that you bore false testimony and he set out to prove it. Had you told him the truth in the first place, the visit to Cambridge would not have been necessary.'

'Heavens above – I'm *married!*'

'At moments like this, I'm pleased I remained a bachelor.'

Lord Hendry frowned. 'Are you mocking me, Mr Tallis?'

'I am simply observing how much easier life is for a single man.'

'I have no interest in your observations, sir.'

'Then I'll keep them to myself.' Sitting behind his desk, Tallis clasped his hands together. 'Now that you've made *your* complaint, Lord Hendry,' he said, 'I'll avail myself of the opportunity to make mine.'

'I haven't finished yet.'

'You have another grievance?'

'I need to report a crime,' said Lord Hendry petulantly. 'That's why I hoped to see Inspector Colbeck. Yesterday, near the stables where my colt is trained, an attempt was made to kill Odysseus.'

'An unsuccessful attempt, I hope.'

'Fortunately, it was. Odysseus was due to be moved to Epsom in his travelling box but my trainer had a strong suspicion that someone was keeping a close watch on the stables. Fearing danger, he took steps to avoid it.'

'In what way?'

'Instead of putting Odysseus in the travelling box, he used a substitute – one of the bullocks from the adjoining paddock. As it was going up a

123

hill, the travelling box was uncoupled from the cart pulling it and it careered down the slope before turning over.'

'Was the bullock injured?'

'One of its legs was broken,' said Lord Hendry. 'Do you see what I am up against, Superintendent? Someone is out to destroy my chances of winning the Derby. Had my horse been in that box, he would have broken his leg instead and we'd have had to put him down. I want you to find the man behind this outrage.'

'We'll do all we can to apprehend him as soon as we can,' Tallis promised him. 'Can you suggest the name of anyone capable of such a heinous crime?'

'Two names command especial attention.'

'And who might they be, Lord Hendry?'

'Hamilton Fido and Brian Dowd.'

'Your great rivals, as I understand it.'

'I mean to win by fair means – they'll resort to foul ones.'

'I'll need to take a fuller statement,' said Tallis, reaching for his pen and moving a piece of paper into position. 'I want the time and place of this incident and the names of any witnesses whom we can contact.'

'First things first, Superintendent – when we do move Odysseus to Epsom, I'll need police protection for the horse. There may be a second attack.'

'We'll look into that, Lord Hendry.'

'Make sure you question Fido and Dowd.'

'Inspector Colbeck has already spoken to both gentlemen.'

'Really?' Lord Hendry was amazed. 'Why did he do that?'

'Because he is accustomed to leaving no stone unturned,' said Tallis. 'There are certain things of which you have clearly not been apprised, my lord, and they may alter your view of events. The severed head has been identified as belonging to John Feeny, a groom at the stables owned, coincidentally, by Hamilton Fido. The hatbox was on its way to Brian Dowd in Ireland before it was intercepted in Crewe. Feeny, it transpires, once worked for Mr Dowd.'

'How do you know all this?' asked Lord Hendry.

'As I told you, Inspector Colbeck is famed for his thoroughness.'

'So both Fido and Dowd are tied in some way to the murder?'

'Let's move one step at a time,' said Tallis, pen poised. 'What brought this crime to light was a hatbox that sprung open on a railway platform. That leads me to a question I'm compelled to ask, Lord Hendry, and I'm sure that you understand why.' He cleared his throat. 'What was the name of the young lady from whom it was stolen?'

'She *has* no name,' retorted Lord Hendry, eyes blazing with defiance. 'The young lady ceased to exist several weeks ago. That being the case, Superintendent, I regret that I'm unable to help you identify that person.' He thrust out his jaw. 'Do I make myself clear?'

The long cab ride back to Scotland Yard gave

Robert Colbeck and Victor Leeming plenty of time to discuss their visit to the Green Dragon. The sergeant was impressed.

'Mr Fido must have made a fortune,' he said enviously. 'He owns a stable of racehorses, a tavern in Bethnal Green and a big house somewhere else. Yet he comes from a poor family.'

'Perhaps that's what spurred him on, Victor. But he's not the only person from the working class who went on to succeed. I'm sitting beside another example right now.'

'Me?' Leeming gave a dry laugh. 'I don't think *I'm* a success.'

'You are, in my eyes,' said Colbeck, letting his affection show. 'Most people with your background never escape it. They're doomed to live the same kind of hard, joyless, unrelenting lives as their parents. By sheer determination, you managed to better yourself and – unlike Hamilton Fido – you did so by entirely legal means.'

'That's no consolation, sir.'

'It is to me, Victor.'

'I'd love to have some of his money.'

'Then back the winner in the Derby.'

'You know what I mean, Inspector,' said Leeming. 'When I see someone like Mr Fido, dripping with wealth, I feel so jealous. I'll never earn that amount of money in the Metropolitan Police Force.'

'Look at it another way,' suggested Colbeck. 'You'll never spend part of your life behind bars.'

'Is that what will happen to Mr Fido?'

'Sooner or later.'

'He seemed so sure of himself.'

'Yes, he was very plausible. That's often a danger sign. He had all the answers. Hamilton Fido is clearly an accomplished liar.'

'What was all that about an anonymous letter?'

'His first and biggest lie,' said Colbeck. 'He must have a source at Scotland Yard and that's worrying. Only a handful of people knew the name of the murder victim and the fact that he once worked for Brian Dowd. It behoves us to move with extreme care, Victor.'

'Why?'

'We have a spy in our ranks – someone who can help Mr Fido to stay one step ahead of us.'

'How, sir?'

'By reporting on our movements, for a start,' replied Colbeck. 'Didn't you notice how un-surprised Mr Fido was when we turned up at his door? He *knew* that we were coming.'

Leeming was unsettled. 'A spy in our ranks – surely not, sir.'

'Mr Fido will employ a whole network of informers, Victor. How can he set the odds for a race if he doesn't have precise details about the runners taking part?'

'What about the Derby?'

'He'll know exactly how the fancied horses fare during their training gallops. A man like Hamilton Fido has eyes everywhere.'

'Do you think he's involved in the murder of John Feeny?'

'He didn't persuade me that he's *not* involved,' said Colbeck, 'so it's an open question. If he is party to the crime, of course, then he may not have a source in the Detective Department, after

127

all. He would know Feeny's name because he ordered his execution.'

Leeming fell silent. A chevron of deep concentration appeared on his brow as he turned something over in his mind. Colbeck waited patiently until his companion was ready to speak.

'I was just thinking,' said the sergeant at length. 'What would have happened if the severed head had not been discovered in Crewe?'

'It would have been delivered to Brian Dowd.'

'Yes – but what would have happened then, sir? Would he have reported it or chosen to keep the whole thing secret?'

'That depends on whether or not he deliberately put John Feeny in a rival stables to act as an informant. If he did,' said Colbeck, 'he might not wish to involve the police at all. Having met Mr Dowd, I'm inclined to believe his explanation – namely, that Feeny left Ireland of his own accord before finding work in England. But,' he went on, 'it's always wise to have a second opinion. That's why I'm sending you to meet Brian Dowd at a secret location.'

Leeming steeled himself. 'Will I have to travel by train, sir?'

'I'm afraid so – but only for a short distance. One thing that even Hamilton Fido doesn't know is the location of Limerick Lad. Mr Dowd confided in me and I've disclosed the address to nobody.'

'Not even to Superintendent Tallis?'

'No, Victor,' said Colbeck, 'and, in hindsight, I'm glad. If we do have a spy in our midst, this is one piece of information that won't fall accidentally into his hands. When we get to Whitehall, you can drop me off and go on to Paddington.'

'What will you be doing?'

'Reporting to the superintendent, in the first instance.'

'Better you than me, sir,' said Leeming gratefully.

'I thought that he'd mellowed of late.'

'Then I'll have to show you the bite marks he left on me.'

Colbeck laughed. 'You'll find Brian Dowd far less intimidating,' he said. 'Sound him out, Victor. See what you make of him.'

'Do you think he'll give me advice about the Derby?'

'You may even be lucky enough to see Limerick Lad now he's in England. That's the advice he'll give you – bet on the Irish horse.'

'Who are you going to put money on, sir?'

'I'm still considering the options,' said Colbeck. 'One of them has to be Merry Legs. When I've spoken to the Superintendent, I'll travel to Hamilton Fido's stables to take a closer look at the filly. I felt from the start that a female would play a crucial role in our investigation.'

Kitty Lavender sat at a table in the corner of the tavern and ignored the curious stares she was getting from most of the men present. As a rule, she enjoyed arousing male interest but she had other things on her mind at that moment. She was grateful when the tall, gangly figure of Marcus Johnson entered the room and crossed over to her. Kitty rose from her chair to accept a kiss on the cheek and an effusive greeting from the new-comer. A collective murmur of disappointment went up from the other tables. She was spoken for.

In fact, Marcus was her half-brother but the familiar way in which he leant across the table towards her hinted at a more intimate relation-ship. He ordered drinks and exchanged niceties with Kitty until they were brought. After clinking glasses, they sipped their respective drinks.

'I haven't seen you for ages, Kitty,' he com-plained.

'I've been busy.'

'On my behalf, I hope.'

'And on my own,' she said tartly. 'I don't see it as my purpose in life to run your errands, Marcus.'

'I'm your *brother*.'

'My half-brother – there's a big difference.'

'Yes,' he said, 'you only love me half as much as I love you.'

He grinned broadly. There were certainly no physical similarities to proclaim their blood relationship. Kitty's beauty was thrown into relief by Johnson's long, thin, bony face with its aquiline nose and prominent chin. While she was poised, his features were mobile. In place of her perfect set of teeth, he had a mouthful of over-large incisors and canines. A few years older than Kitty, he seemed to glow with confidence. He took her hand.

'What can you tell me?' he asked.

'It's far too early, Marcus.'

'You must have picked up some information.'

'I've picked up far too much,' she said. 'I only

have a very limited interest in horses and I'm fast approaching that limit.'

'Think what this could mean to us, Kitty.'

'That's what I have been doing and I'm coming to the conclusion that this is just another of your madcap schemes to get rich. They always fail, Marcus. Why should this one be any different?'

'Because we're working together this time.'

'That's not true,' she denied.

'You swore that you'd help me.'

'First and foremost, I'm in this for myself.'

'I accept that,' he said, squeezing her hand, 'but you ought to remember who contrived the introduction for you. Without me, you might never have got to meet Hamilton Fido.'

'I'd have found a way somehow.'

'But your clever half-brother made it so much easier for you.' He bared his teeth in another grin. 'We both stand to gain, Kitty.'

'That's a matter of opinion.'

'Fido is much more companionable than Lord Hendry.'

'Don't mention him,' she said sharply.

'Too tight with his money?'

'Oh, he was generous enough, I suppose. But he was too frightened to be seen with me at a racecourse. He wanted private pleasure without any public acknowledgement of it. Hamilton is the opposite. He loves to be seen at the races with me.'

'You're gorgeous – any sane man would want to show you off.'

'Lord Hendry didn't.' She sipped her drink and studied him with a blend of fondness and faint

131

despair. 'When are you going to find a profession worthy of your talents, Marcus?'

'I've found a number in my time.'

'But you never stay long in any of them.'

'I'm a restless spirit, Kitty,' he said grandiloquently, 'forever in search of the life on a higher plane that my talents deserve. You've elevated yourself by means of beauty. I'm doing it by other means.'

'By gambling on horses?'

'Fortunes have often been made that way.'

'And lost just as often.'

'Only by people with insufficient information,' he boasted. 'That's why I hold the whip hand over them. I have someone who's in the perfect place to guide me.'

'All I can tell you are the odds that Hamilton is setting.'

'I can get those myself, Kitty. What I need is inside knowledge. Which horse does he *really* think will win the Derby? Those odds might just be a smokescreen to make people back Odysseus or Limerick Lad. That would lengthen the odds on Merry Legs. If I put a heavy bet on the filly, I could be made.' He smiled coaxingly. 'You'll get your share, of course.'

'Fillies never win the Derby – I know that much.'

'Merry Legs could be the exception that proves the rule.'

'Hamilton thinks she has a good chance but no more than that.'

'That's what he says, Kitty, but you should bear in mind that one of his horses won the Derby three years ago. As I recall, he hid his true feelings on that occasion as well, dismissing the colt's chances as no more than average. He *knows*,' insisted Johnson. 'He's already run the race a dozen times in his head. Get me the name of the winner.'

'I like Hamilton,' she pointed out. 'I enjoy his company. I hope to enjoy it for a lot longer. I agree that you helped to get me introduced to him, Marcus, and I'm grateful but I've been increasingly uneasy about what you expect of me.'

'All you have to do is to keep your ears open.'

'I'm worried.'

'Why?'

'Certain things have happened. Frankly, I'm scared.'

'Of what?'

'That's the trouble,' she confessed, 'I don't know. Something very strange and very alarming is going on. My hatbox was stolen from a hotel. It was later found with a man's head in it.'

'Never!' he said, grimacing. 'How perfectly dreadful!'

'It shook me to the core, Marcus.'

'I can imagine. Oh, you poor thing – no wonder you're so uneasy about my plan. Look,' he went on, kneading her hand sympathetically, 'forget all about that wicked half-brother of yours. You have enough to worry about, I can see.'

'I'm afraid of what might happen next.'

'Are you in touch with the police?'

'No – and I don't wish to be.'

'You're like me – you have an aversion to authority.'

'That hatbox belongs to part of my life I'd rather forget.'

'That's readily understandable. But don't trouble yourself on my account. Marcus Johnson will find another way to make his fortune.' He beamed. 'And when I do, Kitty, I promise that *you'll* be a chief beneficiary.'

Robert Colbeck gave the superintendent an edited version of the visit to the Green Dragon and announced his intention to call at the stables belonging to Hamilton Fido that afternoon. Tallis was brusque.

'Be sure to take your handcuffs with you.'

'Why?'

'To effect an arrest, of course,' said Tallis. 'The more I learn, the more convinced I am that Fido is the culprit.'

'He pleaded his innocence.'

'Villains always do that, Inspector.'

'Granted,' said Colbeck, 'but, on this occasion, I pay some heed. While Mr Fido is no candidate for sainthood, there's nothing in his past to indicate he would connive at murder.'

'There's a first time for everything.'

'I'd rather give him the benefit of the doubt.'

'Had you been here earlier,' said Tallis, grinding the remains of his cigar in the ashtray, 'you might not be so ready to give Mr Fido any leeway. I had a visit from Lord Hendry.'

'Indeed – what did he want?'

'To complain about you and Sergeant Leeming, as it happens.'

Tallis sat back in his chair and related the

conversation he had had with Lord Hendry. While he was interested to hear of the attempt to injure Odysseus, Colbeck was not as ready as the superintendent to attribute the blame to Hamilton Fido. One regret was uppermost in his mind. He was sorry that Tallis had been unable to elicit the name of Lord Hendry's former mistress.

'We'll have to find it by other means,' said Colbeck.

'How relevant do you think it will be?'

'Very relevant – the lady may want her hatbox returned.'

'Given what happened to it, I find that highly unlikely.'

'I still wish to talk to her, Superintendent. She will at least be able to tell us when and where the item was stolen. We intercepted it at Crewe on its way to Ireland. Did it begin its journey in London or elsewhere?' Colbeck stood up. 'Perhaps I should speak to Lord Hendry myself,' he said. 'It may be that he'll divulge the name to me.'

'The young lady has vanished forever from his life. I don't think he'd yield up her name if you stretched him on the rack. In his codex, to all intents and purposes, she is dead and buried.'

'Then I may need to exhume her.'

Colbeck bade him farewell and went out into the corridor. He had intended to collect his top hat and leave the building. When he entered his office, however, he found that he had a visitor. A short, plump, middle-aged man leapt to his feet apologetically, as if sitting in a chair were a felony. He had the hunted, hangdog look of man who is uncertain if he is doing the right thing.

135

'Are you Inspector Colbeck?' he asked.

'I am, sir – who might you be?'

'My name is Dacre Radley.'

'Do sit down, Mr Radley,' said Colbeck, wondering why his visitor was so nervous. 'What can I do for you, sir?'

Radley sat down. 'This may be a fool's errand, Inspector.'

'Let me decide that.'

'I can't stay long. I'm on duty again soon.'

'And where would that be, Mr Radley?'

'At the Wyvern Hotel – that's just off the Strand.'

'I know it well,' said Colbeck. 'Expensive but tasteful.'

'We try to maintain high standards.'

'Are you the manager?'

'No, no,' said Radley sheepishly. 'I occupy a more lowly position. The manager is Mr Claude Fielding and – had he been aware of what I proposed – he would certainly have stopped me coming here.'

'Why is that?'

'He believes that the privacy of clients is sacrosanct. And so do I, of course, but not when a murder investigation is concerned. It may just be a weird coincidence, Inspector – I rather hope it is – but I was struck by that article in the newspaper about a stolen hatbox.'

'Go on,' urged Colbeck.

'Well,' said Radley, licking his lips, 'the simple fact is that we had a hatbox taken from the hotel not so long ago. I was on duty when the theft was reported.'

'Do you remember the name of the lady who owned it?'

'No, sir, it was never given to me. But I know the name of the gentleman who booked the room for the night.'

'Well?'

'Mr Hamilton Fido.'

Colbeck shook his hand. 'Thank you, Mr Radley,' he said. 'That information is very valuable. You've rendered us a great service in coming forward like this.'

'You won't mention anything to Mr Fielding, will you?'

'I've no need to speak to him.'

Radley gasped. 'I'm so relieved, Inspector. I've been torturing myself about whether or not I should come. It preyed on my mind, you see. That hatbox *might* have been the one taken from the hotel.'

'I'm fairly certain that it was,' said Colbeck.

'Then I'm glad I came.' He rose to his feet and bit his lip as he wrestled with his conscience. 'There is something else I could tell you, Inspector, though I'm not sure that I should. I hope you don't think I make a habit of this. I'm known for my discretion.'

'Anything you can tell us will be very welcome, sir.'

'The thing is...' Radley bit his lip again before plunging in. 'The thing is that the young lady who accompanied Mr Fido, and whom we assumed was Mrs Fido, had been to the Wyvern Hotel once before.'

'But not with the same gentleman, I take it.'

'No, sir.'

'Who was her husband on that occasion?'

'I'd hate you to think that our hotel caters for such irregular alliances,' said Radley with a simpering smile. 'Most of our guests are highly respectable. We attract only the cream of society. They value the facilities we can offer.' He leant forward. 'It was pure chance that I recognised this particular young lady.'

'With whom was she staying?' prompted Colbeck.

'Lord Hendry.'

CHAPTER SEVEN

Standing in front of the fireplace, Lord George Hendry gazed at the painting with gathering excitement as if seeing it for the first time. It had been an expensive commission but he felt that the money had been well spent on a superb example of equine portraiture. Odysseus looked astonishingly lifelike, ready to leap off the canvas and parade in style around the paddock. The chestnut colt had the unmistakable look of a born winner. Its owner was so enraptured that he did not hear his wife hobble into the library on a walking stick. Lady Caroline Hendry gave a pained smile.

'I still think that you're making a mistake,' she remarked.

He swung round. 'What's that?'

'You're counting your chickens before they're hatched, George.'

'I'm admiring a Derby winner,' he said proudly, 'that's all.'

'But the horse has not yet won the race.'

'I have complete faith in Odysseus.'

'I'm sure that every other owner has complete faith in his horse as well,' she said, 'but none of them would dare to celebrate a triumph that had never actually taken place.'

'You know nothing about racing, Caroline.'

'I know that the favourite does not always win.'

'This one will.'

'How can you be so definite?'

'Because of what happened,' he said, moving across to help her on to a settee. 'Sit down a moment, my dear. I can see it's not one of your better days.' He sat beside her. 'I wasn't going to tell you this in case it upset you but I think you should perhaps know the truth. There's been an incident near the stables.'

'What kind of incident?'

'Someone tried to disable Odysseus.'

'George!' she exclaimed in horror.

'The attempt was foiled,' he assured her, 'so don't be alarmed. I reported it to the police and uniformed officers will protect the horse when we move him to Epsom. At the moment, he's being closely guarded at the stables.'

'I hadn't realised that Odysseus was in any danger.'

'It's one of the penalties of being a favourite, Caroline. And it's clear proof,' he went on, indicating the painting, 'that this year's Derby winner is hanging on the wall. If Odysseus were not feared, nobody would try to put him out of the race.'

'Supposing that they try again?' she asked.

'We'll be ready for them.'

'Do you have any idea who was behind the incident?'

'The choice has to be between Hamilton Fido and Brian Dowd,' he said. 'Each owns another fancied horse. Their only hope of success is to have Odysseus eliminated in some way.'

'Did you give those names to the police?'

'Of course I did. My own feeling is that Dowd

is the snake in the grass. He stands to gain most if Odysseus fails to run. Limerick Lad is the second favourite. I've dealt with Brian Dowd before,' he said with asperity. 'I wouldn't trust that crafty Irishman for a second.'

'What was the other name you mentioned?'

'Hamilton Fido.'

'I thought it sounded familiar. You've spoken of him before. Didn't you tell me that one of his horses was a Derby winner?'

'Yes,' he replied. 'Galliard won by two lengths from Highland Chief. My own horse that year came in third so I have a score to settle with Fido. He's putting a filly in the race, Merry Legs, and she'll never test Odysseus or even put Limerick Lad under any real pressure. Fido must know in his heart that he can never win. No,' he decided, 'on balance, the man behind the attack on us simply has to be Dowd. If my horse does not run, his will take the honours. He suborned some villain to snuff out my chances of winning the Derby.'

'Then why don't the police arrest him?'

'They say that they need clear evidence.'

'Racing seems such a hazardous world,' she said with a sigh. 'Why does it attract so many undesirable characters?'

He chortled. 'Since when have I been undesirable?'

'I was not referring to you, George. I was thinking of all the problems associated with the sport. It's mired in scandal.'

'Great efforts are being made to clean up racing,' he said with easy pomposity. 'I was called

141

upon to offer my advice as how it might happen. One obvious way, of course, is to exclude members of the lower orders from entering horses in major races – social inferiors like Fido and Dowd, for instance. They don't *belong*, Caroline.'

'I'm so glad that I don't have to rub shoulders with people like that. My charity work may not be as exhilarating as watching a horse race but I do have the pleasure of working with kindred spirits.'

'So do I – most of the time.'

'There won't be many archdeacons at the Derby.'

'That's where you're wrong, my dear,' he said. 'Men of the cloth are as addicted to the event as anyone else. We'll have prelates galore on Derby Day and there'll be more than one bishop placing a shrewd bet on the race. If you don't believe me, come and see for yourself.'

'No, thank you, George – you know how much I hate crowds.'

'You ought to be there for Odysseus's crowning moment.'

'Tell me about it after the race,' she said.

'There's still time for you to profit from it, Caroline. I was not joking when I said that you could put a wager on my horse. It's a sure passport to making money.'

'But I don't want to make money,' she said firmly, 'especially not in that way. I've always regarded gambling as rather vulgar. It's the resort of those who want something for nothing.'

'It's a reward for risk,' he explained. 'If people are bold enough to venture a tidy sum on a horse, they have the right to enjoy the winnings. What's vulgar about that?'

'It's something I could never lower myself to, George.'

'Try – just this once.'

'No, I'm sorry. I can't.'

'Wouldn't you even consider giving me a loan so that I can place a bet on your behalf?' She sat up with righteous indignation and he retreated quickly. 'No, no, that was a foolish suggestion. I take it back. Your money is your own and you must be the sole arbiter of how and when it is spent.'

'That's exactly what I intend to be.'

'I'll importune you no more,' he said apologetically. 'Besides, I don't need further capital. I've already placed a substantial bet on Odysseus.' He glanced up at the painting. 'I expect him to win by at least three clear lengths.'

'Then I'll be the first to congratulate you.'

'Thank you, Caroline.'

He touched her hand with distant affection. Having no more money of his own to invest in Odysseus, he had hoped to be able to charm some additional cash from her even though he knew how unlikely that would be. He seethed inwardly at her rejection. Why could his wife have an urge to subsidise a lunatic asylum while denying her own husband the benefit of her wealth? It was unjust.

'George,' she said quietly.

'Yes, my dear.'

'That incident you told me about – it alarms me.'

'I choose to see it as the ultimate seal of approval.'

She was puzzled. *'Approval?'*

'It's startling confirmation from one of my rivals that Odysseus is the undisputed favourite. Since he can't be beaten in a fair race, someone did his best to take him out of it.'

'I'm afraid that *you* might be in jeopardy.'

'No, my dear – Odysseus and his jockey are the targets.'

'And you say they'll be protected by the police?'

'Security will be very tight from now on.'

'Good.' Struggling to her feet, she crossed to the fireplace and looked up at Odysseus. Her husband came to stand beside her. She turned to him. 'Do you really believe he can win?'

'I do, Caroline,' he replied, trying to keep a note of desperation out of his voice. 'Odysseus *must* win. Everything depends upon it.'

'Stay where you are!' ordered the man. 'Or I'll blow your brains out.'

It was not the welcome that Victor Leeming had expected when he stepped down from the cab and walked up the drive. As soon as the sergeant reached one of the outbuildings, a burly individual jumped out to confront him with a shotgun. Staring at the gleaming barrels, Leeming elected to comply with the instruction. The guard ran an unflattering eye over him.

'What's your name, you ugly bugger?' he demanded.

'Detective Sergeant Leeming from Scotland Yard.'

The man sniggered. 'Oh, is that right? Well, if you're a detective, I'm the Angel Bleeding Gabriel.' He jabbed the weapon at Leeming. 'Tell me your real name, you lying devil.'

'I just did.'

'Now you're provoking me, aren't you?'

'What's going on, Seamus?' called a voice.

Brian Dowd ambled down the drive to see what was causing the commotion. Leeming showed proof of his identity and explained that he had come at the instigation of Robert Colbeck.

'Why didn't he come himself?' asked Dowd.

'He had to make enquiries elsewhere – at Mr Fido's stables.'

'That's where the trouble started, Sergeant. John Feeny was murdered by one of Hamilton Fido's henchmen and they sent me the lad's head to frighten me – but I don't frighten that easy.'

'I do,' admitted Leeming, keenly aware that the shotgun was still pointed at him. 'Could you please persuade your friend here to put his weapon away?' Dowd gave a nod and Seamus withdrew into the nearest building. 'Thank you, sir – appreciate that.'

'Nobody gets close to Limerick Lad,' said Dowd.

'I was hoping that I might.'

'You?'

'It's one of the reasons I was glad to be sent here, sir. I know nothing about horses but I do like a flutter on the Derby. The problem is that I'm very confused,' he went on. 'Lord Hendry assured us that Odysseus would be first past the post but, when we met Mr Fido earlier today, I

145

had the impression he felt his own horse would win.'

'Merry Legs doesn't have a prayer.'

'What about Odysseus?'

Dowd was positive. 'Second place behind Limerick Lad.'

'Inspector Colbeck said that you'd commend your horse.'

'I don't commend him, Sergeant – I *believe* in him.'

Turning on his heel, he led his visitor round to the yard. There were a dozen stalls in all and most of them seemed to be occupied. Outside one of them, a groom was cleaning a racing saddle. As the lad bent forward, Leeming noticed that he had a gun tucked into his belt.

'Are all your employees armed, sir?' he asked.

'After what happened with John Feeny, I'm taking no chances.'

'Very wise.'

'Did Inspector Colbeck manage to find the boy's uncle?'

'Yes – the deceased was formally identified by a blood relation.'

'It's not the deceased who needs to be identified but the fiend who killed him and the man who paid him to do it.'

'We know your opinion on that subject, sir.'

'Then arrest Mr Fido and beat the truth out of him.'

He stopped beside one of the stalls and his manner changed at once. Limerick Lad was a bay colt with a yellowish tinge to his coat. Dowd looked at him with paternal pride.

146

'There he is – the next winner of the Derby.'

Hearing the trainer's voice, the animal raised his head from the bucket of water and came across to the door. He nuzzled up against Dowd then let out a loud whinny. Leeming was fascinated. He had never been so close to a thoroughbred horse before and he marvelled at the colt's sleek lines and perfect proportions. The sense of latent power in Limerick Lad was thrilling. Leeming had only heard about the other two potential winners of the Derby. Now he was inches away from the one horse who could challenge them and it made him think again about where he should place his money. He was touched by the affection between horse and trainer. Brian Dowd patently loved his colt but it was equally obvious that he had subjected it to a strict training regime. Limerick Lad was in prime condition.

'Breeding,' said Dowd, stroking the animal's neck. 'That's what's paramount in horseracing – good breeding. Limerick Lad is by Piscator out of Cornish Lass, who ran second in the Oaks. Piscator won the Derby and the St Leger. Do you see what I mean, Sergeant?' he said. 'There's a family tradition to maintain. Limerick Lad comes from the very best stock.'

Leeming was entranced. 'I can see that, Mr Dowd.'

'He won't let us down.'

'I'm sure he won't, sir.'

The trainer gave his horse a final pat on the neck before leading his visitor a few paces away. Then he looked Leeming in the eye.

'Why exactly did you come here?' he asked.

147

'Inspector Colbeck thought that, as a courtesy, you should be kept up to date with our investigation.'

'That was very considerate of him. I'll be interested to hear what progress you've made so far.'

'It's been slow but steady, Mr Dowd.'

Leeming explained what the Detective Department had been doing. On the journey back from Bethnal Green, he had been schooled by Colbeck to release certain facts while holding others back. At the mention of Hamilton Fido's name, Dowd scowled but held his tongue. The sergeant gauged his reactions throughout.

'Inspector Colbeck made one suggestion,' he said, 'and I must confess that it would never have occurred to me.'

'What might that be?'

'That, in fact, Mr Fido is in no way implicated in the murder.'

'He has to be!' cried Dowd. 'John Feeny worked at his stables.'

'You've jumped to the obvious conclusion, sir, as you were meant to do. But supposing that both you and Mr Fido are incidental victims of this crime?'

'Fido as a *victim* – impossible!'

'The inspector thinks otherwise,' said Leeming. 'Since there's bad blood between you and Mr Fido, he wonders if someone is trying to heat it up even more. A third party might have set out to stoke up the mutual antagonism in order to have you snarling insults at each other. That would distract the pair of you from the important job of preparing your horses for the Derby.'

148

Dowd was adamant. 'The man you want is Hamilton Fido,' he said through gritted teeth. 'Over the last couple of years, my horses have consistently beaten his. He's not the kind of man to take that lying down. He had to hit back and he used John Feeny to do it. There's something you ought to know, Sergeant,' he continued. 'The reason that Limerick Lad will win the Derby is not simply because he's the finest horse in the field. He has the best jockey on his back – Tim Maguire. I've lost count of the number of times that Mr Fido has tried to poach Tim so that he'll ride in his colours.'

'There's nothing illegal in that, sir. Every owner would like to have the best jockey riding for him.'

'Only one would offer a huge bribe to make sure that my colt lost the race. That's what was dangled in front of Tim Maguire – five hundred pounds to pull Limerick Lad out of the reckoning.'

'Five hundred!' Leeming whistled in amazement. 'Do you know who made the offer?'

'Hamilton Fido.'

'Are you sure?'

'The letter was unsigned,' said Dowd, reaching inside his coat, 'but I'm sure it had Mr Fido's name on it in invisible ink. Since he couldn't have Tim in the saddle on Merry Legs, he wanted to make use of him another way.'

'That's a very serious allegation, Mr Dowd.'

'Read the letter for yourself.'

'Thank you,' said Leeming, taking it from him and unfolding the paper. The letter was short but explicit. He read it in seconds. 'This is evidence,

149

sir – may I keep it?'

'Please do, Sergeant.'

'I take it that Maguire was not tempted.'

'Tim rides for me and nobody else,' boasted Dowd. 'When he sent that letter, there was something about my jockey that Hamilton Fido obviously didn't know.'

'And what was that, sir?'

'He has the same problem as John Feeny.'

'Problem?'

'He's illiterate. You don't need to be able to read in order to ride a horse. All you have to do is to recognise a winning post when you see one. The joke is on Mr Fido,' said Dowd with a grim chuckle. 'When he received that letter, Tim Maguire didn't have a clue that he was being offered a bribe.'

When he saw Hamilton Fido for the second time that day, Robert Colbeck was not given as cordial a welcome. The bookmaker was at his stables, talking to his trainer, Alfred Stenton, a bear-like man in his forties with a grizzled beard and tiny deep-set eyes. They looked up as the detective approached them across the yard. Stenton showed curiosity but Fido's face registered annoyance until he concealed it behind his practised smile.

'We meet again, Inspector,' he said.

'I remembered your saying that you'd be coming here this afternoon,' said Colbeck. 'Have you established yet how John Feeny got a job here when he'd been in the employ of your fiercest rival?'

'Alfred explained that to me.'

He introduced the trainer and Stenton took

150

over. He had a deep voice, a slow delivery and a bluff manner. Hands on hips, he stood with his legs planted wide apart.

'Don't blame me,' he said stoutly. 'I'd no idea that the lad had worked for Brian Dowd. He told me he came from Cork where he'd been a groom for three years. One of my boys had a nasty accident so I needed a replacement. John Feeny came along at the right time.'

Colbeck wanted to hear more. 'A nasty accident?'

'He was kicked by a horse, Inspector – broke his leg.'

'Was there anything suspicious about it?'

The trainer shook his head. 'If you want to know the truth, the lad deserved what he got. He'd been drinking heavily and he knew I didn't allow beer at the stables. You need a clear head when your dealing with racehorses,' said Stenton. 'They can be a real handful if you get on the wrong side of them. He was grooming Bold Buccaneer and slapped him on the rump. That was asking for trouble.'

'How did John Feeny know there was a vacancy here?'

'A friend recommended him.'

'Someone from the stables?' said Colbeck.

'Yes, Inspector,' replied Stenton. 'Ned Kyle, one of my jockeys, spoke up for him. They grew up together in Cork.'

'Why didn't Kyle warn you?' asked Fido angrily. 'He must have known about Feeny's link with Dowd.'

'He swears that he didn't,' said the trainer, 'and

151

I took him at his word. Ned is as honest as the day is long. He'd not deceive me. In any case, he and John Feeny hadn't seen each other for years. How could Ned possibly know where he'd been working?'

'Feeny was unlikely to tell him,' observed Colbeck. 'He knew he'd never get a job here if Brian Dowd's name was mentioned.'

Stenton snorted. 'I'd have thrown him out on his ear.'

'He winkled his way in here to spy,' said Fido.

'It doesn't look that way,' said Colbeck. 'It seems that he only got the job by default. If another groom hadn't been kicked by a horse, John Feeny would still be looking for work.'

'That's my view as well,' said Stenton.

'On the other hand, *someone* knew about Feeny's past.'

'What do you mean, Inspector?'

'A couple of letters were sent to Jerry Doyle, a lad at Mr Dowd's stables. Since Feeny couldn't write, he must have got a friend to pen the letters for him.'

'Someone from here,' said Fido vengefully. 'Ned Kyle, perhaps.'

'He'd never do such a thing,' argued Stenton.

'Maybe we have *another* spy in the camp.'

'I'd like a word with Kyle, if I may,' said Colbeck.

'I'll see if I can find him for you, Inspector,' said Stenton, moving off. 'But I'll tell you right now – Ned is as clean as a whistle.'

The trainer walked away and left the two men alone.

'It looks as if someone let you down, Mr Fido,' began Colbeck. 'When I arrived here, you were patently surprised to see me. Nobody warned you of my visit this time.'

'After this morning's meeting,' said Fido, 'I didn't think that we had anything more to say to each other.'

'There have been developments, sir.'

'Oh?'

'Your informant at Scotland Yard is obviously unaware of them so I felt it my duty to pass on the information myself. Lord Hendry reported an incident related to the Derby.'

'In what way?'

'Someone did his best to cause Odysseus serious injury.'

'I'm sorry to hear that,' said Fido blandly.

'Luckily, the attempt was thwarted.'

'Why are you telling me, Inspector? You surely can't believe that I'm in any way culpable.'

'I make no assumptions, sir.'

'Lord Hendry pointed the finger at me – is that it?'

'Your name was mentioned to the superintendent.'

'I'm astounded that he didn't have posters printed with a picture of me as the wanted man,' said Fido with a laugh. 'Every time there's a crime or a misdemeanour on a racecourse, Lord Hendry accuses me.'

'Brian Dowd was also named as a suspect.'

'Then he's nearer the mark there.'

'There doesn't appear to be any mutual respect in the world of horseracing,' said Colbeck with disapproval. 'Does the concept of friendly rivalry mean nothing to you?'

Fido was amused. 'Not if you want to be a winner,' he said flatly. 'All's fair in love and racing, Inspector. What about *your* world? Do you regard criminals as no more than friendly rivals?'

'I take your point, sir.'

'There's no virtue in being a gallant loser.'

'Let me change the subject,' said Colbeck, glancing around the yard where several people were busy at work. 'Though you might wish to continue this discussion where we can have a little more privacy.'

'Why?'

'I have to touch on a more personal matter.'

'Touch away,' said Fido, spreading his arms invitingly. 'I've nothing to hide.'

'Then perhaps you'd be good enough to confirm that you stayed at the Wyvern Hotel in London recently.'

Fido bristled. 'What sort of question is that, Inspector?'

'A pertinent one, sir.'

'I often stay at hotels in the city.'

'The one that interests me is the Wyvern – just off the Strand.'

'I can't say that I remember staying there,' said Fido.

'You're a very distinctive figure,' Colbeck pointed out. 'Had you visited the hotel, the staff would doubtless recognise you again. And, of course,' he went on, 'your name would be in the hotel register. In fact, I have it on good authority that that is so.'

'In that case, I suppose I must have spent a night there.'

'You and your companion, sir.'

Fido smiled. 'I've always been a sociable fellow.'

'You were not very sociable on this occasion, it seems. When a hatbox was stolen from your room, you upbraided the hotel staff and demanded restitution.' The bookmaker's smile froze. 'The hatbox later turned up at Crewe with John Feeny's head in it, so you'll understand why we have such an interest in your hotel accommodation on that particular night.'

'What are you after, Inspector?'

'The name of the lady with whom you were staying, sir.'

'It has no relevance whatsoever to your investigation.'

'Let me be the judge of that, Mr Fido.'

'The lady was the victim of a crime.'

'Then it should have been reported to the police.'

'There was no need,' said Fido. 'The manager had the sense to accept responsibility and offer compensation. As far as we were concerned, the matter was closed.'

Colbeck was tenacious. 'It falls to me to reopen it,' he said. 'I believe that there may have been a specific reason why that particular hatbox was stolen. It's therefore important that I know the name of the person who owned it.'

Fido lowered his voice. 'Are you married, Inspector?'

'No, sir, I'm a bachelor.'

'So am I,' confided the other. 'We are two of a

kind – single gentlemen who take their pleasures where they find them and who protect the identity of any lady involved. Such conduct will inevitably attract condemnation from those of more puritanical disposition but, I'm glad to say, it's not an offence that's found its way into the statute book. If it had, some of our most distinguished politicians – the late Duke of Wellington among them – would have been liable to arrest.'

'I'm not hear to discuss the duke's indiscretions.'

'Mine are equally outside your purview, Inspector.'

'I require the name of that young lady.'

'And I decline to give it to you.'

'That's tantamount to obstructing the police,' warned Colbeck.

'I prefer to see it as the act of a gentleman.'

'Your definition of gentlemanly behaviour does not accord with mine, Mr Fido. I thought you were keen for this crime to be solved.'

'I am,' asserted the other. 'I want the killer brought to justice.'

'Then why refuse to cooperate? John Feeny lost his life in the most grisly way. My job,' said Colbeck, 'is to gather every conceivable scrap of evidence. Consequently, I would like to speak to the young lady with whom you stayed at the Wyvern Hotel.'

'I can relay your questions to her, Inspector.'

'That will not suffice.'

'Then you are going to be disappointed.'

'Are you ashamed of the lady for some reason?'

'No,' rejoined Fido, 'and I resent your insinuation. I do not need to buy a lady's favours, Inspector Colbeck. Strange as it may seem, I happen to believe in romance. Do you know what that means?'

'Of course, sir,' said Colbeck, thinking fondly of Madeleine Andrews. 'Being a member of the Metropolitan Police Force does not make us oblivious to emotion.'

'Then see it from my point of view. If a young lady had put the ultimate trust in you, would you break that trust by revealing her identity?'

'Probably not.'

'We agree on something at last.'

'Not exactly, sir,' said Colbeck, 'but I spy a way out of this dilemma. Approach the lady yourself and explain the situation in which we find ourselves. Tell her that she can contact me at Scotland Yard and that I will treat everything she says in strict confidence. Who knows?' he asked meaningfully. 'It may well be that she is more anxious for this murder to be solved than you seem to be.'

Kitty Lavender was in her bedroom, seated in front of the dressing table and looking in the mirror as she fastened her diamond earrings in place. When she heard a knock on the door, she went through to the drawing room to see who her visitor might be. Opening the door, she was taken aback to see Marcus Johnson standing there with a warm and mischievous smile.

'I thought we were going to keep out of each other's way for a while,' she said. 'What brought you here?'

'A hansom cab.'

157

'Don't jest, Marcus.'

'I came on the off-chance of catching you in,' he said, doffing his hat. 'Your landlady recognised me and let me into the house.'

'In that case, you'd better come in.'

Kitty stood back so that he could go past her then she closed the door behind her. She was not sure if she was pleased to see him. Her half-brother tended to vanish from her life for long periods then surface when he needed money or help or both. Kitty wondered what he was after this time.

The drawing room was large, well proportioned and filled with exquisite Regency furniture. Long, gilt-framed mirrors had been artfully used to make the room seem even bigger than it was. Fresh flowers stood in a vase. Marcus Johnson looked around.

'I always like coming here,' he said. 'I just wish that I could afford a suite of rooms like this.'

'You're a nomad. You never stay in one place long enough.'

'That's true – though this house would tempt me.'

'It was recommended to me by a close friend.'

He grinned. 'I won't ask his name,' he said, putting his hat down on a table. 'Well, I won't stay long, Kitty. I just wanted the pleasure of seeing the look of amazement on your face.'

'Why should I be amazed?'

'Because I've not come to borrow money from you.'

'That's a relief,' she said.

'In fact, I've here to do the exact opposite.'

Thrusting a hand into his coat pocket, he extracted a pile of banknotes. 'I'm going to repay in full what I owe you.'

'Marcus!' she exclaimed.

'You see? I knew that you'd gasp with disbelief.'

'It's so ... unexpected.'

'Be honest, Kitty,' he said with a laugh. 'I'm your half-brother. You've no need to mince words with me. It's not only unexpected, it's totally uncharacteristic. Marcus Johnson is one of Nature's borrowers. Until today, that is.' He waved the banknotes. 'Go on – take them.'

'Are you sure?'

'They're not forgeries.'

'Even so,' she said, hesitating.

He laughed again. 'Am I held in such low esteem that you do not believe I could acquire the money honestly? I have to disappoint you,' he went on. 'I neither robbed a bank nor dressed up as a highwayman to waylay an unsuspecting coach. I won at cards, Kitty. I had a run of luck at the card table last night that was unprecedented. And *that*, my dear sister, is how I'm able to pay off my debt to you.'

'Thank you, Marcus,' she said, taking the money and the kiss that came with it. 'But do not fritter away the rest of your winnings.'

'No sermons, please – I know when to stop.'

'Then your judgement *has* improved.'

'I've put youthful impetuosity behind me,' he declared, 'where gambling is concerned, anyway. When it comes to beautiful women, however, it's a different matter. In that regard, I'm ever prey to impulsive action.'

'Does that mean you have someone in mind?'

'I have a dozen ladies in mind, Kitty!'

'For marriage or for pleasure?'

'I'm not the marrying kind,' he said airily. 'I ventured into holy matrimony once and found it a most inhibiting place to be. I like the freedom of the open road. You were right. I'm essentially a nomad.'

'How long will you be staying in London?'

'That depends how well I do during Derby Week.'

'What happens if your run of luck continues?'

'Then I'll probably spend the summer in Paris.'

'And if you *lose* at Epsom?'

'I'll be back to borrow that money off you again.'

'It's no longer available,' she told him, slipping it into the drawer of a mahogany side-table. 'The kindest thing I can do is to refuse you any more loans. That will make you stand on your own feet.'

'I think I've finally learnt to do that, Kitty.'

'I sincerely hope so.'

'Well,' he said, collecting his hat, 'now that I've settled my debts, I'll be on my way. Unless, of course, those keen ears of yours picked up something from Hamilton Fido.'

'I haven't even seen him since we last met.'

'Make a point of doing so.'

'He's too preoccupied with the Derby.'

'Surely he's taking you to Epsom on his arm.'

'Yes, he loves to display me.'

'You're a jewel among women, Kitty. He wears you with pride. But don't forget me, will you? Last-minute information is the best kind. I can

160

place my heaviest bet immediately before the race.' He winked at her. 'Can I count on your help?'

'I don't like to be pestered, Marcus.'

'Blood is thicker than water.'

'As you wish,' she said with a tired smile. 'I'll see what I can find out from Hamilton. How will I get in touch with you?'

'You won't need to,' he told her, 'because I'll get in touch with you. Thank you again for the loan of that money.' He kissed her on both cheeks. 'Take my advice and grow accustomed to the notion that your half-brother will soon be a very wealthy man.'

The Shepherd and Shepherdess was a half-timbered inn, situated on the bank of a river. Built almost three hundred years earlier, it served the needs of the village and also attracted customers from further afield. Since it was only a couple of miles from the stables, it did not take Robert Colbeck long to get there. When they reached the inn, the inspector clambered out of the cab and told the driver to wait.

'How long will you be, guv'nor?' asked the man.

'Long enough,' said Colbeck, understanding the question.

The man jumped quickly down from the cab, tethered his horse and went into the bar to slake his thirst. Colbeck bought drinks for both of them before introducing himself to the landlord. He asked if he might speak to Bonny Rimmer and, moments later, a short, pretty, dark-haired, rosy-cheeked young woman came into the bar, wiping her hands on her apron. She was plainly terrified at having been summoned by a detective from Scotland Yard. After trying to put her at ease with a few pleasantries, Colbeck requested that they move to somewhere other than the bar. Still apprehensive, Bonny took him to a little room at the rear. As they sat down together, Colbeck put his glass of brandy on the table.

'I believe you know a jockey named Ned Kyle,' he said.

'Yes, sir,' she replied. 'He often comes in here.'

'I've just spoken to him at the stables. He struck me as an honest, straightforward person. Would you agree?'

'Oh, I would. Ned is a good man. He never causes trouble.'

'Does that mean some of the others do?'

'They get a bit excited, that's all,' said Bonny nervously.

'What about John Feeny?'

She brightened immediately. 'John?'

'Was he rather boisterous at times?'

'No, sir,' she replied, 'he's always quiet, is John. He likes his beer, mind you – they all do – but he doesn't have the money to drink too much. That'll change when he becomes a jockey, though. He might even earn as much as Ned.'

Colbeck felt a surge of pity for her. She was talking as if John Feeny were still alive and about to fulfil his ambitions. When he had spoken to Ned Kyle at the stables, the inspector had learnt two things. The first was that Kyle was completely unaware of his friend's link with Brian Dowd and the second concerned Bonny Rimmer. During his visits to the inn, John Feeny and the barmaid had developed a close friendship.

From the way she talked about him, it was clear that she was in love with the Irishman. It was equally clear that she believed she would soon see him again. Colbeck had not bought the drink for himself. He moved it across to her before he spoke.

'I have some sad news to pass on, Miss Rimmer,' he said.

'What about?'

'John Feeny?'

She tensed. 'Has he been arrested?'

'It's rather more serious than that, I'm afraid.'

'He's been *injured*?'

'John Feeny is dead,' said Colbeck gently, steadying her with a hand as she reeled from the news. 'He was murdered.'

Bonny Rimmer was stunned. Her mouth fell open, her eyes darted wildly and her whole body trembled. When she began to sob convulsively, Colbeck provided her with a handkerchief and a consoling arm. Since she was in no state to hear the full details of the crime, he decided to keep them from her. He waited until she was over the worst of the shock, then he held the brandy to her lips.

'Drink some of this,' he coaxed. 'It might help you.'

Bonny consented to take a sip. She pulled a face at the sharp taste of the brandy but it helped to bring her to her senses. Of her own volition, she took a second, longer sip before turning her watery eyes on Colbeck.

'Who could possibly want to harm John?' she asked.

'That's what I'm trying to find out, Miss Rimmer, and I'm hoping that you might be able to assist me.' She shrugged hopelessly. 'Ned Kyle told me that you and John were good friends. Is that true?' She nodded. 'According to him, John was always talking about you at the stables.'

'Was he?' The information brought a modicum of comfort and she managed a pale smile. 'We liked each other.'

'When did you last see him?'

'It must have been over a week ago.'

'How did he seem?'

'John was very happy,' she said. 'He was always happy when we were together. But he did warn me that he wouldn't be able to see me for a while because of Derby Week. Mr Stenton wanted the grooms on duty all the time to guard the horses. John said he'd try to sneak off but he never turned up.' She burst into tears again. 'Now I know why.'

Colbeck offered her the brandy once more and she had another sip.

'Did he tell you anything about his work?' he said.

'He told me lots, Inspector. Riding was everything to John. He wanted to be a jockey like Ned. He worked somewhere in Ireland but they wouldn't let him ride. They said he'd never make a jockey and it really hurt John. He came to England to prove himself.'

'Do you know the name of the stables in Ireland?'

'Oh, yes,' she said. 'I wrote letters to a friend of his there.'

'Jerry Doyle?'

She blinked in surprise. 'How do you know that?'

'I spoke to him while I was in Dublin,' said Colbeck. 'He showed me the letters – you have nice handwriting, Miss Rimmer.'

'Thank you, sir – I was taught to read and write proper.'

'In one of the letters, John said that he'd met someone very special but he didn't give your name.' She blushed visibly. 'You did him a great favour in writing on his behalf.'

'John wanted to learn to do it himself. I said I'd teach him.'

'That was very kind of you.'

'I'd do *anything* for John,' she affirmed.

'Did he have any enemies at the stables?'

'No, he got on very well with everyone, Inspector.'

'That was the impression I got when I spoke to some of the other grooms. John Feeny had fitted in very well. He had prospects.'

'He did,' she said, 'and he was about to come into some money.'

'Really?'

'I was the only person he told. He wouldn't even tell people like his uncle or Ned Kyle about it. But he told me,' she went on. 'We had no secrets from each other, you see.'

'And where was this money to come from?'

'A man he'd met.'

'What did John have to do to get it?'

165

'He had to give him as much information as he could about Limerick Lad – that's the Irish horse in the Derby.'

'Yes, I know.'

'John was to see this man somewhere and be paid to talk about the stables where he'd worked. He owed no loyalty to Mr Dowd, the trainer,' she insisted. 'He only held John back. Besides, John was working for Mr Stenton and wanted Merry Legs to win the Derby.'

'Did John say when and where he'd meet this man?'

'No, Inspector.'

'Did he give you the man's name?'

'John didn't know it.'

'What *did* he tell you about him?' Colbeck pressed.

'Only that he was a gentleman and offered a lot of money.'

'Was he English or Irish?'

'Oh, English,' she said, 'and he knew a lot about racing. John told me he was very nice at first but he did threaten him once.'

'Really?'

'When he gave John a job, Mr Stenton warned him that he wasn't to speak to anyone – anyone at all – outside the stables about what went on there. People are always trying to bribe the grooms and jockeys for information. John swore that he'd say nothing,' she said. 'When this man first got in touch with him, John thought it might be best if he said nothing at all to him – not even about a rival stables. It was then the man made his threat.'

'What did he threaten?'

166

'He told John he had a choice,' she recalled. 'He could either talk about Limerick Lad and earn his reward, or, if he refused, then he'd lose his job because Mr Stenton would be told where John used to work in Ireland. John *had* to agree, Inspector,' she said fervently. 'He was afraid that if he lost his job, he'd lose me as well. Besides, he needed the money. So he agreed to do what the man asked.'

'Thank you, Miss Rimmer,' said Colbeck, watching a tear trickle down her cheek. 'You've been very helpful.'

'Can *I* ask *you* a question now, sir?'

'Of course.'

'How was John killed?'

Robert Colbeck took a deep breath before speaking.

CHAPTER EIGHT

Madeleine Andrews was busy in the kitchen when she heard a knock on the front door. Since her father sometimes forgot to take his key with him, she assumed that it was he and went to let him in. Before she did so, however, she decided that it might be safer to see who was outside first. Tugging the curtain back an inch, she peered out into the gloom then let out a cry of joy. Silhouetted against a gas lamp was the familiar figure of Robert Colbeck. She opened the door at once and gave him a radiant smile.

'I was hoping you were still up,' he said, stepping into the house and embracing her. 'I was relieved to see the light still on.'

'I was waiting for Father. I have to cook his supper.'

'Mr Andrews had better come soon.'

'Why is that?'

'It's just starting to rain. I felt the first few spots as I got out of the cab. We're in for a downpour.'

'Father doesn't mind a drop of rain,' she said, shutting the front door. 'He's used to being out in all weathers. But how are you?' she went on, standing back to take a good look at him. 'And how is the investigation going?'

Colbeck whisked off his hat. 'I'm fine, Madeleine,' he said. 'As for the investigation, we continue to gather evidence.'

'Are you close to arresting someone yet?'

'No, but we're eliminating possible suspects one by one.'

'Father still insists that it's a crime of passion.'

'In one sense, he's right – it was certainly instigated by someone who has a passion for horseracing.' An amusing thought struck him. 'Perhaps we should changes places.'

'Who?'

'Your father and I.'

Madeleine laughed. 'What a ridiculous idea!'

'Is it?' he asked. 'Mr Andrews clearly had a detective's instinct and I've always wanted to be an engine driver.'

'I think you're both far better off doing the jobs you have.'

'Perhaps you're right – but what about you, Madeleine? How is your work going?'

'I've all but finished my latest commission.' She took him across to her easel and indicated the painting. 'It's a Crampton locomotive.'

'I can see that,' he said, recognising the distinctive features of Thomas Crampton's design. 'What puzzles me is why so few of them were made for this country and so many for France. When I crossed the Channel last year, I twice travelled on trains that were pulled by a locomotive just like that.' He shot her a look of mock suspicion. 'Don't tell me you're going to export *this* to France as well?'

'Not unless the French start drinking tea.'

'Tea?'

'That's where this may end up, Robert – on a tea caddy. It's a design they want to put on hundreds of them. They intend to sell them at railway stations.'

'*I'd* certainly buy one.'

She giggled and he leant forward to give her a kiss. When they sat beside each other, he put his top hat on her head in fun and it dropped down to her ears. They laughed as she took it off and set it aside. Not having seen her for a while, Colbeck was so pleased to be close to her again, reminded of all the things that had attracted him to Madeleine Andrews in the first place. Her vitality was a positive tonic to him. But he did not forget the main purpose of his visit.

'Do you remember what I asked you?' he said.

She responded eagerly. 'About helping in the investigation?'

'Yes, Madeleine – I may need to call on you now.'

'That's wonderful!'

'You haven't heard what I want you to do yet. I spent a long time at the stables owned by Hamilton Fido today. Then I was driven to an inn called the Shepherd and Shepherdess.'

Colbeck went on to tell her about his meeting with Bonny Rimmer and how devastated she had been by the news about John Feeny. Madeleine was sure that he had been as considerate as always when passing on bad tidings but there was no way that even he could have softened the blow on this occasion.

'I feel so sorry for the poor girl,' she said.

'That's why I want you to speak to her.'

'Me?'

'There's only so much I can do, Madeleine,' he

explained. 'As a detective from Scotland Yard, I must be very intimidating to her. I never felt that I reached Bonny Rimmer, and once she knew the hideous truth about how Feeny died she could not even speak. I left her in a complete daze.'

'What do you think *I* can do, Robert?'

'I felt that she knew more than she actually told me – not because she was deliberately holding anything back but because she was overwhelmed by the situation. Bonny is young and vulnerable. She could simply not cope with the information that the lad she loved had been killed.'

'Very few women could,' said Madeleine, 'especially when they discovered that he'd been beheaded. It must have been horrifying for her. I'm surprised she didn't faint.'

'She came very close to it.'

'I can see why you want me to speak to her instead.'

'You're a woman – that gives you an immediate advantage over me. You can draw her out more easily. Do nothing for a day or so. Bonny needs time to grieve and to get over the initial shock.'

'And then?'

'Go to the Shepherd and Shepherdess and meet her. Talk to the girl about her friendship with John Feeny. How close were they – did they ever think of marriage? Without realising it,' said Colbeck, 'Bonny Rimmer knows things that could be useful to me. I'd hoped you'd be talking to the woman who owned that hatbox but she's yet to be identified. It may be more helpful if you spoke to Bonny.'

'I'll try, Robert.'

'Thank you.'

As he leant across to kiss her again, they heard the scrape of a key in the lock and moved guiltily apart. They got to their feet. The door suddenly opened and Caleb Andrews darted in to escape the rain that was now falling outside. He closed the door behind him.

'It's teeming down out there,' he said.

'I managed to miss it,' said Colbeck. 'I hope it clears up before Derby Week begins.'

'Why?' asked Madeleine.

'I can see you know nothing about horseracing, Maddy,' said Andrews. 'Heavy rain can affect the result of a race. Some horses prefer a hard, dry course. Others do best when the going is soft. If it rains on the morning of the Derby, the betting odds will change.'

'True,' agreed Colbeck. 'Odysseus might drop back and Limerick Lad might replace him as favourite. Brian Dowd told me that his colt liked a soft, damp surface. They have a fair bit of rain in Ireland, by all accounts, so Limerick Lad is used to it.'

'I'm going to bet on an outsider,' said Andrews. 'That way, if I do win, I'll get a decent return on my money.'

'Which horse have you picked?' asked Madeleine.

'Princess of Fire – the name reminded me of you, Maddy. When you're in a good mood, you're my very own princess. And when you're not, it's like being in the middle of a fiery furnace.'

'That's a terrible thing to say,' she protested over his laughter.

172

'Your father is only teasing,' said Colbeck.

'I'm the most tolerant daughter in the world.'

'You are at that,' said Andrews, giving her a kiss of appeasement and soaking her dress in the process. 'I'm sorry, Maddy. I'll get out of these wet things before I have supper.'

'What are the odds on this Princess of Fire?'

'20–1.'

'Good luck!' said Colbeck 'Who owns the horse, Mr Andrews?'

'A man with an eye for fillies – he has two of them in the race.'

'Hamilton Fido?'

'Yes, Inspector,' replied Andrews. 'My reasoning is this, see. No bookmaker would enter a horse unless it had a fair chance of winning. I reckon that he's made sure all the attention has gone on Merry Legs when, in fact, the filly he expects to romp home is Princess of Fire.'

It was her second unexpected visitor that day and Kitty Lavender was torn between pleasure and discomfort. While she was glad to see Hamilton Fido again, she was unsettled by the fact that he had caught her unawares. She was grateful that she was wearing a necklace he had given her. Inviting him into her drawing room, she received a kiss.

'I didn't think to see you for a couple of days,' she said.

'Is that a complaint, Kitty?'

'No, no, of course not.'

'Are your feathers still ruffled?' he said, caressing her shoulders and arms. 'When you came to

173

my office, you were very upset.'

'I had good reason to be, Hamilton.'

'Well, you seem much calmer now, I'm glad to say. And I kept my promise, Kitty. I found out the name of the murder victim even though the police still haven't released it to the press.'

She braced herself. 'Whose head was it?'

'John Feeny's.'

'And who is he?'

'He was a groom at my stables,' said Fido, 'though, in my opinion, he should never have been employed there. Feeny used to work for Brian Dowd. I think he was sent to England as a spy.'

'Who killed him?'

'That's what I came to talk to you about. The man in charge of the investigation is Inspector Colbeck.'

'Yes – I saw his name in the newspapers.'

'His nickname is the Railway Detective but he knows a lot about the Turf as well,' conceded the bookmaker. 'He also knows how to pick up a scent and that's where you come in, Kitty.'

'I don't follow.'

'Colbeck discovered that we stayed at the Wyvern Hotel.'

Kitty was scandalised. 'How on earth did he do that?'

'I wish I knew. The hotel was your recommendation.'

'I'd heard it was very discreet,' she said, not wishing to admit that she'd been there before. 'A woman friend of mine spoke well of it.'

'You can tell your friend that she was wrong.

They let us down badly. Inspector Colbeck came out to the stables this afternoon to question me about our stay there. I must confess that it gave me a bit of a jolt, Kitty. He knew far too much. What he really wanted to find out was your name.'

'She started. '*My* name?'

'It was your hatbox.'

'What difference does that make?'

'Colbeck thought there might be significance in the fact. The only way he can be certain is to talk to you in person.'

'Did you give him my name?' said Kitty anxiously.

'You know me better than that,' he soothed, taking her hands and kissing both of them. 'I refused to tell him, Kitty. The problem is that that could be construed as holding back evidence. If he wants to, Inspector Colbeck could make life very difficult for me at a time when I need to concentrate all my energies on Derby Week.'

'There's nothing I can tell him, Hamilton. My hatbox was stolen. That's the beginning and the end of it.'

'He won't be satisfied until he's heard that from your own lips.'

'I don't want to talk to any detective.'

'It could save me a lot of embarrassment, Kitty. When he saw that I'd never reveal your name, Colbeck suggested a compromise. He said that you could come forward of your own accord and that the meeting with him would be in the strictest privacy.'

'No,' she said, turning away. 'I want no part of this.'

'Not even to help me?'

'I don't wish for any dealings with the police.'

'To give him his due, Colbeck seems very trust-worthy.'

'I don't care what he is.'

'Well, I do,' he said, crossing to turn her round so that she faced him. 'Unless you talk to him, he'll keep hounding me and I simply can't allow that. You know how busy I'm going to be, Kitty. The last thing I need is to be hauled into Scotland Yard.'

'I'm sorry, Hamilton – I just can't do it.'

Their eyes locked and there was a silent battle of wills. They had been together for a relatively short time but it had been long enough for Kitty to glimpse the rewards that might come her way. Fido was rich, amorous and highly indulgent. The few nights they had spent together had been wonderful, marked by pitches of excitement she had never known before. It would be reckless of her to put their friendship at risk. After mulling it over, she gave a noncommittal nod.

'I'll think about it.'

'Thank you,' he said, giving her a warm hug. 'Oh, by the way, I saw your brother last night.'

'Marcus is only my half-brother.'

'I called in at a club I belong to and there he was – sitting at the card table with some of the most notorious gamblers in the city. From what I could see, Marcus was doing quite well.'

'He had a lucky streak. He told me about it.'

'That's a good omen for Derby Week.'

'He means to bet heavily.'

'Then send him to me,' said Fido. 'I like a man

who knows how to throw his money around. Cautious punters are the bane of my life.'

'Marcus is never cautious.' She remembered her discussion with him and saw an opportunity to probe a little on his behalf. 'And neither are you, Hamilton. Because you've taken big chances, you've reaped big rewards.'

He grinned at her. 'You're one of them, Kitty.'

'I may place a small bet myself.'

'Then don't come to me. Small bets are for small bookmakers.'

'They all agree that Odysseus is the favourite.'

'Put your money on him and you'll lose it.'

'What would you advise?' she asked, nestling up to him.

'Look to the lady,' he suggested. 'It's high time that a filly won the Derby again and that's exactly what Merry Legs will do. I saw her being put through her paces today and she reminded me of you.'

She spluttered. 'A *horse* reminded you of me?'

'A filly,' he corrected with a wicked smile. 'Merry Legs was sleek, beautiful and a class apart from all those around her – just like you.'

Robert Colbeck and Victor Leeming arrived early at Scotland Yard next morning so that they could compare notes about their respective visits the previous day before reporting to the superintendent. Colbeck was interested to hear Leeming's assessment of Brian Dowd.

'He's a hard man,' said the sergeant. 'Mr Dowd was pleasant enough to me but I'm not sure I'd like to work for him.'

'Why not, Victor?'

'He has a real temper. One of his stable lads felt the full force of it. The last time I heard that kind of language was in a dockyard. He cursed him until the lad was shaking.'

'Brian Dowd likes to assert his authority. I saw that in Ireland.'

'There's no love lost between him and Hamilton Fido.'

'I know,' said Colbeck. 'They loathe each other and neither of them has a good word to say about Lord Hendry. Of the three of them, I think I liked Dowd the best.'

'He seemed the most straightforward of them to me.'

'And he obviously inspires loyalty. That's why Tim Maguire has stayed with him. If I owned a racehorse, Maguire would always be my first choice as a jockey. I've seen him ride before.'

'No wonder Mr Fido tried to bribe him.'

'We don't know that he did,' said Colbeck, glancing at the letter again. 'That was an assumption that Dowd made when he saw that. The offer could have come from one of the many owners who'd love to have Maguire in their colours.'

'It didn't come from Lord Hendry,' said Leeming.

'How do you know?'

'Because of something Mr Dowd told me. According to him, Lord Hendry is always short of money. He certainly couldn't afford the five hundred pounds to tempt Maguire.'

'He could afford to keep a mistress – until she walked out.'

'How could he manage that?'

'On credit, probably,' said Colbeck. 'People still respect a title. It can buy a lot of financial leeway.' He handed the anonymous letter to Leeming. 'Time to face the wrath of Mr Tallis,' he added, getting up from his chair. 'He expected arrests long before now.'

When they entered the superintendent's office, they walked into a fug of cigar smoke. Tallis was behind his desk, glowering at one of the newspapers on the pile in front of him. After puffing on his cigar, he looked up at them with controlled fury.

'Which one of you idiots did this?' he demanded, tapping the newspaper. 'Who released the name of John Feeny to the press?'

'Not me, sir,' said Leeming.

'Nor me,' said Colbeck.

'It must have been one of you. Nobody else outside this room knew who the murder victim was and I wanted to keep it that way until I felt it appropriate to identify him publicly. Admit it,' he went on, rapping his desk. 'Which one of you let the name slip?'

'Neither of us, Superintendent,' said Colbeck, 'and you're wrong to think that we are the only three people aware of Feeny's identity. You're forgetting his uncle and Brian Dowd. More importantly, you're forgetting his killer – he was very much aware of who and what the lad was. You can add someone else to that list as well.'

'And who might that be?' said Tallis.

'Hamilton Fido.'

'The bookmaker?'

'When we called on him this morning, he already knew that it was John Feeny's head in that hatbox.'

'Incredible!'

'Not if you've met Mr Fido,' said Leeming.

'He has agents everywhere, sir,' said Colbeck. 'One of them, I'm ashamed to tell you, works in this very building.'

Tallis was rocked by the news. 'Are you certain, Inspector?'

'Beyond a shadow of a doubt,' Colbeck assured him. 'We need to flush him out and I have an idea how it might be done. Before we get diverted by that, however, I think you should hear what Victor and I managed to find out yesterday afternoon.'

'Yes, yes, please go ahead.'

'Victor,' prompted Colbeck.

'Oh, I see,' said Leeming uneasily. 'You want me to go first.' He launched into a long, rambling account of his visit to Brian Dowd's stables and he handed Tallis the anonymous letter sent to the jockey. When the report finally came to an end, the superintendent waved the letter in the air.

'Five hundred pounds for a jockey?' he bellowed. 'Is any man worth that amount for simply riding in a horse race?'

'Tim Maguire is worth every penny,' said Colbeck. 'He's ahead of his rivals in both skill and experience. The Derby is not an ordinary race, sir. Apart from bringing great kudos to the winner, there's prize money of over six thousand pounds this year.'

'Six thousand!'

180

'That's in addition to what the owner can make by betting on his horse,' said Leeming. 'You can see why they all want the best jockey. Mr Fido has tried to lure him away before.'

'Is Dowd certain that Hamilton Fido offered this bribe?'

'Yes, sir.'

'Then all we need to do is to get another sample of Mr Fido's handwriting in order to compare it with this letter.'

'With respect,' said Colbeck, 'that would be utterly pointless. If Hamilton Fido *is* the man behind the bribe – and there's no proof of that – he'd never risk penning the letter himself. He's too guileful.'

'I agree,' said Leeming. 'He's the sort of man who could walk through snow without leaving a single footprint.'

'*Somebody* wrote this letter,' insisted Tallis.

Colbeck took it from him. 'It's an educated hand,' he noted, 'and he's used stationery of good quality. Lord Hendry, perhaps – now there's a thought! If he had Tim Maguire in the saddle, Odysseus really would be unbeatable.'

'Tell me about your visit to Mr Fido's stables.'

'It was very productive, sir.'

Unlike the sergeant, Colbeck had taken the trouble to prepare his report beforehand so that it was clear and succinct. Though he told the superintendent about his meeting with Bonny Rimmer, he omitted all reference to the fact that he would be using Madeleine Andrews to extract further information from the barmaid. It was another woman who excited Tallis's curiosity.

'Mr Fido spent the night in a hotel with this person?' he asked censoriously. 'Whatever happened to Christian values?'

'He *is* a bachelor,' said Colbeck.

'My point exactly.'

'He refused to give me the young lady's name.'

'Then he must be compelled to do so, Inspector.'

'I think I found a way around that particular problem, sir. Mr Fido will advise her to come forward voluntarily. I've every hope that she'll take his advice.'

'Gentlemen consorting with unmarried women,' said Tallis, exhaling a cloud of smoke. 'Where will it end? First of all we have Lord Hendry sharing a bed with his mistress in Cambridge and now we have Fido indulging in lewd conduct here in London.'

'It's an intriguing coincidence, isn't it?' said Colbeck.

'I think it's abominable!'

'I don't hold with it myself,' said Leeming. 'Especially in the case of Lord Hendry – he's married.'

'There's something that both of you should know,' said Colbeck who had been saving the revelation until he could spring it on the two of them at once. 'The young lady involved with Lord Hendry was, in point of fact, the same one who had her hatbox stolen from the Wyvern Hotel where she had been staying with Hamilton Fido.'

Tallis was flabbergasted. 'The same one?'

'That's indecent!' gasped Leeming. 'She must be a prostitute.'

182

'I fancy she'd prefer to be called a courtesan,' said Colbeck, 'and considers herself to be continuing a long and honourable tradition.'

'Honourable!' The superintendent almost exploded.

'In *her* eyes, sir.'

'Sheer depravity!'

'You can see why I'm so keen to meet her.'

'I'll leave that disagreeable task to you, Inspector,' said Tallis with disdain. 'I don't want the creature near me.'

'As you wish, sir.'

'Wait a moment,' said Leeming, weighing up the possibilities in the situation. 'Did both gentlemen realise what was going on?'

'I doubt it very much, Victor.'

'What if she was being used as a spy?'

'At whose behest?'

'Mr Fido's,' said Leeming. 'What better way to learn how Odysseus is faring than by getting someone to win Lord Hendry's confidence?'

'No,' decided Colbeck. 'Hamilton Fido may be manipulative but I don't believe that even he would loan a young lady for whom he really cares to another man. I learnt today that he has a romantic streak.'

'Romantic!' echoed Tallis incredulously. 'What's romantic about fornicating with a fallen woman? I saw too much of that in the army. I lost count of the number of drunken fools in the lower ranks who persuaded themselves they were in love with some damned whore because she offered them forbidden pleasures.'

'I think you're being unkind to Mr Fido, sir,'

warned Colbeck.

'If the caps fits, Inspector, the man must wear it.'

'I've just had another thought,' said Leeming. 'Suppose that a third person is involved here.'

Tallis rounded on him. 'Third, fourth, fifth and all the rest of them, sergeant,' he said harshly. 'This woman is no vestal virgin.'

'Hear me out, please, sir. My feeling is this, you see,' continued Leeming. 'A third person could be using this young lady to get information about the Derby from the two people who are his closest rivals. In other words, the man we should look at is Brian Dowd.'

'I've already done that,' said Colbeck, 'and dismissed the notion at once. He has all the information he needs about the other horses and he would never resort to the tactics you suggest, Victor. Well, you've met the man. What was your overriding impression?'

'He was blunt and direct.'

'What about Hamilton Fido?'

'I've never met anyone so sure of himself.'

'Exactly,' said Colbeck. 'He's supremely confident, clever and well acquainted with the ways of the world. A man as urbane as Fido would never let a woman be planted on him by a rival, however skilful she might be in the arts of deceit. He's a handsome man who could have his pick of the most attractive young ladies in London. Since he chose this particular one, she must have outstanding appeal.'

'Yes,' added Tallis, putting his cigar down. 'And we can all guess the nature of that appeal. Find this person, Inspector,' he ordered. 'We must know where she fits into the picture.'

'Before I do that, sir,' said Colbeck, taking a slip of paper from his pocket, 'I wonder if I might remind you of the amount you owe me for my travel expenses to Ireland. As you will recall, I met them out of my own pocket.'

'I'm still not convinced your journey was entirely necessary.'

'I brought back the name of the murder victim.'

'What I'm after is the name of the killer,' said Tallis.

'That will come in time, sir.'

'Then we'll defer any reimbursement until then, Inspector. If and when we do finally put someone behind bars, I'll accept that your jaunt to Ireland should be paid out of our budget.'

'Thank you,' said Colbeck, putting the piece of paper on the desk. 'This is a record of my expenses. I think you'll agree that a small investment of time and money yielded a large reward.'

'Make an arrest and secure a conviction.'

'We're bending all our energies to that end, sir. However,' Colbeck went on, 'it might be sensible to take time off to confront the problem we have here at Scotland Yard – namely, a spy.'

'A traitor in our ranks?' said Tallis. 'He must be rooted out.'

'That's easier said than done,' Leeming commented.

'I don't think so, Victor,' said Colbeck. 'We can catch him very quickly and you are the person to help us do that.'

'Am I, sir – how?'

'There are four people here who are above suspicion – we three and the commissioner. Somewhere among the rest of our colleagues is Hamilton Fido's source. The bookmaker operates on the principle of *scientia est potentia*.'

'What's that?' rasped Tallis.

'Knowledge is power. Fido collects intelligence all the time from his network of spies. That's why he's so well informed. I suggest that you gather the detectives together, sir,' said Colbeck, 'and give them a piece of information that would be very valuable to Fido. His informer will want to communicate it as soon as possible to him. Victor will be watching from an upstairs room in the Lamb and Flag. When someone leaves surreptitiously, we'll know who our man is.'

Leeming liked the idea. 'Do I arrest him, Inspector?'

'You follow him until he meets up with Fido.'

'Right.'

'And when the rogue is apprehended,' said Tallis mercilessly, 'hand him over to me. I'll make him wish he was never born.'

'You approve then, sir?' asked Colbeck.

'I do, Inspector. We'll put the plan into operation at once.'

'Give Victor time to get across to the Lamb and Flag first.'

'Off you go, Leeming,' instructed Tallis.

The sergeant went to the door. 'Yes, sir.'

'And remember that you're in that tavern to watch out for the criminal in our midst – not to sample the beer.' Leeming nodded and left the room. 'What is it that I'm supposed to tell my

186

men, Inspector?' continued Tallis. 'You called it a valuable piece of information.'

'Were it true,' said Colbeck, 'it would certainly be valuable to Hamilton Fido. When you tell the others about the progress we've made in the investigation, go on to say that I intend to arrest Mr Fido this very afternoon.' He smiled conspiratorially. 'That should inject a note of urgency.'

Victor Leeming was delighted with his assignment. He would be helping to unmask an informer, he would be doing so from the vantage point of his favourite establishment and no train journey was required of him. As he took up his position at the window in an upstairs room of the Lamb and Flag, the landlord came in with a tankard of beer for him.

'I'm not allowed to drink on duty,' said Leeming.

'This is on the house, Sergeant.'

'Then it would be rude to refuse.'

The landlord handed him the tankard. 'You've been such a good customer for us over the years – so have your colleagues. We always like to keep on the right side of the law.'

'I wish everyone had that attitude.' Leeming took a long sip of his beer then licked his lips appreciatively. 'This is good.'

'We aim to please.'

'Well, you've certainly pleased me.'

'Recommend my beer, that's all I ask.'

'Oh, I always do,' said Leeming, gazing through the window. 'I sing your praises to everyone. Though I have some bad news, I fear.'

187

'Oh dear – what's that?'

'I may have to deprive you of one of your regular customers.'

Quaffing some more beer, he remained vigilant.

White's was the oldest and most celebrated gentlemen's club in St. James's Street. It was renowned for its illustrious history, its elite membership and its penchant for gambling. Prime Ministers, generals, admirals, poets, diarists, Regency bucks and other luminaries had belonged to it in their time and left the place charged with their memory. Some had joined in search of civilised conversation while others had wanted a desirable refuge from their wives and children. Once a member of White's, they entered a magic circle.

Lord Hendry had belonged to the club for many years and was a familiar sight at the card tables. That morning, he was enjoying a drink with friends and fending off their enquiries about the Derby. A uniformed steward soon entered with a business card on his silver tray. He offered the card to Lord Hendry.

'The gentleman wishes to speak to you now, sir,' said the man.

Lord Hendry read the name on the card. 'Very well,' he agreed.

Excusing himself from his friends, he followed the steward to an anteroom near the vestibule. When he went in, Lord Hendry found Robert Colbeck waiting for him. After an exchange of greetings, they sat down opposite each other. Lord Hendry adopted a patrician tone with his visitor.

'At least you didn't bother me at home this time,' he said loftily.

'I recalled your saying how often you came to your club, my lord,' said Colbeck, 'and you indicated to Superintendent Tallis that you'd rather be contacted here.'

'How did you know I was a member of White's?'

'It seemed the most likely place for someone of your eminence.'

'I divide most of my time between here and my stables.'

'I trust that Odysseus is still in fine fettle.'

'He's fully justified his position as Derby favourite,' said Lord Hendry, 'and that's why our rivals are so worried. I hope you've come to tell me that you've arrested the man who tried to put my horse out of the race altogether.'

'I wish that I had, Lord Hendry, but it's not the case.'

'Fido and Dowd are the chief suspects.'

'Both of them have been interviewed at length,' said Colbeck. 'I spent yesterday afternoon at Mr Hamilton's stables and he denied all knowledge of the attack on Odysseus.'

'He *would*,' snarled the other.

'As it happens, I've come here on another errand.'

'And what, pray, is that?'

'To discuss your visit to the Wyvern Hotel,' said Colbeck.

'I've never been anywhere near such a place.'

'Then let's start with the Angel Hotel in Cambridge, shall we? Or perhaps you've never heard of that either.'

'You're being impertinent, Inspector Colbeck.'

'I am merely trying to save time.'

'By resorting to insolence?'

'No,' said Colbeck, 'by reminding you how thorough we are. I sent my sergeant to the Angel Hotel to confirm that you stayed there. And I'm equally satisfied that you stayed at the Wyvern Hotel. I can tell you the precise date, if you wish.'

'I warned your superintendent about this,' railed Lord Hendry, cheeks reddening by the second. 'It's intolerable! I demand the right to privacy. I'll not have the police intruding into my life like vultures pecking at a carcass. Damn it all, Inspector! You're supposed to be tracking a vicious killer, not checking up on where I choose to stay.'

'The murder and the Wyvern Hotel are inextricably linked.'

'I fail to see how.'

'It was from the hotel that the hatbox was stolen.' He saw the way that Lord Hendry winced. 'But you already knew that, didn't you? In the interests of solving this crime, you should have come forward with that information instead of letting us find out for ourselves.' Colbeck waited for a response that never came. 'I know this must be embarrassing for you,' he said at length, 'but there's a question you refused to answer when Superintendent Tallis put it to you.'

'And I *still* refuse,' asserted Lord Hendry.

'The name of that young lady is of great interest to us.'

'And none whatsoever to me.'

'We'll find her one way or another,' said Colbeck. 'If she proves instrumental in helping us to solve this murder, then your refusal to name her will be taken as an act of wilful obstruction. There could be consequences.'

'I don't give a fig for your consequences!' yelled Lord Hendry, snapping his fingers. 'And I don't accept that this person can be of any value to you. She neither beheaded the murder victim nor planned the attack on Odysseus. Look elsewhere, Inspector. I've told you who the likely villains are.'

'They appear to be injured parties, my lord.'

'Dowd and Fido are the two biggest rogues in horseracing.'

'That doesn't stop them from being a target for their rivals,' said Colbeck. 'Did you know that someone has been trying to entice Tim Maguire away from Mr Dowd with an offer of five hundred pounds?'

'No,' admitted Lord Hendry. 'I didn't.'

'And did it never occur to you that the reason John Feeny was killed was to throw suspicion on to Hamilton Fido? He resents that.'

'Don't believe his protestations of innocence. Fido is a two-faced villain of the first water. It wouldn't surprise me if he's behind the murder *and* the assault on Odysseus. He's an appalling fellow. How anyone can have any dealings with him is beyond me.'

Colbeck was about to tell him that his former mistress did not share his low opinion of Fido but he changed his mind. He felt that it would be too cruel and that the information should not

191

come from him. It would certainly not encourage Lord Hendry to divulge the name that he was after. His only hope was that the young lady would come forward at the prompting of Hamilton Fido. He shifted his interest to another racehorse owner.

'Why do you dislike Brian Dowd so much, Lord Hendry?'

'I don't dislike him – I hate, detest and revile the man!'

'On what grounds?' asked Colbeck.

'He's beneath contempt.'

'Yet every racing correspondent describes him as a brilliant trainer. How did he achieve that reputation?'

'By dint of cheating and connivance,' said Lord Hendry. 'Dowd can pick out a good horse, I'll grant him that. But he can also make sure that lesser horses somehow contrive to win races. Exactly how he does it is a mystery to me – but it's criminal.'

'Has he ever been charged with any offence?'

'I've made frequent allegations against him, Inspector, but I've been unable to back them up with firm evidence.'

'Evidence should come *before* any allegation, Lord Hendry.'

'He *must* be cheating – his horses win too many races.'

'What about the Derby?'

Lord Hendry was unequivocal. 'That's one race he won't win.'

'Limerick Lad is a fine colt – my sergeant has seen him.'

'But did he time him over the Derby distance, Inspector? I think not. I know exactly how fast the Irish horse can run on that course and it puts him seconds behind Odysseus.'

'I can't believe that Mr Dowd was kind enough to tell you about Limerick Lad,' said Colbeck. 'You must have obtained details about the horse's speed by underhand means.'

'My trainer likes to weigh up the competition.'

'I'd be interested to hear how he goes about it, Lord Hendry. But I've detained you far too long,' he continued, getting up and reaching for his top hat. 'I'm sorry that you feel unable to assist us in our enquiries.'

'I *have* assisted you, Inspector,' said the older man. 'I pointed out the two obvious culprits – Brian Dowd and Hamilton Fido.'

'Having met Mr Dowd, I'm inclined to absolve him of the charges you make against him. Mr Fido, however is a different matter. He sails very close to the wind. In fact,' said Colbeck, 'I expect to be speaking to him on that very subject in the near future.'

Sergeant Leeming's vigil did not last long. Twenty minutes after he had taken up his post in the Lamb and Flag, he saw someone coming out of Scotland Yard and glancing around furtively. When he recognised the man, the shock momentarily took his breath away. It was Detective Constable Peter Cheggin, a friend of the sergeant's. They had served in uniform together and, since their move to the Detective Department, they had often chatted over a drink in the very public house where Leeming was concealed. As a policeman, Cheggin had always been fearless and reliable. Leeming was distressed to learn that his friend had been corrupted.

He left the room at speed and raced down the stairs. Opening the front door, he slipped through it and hid in the porch of the neighbouring building. There was no danger of his being seen. Peter Cheggin was too preoccupied with trying to find a cab. When one finally came along White-hall, he stepped out to flag it down. Leeming was afraid that a second cab would not come in time for him to follow the first but his fears were groundless.

Cheggin did not climb into the cab. He merely gave something to the driver and issued some instructions. When the driver was paid, he nodded his thanks. Cheggin hastened back to his office. A message was being sent. Leeming knew that he had to intercept it. As the cab set off, therefore, he dashed out into the middle of the road and held up both arms. The driver pulled the horse to a halt and rid himself of a torrent of expletives. His rage turned to meek apology when Leeming identified himself as a detective.

'I want that letter you were just given,' said Leeming.

'But the gentleman paid me, sir,' wailed the driver.

'That was Constable Cheggin and he was break-ing the law in sending that message. If you deliver it, you'll be arrested and charged as an accom-plice.'

'I did nothing wrong, sir!'

'Then give me the letter and be on your own way.'

The driver was downcast. 'Do I have to give the money back as well?' he asked morosely.

'What money?' said Leeming, feeling that the driver deserved to keep it. 'I didn't see any money being exchanged between you. All I need is that letter.'

'Then it's yours.'

The driver handed over the missive and flicked the reins to set the horse off again. Leeming, meanwhile, glanced at the name and address on the letter. It was being dispatched to Hamilton Fido. The ruse had worked. Anger bubbled inside Leeming. He knew that he should report what he had seen to the superintendent but this was no time to follow instructions. Putting the letter in his pocket, he went after the man who had written it.

Peter Cheggin was a tall stringy man in his thirties. He was in the office belonging to Robert Colbeck, leafing through the case file that related to the murder investigation. When Leeming walked in, the other man immediately put the file back on the desk and pretended to move a few other items around.

'Hello, Victor,' he said cheerfully. 'I was told to tidy up in here.'

'Not by Inspector Colbeck – he keeps the place spotless.'

'That's why there was so little to do.'

'I'm glad I bumped into you, Peter,' said Leeming. 'Some mail arrived for you.' He took out the letter and held it out. 'A cabman delivered it just this minute.'

Cheggin turned white. Seeing the letter, he knew at once that he had been caught. He shrugged, gave a strained smile then, without warning, hurled himself at Leeming, intending to push him aside so that he could make his escape. The sergeant was ready for him. Moving swiftly to one side, he grabbed Cheggin by both arms and swung him hard against the wall before using both fists to pummel him. Cheggin fought back and they grappled wildly in the middle of the room. A chair was knocked over, a potted plant was toppled from its perch and all the papers on Colbeck's desk went flying as the two men flailed about.

Cheggin had the strength of desperation but Victor Leeming slowly got the upper hand. Subduing an offender was the part of police work that he liked best. Fuelled by resentment and by a sense of betrayal, he shoved, shook, punched, pulled and squeezed hard before using his knee to explore Cheggin's groin. When the constable doubled up in agony, Leeming took his opportunity to fell him with a swift uppercut. Cheggin collapsed in a heap on the floor and groaned. Breathing hard, Leeming stood over him.

'You were one of us, Peter,' he said, 'and you let us down.'

'I needed the money,' croaked the other.

'You won't need money in prison and that's where you're going for this.' Leeming glanced at the debris they had caused. 'Look at the mess you made. Inspector Colbeck won't like that at all.'

The noise of the fight had brought a knot of onlookers and they stood at the open door. Super-intendent Tallis pushed through them and came into the office. He looked with dismay at the dishevelled state of the two men.

'What, in heaven's name, is going on here?' he shouted.

'I made an arrest, sir,' explained the sergeant, taking Cheggin by the scruff of the neck to hoist him to his feet. 'This is the man who's been spying on us, Superintendent – he's all yours.'

CHAPTER NINE

Kitty Lavender spent most of the morning on a shopping spree, buying what she considered to be the last few vital accessories for her visit to Epsom Downs during Derby Week. She wanted to look at her best for the occasion. A hansom cab returned her to her lodgings and, when she alighted from it, she was laden with boxes and packages. Her landlady was at the window as she arrived and, seeing what Kitty was carrying, she came to open the front door for her.

'Thank you, Mrs Collier,' said Kitty, stepping into the house. 'I didn't have a spare hand to ring the doorbell.'

'You have a visitor, Miss Lavender,' said the landlady, a small, rotund, motherly woman. 'I showed him up to your room.'

Kitty was wary. 'It's not Mr Johnson again, is it?'

'No, Miss Lavender.'

'Then it must be Mr Fido.'

'It's not him either.'

'Oh – then who is it?'

'Your father.'

Kitty was nonplussed. Since her father had died years before, she knew that it could not possibly be him. Somebody had entered her lodgings under false pretences and that disturbed her. Hiding her alarm from the landlady, she struggled upstairs with her shopping then put down one of the boxes so that she could open the door of her drawing room. Lord Hendry was sitting in a chair. When he saw how burdened she was, he got up and walked over to her.

'Let me help you, Kitty,' he volunteered.

She was shocked. 'What are *you* doing here, George?'

'Let's get everything inside first, shall we?' he said, picking up the box from the floor and ushering her into the room. He closed the door behind him. 'We don't want your landlady to overhear us. She believes that I'm your father. We can't have her thinking that we committed incest.'

Kitty put her shopping down. 'You've no right to be here,' she said belligerently. 'Even when we were friends, I kept you away from my lodgings. I like to preserve some privacy.'

'I needed to speak to you, Kitty.'

'Then you should have asked me to meet you somewhere.'

'After what happened last time,' he said reasonably, 'I had no guarantee that you'd agree to see me again.'

'So you tricked your way past my landlady with an arrant lie.' She became suspicious. 'How long have you been here?'

'Long enough to have a good look around.'

'I hope you didn't dare go into my bedroom.'

'Why – what secrets have you got hidden in there?'

'Is that why you came?' she demanded. 'To snoop on me?'

'Calm down, Kitty,' said Lord Hendry, putting

a hand on her shoulder. 'I've only been here five minutes or so.'

Reacting to his touch, she pulled away smartly and went to open the door of her bedroom. She glanced inside to make sure that nothing had been moved or taken. Satisfied that all was well, she turned back to face him again.

'I was interested to see where you lived,' he said. 'It's exactly the kind of place I imagined – comfortable, tasteful and essentially feminine.' He became serious. 'I had a visit from Inspector Colbeck this morning. Does that name mean anything to you?'

'Yes – he's leading the murder investigation.'

'God knows how but he somehow discovered that you and I spent that night at the Wyvern Hotel. He asked me to divulge your name. I refused to give it, of course, but he's the kind of man who won't let the matter rest there.'

'He has no need to speak to me,' she said irritably.

'Colbeck believes that he does.'

'I have nothing whatsoever to do with the crime.'

'Unfortunately, you do,' he told her. 'It was your hatbox that contained the severed head. The Inspector feels that it was no random choice. Your property was stolen for a specific purpose.'

'How could it have been? Nobody knew I was at that hotel.'

'Someone must have done.'

'No,' she stressed, walking across to him. 'For obvious reasons, I didn't tell a soul that I was going there.'

'What about the person who accompanied you?'

'He was equally circumspect.'

'That's what he claimed, I daresay, but men are men, Kitty. Some of them simply can't resist boasting about their conquests. It may well be that this fellow unwittingly let the cat out of the bag.'

'He'd never do that, George.'

'How do you know?'

'Because he's very discreet.'

'By instinct or necessity?' he asked, eyelids narrowing. 'Is he married? Having a wife forces a man to be extremely discreet.'

'You'd know more about that than I do, George.'

'So who *is* your mysterious lover?'

'Mind your own business.'

'You won't be able to say that to Inspector Colbeck,' he warned. 'He'll find out who the man is and follow the trail to you. One thing is certain. Your new admirer is patently not accustomed to clandestine encounters in hotels or he'd have known exactly where to take you. Instead of that, he let you recommend the Wyvern.'

Kitty flared up. 'I did that with good reason, George.'

'Did you?'

'I wanted to purge the memory of spending time there with you. In fact, I'd like to forget every single thing that ever happened between us. It was all a regrettable mistake.'

'You didn't think so at the time.'

'I didn't know the sort of person you really

were then.'

'I *cared* for you, Kitty. I indulged your every whim.'

'But you didn't,' she countered. 'You denied me the thing that I coveted most and that was a public acknowledgement of my status. You kept me out of sight because you were ashamed of me.'

'Ashamed of myself, more likely,' he said under his breath. 'How could I be seen with you in public? I have a wife. That fact inevitably imposed restrictions on our friendship. I told you from the start that Caroline's feelings had to be considered.'

'What about *my* feelings?'

'You seemed happy enough to me.'

'Did you ever ask how I felt? Did you ever show any real interest in what I actually wanted? No, George – you simply wished to have me at your beck and call.' She struck a dignified pose. 'I'm worth more than that.'

'I took you for what you were, Kitty – a scheming adventuress.'

She pointed to the door. 'I think you should leave.'

'I'll not depart until I find out who he is,' he resolved. 'I don't believe that you deserted me because I didn't take you with me to the races. There was someone else, wasn't there? All the time we were friends, you were intriguing behind my back with another man.'

'I'm not that unprincipled, George.'

'Who is the fellow?'

'We only met after I'd parted company with you.'

'I want to know his name!' he howled, stamping

202

a foot.

Kitty was shaken by the intensity of his anger and she took a precautionary step backwards. There was no way that she could conceal her relationship with Hamilton Fido indefinitely and she had no wish to do so. It had been her intention to flaunt it at the Derby when everyone would see her and where it could be used as a potent weapon against Lord Hendry. Nothing would hurt him more than the realisation that the woman he had lost was now on intimate terms with a despised rival. The revelation could not be postponed until then. Cornered in her own lodgings, she responded with spirit.

'I'll tell you his name,' she said, raising herself up to her full height, 'but I'll only do so on one condition.'

'What's that?'

'That you leave this house immediately.'

'With pleasure,' he said, picking up his top hat and cane. 'Now, then, what benighted fool have you enticed into your bed this time?'

'Hamilton Fido.'

He was stunned. 'You'd never do that to me, Kitty.'

'Hamilton Fido,' she repeated with a smirk of delight. 'You'll see us both at the Derby next week. What do you think of that, George?'

Unable to find words to express his fury, Lord Hendry resorted to actions. Drawing back his cane, he used it to hit her across the side of the head and knock her down. Then he stormed out of the room and slammed the door after him.

Derby Week did not begin until the following Monday but preparations were already well under way. When he took the train to Epsom that Saturday, Robert Colbeck found that it was already covered with tents, marquees, stalls, sideshows and gypsy caravans. It was a sunny afternoon in late May and more people were arriving in carts, wagons, drays, cabs and coaches or on horseback and foot. Even at that early stage, a carnival atmosphere prevailed. By the time the Derby was run on Wednesday of the next week, the whole place would be transformed into a giant fairground.

Like Victor Leeming, Colbeck had been saddened to learn that the informer inside Scotland Yard was Constable Peter Cheggin, a competent and hard-working detective, but he was relieved that the man had been caught. The letter that Cheggin had tried to send to his paymaster was addressed to the office in Bethnal Green and Colbeck had dispatched his sergeant there, choosing himself to seek Hamilton Fido at the venue where the bookmaker would be working during the races. He was in luck. Fido was there. After making enquiries, he was directed towards the betting office.

Hamilton Fido was outside the grandstand, talking to Marcus Johnson with an affability that suggested a measure of friendship. The bookmaker was displeased to see Colbeck again but he performed the introductions with suave politeness.

'I've read about you, Inspector,' said Johnson, pumping his hand. 'You are the celebrated Railway Detective.'

Colbeck was modest. 'That's not a title I ever use, sir.'

'Have you come to place a bet on the Derby?'

'Not yet, Mr Johnson.'

'I've been trying to get some guidance from Hamilton but he's too canny to give it. His only advice is to bet on the horse I fancy.'

'Look at the odds I've set,' said Fido. 'They tell you everything.'

'But they don't,' said Johnson, displaying his teeth. 'They tell us enough to mislead us. Do you know what I think, Inspector?'

'What, sir?' said Colbeck.

'I believe that Hamilton is playing a deep game. Merry Legs is only 8–1 but her chances are much better than that. Did you know that he has a second horse in the race?'

'Yes, sir – Princess of Fire.'

'One filly might not win against all those colts but two might. That's his plan, I suspect,' argued Johnson. 'He'll use Princess of Fire to set the pace so that Merry Legs can sit in behind her until the final couple of furlongs. Am I right, Hamilton?'

Fido's smile was enigmatic. 'Put your money where your mouth is, Marcus,' he counselled. 'Rely on your instinct.'

'I did that two years ago,' boasted Johnson, 'when the favourite was Little Harry. My instinct told me that Daniel O'Rourke was a tempting bet at 25–1 and I walked off with a full wallet when he won by half a length. Little Harry, by the way, was unplaced.'

'I remember it only too well,' said Colbeck. 'I had money on Little Harry that day. If my memory serves, there were over thirty runners in that race. Merry Legs will have fewer to contend with this year.'

'Twenty other runners in all.'

'Nineteen,' corrected Fido.

'Since when?'

'Since this morning, Marcus.'

'Oh?'

'My spies tell me that Tambourine has sprained a tendon and been withdrawn. His owner, Sir Richard Duggleby, will be livid – he had high hopes of Tambourine.'

'That means we only have twenty runners.'

'A much smaller field than usual,' observed Colbeck, 'but it's still infernally difficult to pick the winner.'

'Not unless you're a bookmaker,' said Johnson, clapping Fido on the back. 'However, I can see that the inspector wants a private word with you, Hamilton, so I'll make myself scarce.'

There was a flurry of farewells then Johnson withdrew. Colbeck watched him bounding off with a spring in his step then raising his hat to two ladies who walked past.

'A born gambler, by the sound of it,' he said.

'Marcus Johnson lives off his wits,' observed Fido. 'If he's not at the races, he'll be at the card table. If not there, he'll be betting on something else.'

'Illegal blood sports, for instance?'

Fido laughed. 'You'll have to ask him yourself, Inspector.'

'You're the only person who interests me at the moment, sir. It's odd that you mentioned spies a moment ago because that's exactly what I came to talk to you about. First,' he went on, taking a letter from his pocket, 'I'm delivering this on behalf of Detective Constable Peter Cheggin. He was unable to come here as he's now in custody.'

'I see,' said Fido calmly, taking the envelope and opening it to read the letter. He grinned. 'Is this some kind of joke, Inspector?'

'I'm here to do exactly what he says – to arrest you.'

'On what charge?'

'Corrupting one of our detectives so that he passed on privileged information from Scotland Yard.'

'Is that what I did?'

'The letter is proof of that.'

'I don't think so, Inspector. Have you talked to Peter Cheggin?'

'Of course.'

'Did he say that I *asked* him to act as an informer?'

'He didn't need to do that.'

'Did he claim that I paid him for information?'

'Cheggin is being rather bloody-minded at the moment,' said Colbeck. 'He'll admit nothing beyond the fact that he wrote that letter.'

'I wish that it had arrived before you did, Inspector.'

'So that you could take to your heels?'

'On the contrary,' said Fido. 'I'd have saved you the trouble of coming here by giving myself up. Then I could have told you the story that lies behind this letter.'

'That's only too apparent, Mr Fido.'

'Is it? How well do you know Peter Cheggin?'

'Reasonably well. I judged him to be a good officer.'

'I've no doubt that he is but Peter has two glaring problems. The first is that he loves to gamble and the second is that he doesn't earn enough to cover his losses. Peter Cheggin owes me money,' said Fido quietly. 'A fair amount of money, as it happens. Most bookmakers are not as patient as I am, Inspector. If someone can't settle his debts, he gets a visit from two strong men with the gift of persuasion. I prefer to do business on a more civilised basis.'

'Very noble of you, sir,' said Colbeck with light sarcasm.

'Peter is obviously so grateful that he sends me the occasional nugget of information as a sign of goodwill. I don't *ask* for it and I most certainly don't pay for it. Did I corrupt one of your men?' he asked rhetorically. 'No, Inspector – he was already corrupted by the desire to gamble and that's what landed him in debt.'

'I only have your word for that, Mr Fido, and – if you'll forgive my saying so – I don't accept that at face value.'

'In that case,' said Fido, enjoying the situation, 'you must do your duty and arrest me so that you can question me at Scotland Yard. But bear this is mind – the burden of proof lies with you. And there is no court in Creation that can prove I paid Peter Cheggin to act as a spy. He did it entirely of his own accord.'

His readiness to be arrested rang a warning bell for Colbeck. Before he had joined the Metropolitan Police Force, the inspector had been a successful barrister, spending every day in court and testing the limits of the English legal system with regularity. He knew how difficult it sometimes was to persuade juries of a malefactor's guilt even when the evidence against him was fairly strong. In view of what Fido had just told him, the evidence against the bookmaker could look decidedly flimsy in court. Though he had certainly encouraged a detective to act as an informer, proving it would be difficult. Hamilton Fido was a wealthy man who would retain the ablest defence counsel he could find. The case against him would be ripped to shreds and Colbeck did not want that to happen.

'How many of them are there, Mr Fido?' he asked.

'How many what?'

'People like Peter Cheggin – decent men who get led astray by you and who end up taking the punishment that should really be yours alone.'

'I told you once before, Inspector,' said Fido gleefully. 'I have a gift for survival. When others fall by the wayside, I carry on unscathed.' He thrust out both wrists. 'Well – come on,' he goaded. 'Aren't you going to put handcuffs on me?'

Late that afternoon, Brian Dowd had ridden over to Epsom to inspect the course and get a feel of the place where he expected Limerick Lad to achieve a resounding success. He talked to some of the officials who were there and also chatted to a couple of the men whose job it was to cut the grass and ensure that the course was in good condition. Dowd was standing reflectively near the winning post when a carriage pulled up beside him. Sitting in the back of it was Lord Hendry, still smarting from his earlier encounter with Kitty Lavender. The sight of his rival enraged him.

'That's the closest you'll get to the winning post, Dowd,' he said with condescension. 'Odysseus will flash past it first.'

'Really?' said Dowd, looking up at him. 'How do you know that, my lord? You've never trained a racehorse. I've trained dozens and I can tell you now that Limerick Lad is the finest three-year-old I've ever had in my stables. I've brought him to his peak for the Derby so I know what he'll do. You, on the other hand, rely solely on the word of your trainer.'

'He happens to be a master at his trade.'

'Then why have none of your horses won a major race?'

'They've been unlucky,' said Lord Hendry, stung by the remark.

'I don't believe in luck.'

'No, you believe in gaining the advantage by unfair means. What tricks have you got up your sleeve this time, Dowd? I haven't forgotten that race at Doncaster in which one of your jockeys – acting on your instructions, no doubt – forced my horse against the rails.'

'Your horse tried to come through a gap that did not exist.'

'That's not how I saw it.'

'You're a poor loser, my lord,' said the Irishman with a grin. 'That surprises me, considering how much practice you've had at it.'

'Sneer, if you must,' said Lord Hendry. 'You'll change your tune on Wednesday when Odysseus leaves your horse standing.'

'I admire your confidence.'

'It's shared by every bookmaker of note.'

'Never trust bookmakers,' said Dowd. 'They work on incomplete information. Look how many favourites are beaten out of sight. You'll see another come to grief in the Derby.'

Lord Hendry flicked a hand. 'I'm not here to bandy words with the likes of you,' he said scornfully.

'I assumed you'd come to see Odysseus. Has the horse been moved to Epsom already?'

'He arrived this morning under police guard.'

'Yes, I heard that you'd a spot of trouble.'

'Is that because you incited it?' challenged Lord Hendry.

Dowd's face was impassive 'Now why should I do that?'

'For the reason you always resort to criminality – to gain an unfair advantage.'

'But I already have an advantage, Lord Hendry. I own better horses than anyone else. I'm far too busy protecting them to worry about anybody else's stables. Before you portray yourself as a victim,' said Dowd forcefully, 'look at my problems. Someone tried to send me the severed head of a groom I used to employ. How would you like to open a lady's hatbox and find *that* inside?'

211

Lord Hendry flinched at the mention of the hatbox. It brought back painful memories of Kitty Lavender's betrayal of him. It also made him wonder who had committed the murder and why he had sent such a chilling memento of it to Ireland.

'Then we come to Tim Maguire,' continued Dowd. 'Even you must admit that he's the best jockey alive.'

'One of them, I grant you.'

'Someone offered him five hundred pounds if he refused to ride for me. When that bribe failed,' said Dowd with rising anger, 'they set a couple of ruffians on to him last night. They were supposed to make sure that he was unfit to ride in the Derby. But I keep my jockeys well guarded so the attackers were frightened off with a shot or two.' He stepped closer to the carriage and fixed Lord Hendry with an accusatory stare. 'The location of those stables was supposed to be a secret,' he added. 'How did anyone know where Tim Maguire was?'

'Don't look at me like that,' said Lord Hendry. 'I'd never hire ruffians to assault a jockey. As for your stables, I haven't the slightest clue where they are.'

'Someone does. If it's not you,' said Dowd, still subjecting him to a piercing stare, 'then who the devil is it?'

They left early on Sunday morning. Robert Colbeck had hired a trap so that he could drive Madeleine Andrews to her rendezvous with the barmaid at the Shepherd and Shepherdess. On the ride there, he explained precisely what he wanted her to do when she met Bonny Rimmer. Madeleine was attentive. It was not the first time she had been given this kind of unofficial assignment so she had a degree of experience on which she could draw. Talk soon turned to the progress of the investigation. Colbeck told her about his visit to Epsom Downs.

'Why didn't you arrest Mr Fido?' she said.

'Because I could not build a convincing case against him in court,' he confessed resignedly. 'I'd need firmer evidence.'

'You had that letter sent by one of your detectives.'

'It would be almost impossible to establish that he ordered Peter Cheggin to provide the information. Hamilton Fido is far too clever. There'd be no direct link between him and Cheggin. Fido would always use intermediaries and I have no idea who they might be.'

'Couldn't your prisoner tell you?'

'He's too ashamed of what he did, Madeleine. I feel sorry for him. Cheggin has a wife and children. When he's sentenced, they'll be left to fend for themselves. In fact,' he went on, 'knowing Fido, he'll probably try to force Mrs Cheggin to pay off her husband's debts.'

'There must be *something* you can arrest him for, Robert.'

'I'm sure it will emerge in the fullness of time.'

When they got to the village, Colbeck did not head for the inn. He drove on to the little church at the top of the hill. Its bell was ringing sonorously in the tower. As he brought the trap to a halt, Colbeck saw a few people going in through the porch.

'How did you know what time the service was?' she said.

'I took the trouble to find out when I was last here.'

'Why?'

'Because that's where we'll find Bonny Rimmer.'

'How do you know?'

'She's mourning a loved one,' said Colbeck. 'She needs help. My guess is that she'll turn to the church.'

He got out of the trap, tethered the horse then offered a hand to assist her down. When Madeleine stepped on to the ground, she straightened her dress and adjusted her hat. She was thrilled when he extended an arm for her to take. They went through the lychgate together and into the little churchyard where tombs, monuments and stone crosses were clustered together at odd angles and surrounded by uncut grass and bramble. The church itself had stood on the same spot for over five hundred years and it showed clear signs of decrepitude.

When they left the morning sunshine, they entered the chill interior of the building. Wooden pews ran down either side of the nave and there was a scattering of worshippers there. Colbeck could not identify the woman who knelt in the front pew wearing black but he was certain that it was Bonny Rimmer. He and Madeleine sat halfway down the nave and bent their heads in prayer. It was the first time they had been in a church together and the significance of attending morning service as a couple was lost on neither of them.

The vicar was a white-haired old man who took the service briskly and who preached a combative sermon as if addressing a full congregation rather than a mere nine parishioners. When it was over, he stood at the door to bid farewell to people as they left. Bonny Rimmer remained immoveable in her pew. Colbeck and Madeleine shook hands with the vicar and made complimentary remarks about the service before moving out into the porch. Most of the others had drifted away but they lingered in the churchyard.

'Wait for her here,' said Colbeck. 'She stayed behind for some words of comfort from the vicar.'

'Where will you be, Robert?'

'In the trap – I'd only be in the way.'

'Suppose that she won't speak to me?'

'I think she'll be grateful for sympathy from anyone.'

'I'll do my best,' said Madeleine.

He touched her arm. 'That's why I brought you.'

Putting on his hat, he went out through the lychgate and took up his position in the trap. Madeleine, meanwhile, read some of the inscriptions chiselled into the stone and let her thoughts turn to the death of her mother. It had been so sudden and unexpected that it had left her father in a daze for weeks. Though trying to cope with her own bereavement, Madeleine had also had to help him through his despair. It had forged a strong bond between father and daughter. As she read some of the elaborate and sentimental epitaphs, she remembered the simplicity of the inscription on her mother's tombstone and wished that these neglected graves could be tended with as much loving care as she and her father always showed.

It was some time before Bonny Rimmer came out of the church. When she did so, her head was down and she clutched a prayer book in her hand. Madeleine stepped back on to the path to intercept her.

'Miss Rimmer?' she began.

'Oh!' cried Bonny.

She looked up in dismay as if someone had just bumped into her. Madeleine saw the oval face, drained of colour and framed by the black bonnet. The girl had been crying and there were dark patches beneath her eyes. She was patently bewildered.

'My name is Madeleine Andrews,' said the other, 'and I'd like to offer my sincerest condolences. I know that you've suffered a terrible loss and I'm sorry to intrude on your grief.'

'You knew John?'

'No, but I'm aware of what happened to him. I'm a friend of Inspector Colbeck's. He told me what had happened.'

'He was kind,' murmured Bonny.

'I wonder if I might talk to you for a moment?'

The girl's face was blank. 'Talk?'

'About your friendship with John Feeny.'

'He was a wonderful person, Miss Andrews.'

Madeleine gave a gentle smile. 'Tell me about him.'

Taking her by the elbow, she led Bonny across to a wooden bench that had been stained by age and autographed by youthful parishioners with sharp knives. They sat down together. Bonny gazed at her with a curiosity tempered by anxiety.

'What do you want?' she said.

'I want to do all I can to help the police catch the man who killed your friend. I'm sure that you want to do the same.'

'Yes, yes, I do.'

'Then talk to me about John.'

Bonny was lost. 'What am I to say?'

'Tell me how you first met him.'

The barmaid began slowly, stopping from time to time as the pain of recollection became too acute. Madeleine said nothing, sharing her anguish, offering solace, acting as a silent and uncritical witness. The tale eventually gathered pace. Bonny had met John Feeny when he came to the inn with a group of other lads from the stables. He had seemed quieter and more thoughtful than the others. While they had flirted with her, Feeny stood shyly on the side and watched.

Then the day came when one of the grooms tried to molest her. He was very drunk and the others had egged him on. He caught Bonny in the yard at the rear of the inn and pounced on her. John Feeny was the only person who responded to her scream. Rushing out of the bar, he tore her attacker off and flung him to the ground. A fierce struggle ensued. The other groom was bigger and older than Feeny but that made no difference. The Irish lad was so incensed that Bonny had been assaulted that he fought like a demon and put his opponent to flight. Full of gratitude, the barmaid had washed the blood from Feeny's face.

'So he wasn't quiet *all* the time,' she said softly. 'John had a real temper. He never turned it on me but it was there. He wasn't afraid of getting hurt – that's why he'd have made a good jockey. And he was so brave, Miss Andrews.'

'Brave?'

'Yes,' replied Bonny. 'Do you know how he came to England?'

'On a boat, I suppose.'

'But he had no money for the passage. John had a row with Mr Dowd – that's the man who owned the stables – and walked out. John was so keen to get to this country that he sneaked aboard a boat and hid under a tarpaulin.' She smiled for the first time. 'Now isn't that brave?'

'Brave but foolhardy.'

'That's what John was like. He took chances. When the boat was a mile or so away from Anglesey, they caught him. Do you know what the captain told him? He said that if John was that keen to get here, he could swim. So they threw him overboard.'

Madeleine was shocked. 'He might have drowned.'

'Not him,' said Bonny. 'He swam ashore and dried himself off. Then he made his way to London by walking and begging lifts off carters. At long last, he found his uncle and started to look for work. Weeks and weeks later, he got a job at the stables down here.'

'And he met you.'

'Yes – we made so many plans together.'

218

'Plans?' repeated Madeleine.

'For when he became a jockey,' explained Bonny. 'John said he'd make enough money to look after me. I wouldn't have to work at the inn any more. He wanted me all to himself.'

Madeleine was deeply moved by the tenderness with which she spoke of John Feeny and she learnt far more about the groom than Colbeck had done when he spoke to Bonny Rimmer. The presence of another woman had unlocked memories that the girl would otherwise have kept to herself. Uncertain at first, she was now eager to talk about her relationship and the facts tumbled out. She talked of secret meetings, bold ambitions and an exchange of vows. Bonny and the young Irishman had decided to get married one day.

'Who could possibly have wanted to hurt him?' said Madeleine.

'Nobody – he was the kindest person I ever met.'

'What about the groom who had a fight with John?'

'Oh, he was sacked a long time ago.'

'He could have come back to get his revenge.'

'He'd never do a thing like that.'

'You told Inspector Colbeck about a man that John had met.'

'A real gentleman, he was,' said Bonny, 'or so John thought at first. He wanted information about Limerick Lad – that's one of the runners in the Derby. He offered him money but John refused. The man wasn't so friendly then – he threatened John.'

'So I understand.'

'He had no choice, Miss Andrews,' said Bonny defensively. 'If it was known that he'd worked for Mr Dowd, he'd have been kicked out of the stables. They'd have thought he was a spy.'

'Instead of which,' noted Madeleine, seeing the irony of the situation, 'he was being asked to spy on Mr Dowd himself.'

'John was helping to look after Mr Hamilton's horse, Merry Legs, but the man wasn't worried about him in the Derby. All he wanted to hear about was Limerick Lad.'

'What did he tell you about this man?'

'Very little.'

'Was he young or old, tall or short? How did he dress?'

'John said he was well dressed,' she recalled. 'He wasn't old but I've no idea how tall he was. The man had money. He gave some to John and told him there'd be a lot more when they met to have a long talk about Mr Dowd's stables.' She pulled the sleeve of her dress back to expose a delicate silver bangle. 'John used the money to buy this for me. Then he went off to meet this man in London.'

'Did he say where the meeting was to take place?'

'No, Miss Andrews,' said Bonny, brightening for a moment, 'but he promised to buy me another present when he got the rest of the money.' Her face clouded. 'I never saw John alive again.'

Surprised to receive the summons, Marcus Johnson responded to it at once. He went to the house to see Kitty Lavender, kissing her on the cheek when they met. She let him into her drawing room and shut the door. Putting his hat down, he beamed at her.

'Three meetings in a week,' he said. 'This is a treat. We rarely see each other more than three times in a year.'

'I wanted your advice, Marcus.'

'I'm always ready to give that, bidden or unbidden.'

'Sit down,' invited Kitty, taking a seat well away from him. 'And thank you for coming so promptly.'

'I hoped you might have gleaned some information for me,' he said, settling into his chair. 'That's why I rushed here. Any warm hints from Hamilton?'

'He still believes that Merry Legs will win.'

'I want to know why. When I met him at Epsom yesterday, he'd tell me nothing. It was like trying to get blood from a stone. However,' he went on, sensing her concern, 'you obviously don't want to hear any more about the Derby. What's this about advice?'

'Do you remember my telling you about that missing hatbox?'

'Yes – it was stolen from some hotel or other, wasn't it?'

'The police wish to speak to me about it.'

'How do you know?'

'Because that's what Inspector Colbeck said both to Hamilton and to Lord Hendry. Somehow he found out that I was connected with both of them and tried to get my name from them.'

'I hope they had the decency to refuse,' said

221

Johnson sharply. 'I'd certainly have done so in their position.'

'They didn't give me away, Marcus.'

'Good for them! You're an innocent party here, Kitty. You don't want your name entangled in a murder investigation. If it got into the papers, it could be very embarrassing for you.'

'That's my fear. I'm worried.'

'About what?'

'Inspector Colbeck,' she said. 'Lord Hendry came here to warn me that he was looking for me and Hamilton actually urged me to go to Scotland Yard.'

'Why did he do that?'

'When he was questioned by Inspector Colbeck, he refused to give my name. That could be seen as withholding evidence. On the eve of Derby Week, the worst thing for Hamilton is to get embroiled with the police.'

Johnson laughed. 'He's spent most of his life getting embroiled with the police, Kitty. That's why I like him so much – he outwits them at every turn. I wish I had his effrontery.'

'What would you advise me to do?'

'Stay in the shadows and say nothing.'

'Even if this detective is looking for me?'

'Forget about Inspector Colbeck,' he said expansively. 'He's no threat to you. As it happens, I met the fellow myself only yesterday when I was chatting to Hamilton at the racecourse. He didn't impress me, Kitty. He's like all policeman – plodding and slow-witted. If neither Hamilton nor Lord Hendry surrenders your name, Colbeck would never be able to identify you.'

'Yet he knows I befriended both of them.'

'That's all he knows and all he will know. What purpose can be served by questioning you?' he asked with a grin. 'Unless he wants you to discuss their respective merits in the boudoir, that is.'

'Don't be unseemly, Marcus.'

'I'm only trying to look at the situation through your eyes. If you were able to help the police solve this horrendous murder, then I'd take you to Scotland Yard myself. But that's not the position you're in. As far as I know, you can't shed any light on the crime.'

'None at all,' she said plaintively. 'What I want to avoid at all costs is facing Inspector Colbeck and enduring his disapproval at the way I choose to live.'

Johnson guffawed. 'If he disapproved of *you*,' he said, 'then he'd hold up his hands in horror at the kind of existence I lead. It may be sinful to say this on the Sabbath but I believe moral standards are nothing but silly impediments to happiness.'

'There's nothing useful I can tell the police.'

'Then steer clear of them.'

'What about Hamilton?' she said, still worrying. 'Unless I go to Scotland Yard, they may harass him again.'

'He can run rings around a man like Inspector Colbeck.'

'What if the inspector sees the two of us together at the Derby?'

'Make sure that he doesn't, Kitty. Exercise discretion – you're an expert at that. My feeling is this,' he went on, rising to his feet. 'The only time we should get involved with the police is when we are in danger. Otherwise, the less the Inspector Colbecks of this world know about us, the better.' He flashed her a smile. 'Have I answered your question, Kitty?'

'Yes, Marcus,' she said. 'You've put my mind at rest.'

'Then I'd like you to do the same for me.'

'What do you mean?'

'I want you to tell me why you behaved so oddly when I arrived,' he said. 'Why you only offered one cheek for me to kiss and why you sat just as far away from me as you could. I'd also like to know why you're wearing so much powder on your face today. What's wrong?'

'Nothing – nothing at all.'

'I don't believe you, Kitty.'

'I'm fine, I tell you.'

'That's not the feeling I get,' he said, crossing over to her and pushing back the hair from one temple to reveal a bruise that was only half-hidden by cosmetics. He was shocked. 'Who did this to you?'

'Nobody – I slipped and fell.'

'You're far too sure-footed for that.'

'It was a stupid accident,' she said with a shrill laugh.

'You're lying to me, Kitty. I think somebody hit you.'

'No!'

'Was it Hamilton?' he asked, letting the hair fall back over the bruise. 'If he's been knocking you about, he'll suffer for it. Tell me the truth – was it him?'

'No, Marcus.'

'Do you swear that?'

'Yes – Hamilton is considerate. He'd never lay a finger on me.'

'Then who was responsible?'

'It was my own fault, I tell you.'

'But I don't believe you,' he said, trying to contain his anger. 'Somebody else gave you that bruise or you wouldn't be so eager to disguise it from me. Who was it, Kitty? I insist on being told.'

There was no chance of deceiving him. Marcus Johnson was too sharp-eyed and too familiar with his half-sister's manner to be fooled. All his protective instincts had been aroused. Kitty was touched but she was still reluctant to tell him the truth. When she remembered what had happened, she was filled with shame and discomfort. She could feel the stinging blow from the cane all over again.

'Tell me his name, Kitty,' he demanded. 'This is one time when I might actually be able to be useful to you. Who is he?'

She swallowed hard. 'Lord Hendry,' she said.

Sunday was no day of rest for Edward Tallis. A deeply religious man, he first attended a service of Holy Communion at his parish church. It left him both spiritually replenished and reinvigorated to continue the unending fight against crime. He adjourned to Scotland Yard. Most of the day was spent reviewing the security arrangements for Derby Week. In the evening, by prior arrangement, he had a meeting in his office with Robert Colbeck and Victor Leeming. The

225

superintendent was used to seeing Colbeck look immaculate but the sight of Leeming in his best suit was something of a novelty. For once in his life, the sergeant had achieved a miraculous smartness.

Predictably, the meeting began with a rebuke for Colbeck.

'You made a bad mistake, Inspector,' he said, using a paper knife to wag at Colbeck. 'You should have arrested Hamilton Fido.'

'On what charge, sir?'

'Keeping a paid informer in the Detective Department.'

'I explained that,' Colbeck reminded him. 'I lacked sufficient evidence to convict him. He argues that Cheggin provided information voluntarily as a means of settling his gambling debts.'

'Gambling is a disease,' said Tallis, gaze shifting to Leeming, 'and we see what havoc it can wreak in the life of a man like Constable Cheggin. Next time you have the urge to bet on the Derby, Sergeant, call that to mind or you'll end up in the same cell as him.'

'Hardly, sir,' said Leeming, aggrieved. 'I only have a bet once in a blue moon and always with small amounts of money. There's no danger of me going the same way as Peter.'

'Once the disease gets hold of you, there's no cure.'

'Victor knows that full well,' said Colbeck, heading off another homily from Tallis, 'and is too aware of his family responsibilities to get infected. His study of the Derby field has not only been for the purposes of selecting a winner,

226

sir. At my suggestion, he's been doing something else as well.'

'What's that?' asked Tallis.

'Trying to sift out possible suspects. Consider the situation that we have before us. Three horses stand out from the rest. Each of their owners has – to put it mildly – experienced difficulties of late. Each one has accused his two rivals of the various crimes committed.'

'What we have to ask,' Leeming interjected, 'is *cui bono.*'

Tallis's mouth dropped open in wonderment. The sergeant had many sterling virtues but knowledge of Latin was not one of them. His strengths lay in his tenacity and courage.

'Who stands to gain?' Leeming continued. 'That's what it means – or so the inspector tells me, anyway. If all three fancied horses were put out of the race, who would be the likely winner?'

'Don't ask me, man!' scolded Tallis.

'According to the odds, sir, Aleppo, Gladiator and Royal Realm would come to the fore. Someone connected with one of those horses could be behind all the upset.'

'A vicious murder is rather more than an upset, Leeming, but I take your point. The owners of those three horses must be kept under suspicion. Indeed,' said Tallis, 'it seems to me that anyone involved in the Derby must be watched carefully. I did a little research into the event and it confirmed my long-held belief that horseracing is a sordid business.'

'It has its darker side, sir,' conceded Colbeck.

'Ten years ago, in 1844, the winner of the

Derby was a four-year-old called Maccabeus, masquerading under the name of Running Rein. It was a year older than any other animal in the race.'

'The fraud was eventually exposed, Superintendent, and it left a stain on the event that will be difficult to eradicate. I think we face an even more blatant example of villainy and intrigue this year. For the sake of the Derby, we must catch the people behind these crimes.'

'For the sake of our reputation, you mean,' corrected Tallis.

'That goes without saying, sir.'

'So what have you learnt since we last met?'

'I made some more enquiries about John Feeny,' said Colbeck, 'and discovered new facts that altered my view of him slightly.'

Without mentioning that he had been there with Madeleine Andrews, he talked about his visit to church that morning and related what Bonny Rimmer had disclosed. Feeny was no longer the hapless victim they had assumed him to be. The person who got closest to him described an ambitious, dedicated, brave young man given to fits of temper and unwilling to take criticism.

'Brian Dowd told me that he and Feeny were on good terms when the lad left his stables,' said Colbeck, 'but that's not true. They had a violent row, it seems, and Feeny stormed out. He stowed away on a boat sailing for Anglesey.'

'As if we didn't have enough Irish over here!' sighed Tallis.

'I think the man we're looking for is the one

228

who claimed to be seeking information about Limerick Lad. Once he'd lured Feeny away from the stables, he killed and beheaded him. The same man probably tried to cripple Odysseus and he may even have sent that anonymous letter to Tim Maguire. One way and another,' said Colbeck, 'he's determined to stop the fancied horses from winning.'

'Who's paying him, Inspector?' asked Leeming.

Tallis had the answer. 'I'm certain it was Hamilton Fido,' he said, slapping the paper knife down on the desk. 'You should have arrested him when you had the chance, Inspector, instead of letting him stay free to cause more trouble.'

'We could never prove that he instructed Peter Cheggin to act as his spy,' said Colbeck. 'Our case would be laughed out of court.'

'Then arrest him for refusing to name the young lady with whom he spent the night at the Wyvern Hotel. In remaining silent,' said the superintendent, 'Fido is denying us the opportunity to collect evidence that might be of critical importance in a murder investigation.'

'You wish me to arrest him now, sir?'

'Yes, I do.'

'Then I'll also have to take Lord Hendry into custody on the identical charge,' said Colbeck, 'for he has also declined to cooperate with the police. What good that will do, I fail to see, but it would have one immediate effect.'

'What's that?'

'To frighten away the young lady we're anxious to speak to, sir. She'll disappear completely and we'll be left to fight a ferocious battle against the respective lawyers of Lord Hendry and Hamilton Fido.'

'I agree with the inspector,' said Leeming.

'Was your opinion sought?' asked Tallis nastily.

'No, sir.'

'Then keep it to yourself.'

'We could be sued for wrongful arrest,' warned Colbeck. 'Lord Hendry is a man of considerable influence and Fido exerts power of another kind. Both are staking an enormous amount on this year's Derby. If they're languishing in a police cell while the race is being run, there'll be serious repercussions.'

Before he could signal his agreement, Leeming was quelled with a glance from the superintendent. Tallis was forced to rethink his tactics. He was under severe pressure from the commissioner and from the press to solve the murder of John Feeny and he wanted to be seen to be taking positive steps. At the same time, he did not wish to end up in a legal wrangle that would simply hamper the inquiry. With reluctance, he accepted what Colbeck had just told him.

'What would you advise, Inspector?' he said.

'Let them stay free,' urged Colbeck. 'We'll find out the young lady's name without their help. What we need to do is to keep an eye on all three owners, Lord Hendry, Fido and Brian Dowd. It's only a matter of time before one of their horses is in danger again.'

Sidney had worked at the stables for years. The little terrier acted as a guard dog, kept the place free of vermin and made a nuisance of himself whenever the yard was full of horses. The rest of the time, he liked to curl up in the straw in one of the stalls and sleep. That was exactly where the groom found the dog when he brought Merry Legs back from her morning gallop. As he led the animal into the stall, he gave Sidney a friendly kick to get rid of him but there was no response. A harder kick made the dog roll over limply.

The groom was alarmed. Sidney was clearly dead. In the corner of the stall was a pail of water from which the dog might well have drunk. Realising that, the groom flew into a panic. He led the filly quickly back into the yard and called to the trainer.

'Mr Stenton!' he yelled at the top of his voice. 'Come quickly, sir. I think someone tried to poison Merry Legs.'

CHAPTER TEN

When the detectives eventually reached the stables, Alfred Stenton was still shuttling between blind rage and deep sadness. Robert Colbeck introduced his sergeant but the trainer was too preoccupied even to shake hands with Victor Leeming. The death of his dog had shaken him badly and left him lusting for vengeance.

'They poisoned Sidney,' said Stenton, grief-stricken. 'I've had him for years. He's been our mascot here at the stables.'

'What exactly happened?' asked Colbeck. 'All that the message told us was that an attempt had been made to kill Merry Legs.'

'A failed attempt,' added Leeming.

'We'd appreciate more details, Mr Stenton.'

The trainer nodded. It was Hamilton Fido who had reported the crime and the detectives had set out immediately for the stables. Only two days after he had tried to arrest the bookmaker, Colbeck had now been summoned to help him. Breaking the law when it suited him, Fido was obviously not slow to call in those who enforced it when he felt the need to do so. Stenton escorted his visitors to the stall where his dog had perished and indicated the pail of water.

'Sidney must have drunk from that,' he said. 'He shouldn't even have been in here but somebody left the door open and in he came. One of the grooms found him dead in the straw.'

Colbeck bent beside the pail. 'I take it that this stall was occupied by Merry Legs?'

'Until this morning – I've had her moved.'

'I'm glad you didn't throw the water away, Mr Stenton. We'll take a sample with us so that it can be analysed.' He stood up. 'I'll leave that to you, Victor.'

'Yes, Inspector,' said Leeming, producing a small bottle from his pocket and dipping it in the water. 'I'm sorry about your dog, sir, but at least it wasn't Merry Legs.'

'I'll kill the man who did this!' vowed Stenton.

'He'll have to face proper judicial process,' said Colbeck. 'First of all, of course, we have to catch him. He's clearly someone familiar with your stables or he wouldn't have known in which stall to poison the water. And he's obviously aware of your daily routine. He struck when the yard was virtually deserted.'

'There were a couple of lads about.'

'Did they see anything unusual?'

'Nothing,' said Stenton. 'My first thought was that one of them had been responsible and I put the fear of death into them. I'm sure they were both innocent. They were as upset about Sidney as me.'

'What did you do next, sir?'

'I sent word to Mr Fido then I spoke to every single person here, one by one. We've already had one spy at the stables and I wanted to make certain that we didn't have another. I really interrogated them, Inspector.'

'I can well imagine.'

'So I know that none of them was involved.'

'What about John Feeny?' asked Leeming, slipping the bottle and its contents into his pocket. 'Perhaps he was linked to this in some way. We know that a man arranged a secret meeting with him. He could have got details about the running of the stables out of the lad before he killed him.'

Stenton frowned. 'What's this about a secret meeting?'

'It's something I discovered from the barmaid at the Shepherd and Shepherdess,' explained Colbeck. 'She and Feeny were close friends, it seems. He told her about a man who demanded information about Limerick Lad. Feeny had to comply. The man threatened to reveal that he had once worked for Brian Dowd and get him sacked.'

'Sacked!' exclaimed the trainer. 'Torn limb from limb, you mean!'

'Don't speak ill of the dead, sir.'

'Feeny got what he deserved.'

'I'm sorry that you can mourn a dog and find no sympathy for a human being who was brutally murdered,' said Colbeck, shooting him an admonitory look. 'The sergeant makes a valid point, however. Before he was killed, John Feeny might well have had everything he knew about your stables wrung out of him. Though, from what I've heard about Feeny, he would never have given that information freely.'

'All I'm worried about now is Merry Legs,' said Stenton.

'Understandably.'

'I'm having her watched night and day and I'm

234

supervising her food and her water myself.'

'A sensible precaution,' said Colbeck. 'What troubles me are the lengths to which someone is prepared to go. Why use poison when something less lethal could have been put in that water? Why try to kill Merry Legs when you could keep her out of the race simply by giving her some kind of abdominal disorder?'

'That's what I was thinking, Inspector,' said Leeming. 'Whoever he is, this man does not believe in half-measures.'

'Arrest the person who set him on to do this,' urged Stenton.

'We would if we knew who he was, sir.'

'Brian Dowd is behind this. Find him before I do.'

'Do you have any proof that Mr Dowd is implicated?' said Colbeck calmly. 'If so, we'd be very glad to see it.'

'It *has* to be him, Inspector.'

'I'd doubt that, sir. Victor and I have both met the gentleman and one thing was clear to both of us. Mr Dowd loves racehorses. I can't believe that he would deliberately harm one of them, whatever his feelings about its owner.'

'I agree,' said Leeming. 'I saw Mr Dowd at his stables. He lives and breathes racehorses. Why should he pay someone to attack Merry Legs when he's so convinced that Limerick Lad can beat her easily in the Derby?'

'If you two don't tackle him,' warned Stenton, 'then I will.'

'You'd never get close to him, sir. He has a bodyguard called Seamus who carries a loaded shotgun. I don't think he'd need much excuse to use it.'

'Besides,' said Colbeck, 'we don't want you trying to do our job for us, Mr Stenton. We'll be speaking to Brian Dowd very soon.'

'Make sure that you do.'

'Before that, I'd like to talk to the groom who actually found your dog in here. With your permission, Victor and I will then take a look around to see if we can find the most likely place of access for any intruder.'

'When you've done that, put the handcuffs on Brian Dowd.'

'He'll have to wait his turn in the queue, sir,' said Colbeck. 'It was Mr Fido who called on us and I feel duty bound to report to him. No need to ask where he'll be at this moment.'

'No, Inspector,' said Stenton. 'He's at Epsom.'

Derby Week was a gambling extravaganza. Betting was brisk on all the races on the various cards but it was the Derby itself that commanded most attention. Sums ranging from the spectacular to the paltry had already been waged though wiser heads were reserving their options by delaying any decision until much nearer the event. Caught up in the frenzy of betting, Hamilton Fido was working at full tilt all morning and only allowed himself a small break for luncheon. He was annoyed to see Marcus Johnson heading in his direction.

'Stop right there!' he ordered, holding up a palm. 'I've told you a hundred times, Marcus. I'm not giving you any advice.'

'You don't need to, Hamilton. I've got some for you.'

'Oh?'

'This is personal,' said Johnson.

'How personal?'

'It concerns Kitty. We need to talk in private.'

'What's going on?'

'I can't tell you here.'

Fido got up from his chair and the two men left the refreshment room. They found a quiet corner behind the grandstand. Johnson's face was grim. His normal ebullience had deserted him.

'Before we go any further,' he said, 'I must tell you that Kitty doesn't know I'm here. In fact, she begged me not to talk to you.'

'Why not?'

'You'll soon understand why.'

'Is she in trouble of some kind?' asked Fido.

'A small problem has arisen, Hamilton.'

'Problem?'

'It goes by the name of Lord Hendry,' said Johnson. 'I'm sure that you're aware he once took an interest in Kitty.'

'In my eyes,' said the other, 'it added to her attraction – not that she needed any additional appeal, mark you. I rather relished the idea of snatching her away from Lord Hendry. I can't wait to dangle Kitty in front of him. It will be the first of two humiliations for the old goat.'

'What's the other one?'

'Having to watch Odysseus being beaten by Merry Legs.'

'Any other time,' said Johnson with a half-smile, 'I'd seize on that as reliable advice about where to place my bets. As it is, Kitty's welfare comes first.'

'Why – what's happened to her?'

Johnson told him about his visit to the house the previous day and how he had sensed that his half-sister was trying to hide something from him. Once he had forced the truth out of her, she had gone on to explain the circumstances of the assault in more detail. He passed them on to Hamilton Fido. Simmering with fury throughout, the bookmaker at last erupted.

'He actually struck Kitty?' he said in horror.

'Across the side of her head with his cane,' replied Johnson.

'The bastard!'

'He went there to bully her into going to the police and ended up attacking her. Apparently, it was the mention of your name that really set him off. Lord Hendry went berserk.'

'*I'll* go berserk when I catch up with him,' growled Fido.

'My first instinct was to charge off to confront him but I thought that you ought to know what was going on.'

'Thank you, Marcus – I'm very grateful.'

'Lord Hendry's assault was utterly unforgivable.'

'Cruel, undeserved and unbecoming a gentleman.'

'Kitty said that the pain was excruciating.'

'The old fool will pay for this!' said Fido.

'There's only one thing to decide,' said Johnson solemnly.

'Is there?'

'Who challenges him to a duel first – you or me?'

Brian Dowd had brought a number of horses from Ireland with him and he had moved all of them to the racecourse over the weekend. Robert Colbeck and Victor Leeming found him at the stables allocated to him. He gave them a cheery welcome.

'The two of you have come this time, have you?' he said.

'I didn't want to get shot at by Seamus,' joked Leeming, 'so I made the inspector come with me in order to draw his fire.'

'Oh, Seamus won't bother you.'

'It looks as if you got here safely, Mr Dowd,' said Colbeck.

'Yes, the journey was entirely without incident, I'm glad to say. Limerick Lad and the rest of my horses are all safely locked up.'

'You might consider looking to your own safety, sir.'

'Why is that, Inspector?'

'Because you may get an unwelcome visitor,' said Colbeck. 'When we left Alfred Stenton a while ago, he was breathing fire through his nostrils.'

Dowd cackled. 'That's nothing new for Alfred!'

'He blames you for what happened at his stables.'

Colbeck went on to tell him about the poisoned water that killed Sidney and how the trainer had immediately identified Dowd as the likely culprit. The Irishman was offended.

'Accuse me, did he?' he said indignantly. 'I haven't been anywhere near his stables and I certainly didn't try to get his horse poisoned. Jesus – that's a terrible crime, to be sure! Horses are wonderful animals. I'd never let one of them suffer like that.'

'That's what we told Mr Stenton, sir.'

'Alfred wants to watch that loud mouth of his.'

'You and he have often tussled in the past, I believe.'

'I've taken on every trainer in England,' boasted Dowd, 'and, as often as not, I've put them to shame. When he was a two-year-old, Limerick Lad won the Champagne Stakes at Doncaster. Merry Legs, trained by Alfred Stenton, came in fourth. My horse went on to win the Criterion Stakes at Newmarket and Merry Legs was three lengths behind him. That's why he's throwing these foul accusations at me, Inspector. It's pure spite.'

'He still reckons that his filly will win the Derby,' said Leeming.

'You need three things to do that, Sergeant – the best horse, the best jockey and the best trainer. I have the first two of those things and I happen to be the third.'

'Thing could still go wrong, sir.'

'Yes,' said Colbeck. 'I watched the Derby one year and a horse ran amok at the start, unsaddling his jockey and causing mayhem among the other runners.'

'Tim Maguire knows how to keep Limerick Lad out of trouble.'

'Is there no horse in the field that you fear?'

240

'None.'

'What about Odysseus?'

'The odds have shortened on the favourite,' said Leeming. 'Lord Hendry is so convinced that he'll win that he's had Odysseus's portrait painted. We saw it hanging on the wall of his library.'

Dowd grinned. 'Then he'll soon have to take it down,' he said. 'As luck happens, I chanced to meet Lord Hendry myself. He's as bad as Alfred Stenton – he accused me of trying to injure his horse. The nerve of it!' he went on. 'I *want* Odysseus and Merry Legs in this race so that Limerick Lad can show them a clean pair of heels.'

'Have any more approaches been made to your jockey?'

'I'll say they have, Sergeant Leeming. Two ruffians called on Tim the other night to cudgel him out of the race. We saw them off with a shotgun. I keep my leading jockey well guarded.'

'Why didn't you report the attack to us?' asked Colbeck.

'We took care of it ourselves.'

'A serious crime might have been committed. A record should be made of that, Mr Dowd. As soon as there was trouble at Mr Fido's stables, he sent for us at once.'

'I think that's rich,' said Dowd, laughing derisively. 'A black-hearted crook like Hamilton Fido, calling on the police – now I've heard everything!'

'We've just been looking for him but Mr Fido has disappeared for some reason. His assistants are taking bets in his stead. That being the case, we thought we'd talk to you first.'

'Always nice to see the friendly face of the law.'

'There aren't many who think that,' said Leeming.

'Other people don't have clear consciences, Sergeant.'

'Do you, sir?'

'My mind is entirely free of guilt.'

'Really, sir?' said Colbeck. 'Didn't you feel even the tiniest twinge of guilt when you lied to me about John Feeny?'

Dowd stiffened. 'I did nothing of the kind, Inspector.'

'You told me that you'd parted on good terms.'

'That's true. I held no grudges.'

'Then why didn't you give him his full wages? According to you, before he left Dublin, you handed him some extra money to help him on his way.' Colbeck watched him closely. 'Do you remember telling me that, Mr Dowd, or do you think I'm misrepresenting you?'

'That's what I said and that's what I stand by.'

'Feeny left your stables after a violent row with you.'

'A few hot words were exchanged, maybe, but that was all.'

'You held back all of the money you owed him.'

'Who's been telling you all this baloney?' said Dowd truculently, 'That's what it is, Inspector. I was there with the lad so I know what happened. Nobody can gainsay it.'

'One person can,' rejoined Colbeck, 'and that's Feeny himself. He found himself a sweetheart when he was here and told her his story. It was she who wrote those letters to Jerry Doyle. I've spoken to the girl and her version of events is very different to yours.'

'Who is this creature?'

'She's a barmaid at an inn that Feeny frequented.'

'A *barmaid!*' Dowd was contemptuous. 'You'd take the word of a barmaid against that of someone like me? Thank you very much!' Arms akimbo, he spoke with feeling. 'John Feeny left my stables under a cloud because he made the mistake of answering back to me. I don't allow that in my yard, Inspector. When I told him that he didn't have the talent to become a jockey, he lost his temper and swore at me. I threw him out there and then but had second thoughts later on. I liked the lad and didn't want us to part like that. I made my peace with him and gave him some cash.'

'If he had money in his pocket,' said Colbeck, 'why did he have to stow away on a boat?'

'Because he probably spent what I gave him on drink,' retorted Dowd. 'That's what he'd always done in the past. He had a streak of wildness in him, did John Feeny, or maybe the barmaid forgot to mention that? Good day, gentlemen,' he said pointedly. 'Instead of making false allegations against me, why don't you spend your time hunting for the man who sent me Feeny's head in a hatbox? Then you might actually be doing something useful. Excuse me,' he added, turning on his heel to walk away. 'I have work to do.'

'I think you upset him, sir,' said Leeming.

'I must have caught him on a raw spot.'

'I didn't see any sign of guilt in him.'

'No,' said Colbeck. 'You wouldn't, I'm afraid. Whatever he's done, I don't think that Brian Dowd would have one iota of guilt.'

'Is it something to do with being Irish, sir?'

'No, Victor, it's something to do with being involved in the world of horseracing. It's a hard, cold, strange, unforgiving, venal world that operates by its own peculiar rules. Let's see if we can find another of its denizens,' he suggested. 'The elusive Mr Hamilton Fido.'

Hamilton Fido maintained his surface bonhomie but he was seething inside. After being told about the way that Kitty Lavender had been treated, he was determined to strike back at Lord Hendry. He was glad that Marcus Johnson had informed him about an incident that his half-sister would have tried to conceal out of embarrassment. Fido not only felt an urge to leap to her defence, he realised how fond he had become of her during their short time together.

When they had first met, he had no illusions about the sort of woman that Kitty was and he accepted her on those terms. Their relationship was only the latest in a long series of *amours* that he had enjoyed over the years and none of them had lasted very long. Kitty Lavender was somehow different to the other women. She had a vivacity and intelligence that set her apart. The news that someone had hit her with his cane had awakened feelings in him that he had not believed were there. He experienced a new intensity. Hamilton Fido was hurt, proprietorial, bent on revenge.

The bookmaker knew where to find Lord Hendry but he did not want to accost him in public. Causing a scene would be foolish and unnecessary. Instead, he bided his time. Lord Hendry was surrounded by acquaintances in the grand salon, discussing the prospects of Odysseus and making predictions about other races during the week. It was over an hour before he broke away and headed for the door. As the older man came through it, Fido was waiting for him in the narrow passageway, blocking his path.

'Out of my way, man!' snapped Lord Hendry.

'I want a word with you first.'

'I've nothing to say to people of your ilk.'

'Oh, I think you do,' said Fido, squaring up to him. 'It concerns a young lady named Kitty Lavender. I believe you paid her a visit recently.'

'Stand aside,' ordered Lord Hendry, 'or I'll report you to the Jockey Club for menacing conduct.'

'It was you who resorted to menacing conduct with Kitty. Is it true that you struck her across the face?'

'That's my affair.'

'And mine,' said Fido, holding his ground. 'I've come to exact retribution on her behalf.'

Lord Hendry sniggered. 'Retribution – for a whore?'

'Show more respect or you'll regret it.'

'It's you who needs to show respect. Do you know who I am?'

'Only too well,' said Fido, looking him up and down. 'I know who you are and what you are, Hendry – a coward, a bully and a damn rogue. You're not fit to be called a gentleman. You're a disgrace to the title you bear and it's high time somebody told you.'

'What happened to Kitty was long overdue.'

'Do you have no remorse at all?'

'None whatsoever,' said the other, roused by the verbal attack on him. 'I'd do exactly the same again. I'd never apologise to her or to you, for that matter. You're two of a pair – loathsome, uneducated creatures who've dragged yourselves up from the gutter and learnt a few airs and graces. You'll never be accepted in society. The stink of inferiority remains on both of you and always will.'

Fido had heard enough. Snatching the older man's cane from him, he used it to knock off his top hat then he prodded him hard in the chest. Lord Hendry was frothing with outrage.

'I'll have the law on you for that!' he cried.

'If we're talking about litigation,' said Fido, tossing the cane aside, 'then Kitty could bring an action against you for assault and battery. But this is a matter that can be settled out of court.'

'What are you talking about?'

'I demand satisfaction,' he went on, waving a fist. 'Meet me at a time of your convenience and have the choice of weapons.'

Lord Hendry gasped. 'You're challenging me to a duel?'

'I want to see if you have the courage to turn up.'

'I'd never lower myself to fight with you.'

'You'll have to – I insist upon it.'

'This is absurd!'

'Select the time and place, Lord Hendry.

Remember one thing.'

'What's that?'

'You won't be up against a defenceless young woman this time,' said Fido warningly. 'You'll be facing another man.'

Lord Hendry was dumbstruck. Rooted to the spot, he could not hide the trepidation in his eyes. As he walked away, Hamilton Fido deliberately trod on the top hat as a signal of his future intent. The challenge had been issued. He wanted blood.

Travelling by cab, it had taken Kitty Lavender a long time to reach Epsom because of the huge volume of traffic on the road. She was staying in rooms that had been rented for her by Hamilton Fido and the first thing that she did when she got to the house was to change into her dressing gown and lie down for a rest. After a while, there was a knock on her door. Fearing that it might be Fido, she got up and hurried across to the mirror to adjust her hair so that it covered the bruise on her temple. There was a second knock.

'Just a moment!' she called.

She examined herself in the mirror until she was satisfied that her injury was all but invisible then she opened the door. Instead of the bookmaker, it was Marcus Johnson. Kitty was disappointed.

'Oh!' she sighed. 'It's you.'

'I've had better welcomes than that,' he complained.

'I'm sorry, Marcus – come on in.'

'Thank you.' He entered the room and weighed it up at a glance. 'This is quite luxurious. Hamilton has spared no expense. Prices for accommodation shoot up like rockets in Derby Week so he must love you.' He took off his hat with a flourish and studied her face. 'It hardly shows at all now, Kitty. It's only your heart that's still bruised.'

'I prefer to forget that it ever happened,' she said.

'Well, I don't – and neither does Hamilton.'

Kitty tensed. 'You've *told* him?'

'I felt obliged to do so,' he replied. 'If someone had assaulted a woman I adored, then I'd want to know about it.'

'But I told you to keep it from him.'

'That would have been unfair on Hamilton. It would also have let Lord Hendry off the hook and I was not going to allow that.'

'How did he receive the news?'

'With the same horror and disgust that I did.'

'Oh, dear!'

'I mean to confront Lord Hendry myself but I fancy that Hamilton will get there first. He was absolutely furious.'

She was alarmed. 'What's he going to do?'

'I know what he ought to do,' said Johnson savagely, 'and that's to horsewhip him ten times around the Derby course. The very least he'll demand is an apology and some kind of reparation.'

'He won't get a penny from George,' she said. 'Nor an apology.'

'Then the old roué will have to suffer the consequences.'

'Consequences?'

'If I know Hamilton Fido, he'll challenge him

248

to a duel.'

'He mustn't do that, Marcus!' she protested.

'It's a matter of honour.'

'Duelling is illegal. I don't want Hamilton arrested.'

'I'm sure they'll find a venue that's well hidden from the prying eyes of the police. Lord Hendry will be shaking in his shoes.'

'I don't care about him,' said Kitty anxiously. 'It's Hamilton that I fear for. What weapons will they use?'

'Pistols, most probably.'

'Then I must warn him that George was in the army. He knows how to handle guns of all kinds. Shooting is one of his hobbies.'

'Hamilton is much younger than he is,' said Johnson. 'His eyesight is better, his aim straighter and he'll be the first to pull the trigger. Put your money on him.'

'I don't wish to put it on anyone. I want this duel stopped.'

'But he'll be protecting your honour, Kitty.'

'That makes no difference,' she said. 'If he's not killed, Hamilton could be wounded. And if he kills George, then he'll be liable to arrest on a charge of murder. I don't want him hanged.'

'It will never come to that,' he assured her. 'A duel carries its own code. Whatever the outcome, nobody will be reported to the police. Have no qualms about Hamilton. He's perfectly safe.'

'Unless he's shot dead by George.'

'There's no danger of that.'

'But suppose that he was, Marcus,' she said, trying to envisage the situation. 'I'd lose Hamilton and George would get away scot-free.'

'I could never allow that to happen.'

'What do you mean?'

'You're my half-sister, Kitty. We may spend most of our time apart but I'm devoted to you and I'll not have you maltreated by anyone. There's only one course of action for me to follow,' he said, straightening his shoulders. 'If Hamilton Fido doesn't kill that aristocratic bastard – then I will.'

It was not until late afternoon that they ran the bookmaker to ground. They found it difficult to move in the swirling crowds. There were too many distractions. Left to himself, Victor Leeming would have explored the fairground and sampled some of the food and drink that was on sale. He was particularly interested in seeing the tattooed Polynesian lady, a woman of massive proportions, whose nude portrait was painted in lurid colours on a board outside one of the booths. But he and Robert Colbeck were there on duty and there was no time for entertainment. Making their way through the mass of people, they visited the betting office for the third time in a row and found that Hamilton Fido had at last returned.

When he saw the detectives approach, Fido excused himself from the man to whom he was talking and came over to them. Since the crowded room was no place for a private conversation, he led them out of the grandstand altogether and stood in the shadows at the rear.

'You're a difficult man to find,' said Colbeck.

'I've been very busy,' explained Fido.

'We came in response to your message. We

spoke to Mr Stenton and he gave us the details of the crime. There's no doubt that an attempt was made on the life of your filly.'

'Someone should swing for this, Inspector.'

'The least he can expect is a very long prison sentence.'

'I want more than that.'

'The law does not exist for the personal gratification of those, like yourself, who've been victims of a particular offence. Punishment is designed to fit the crime.'

'Otherwise,' said Leeming, 'everybody we arrested would be dangling at the end of a rope, however minor his or her offence. The judge is there to impose the appropriate sentence.'

'There's only one thing appropriate for this villain,' said Fido with vehemence, 'and that's a visit to the hangman. Do you know how much Merry Legs cost me? Do you know how much I've invested in training her? Do you realise how much I'd stand to lose if anything untoward happened to her?'

'A lot of money, I suspect, sir.'

'A fortune, Sergeant.'

'That's why we must look at those who'd stand to gain at your expense,' said Colbeck. 'Your trainer had no hesitation in singling out the man who instigated the attempted poisoning – Brian Dowd.'

'That was the first name that popped into my mind.'

'Has Mr Dowd ever done anything like this before?'

'No,' admitted Fido.

'Have you ever known him injure a horse on purpose?'

'I can't say that I do.'

'Then why do you assume that he must be behind this crime?'

'Past experience,' said Fido. 'Every time our horses have been pitted against each other, we've had trouble from Dowd. If he can stoop to putting a spy in my stables, you can see how desperate he is.'

'You're wrong, sir,' Colbeck told him. 'John Feeny was no spy. My belief is that the killer wanted him to act as spy *against* Brian Dowd. We spoke to Mr Dowd earlier. He's a shrewd man.'

'Shrewd and slimy.'

'There seem to be a lot of slimy individuals on the Turf, sir,' said Leeming. 'Our superintendent holds the view that horseracing is only a polite word for criminal activity.'

'Yes,' said Fido, 'from people like Brian Dowd.'

'Let's put one myth to rest,' said Colbeck, 'because it's patently clouding your judgement. When he worked at your stables, John Feeny developed an attachment to a young lady at a nearby inn. They even talked of marriage. She told me categorically that Feeny left Ireland after an argument with his employer and Mr Dowd now admits as much. Feeny was loyal to your stables, Mr Fido – he told the girl how much he'd love to see Merry Legs win the Derby instead of Limerick Lad.'

'She *will* win, Inspector.'

Leeming grinned. 'Do I have your word on that, sir?'

252

'I wouldn't put her in the race if I expected her to lose.'

'That's what you're doing with Princess of Fire.'

'She's only in the Derby for experience. Merry Legs is there to wipe the smiles off the gloating faces of Brian Dowd and Lord Hendry.'

'That's in the lap of the gods at the moment,' said Colbeck. 'With regard to the poisoning of the dog, however, my own theory is that the person responsible is the same man who murdered John Feeny and who may also have tried to eliminate Odysseus from the Derby. Not content with those crimes, he's made two attempts to ensure that Tim Maguire will not ride in Mr Dowd's colours on Wednesday.'

'Catch him before he causes any more damage,' said Fido.

'That's our intention, sir,' Colbeck promised. 'Turning to another but not unconnected matter, we're still waiting for the young lady who owned that hatbox to come forward.'

'I've advised her to do so.'

'She seems disinclined to take your advice, Mr Fido.'

'I can't compel her, Inspector.'

'Perhaps not but you could apply more pressure, I feel. Point out to her that it's in her best interests to assist us. Her hatbox was stolen and used in the course of a heinous crime. Surely she would want the killer to be apprehended.'

'She does – it would relieve her mind greatly.'

'Relieve mine by making her cooperate with the police. If she persists in avoiding us,' said Colbeck, 'we are bound to think that the lady has something she prefers to keep hidden.'

'That's not the case at all.'

'Then use your influence over her, Mr Fido.'

'My hands are rather full at the moment,' said the other. 'This is the most frantic time of the year for me.'

'We're not exactly short of work ourselves, sir,' Leeming put in.

Colbeck smiled wryly. 'That's an understatement, Victor,' he said. 'This year's Derby is keeping us well and truly on our toes. I still have hopes of watching the race itself but I'll not enjoy it if the killer is still at large. He'll be *here*, Mr Fido, ready to create more chaos for all of us. We need every ounce of help we can get from every available source. Tell that to the young lady,' he ordered. 'Either she comes forward voluntarily or we go looking for her with a warrant.'

The first day of Derby Week had been a sustained ordeal for Lord Hendry. Outwardly, it was a story of gain. He gained respect, flattery and admiration. Everyone he knew sought his advice. All of them congratulated him on the position that Odysseus held in the betting. He should have sailed through the day on recurring waves of affection and goodwill. Inwardly, however, he was contemplating a story of loss. He had failed in his attempt to borrow money from various friends. Pleasant discussions over glasses of champagne had all ended in polite refusal. Even his brother-in-law had turned down his request. As a gambling man, Lord Hendry had endured serious losses in recent months and he needed to recoup them on the Derby but he could only do that if he had enough capital to place on his horse. Everything depended on that one headlong race.

Another loss that troubled him was that of Kitty Lavender. He had been shocked to learn that she had betrayed him by turning to the one man he detested above all others. Lord Hendry's loss was accentuated by Hamilton Fido's gain. It was the bookmaker who would now enjoy her luscious kisses, her soft caresses and all of her unparalleled skills as a lover. Rather than yield her up to Fido, he would have preferred to keep her as his mistress and allow her to be seen with him in public.

Overarching all the other losses was the imminent loss of his life. He was a good shot but, if he fought a duel against a younger man, there was no guarantee that he would come through it alive. Lord Hendry could see only two ways out of his predicament. He could try to appease Kitty by writing her a letter of abject apology, hoping that she would make Fido stay his hand. Or he would have to make sure that the duel never took place by having his opponent disabled beforehand. Of the two possibilities, the second had more attraction. He had never apologised to one of his mistresses and did not wish to set a precedent with Kitty Lavender. Causing pain to a disagreeable bookmaker, on the other hand, would be pleasurable.

Though he wore a benign smile and waved to acquaintances on all sides, he was glad to be leaving Epsom at the end of the day. His carriage was waiting for him and he clambered into it. No sooner had he settled back than a man appeared beside him.

'Lord Hendry?' he enquired.

'I have that honour, sir.'

'It's a dishonourable name, in my opinion,' said Marcus Johnson baldly. 'Titles should be bestowed on those who deserve them and who learn to behave with the dignity commensurate with their station. You are unable to do that.'

'Who the devil are you?' demanded Lord Hendry.

'My name is Marcus Johnson.'

'Then I bid you good day, Mr Johnson.'

'Not so fast,' said Johnson, reaching into the carriage to grab his arm. 'I haven't introduced myself fully yet. I'm surprised that Kitty hasn't mentioned me to you. I'm her half-brother.'

'I don't care who you are – take your hand off me.'

Johnson released him. 'Kitty told me what you did to her.'

'I'm done with the woman. She belongs to my past.'

'You can't shake her off like that, my lord. It's unkind, ungrateful and monstrously unfair. Have you had a visit from Hamilton Fido yet?' Johnson laughed at his startled reaction. 'Yes, I see that you have. As a matter of record, I was the one who told him how you struck Kitty.'

'It was a glancing blow – nothing more.'

'If it were the slightest touch, it would be unpardonable and we both know that it was far more than that. You might have cut her face open or taken her eye out. Did that never occur to you?'

'You heard what I said, Mr Johnson – good day to you.'

'You'll not escape me that easily,' said Johnson, opening the door to jump into the carriage.

'Get out or I'll have you thrown out!'

'I'll leave when I'm ready, Lord Hendry.'

'I'll stand no more of this infernal impudence.'

'What are you going to do?' taunted Johnson, grabbing the cane from the other man. 'Hit me with this?' He snapped the cane across his knee and tossed both pieces on to the ground. 'I just wanted to deliver a message,' he went on, leaning over to whisper in Lord Hendry's ear. 'I know that Hamilton planned to challenge you to a duel. I hope you survive – then I can have the supreme pleasure of shooting you myself.'

It was mid-evening by the time that Robert Colbeck and Victor Leeming returned by train to London. After sending the sergeant home to his family, Colbeck first delivered the bottle of poisoned water to a chemist for analysis then went off to give his report to Edward Tallis. The superintendent was not impressed with what he heard.

'Is there no end to this?' he grumbled. 'One crime follows another in quick succession. As if a murder were not bad enough, we now have to investigate the attempted crippling of one racehorse, the attempted poisoning of another, a plot to suborn a jockey and, since that failed, a plan to beat him with cudgels. What's next, Inspector?'

'The arrest of the culprits, sir.'

'I see no sign of that.'

'We are getting closer all the time,' said Colbeck. 'And I doubt if there'll be any more incidents involving the racehorses. Odysseus, Merry Legs and Limerick Lad are all being guarded with extreme care. Their respective owners will not let any unauthorised person near them. I've deployed some of our men to provide additional protection.'

'I wish the Derby had never been invented!' moaned Tallis.

'Tens of thousands of people would disagree with that sentiment, sir. They'll come from all over the country to see the race and there'll be lots of people from abroad as well.'

'Foreigners and Irish always bring trouble. The government should ban horseracing forthwith and keep out the riffraff from across the water altogether.'

'I don't think you'll find a single Member of Parliament to support that idea,' said Colbeck with amusement. 'Derby Day is a national holiday. Parliament is suspended and many of the people who sit on its benches will be heading for Epsom. It's a wonderful occasion, Superintendent. You'd enjoy it.'

'I never enjoy uncontrolled revelry,' said Tallis with distaste. 'It leads to crime, drunkenness and fornication. It encourages the lower orders to take gross liberties. I'm surprised that someone as fastidious as you takes an interest in such a despicable event.'

'There's nothing deplorable about watching racehorses at full gallop, sir. It's an inspiring sight. My interest in the Derby began some years ago,' explained Colbeck, 'when I was first called to the Bar. You've no idea how much litigation surrounds the race. It may delight the spectators who flock to Epsom but it also enriches the lawyers who are involved in the countless bitter disputes. When the Derby is at hand, passions run high. That's why the courts are always full.'

'Don't talk to me about passions, Inspector. We're the victims of them. Were it not for someone's passion to win the Derby, we wouldn't have this daunting catalogue of crime to deal with.'

'I can't say that I feel daunted, sir.'

'Well, I do.'

'Never a day passes but we gather important information.'

'But look where it comes from,' said Tallis. 'That's what worries me. The most important information to date has come from a clerk at the Wyvern Hotel and a barmaid at some country inn. Neither of them has taken us any closer to apprehending the killer.'

'That's not true,' argued Colbeck. 'Because he was vigilant, Dacre Radley noted that the same young woman stayed at his hotel with both Lord Hendry and Hamilton Fido. That was significant.'

'It might be if you were able to question the woman but you seem unable to do so. Why is that?'

'I'm addressing that problem, sir.'

'Address it more robustly.'

'Yes, Superintendent,' said Colbeck. 'As for the barmaid at the Shepherd and Shepherdess, she supplied us with valuable insights into the character of John Feeny and she may yet do more for us.'

'In what way?'

'You must understand her state of mind. When I told her about Feeny's death, Bonny Rimmer was all but knocked senseless. All of the plans she had made with Feeny disappeared in an instant. It left her hurt, bewildered and consumed by grief. Days later, the girl had still not recovered from the blow. What I learnt from her,' said Colbeck, relaying what Madeleine Andrews had, in fact, discovered, 'was only part of the story. There's more to come. Bonny Rimmer promised to contact me when she could think more clearly. She talked of keepsakes that Feeny had given her, for instance.'

'Keepsakes?' snorted Tallis. 'What use are they?'

'They're clues to the sort of person Feeny really was, sir.'

'We know the sort of person he is – a dead one. He's a murder victim, Inspector. Instead of worrying about him any more, you should concentrate solely on his killer.'

'I need the lad's help to do that,' said Colbeck, 'and I have every hope that he'll give it to me. Dead men should never be discounted as a source of information. John Feeny is a case in point, sir. My belief is that he will rise from the grave to assist us.'

'Let me see it, Kitty.'

'No,' she replied.

'Show me where he hit you.'

'There's no point, Hamilton. The bruise has

gone now.'

'Which side of the head was it?'

'Leave me be. It doesn't matter any more.'

'Oh, yes, it does,' said Hamilton Fido sternly. 'It matters a great deal to me and to Marcus. Nobody touches you with impunity. Now, *please* – let me see.'

Kitty Lavender and the bookmaker were in one of the rooms he had rented for her near the racecourse. All her attempts to conceal her injury were in vain. He was insistent. After another round of protests, she eventually gave in.

'You're making far too much fuss over it,' she said.

'Which side?'

'On the left.'

He pushed her hair back gently and saw how much powder she had used on her temple. Taking out a handkerchief, he first licked it then applied it gingerly to her head. As the powder was wiped off, the vestigial bruise slowly came into view. Fido was incensed.

'Lord Hendry did *this* to you?' he exclaimed, standing back.

'Yes.'

'I'll murder him!'

'Calm down, Hamilton.'

'Why didn't you tell me about this?'

'Because I was afraid of the way you'd react,' she said, 'and I was right to do so. Both you and Marcus flew off the handle.'

'Do you blame us?'

'No – I blame myself.'

'*Yourself?*'

'I provoked him, Hamilton. I couldn't resist hurling your name at him. That was too much for George to bear.'

'Nothing can excuse what he did, Kitty.'

'Oh, I don't excuse it,' she said ruefully, 'believe me. I intended to get my revenge on George but I meant to do it in my own way.'

'I'm doing it on your behalf.'

'Is it true that you've challenged him to a duel?'

'Yes,' said Fido. 'First of all, I'll let him watch Odysseus get beaten in the Derby then I'll send him off to Hell with whichever weapon he chooses.'

'You'll need to watch him. George comes from military stock.'

'He'll be no match for me, Kitty. He's at least twenty years older and he drinks far too much. When I issued my challenge, I could sense that he was terrified.'

'I'm the one who's terrified. You might be wounded.'

'I've fought duels before,' he told her, 'and I've always emerged from them without a scratch. Why are you so upset? Don't you want Lord Hendry to be killed?'

'Yes!' she said with sudden rage. 'Cut down without mercy.'

'Leave it to me.'

'I hate him. I don't know why I ever got involved with George.'

'You were dazzled by his title and his wealth.'

'The title, perhaps,' she confessed, 'not by his money. He always seemed to be prosperous but I found out that he'd run up sizeable debts. It's the reason he's staking so much on the Derby. George believes it will help him pay off his creditors and still leave him with a substantial amount.'

'Then he's in for a massive disappointment, Kitty.'

'Is there no way that Odysseus will win the race?'

Fido smirked. 'Not if I have anything to do with it.'

'George thinks the result is cut and dried. He's so confident that his horse will be first that he's even had a portrait of Odysseus painted. It's already hanging somewhere in his house, I daresay. He said that I'd share in his triumph,' she recalled with a cynical smile. 'After the race, George promised to take me to Paris with the proceeds. Instead of that, I end up getting beaten across the head with his cane. Yes, I *do* want him killed, Hamilton,' she said, clenching both fists. 'My only regret is that I'm not the person to do the deed.'

Admiring her spirit, Fido kissed her impulsively. Then he walked across to a side-table and poured two glasses of brandy out of a crystal decanter. He handed one to Kitty and became pensive.

'Tell me about this portrait of Odysseus,' he said.

A heavy drizzle was falling when he arrived at the house in Camden. As she let him in, Madeleine Andrews sounded a note of mock reproof.

'This is the second time you've brought rain, Robert.'

'I'd hate you to associate me with bad weather,' he said with gallantry, 'because you always bring sunshine into my life.'

She laughed, thanked him for the compliment and accepted his kiss. Then she hung his damp hat on a peg behind the door. Sitting down beside each other, they held hands.

'Have you been at Epsom all day?' she asked.

'Yes,' he answered. 'There were more people there than ever.'

'You did say that I might get to see the Derby this year.'

'And I hope to honour that promise, Madeleine.'

'What happened today?'

He told her about the attempted poisoning of Merry Legs and about his meeting with Brian Dowd. Shocked by news of the crime, she reserved her main interest for the comments about John Feeny.

'He and Mr Dowd parted on friendly terms?' she said.

'That's what Dowd claims.'

'Well, it's not what Bonny Rimmer told me. She heard it from Feeny himself and he had no cause to lie to her. He had to leave Ireland because he'd no chance of finding another job there. Mr Dowd said he'd make sure of that.' She pulled a face. 'Is that what he calls parting on friendly terms?'

'I suppose there's been no word from Bonny,' said Colbeck.

'Not yet.'

'Do you expect to hear from her?'

'I'm depending on it,' said Madeleine. 'When I

264

spoke to her on Sunday, she was very emotional. She still hadn't resigned herself to the fact that she'd never see John Feeny again. She wanted time to collect her thoughts. When she'd done that, she said she'd be in touch with me. I told her how vital that was.'

'Did you give her this address?'

'Yes, Robert, and I gave her the directions to get here. At first she was frightened at the idea of coming to a big city but I managed to still her fears. Since I knew she'd worry about the cost of travel, I took your advice and gave her the money you provided.'

'It was the least I could do for her,' he said.

'That was typical of you.'

'She's a key witness, Madeleine. Bonny Rimmer knows things about John Feeny that nobody else could tell us. I'll pay any travel expenses that she incurs.'

'Has the superintendent given you *your* money yet?'

'No,' replied Colbeck dolefully. 'I have to find the killer before Mr Tallis will refund my expenses. He still claims that my visit to Ireland was largely a waste of time.'

'That's ridiculous!'

'Try telling that to him.'

She giggled. 'After listening to some of the things you've said about him,' she recalled, 'I'll avoid him like the plague.'

'Even though he's a colleague of yours?'

'I don't work for the Detective Department.'

'Not officially,' he said, 'but you work for me and that amounts to the same thing. You're the

265

most charming assistant I've ever had.'

'What about Sergeant Leeming?'

Colbeck laughed. 'Even his wife wouldn't dare to call Victor charming. Nature decided that. However, he's everything a policeman should be and that's all that matters in the long run.'

'Where will you be tomorrow?'

'Back at Epsom with Victor.'

'Have you heard any talk about the Derby?'

'We've heard little else, Madeleine. Everyone is talking about the prospects of Lord Hendry's Odysseus – except Hamilton Fido, that is. He is as certain as can be that the favourite will be beaten. The odds may not reflect this but, in his heart – if a bookmaker can be said to possess such a thing – he believes that Merry Legs will win.'

'Father is tempted to back Princess of Fire.'

'Mr Fido says she's only in the race for experience.'

'Who will you be backing, Robert?'

'I really don't know,' he admitted. 'I've been trying to separate the horses from their owners in my mind and I'm finding that difficult. The horses are all fine animals, I daresay, but the owners are a rather unprepossessing trio. Lord Hendry is dry and aloof. Hamilton Fido is as trustworthy as a paper bucket filled with sea-water. And Brian Dowd, I learnt today, doesn't always tell the truth.'

'So where will you put your money?'

'I'm rather tempted by Aleppo.'

'If I come to the Derby, I'll cheer him to the echo.'

'Don't be so hasty, Madeleine. I haven't

decided on a horse yet. As for the Derby,' he went on, 'you'll be there one way or another.'

'Father will be very jealous. He's working that afternoon.'

'Then he should be grateful he's not driving one of the special trains to Epsom. We travelled on one today. It was packed to capacity.'

'But at least the trains do go to Epsom now.'

'Yes,' he agreed with a nod. 'In the old days, you had to take the train out of Nine Elms Station, courtesy of the Brighton and South-ampton Railway. When you got out at Kingston, the cab drivers charged you the most exorbitant fees to drive you the few miles to Epsom. All that's changed now. You can catch a train at London Bridge Station and go all the way.'

'I hope to do exactly that on Wednesday, Robert.'

He responded to her smile. 'You will, Madeleine,' he said fondly. 'I just hope and pray that Bonny Rimmer comes to see you before then. We need her help. And there's something else we need as well.'

'What's that?'

'A period of calm before the Derby is run,' he told her. 'We've had enough crimes to deal with already. What we require now is a long, quiet, restful, law-abiding passage of time.'

Drizzle had turned into driving rain. It was so persistent that the dogs were locked in their kennels instead of being let out to roam around the house. In the middle of the wet, blustery night, everyone was fast asleep in bed. Nobody heard the shutters being forced nor the tinkle of glass as a panel was smashed to allow a hand to reach through. When the catch was released, the sash window was lifted right up and the thief clambered over the sill. Glad to be out of the rain at last, he looked around in the gloom.

'Now, then, Odysseus,' he said to himself, 'where *are* you?'

CHAPTER ELEVEN

Lord George Hendry was absolutely distraught. Stunned, wounded and hollow-eyed, he sat in his library and stared up at the gilt frame that had once surrounded the portrait of Odysseus. The horse had now bolted. The frame still hung over the marble fireplace but the oil painting had been cut out and removed. He was inconsolable. Lord Hendry was not simply mourning the loss of his colt and of the large amount of money it had cost to immortalise the animal on canvas. To him, the theft was a dreadful omen. Odysseus might not, after all, win the Derby. Its owner was facing ruin.

It was still early morning when Inspector Robert Colbeck arrived at the house in response to the urgent summons. A servant showed him into the library but Lord Hendry did not even notice him at first. Colbeck had to clear his throat to gain his attention.

'Good morning, my lord,' he said.

The other looked up. 'Ah, you're here,' he said dully.

'When I heard the news, I came as quickly as I could.' Colbeck glanced at the empty frame. 'I can see why you're so distressed.'

'Distressed?' Lord Hendry gave a mirthless laugh.

'When was the theft discovered?'

'Not long after dawn – one of the servants heard the shutters banging and got up to investigate. He found that someone had broken into the house through the dining-room window.'

'I'll need to see the exact spot.'

'The alarm was raised and I came downstairs to face this catastrophe,' said Lord Hendry, rising from his chair to point at the gilt frame. 'Odysseus has been stolen.'

'Was anything else taken?'

'Isn't this bad enough, man!'

'Yes, yes,' said Colbeck, 'of course, it is, Lord Hendry. But I want to establish if the thief came for the sole purpose of stealing the painting or if it was only one of many items that went missing.'

'Nothing else was taken, Inspector. He was after my horse.'

'You have my sympathy – it was a magnificent painting.'

'Odysseus is a magnificent colt,' asserted Lord Hendry. 'That's something my wife has never been able to appreciate, I fear. When she saw what had happened, she was more concerned about the muddy footprints left on the carpets than about the theft.'

'They could help us,' said Colbeck, noting the clear footprints that led to and from the fireplace. 'From the size of his boots and the length of his stride, I can see that we're looking for a tall man with large feet. There'll be more footprints in the mud outside to show from which direction he approached the house and where he left it.'

'What use is that? It won't bring my painting back.'

'Oh, I think it will be returned eventually.'

'Balderdash! It's already been destroyed.'

'I disagree, Lord Henry. If the thief were intent on destruction, then he'd simply have slashed the canvas to shreds. Instead of that, judging by the way it's been cut out, he's removed it with great care.'

'What does that tell you?'

'That you may well be offered the portrait back,' said Colbeck. 'At a high price, naturally.'

Lord Hendry shuddered. 'I can't afford to pay for it *twice*.'

'You can if Odysseus wins the Derby.'

'Yes,' said the other, rallying slightly. 'I can, Inspector. I can pay for anything then. The horse will get that painting back for me.'

'God willing!'

'I don't have to call on the Almighty. I rely entirely on form. Odysseus has been consistently faster than his nearest rivals. Over the same distance, he was even fleeter of foot than last year's Derby winner, West Australian.'

'But not in race conditions,' said Colbeck. 'In the heat of a Derby, form is not the only telling factor.'

'It will be tomorrow,' said Lord Hendry in a conscious effort to raise his own spirits. 'My trainer has never been so positive about a result before and he's handled dozens of three-year-olds.'

'I wish you luck.'

'Thank you.'

'Incidentally,' said Colbeck, 'when I heard about this theft, my immediate concern was for Odysseus himself. I thought that he might be in danger

271

as well. I know that you have him under armed guard, but I dispatched Sergeant Leeming to your stables to verify that there have been no problems during the night.'

'That was considerate.'

'Has your trainer been made aware of what happened here?'

'Not yet,' said Lord Hendry, 'and my instinct is to keep the news from him and from my jockey. They're both very superstitious. They'll interpret the theft in the way I've been doing – as an evil portent.' He was worried. 'I hope your sergeant will not tell them about what occurred here last night.'

'I told him not to, Lord Hendry. His job is simply to check on the safety of Odysseus. When all is said and done, the horse is far more important than the portrait of him.'

'Quite so.'

'Do you have any clue as to the thief's identity?'

'I could hazard a guess at his paymaster.'

'Brian Dowd?'

'Not in this instance, Inspector,' said Lord Hendry thoughtfully. 'He wouldn't even know that I had the painting. Besides, he's never been anywhere near this house. Because Odysseus stands between him and a Derby win, Dowd is much more likely to try to injure the horse himself than steal his portrait. No,' he continued, 'I spy the grasping hand of Hamilton Fido behind this.'

'How would *he* know that the painting existed?'

'Someone could have told him,' replied the other, thinking of Kitty Lavender. 'Someone in whom I unwisely confided at one time.'

'Are we talking about the young lady at the Wyvern Hotel?'

Lord Hendry glanced anxiously towards the door. 'Keep your voice down, man!' he ordered. 'This is my home.'

'I'm sorry, sir,' said Colbeck, speaking in a whisper. 'But the question cannot be avoided. Is it the lady we've discussed before?'

'Yes, Inspector.'

'You seem to have discovered that she's formed a liaison with Mr Fido. Am I right in thinking that?' Lord Hendry nodded sullenly. 'Could there be an element of spite in this? Given the circumstances, could this person have urged Mr Fido to arrange the theft of the painting out of pure malice?'

'She could and she did, Inspector,' said Lord Hendry, deciding that Kitty wanted her revenge for the blow he had given her. 'That must be what happened. She instigated the whole thing.'

'Then she committed a criminal act,' said Colbeck. 'That being the case, it's even more crucial that I know her name so that I can speak to her as soon as possible. If your supposition about her is correct, it may be a way to retrieve the painting sooner than I thought. Well, Lord Hendry?' he pressed. 'Are you going to tell me who she is?'

Still in her night attire, Kitty Lavender was propped up in bed as she watched Hamilton Fido putting on his frock coat. She was peevish.

'Do you have to leave so early?' she complained.

'Needs must when the devil drives, my darling.'

273

'Let your assistants do all the work.'

'I like to be at the course first thing to give them instructions,' said Fido, adjusting his coat in the bedroom mirror. 'One of the rules of bookmaking is to be constantly visible. It inspires trust.'

'Come here and inspire me,' she said, patting the bed.

He blew her a kiss. 'I'll have to postpone that delight until this evening, Kitty. I have too many people to see and too many bets to take. I also need to find a moment to go across to the stables to check on Merry Legs. That attempt at poisoning her scared me.'

'Do you still think that Mr Dowd was responsible?'

'I'd put money on it.'

'You'd never do that unless you were very confident.'

'My motto is simple,' he said, coming to sit on the bed. 'I only back certainties – like Kitty Lavender.' She gave a brittle laugh. 'How are you feeling this morning?'

'Pleasantly tired,' she purred.

'Then you can go back to sleep. While you slumber away, I'll be plying my trade at the racecourse and hoping that Inspector Colbeck will be able to find the villain who put that poison in the water.'

'What are the chances of that happening?'

'We shall see. Colbeck is an astute man.'

'Marcus doesn't think so. He said you'd outwit him every time.'

'I'd outwit any policeman, Kitty,' he said cheerily, 'which is why I've never seen the inside

274

of a courtroom. But this crime is something I can't solve on my own. I need an able detective.'

'What sort of person is Inspector Colbeck?' she asked.

'You'd like him – he's a real dandy. He sticks out from every other policeman I've met whereas his sergeant is more typical of the breed. To be honest,' he went on, 'I enjoyed crossing swords with Colbeck. He's a worthy opponent – unlike Lord Hendry.'

She was uneasy. 'Do you still mean to go ahead with the duel?'

'I can't pull out of it now, Kitty.'

'But you could be putting yourself in jeopardy.'

'He'd never get the better of me with a pistol.'

'If he believes that, George will look for a way to ensure that the duel never takes place.'

'You mean that he'll go into hiding somewhere?'

'No,' she said, stroking his arm. 'George won't run away – that would look bad. He's more likely to hire some ruffians to break a few of your bones so that you're frightened off.'

Fido laughed. 'He'll need a whole army to get close to me,' he boasted, tapping the bulge at his waist. 'Apart from the fact that I carry a loaded weapon, I have a bodyguard watching my back. The moment I leave here, I'm under his protection.'

'That won't stop me worrying.'

'Lord Hendry deserves a bullet between his eyes.'

'I want you to stay alive in order to put it there.'

'One of us will finish him off,' he said with con-

275

viction. 'If some mishap should befall me, Marcus will take my place. From what you've told me about him, he's an excellent shot.'

'He is,' said Kitty. 'Gambling is his first love but, when he takes time off from that, it's to join a shooting party somewhere. Though he's desperately short of money most of the time, he somehow manages to maintain a very comfortable existence. He trades on his charm and lives off his wealthy friends.'

'He's a silver-tongued social parasite and I admire him for that. It takes skill and daring to do what he does. I was also touched by the way he came to your defence.'

'I just wish that he hadn't told *you* about it.'

'Somebody must call Lord Hendry to account.'

'I'd rather it wasn't you, Hamilton. I know the way that George's mind works. If the duel did actually take place,' she warned, 'he'd be ready to fall back on unfair means.'

Fido grinned. 'That makes two of us – so will I.' Holding her by the chin, he gave her a gentle kiss then stood up. 'When are you going to speak to Inspector Colbeck?'

'Never – if I can help it.'

'He won't give up, Kitty. The longer you keep dodging him, the meaner he'll be when he finally does catch up with you. It's only a matter of time before he does that,' he pointed out. 'As soon as he sees us together, he'll know that you're the lady from the Wyvern Hotel.'

'There's no reason why he *should* see us together – not alone, anyway. I've got myself another beau to hide behind.'

'Oh – and who might that be?'

'Marcus, of course,' she said. 'He told me to avoid the police at all costs or my name might finish up in the newspapers. I don't want to become a public spectacle, Hamilton.'

'I rather hoped that you did – on my arm.'

'When I've shaken off Inspector Colbeck, there's nowhere I'd rather be. Above all else, I want George to see us together. After what he did to me, I want him to writhe in pain.'

'He's already been doing that, Kitty,' he said, reaching for his hat. 'My guess is that Lord Hendry didn't get a wink of sleep last night. He'd have been tortured by the thought of fighting a duel against me. He knows how that will end. And if he was kept awake, he'll have heard the sound of the downpour we had. It rained hard for hours and hours. That means the going will be soft at the racecourse and that won't suit Odysseus at all.' He put his hat on at a rakish angle. 'One way or another,' he said cheerfully, 'Lord Hendry must have had the worst night of his life.'

Victor Leeming was making his way through the crowd when he saw the woman. Short, dainty and with a look of sublime innocence on her face, she was accompanied by a small boy. Speaking to an elderly gentleman who was just descending from his carriage, she asked directions from him. He was happy to oblige. He was entranced by her pretty features and beckoning smile. Victor Leeming was more interested in what the boy was doing. When the directions had been received, the woman thanked her guide and led the boy away.

The sergeant moved swiftly to intercept them. Fixing the boy with a knowing look, he held out the palm of his hand.

'Give me the wallet,' he ordered.

'What are you talking about?' demanded the woman haughtily.

'The wallet that he took from that gentleman while you distracted him. This lad is a pickpocket and you're his accomplice.'

'How dare you! I'm David's mother!'

'Then you should be ashamed to bring him up in this way.'

'If you don't leave us alone,' she said, putting a maternal arm around her son, 'I'll call a policeman.'

'You're already talking to one,' said Leeming, enjoying his moment. 'I'm Detective Sergeant Leeming from Scotland Yard.'

He waved a hand to a uniformed policeman who stood a dozen yards away. Recognising him, the man came briskly over to him.

'Good morning, sir,' he said.

'Here's your first arrest of the day, Constable. I caught a pair of pickpockets. The lad has just stolen a wallet from that gentleman standing beside his carriage. Return his property to him,' said Leeming, 'then find out what else these two have purloined.'

The woman and her son made a sudden dash for freedom but the policeman restrained them both. Turning on the sergeant, she unleashed a stream of vile abuse and had to be dragged away. Leeming was about to move off when Brian Dowd came over to him.

'I saw that, Sergeant,' he said with a complimentary smile. 'You did very well. I'd never have known what those two were doing.'

'You didn't spend as many years in uniform as I did, sir. When you get big crowds, the pickpockets come out in their hundreds.'

'That boy could have been no more than six of seven.'

'Children younger than that have been trained to steal,' said Leeming sadly. 'They're corrupted at an early age. I don't blame the lad. It's the mother who should take the punishment.'

'I hope you don't spend all your time looking for pickpockets.'

'By no means, sir.'

'There are more important crimes to solve.'

'Inspector Colbeck and I are well aware of that,' said Leeming, 'and we have our superintendent snapping at our heels to make us find the killer of John Feeny. Our problem is that we keep getting distracted by related crimes.'

'Such as?'

'The attacks on both Odysseus and Merry Legs – someone is determined to keep them out of the Derby.'

'Don't forget what happened to me,' said Dowd. 'Limerick Lad can win the race but I'm honest enough to admit that he might not do it unless he has Tim Maguire on his back. That's why my jockey has been the target, Sergeant. Tim is my guarantee of success.'

'Limerick Lad likes soft going, I'm told.'

'The more rain we have, the better.'

'I hope that it holds off for the race itself.'

'Yes,' said Dowd. 'The world and his wife will be here tomorrow. There's nothing quite like Derby Day. I hope that the sun shines brightly during the races but I'll be praying for more rain tonight.'

'Were you on your way to the grandstand?' asked Leeming, glancing towards it. 'If you are, I'll walk with you, if I may.'

'Please do, Sergeant. I have some friends to meet there.'

Leeming fell in beside him. 'I've arranged to meet Inspector Colbeck,' he said. 'Left to myself, I'd rather see some of the sights. There's a six-legged pig on display and the Smallest Man in England is in one of the booths. Then there's a huge Polynesian woman who has tattoos *everywhere*. Duty calls, however,' he sighed. 'And the inspector should be back from Lord Hendry's house by now.'

'Oh?' Dowd was curious. 'What was he doing there?'

'We had a report of a crime that took place last night.'

'Indeed?'

'Lord Hendry's painting of Odysseus was stolen,' said Leeming. 'Other things may have been taken as well, for all I know, but it was the loss of the painting that sent the inspector haring over there.'

'I'll be interested to hear what transpired.'

They picked their way through the crowd. Races were not due to begin for a couple of hours yet but Epsom Downs were already submerged beneath a rippling sea of humanity. The noise

280

was deafening and the buzz of excitement was almost tangible. The two men chatted about the races on the day's card and Dowd recommended a bet on one of his own horses, Quicklime, in the last event of the day. As they got near the grandstand, they saw Robert Colbeck waiting at the appointed place. After an exchange of greetings, the inspector looked enquiringly at Leeming. The sergeant shook his head.

'There are no problems at the stables, sir. Odysseus is fine.'

'Thank you, Victor,' said Colbeck.

'What's this about a painting being stolen?' asked Dowd.

'It was taken in the night, sir. Lord Hendry is heartbroken.'

'Don't look to me for sympathy. It was rash of him to have a portrait of his horse painted before the race was even run. That was tempting Fate. But I'm surprised that anyone was out and about last night,' he went on. 'That storm should have kept everyone indoors.'

'Unfortunately,' said Colbeck, 'it kept the dogs indoors or they would have been guarding the house.'

'It's not a disaster,' said Leeming. 'Lord Hendry could always have another portrait painted.'

'Only if Odysseus wins the Derby,' said Dowd waspishly, 'and *you'd* have a better chance of doing that, Sergeant.'

'Then why is Odysseus still the favourite?'

'Wonders never cease.'

'Limerick Lad has dropped back slightly in the betting.'

'That suits me – we get better odds. But you must congratulate your sergeant,' said Dowd, turning to Colbeck. 'I watched him catch a couple of pickpockets in the crowd just now.'

'Well done, Victor,' said Colbeck. 'You always had sharp eyes.'

Leeming shrugged. 'I just happened to be in the right place, sir.'

'That's an essential part of policing.'

'I hope you're both in the right place when it comes to catching John Feeny's killer,' said Dowd earnestly. 'I want to know who that merciless bastard is.'

'So do the rest of us, sir.'

'Well, I must be off – don't forget what I told you, Sergeant.'

'Quicklime in the last race,' said Leeming.

'Tim Maguire is riding him.'

'Then I'll be sure to put a bet on him. Goodbye, Mr Dowd.' They waved the Irishman off. 'I'm glad I saw him this morning.'

'He was in a better mood than when we last met,' said Colbeck.

'You didn't accuse him of lying this time, Inspector.'

'That's true.'

'What happened at Lord Hendry's house?'

Colbeck told him about his visit and how profoundly depressed the owner had been at the theft of his beloved painting. The piece of information that Leeming seized on was the suggestion that a woman might be implicated in the crime.

'Did you get her name, Inspector?'

'Only after a long battle,' said Colbeck.

'Who is she?'

'Kitty Lavender.'

'Do you have an address?'

'She lives in London but Lord Hendry was certain that she'd be staying somewhere nearby during Derby Week.'

'How do we find her?'

'By speaking to Hamilton Fido,' said Colbeck. 'He and Miss Lavender will doubtless be sharing the same accommodation.'

'Do you think she had anything to do with the theft of that painting?' said Leeming.

'I'm keeping an open mind about that. What I do think is that last night's incident is related to all the others. If we solve one of the crimes, we will effectively be solving them all. The same person is behind them. Who knows? Her name may even be Kitty Lavender.'

'You did say that a woman might help to unravel this mystery.'

'I still hold to that view,' said Colbeck. 'In fact, we may find that we get help from more than one woman.'

Having packed the food into his satchel, Madeleine handed it to her father. Caleb Andrews thanked her with a kiss then slung the satchel from his shoulder. He was just about to leave the house to go to work.

'You'll have to make your own lunch tomorrow,' she warned.

'Why?'

'Robert is taking me to Epsom.'

'Then you'll be able to see your father making

money,' he said chirpily. 'I picked out the winner.'

'Which horse did you bet on – Princess of Fire?'

'I was going to bet on her but I remembered that colts always win the Derby so I've gone for Aleppo instead at 12–1. I read in my newspaper that he's the most likely to upset the favourites in the race. Help me tomorrow and shout for Aleppo.'

'Whoever I shout for, my voice won't be heard in that crowd. Oh, I'm so excited, Father. I just can't wait to get there.'

'You'll enjoy every minute of it, Maddy.'

'It's such a wonderful present for me.'

'I'm glad to see that Inspector Colbeck is treating you in the way you deserve. The only time you've ever been to Epsom was years ago when you were a baby and your mother and I took you on Derby Day.' He tapped his chest and chortled. 'I backed the winner then as well. I bought you a new rattle out of my winnings.'

Madeleine giggled. 'I won't need one of those this year,' she said. 'According to Robert, Aleppo might be a wise choice.'

'Why?'

'The three horses ahead of him in the betting are the ones that have been having trouble. There have been attempts to kill two of them and to bribe the jockey riding the third. Robert says he'll be grateful if he can get Odysseus, Merry Legs and Limerick Lad to the starting post.'

'Is he anywhere nearer making an arrest yet?'

'He thinks so.'

'I've told him before, Maddy – the killer is a jealous husband.'

'You're wrong about that, Father,' she said. 'The victim was a young Irish groom who was walking out with a barmaid called Bonny Rimmer. They worshipped each other. John Feeny would never have looked at another woman, certainly not at someone's wife in Crewe.'

'That's where the inspector should be continuing his search.'

'The murder has nothing to do with Crewe. Feeny probably had no idea where the place is. Everything that Robert has discovered so far is connected with the Derby. The answers lie there.'

'I'll believe that when I see the proof. But I wish I was going with you tomorrow,' he said enviously. 'I'm probably the only person in London who won't be there.'

'When will you learn the result?'

'When I get back to Euston.'

'How?'

'Carrier pigeons will bring the result to London and it will be posted up in various places. Next day, I'll collect my winnings.'

'From where?' she asked. 'I thought the only betting that was allowed was on the course itself.'

Andrews cackled. 'Some rules are made to be flouted.'

'Do you mean that that you've deliberately broken the law?'

'I've just bent it a little, that's all – like everyone else.'

'What will Robert say if he knew that my father was a criminal?' she teased. 'If you break a law, it's his duty to arrest you.'

'Then he'll have to arrest thousands of other

people as well, Maddy. A stupid law won't stop us putting money on the Derby. It's every Englishman's right to have a bet.'

'Time to go,' she said, glancing at the clock on the mantelpiece. 'I'll come part of the way with you, Father. I need to go to the market.'

He put a hand to his wallet. 'Do you have enough money?'

'Plenty, thank you.'

Madeleine went into the kitchen to collect a large wicker basket then they left the house together and strolled along the street.

'Who was that woman you mentioned earlier?' he said.

'Bonny Rimmer? She was Feeny's sweetheart.'

'And you've met her?'

'We went to church together last Sunday.'

'Is that where you and Inspector Colbeck were?' he said. 'When he took you off in that trap, I was bound to wonder. What's so special about this girl, Maddy?'

'Robert thinks she'll help us solve the murder.'

'What do *you* think?'

'I was very hopeful at first,' she said, 'but not any more. If she was going to come forward, she'd have done so by now. To be honest, I don't believe we'll ever see Bonny Rimmer again.'

As soon as he noticed the two detectives coming into the crowded betting room, Hamilton Fido got up from his table and let his assistant take over. Crossing the room, he gave Robert Colbeck and Victor Leeming a cordial greeting and a warm handshake.

'You seem in good spirits this morning, sir,' noted Colbeck.

'I'm always in good spirits, Inspector,' said Fido. 'The Derby gets closer and closer and the money keeps rolling in.'

'Some of it will have to be repaid.'

'Not if it's been wagered on Odysseus or Limerick Lad.'

'I see that the odds have shifted slightly, sir,' said Leeming. 'Your horse is now only 6–1.'

'Are you tempted, Sergeant?'

'Very tempted.'

'But we're not here to place any bets at the moment,' said Colbeck briskly. 'Is there somewhere a little quieter where we might talk to you, Mr Fido?'

'Of course,' said the bookmaker. 'Follow me.'

He took them through a door, along a passageway and into a room that was used for storage. Fido was dressed more ostentatiously than ever and there was even more of a swagger about him.

'How can I help you, gentlemen?' he said obligingly.

Colbeck was direct. 'Tell us how to find Miss Kitty Lavender.'

'Kitty?'

'She is the young lady with whom you stayed at the Wyvern Hotel, is she not? There's no point in prevarication. My information comes from an unimpeachable source.'

'Lord Hendry, no doubt!'

'He was as unwilling as you to divulge her name at first, Mr Fido, even though he'd once tried to pass her off as Lady Hendry. The turn of events forced him to change his mind.'

'What events?'

'I'll tell you that in a moment, sir. First, we'd like to know how we can make contact with Miss Lavender.'

'I'm sorry, Inspector Colbeck,' said Fido, trying to protect her until she was ready to come forward. 'I'm not sure where Kitty is.'

'We assumed that she'd be with you,' said Leeming.

'There are no women bookmakers, Sergeant.'

'*Staying* with you, Mr Fido.'

'I forego such delights during Derby Week,' said the other with a grin. 'A man in my position can afford no distractions whatsoever at such a busy time, however pleasurable they might be. No matter – I'm consoled by the fact that self-denial is good for the soul but, then,' he added with a wicked smile, 'I don't suppose that you believe we bookmakers *have* souls, do you?'

'Let's talk about Kitty Lavender,' said Colbeck. 'It seems highly unlikely that she would want to miss the excitement of Derby Week. Do you happen to know if the young lady is here?'

'I've not set eyes on her, Inspector.'

'I understood you were on close terms.'

'By the grace of God, we are.'

'I'm not sure that God would approve of the attachment, Mr Fido,' said Leeming, irritated by the glib reference to the Almighty. 'Your union has not been blessed in His sight.'

'That doesn't prevent either of us from enjoying it, Sergeant.'

'It would prevent me, sir.'

'I'll mention that to Kitty when I see her.'

'And when will that be?' asked Colbeck.

'When this week is over, Inspector.'

'Not before?'

'Only if we should chance to meet.'

'Where are you lodging at the moment?'

'In my own home,' replied Fido. 'My coachman drives me back to London every evening and gets me here early in the morning.'

'Would it not be more sensible to stay near Epsom?'

'Accommodation is almost impossible to find.'

'Do you know if Miss Lavender found any?'

'I've no idea.'

'You seem singularly uninformed about her movements, sir.'

'Kitty is a friend,' said the bookmaker, 'and a rather special friend at that. Yet I don't keep her on a leash. Kitty likes her freedom. She comes in and out of my life at will.'

'I don't think that anyone would be allowed to do that somehow,' said Colbeck levelly. 'You're a man who prefers to exercise control. We saw that in the sad case of Peter Cheggin and the same rule no doubt obtains with Miss Lavender. You never fit into anyone else's plans, Mr Fido – they fit into yours.'

'You're getting to know me too well, Inspector.'

'Well enough, sir.'

'What this about Lord Hendry and the turn of events?'

'His house was broken into last night,' said Colbeck. 'His portrait of Odysseus was stolen.'

Fido laughed harshly. 'He was less amused by the

289

crime. We saw the painting. It was an outstanding piece of portraiture.'

'What use is the portrait of a losing horse?'

'Odysseus has not lost the race yet, sir, and Merry Legs has not won it. May I ask if you were aware that the painting existed?'

'I was, Inspector.'

'How did you come to know about it?'

'Kitty mentioned it to me. She heard about it from Lord Hendry himself. He was inordinately proud of it.' He looked from one to the other and saw their stern expressions. 'Ah – so that's why you've come to see me, is it? Lord Hendry has accused me of arranging the theft. Or perhaps he thinks I broke into the house myself.'

'No,' said Colbeck, 'that's not the allegation he made.'

'Then what is he alleging?'

'He feels that Miss Lavender was involved in some way.'

'Kitty?' Putting back his head, Fido laughed aloud. 'What would she want with the painting of a horse?'

'To cause Lord Hendry pain and embarrassment.'

Fido became serious. 'She's every right to do that, Inspector, and I'd back her to the hilt when she did so. But she's no thief – nor would she know where to find one skilful enough to get in and out of the house without being caught.'

'Would *you* know where to find one, sir?' asked Leeming.

'I know where to find whatever I want, Sergeant.'

'So you could have advised Miss Lavender.'

'The only advice I gave to Kitty was that she should speak to you. When she's done that, and when you realise that she's had nothing to do with any of the crimes committed, you might stop pestering the two of us.'

'You were glad enough of our help when someone tried to poison your horse,' said Colbeck.

'In times of trouble, I always turn to the law, Inspector.'

'That's what Lord Hendry has done.'

'Well, you can tell him to stop looking in my direction,' said Fido irritably. 'I didn't steal his painting and nor did Kitty. You ought to be talking to Brian Dowd. He has good reason to upset Lord Hendry. So do lots of other people, for that matter. Lord George Hendry is not the most popular man in horseracing.'

'We've learnt that, sir,' said Colbeck. 'Well, you must get back to the betting office. But if Miss Lavender *should* cross your path...'

'I'll be sure to point her in your direction, Inspector.'

'Thank you.'

Fido gave them a smile of farewell before hurrying off down the passageway. Colbeck rubbed a hand across his chin and reflected on the conversation with the bookmaker. Leeming was terse.

'He's a liar.'

'I don't think Mr Fido has ever been acquainted with the truth.'

'My guess is that Kitty Lavender travels back to his house with him every evening. A man like that just has to wear the trappings of success and the

291

lady is one of them.'

'Granted,' said Colbeck, 'but I don't accept that he lives at home during Derby Week. It would be absurd to travel back and forth to London when the roads are so congested. He'll have found a hotel or lodgings close to the racecourse. Find out where it is, Victor.'

'How, sir?'

'By following him when he leaves at the end of the day. With luck, Hamilton Fido will lead you all the way to Kitty Lavender.'

'May I say how ravishing you look, Kitty?' he remarked, appraising her with beaming approval. 'At times like this, I begin to wish that we were not related.'

'Whereas I'm grateful that we are,' she said.

'I thought I was your beau for the day.'

'You are, Marcus.'

'Then we must look as if we're together,' said Marcus Johnson. 'Not as children of the same mother but as man and mistress.'

'Why not husband and wife?'

He brayed at her. 'Neither of us could manage that deception with any degree of success. It's far too much to ask. Even when I was married, I never contrived to *look* like a husband and your blend of beauty and voluptuousness would rarely be found in a wife.'

He had come to pick her up from the house to take her to the racecourse. Kitty Lavender had, as usual, taken great pains with her appearance, wearing a dress of light blue shot silk with pagoda sleeves and a hooped skirt with several flounces.

To complement the dress, she had chosen a round hat of leghorn straw, trimmed with flowers at the front and a large blue velvet bow at the back. Marcus Johnson wore a well-cut frock coat, fawn trousers and a purple cravat. As she took a final look in the mirror, he put on his top hat.

'What a handsome couple we make!' he declared, looking over her shoulder. 'If he could see us now, Hamilton would be green with jealousy.'

'He won't be jealous of my half-brother.'

'What a pity! I love exciting envy.'

'How did you first come to know him?' she asked.

'I met him at Newmarket when I placed some bets with him. I was staying with friends near Cambridge at the time and I got Hamilton invited back for a night at the card table. He was impressed that I moved so freely among the aristocracy.'

'Did he win at cards?'

'Yes, Kitty,' he replied, 'but only modestly. He played like the bookmaker he is and hedged his bets. Had he been bolder and more venturesome, he would have won far more.'

'Were you bold and venturesome?'

'Of course – but, as it happens, I lost.'

'That's nothing new,' she said, turning to look at him. 'Yet you've had successes at the card table as well, I have to admit that.'

'Good fortune comes in waves. I'm riding one at the moment.'

'So am I, Marcus – thanks to you.'

'Hamilton Fido seemed the obvious choice for you, Kitty,' he said, 'and you were in need of some adventure after wasting your favours on Lord Hendry.'

'I regret ever meeting George now though there were some good times at the start. And like you, I do have a weakness for hobnobbing with the nobility. For that reason,' she said, 'I was prepared to endure some of George's obvious defects.'

'Too old, too ugly, too mean-spirited.'

'And far too married.'

'Why does his wife put up with the old rake?'

'The wonder is that *I* endured him for so long,' said Kitty with rancour. 'My prospects have improved in every way since I met Hamilton. He's ten times the man that George ever was.'

They left the house and climbed into the waiting cab. As it set off, Kitty adjusted her dress and tried to ignore the dull ache in her temple. Days after she had received it, the bruise caused by the slash of a cane reminded her that it had not yet healed.

'Hamilton keeps on at me about Inspector Colbeck,' she said.

'Why?'

'Because the inspector is determined to speak to me.'

'You know my advice, Kitty,' he said. 'It was bad enough having your hatbox turn up in the middle of a murder investigation. Do you want to make it worse by facing the press? That's what will happen if you cooperate with the police.'

'Hamilton said that Inspector Colbeck is very discreet.'

'He has reporters watching his every move. The moment you talk to him, someone will release your name to the newspapers and that could well bring some adverse publicity. You and I are twilight creatures, Kitty. We operate best in the half-dark of anonymity. If names and descriptions of us appear in newspapers, they could be read by people we are anxious to avoid.'

'There are several of those in my life,' she said, rolling her eyes, 'and I daresay you've left a trail of disappointed ladies in your wake.'

'I have,' he said. 'All the way from Paris to Perth.'

'What were you doing in Perth?'

'I had a brief dalliance with a countess.'

Kitty laughed. 'You are incorrigible, Marcus!'

'That makes two of us. We both have a ruthless streak. But you can rid your mind of Inspector Colbeck,' he went on. 'He won't be able to find you in a month of Sundays. When the murder is eventually solved, your unfortunate connection to it will be soon forgotten.'

When she returned from the market, Madeleine Andrews did her household chores then spent the rest of the time working at her easel. It was late afternoon before she had a visitor. Having given up all hope of seeing Bonny Rimmer again, her spirits soared when she heard a tentative knock on the front door. She opened it at once and saw the girl standing there, nervous, frightened and overawed.

'I'm sorry,' said Bonny. 'I was lost.'

'You got here and that's the main thing. Come on in.'

The barmaid stepped into the house and looked

around. The living room was small but it was larger and more comfortable than the bare room that Bonny occupied at the Shepherd and Shepherdess. The place was neat and tidy. Everything had been recently polished. She stared at the painting of a locomotive on the wall.

'It's the Lord of the Isles,' explained Madeleine.

'Oh, I see.'

'It was on display at the Great Exhibition and a friend kindly bought this for me.' She was about to mention that the friend was actually Robert Colbeck but she thought better of it. 'I have a keen interest in railways. My father's an engine driver and I like to draw locomotives.'

She indicated the easel near the window. Bonny went across to inspect the drawing and stood back in amazement. She shook her head in disbelief.

'*You* did this, Miss Andrews?' she said.

'Yes.'

'It's so clever. I could never do anything like that.'

'I didn't know that I could until I tried.'

Seeing how anxious her visitor was, Madeleine took her into the kitchen and made a pot of tea. When she had taken a few sips from her cup, Bonny Rimmer slowly began to relax. Coming to London for the first time was an unsettling experience for a country girl. The size and speed of everything was terrifying to her, and she felt as if she had stumbled into a foreign country. Madeleine tried to reassure her.

'I'll walk you to the station afterwards,' she said.

'Thank you, Miss Andrews – getting here was a

real trial.'

'London can be overpowering for all of us sometimes.'

'It scares me.'

'Did you bring anything with you?'

'Oh, yes,' said Bonny, putting down her cup to open her handbag. 'There's not much, I'm afraid.' She took out a handful of items and put them on the table. 'John asked me to look after these letters from his friend because he couldn't read.' A forlorn smile brushed her lips. 'I was going to teach him.'

Madeleine looked at the meagre legacy of John Feeny. Apart from the letters, a few trinkets bought for Bonny and a rabbit's foot he had given her for luck, the only thing there was a short note, written by Brian Dowd, confirming that Feeny had been taken on his payroll.

'He was so proud to get that job,' said Bonny. 'Dozens of lads wanted to work at Mr Dowd's stables but John was the one he chose. It was hard work but he liked it there – at first. He had dreams of riding in Mr Dowd's colours and winning big races.'

'It was not to be.'

'No, Miss Andrews.'

'But he lasted a couple of years,' said Madeleine, seeing the date at the top of the paper. 'Since he fell out with Mr Dowd, I'm surprised he kept this record of working there.'

'He needed the address so that he could write to Jerry Doyle.' Bonny gave a shy smile. 'Or get someone else to write for him.'

'I'm surprised the note was not damaged when

he swam ashore.'

'John was not stupid. He knew he might get wet on the voyage so he wrapped everything he had in a piece of oilskin. That includes this,' she said, holding up a misshapen gold ring. 'It belonged to John's mother. He wanted me to take care of it until the day I could wear it as Mrs Feeny.' Bonny slipped it on the appropriate finger. 'You see, Miss Andrews? It fits.'

Madeleine was disappointed. She could see nothing there that would be of any use to Colbeck but she decided to hold on to some of it nevertheless. Bonny was quite happy to leave the letters and the note behind as long as she could take the wedding ring and the trinkets with her. They were her only mementoes of the young man she had loved. Madeleine thanked her.

'When Inspector Colbeck has looked at these other items,' she said, 'I'll make sure that you get them back.'

'Will they be any use?'

'That's for the inspector to decide.'

'You like him, don't you?' said Bonny.

'Well, yes,' replied Madeleine, caught unawares by the bluntness of the question. 'I suppose that I do.'

'I can hear it in your voice when you say his name.'

'He's been very kind to us.'

Madeleine gave her a brief account of how Robert Colbeck had come into her life and how he had solved the series of crimes that started with a train robbery in which Caleb Andrews was badly injured. Bonny listened with fascination.

'Does that mean he'll be able to catch John's killer?' she said.

'I have no doubt about it.'

'What will happen to him?'

'He'll be hanged.'

'I wish I was there to see it,' said Bonny with unexpected anger. 'He deserves terrible pain for what he did to John. I hate him. He'll roast in Hell for this crime.'

Madeleine was surprised by the outburst from such a placid girl but she understood the strain that Bonny Rimmer must be under. As they drank their tea, she moved the conversation to more neutral topics and her visitor calmed down. Before they left, however, Madeleine returned to the subject that had brought them together.

'You told me that John had no enemies.'

'None to speak of,' said Bonny. 'He always got on with people.'

'He didn't get on with Mr Dowd.'

'That was because he ran out of patience. Mr Dowd made all sorts of promises to him about how he'd be a champion jockey one day but they were just lies. He never let him ride in a single race and John realised that he never would.'

'Was that when they had their argument?'

'Yes,' said the other. 'John used bad language to Mr Dowd and that was that. He was thrown out of the stables without any pay. You know the rest, Miss Andrews.'

'I can see why John was so grateful to meet a friend like you,' said Madeleine. 'For the first time in his life, he had something to look forward to.'

'Oh, he did. John didn't just want to prove to everyone that he could be a good jockey. He wanted to beat Mr Dowd's horses in every race he could. That's what kept him going,' said Bonny. 'He told me that he'd never be really happy until he could get his own back on Mr Dowd. It was like a mission.'

Brian Dowd had had a more than satisfactory day at the races, One of his horses had come second in the opening race and Quicklime, as he had predicted, won the last race on the card. Wearing a frock coat and top hat, he sat among the privileged spectators in the grandstand and relished his position. Lord Hendry, by contrast, had had a miserable afternoon. All of his bets were misplaced, especially the one on his own horse, Darius, in the final race. After a promising start, the animal had pulled up lame three furlongs from home. It was irksome. As he made for the exit, the last person he wanted to encounter was the smirking Irishman.

'It was a rehearsal for tomorrow,' said Dowd.

'What was?'

'That last race – my horse winning by a mile from yours.'

'Darius went lame,' said Lord Hendry.

'A sure sign of lack of fitness – he was badly trained.'

'I need no advice from you about training horses, Dowd.'

'Apparently, you do,' taunted Dowd. 'You can't even train Odysseus to stay on your wall. He galloped off somewhere, I hear.'

'Who told you that?' snarled Lord Hendry.

'You'd be surprised what I get to hear. The rumour is that the painting was stolen in the night. True or false?'

'You ought to know the answer to that.'

'Why?'

'Because it's just the kind of thing you'd do. When you failed to cripple Odysseus in his travelling box, you paid someone to steal that portrait of him instead. It's typical of your low Irish cunning.'

'I wondered how long it would be before you started abusing my country,' said Dowd cheerfully. 'You English are so ungrateful. We dig your canals for you, we build your railways and we show you how to train racehorses properly yet you still sneer at us.'

'Do you have my painting?' demanded Lord Hendry.

'I wouldn't touch it with a barge pole.'

'Do you know where it is?'

'No, Lord Hendry, and, quite frankly, I don't care. The only horse that interests me at the moment is Limerick Lad. When he runs in the Derby tomorrow, you'll see why.'

Dowd walked away before the other man could speak. Lord Hendry muttered a few obscenities under his breath then joined the queue at the exit. His first thought had been that Hamilton Fido was behind the theft of the painting but he now felt that Dowd was a likely suspect as well. He believed that the Irishman had deliberately sought him out to gloat over the loss of the portrait. Lord Hendry decided to report that fact

301

to Robert Colbeck.

Before he could do that, another shock awaited him. As he left the grandstand, an official walked across to him and handed Lord Hendry a letter.

'This was left for you in the office, my lord,' he said.

'By whom?'

'I've no idea. It just appeared.'

Without even thanking the man, Lord Hendry tore open the envelope. His blood froze as he read the single sentence inside.

'Your painting will be returned for £3000.'

Victor Leeming was smiling complacently. Having taken Brian Dowd's advice, he had bet on Quicklime and won himself over twenty pounds. He planned to spend it on gifts for his wife and children but, before he could decide what they would be, he saw that Hamilton Fido was about to leave at last. There had been no point in watching the man while he was in the betting room. Leeming waited until all the races had been run and all bets paid off. Then he lurked behind a coach and waited for the bookmaker to appear. Fido came out with a group of acquaintances but they soon dispersed.

Leeming trailed his man from a reasonable distance, close enough to keep him in sight but far enough behind him to eliminate any risk of being seen by Fido if he suddenly turned round. The thick crowd was both a hazard and help, impeding his progress yet offering him a welcome screen should he need it. The bookmaker seemed to be heading for a line of cabs that stood waiting for business. Leeming was pleased. Once Fido had taken a cab, he could easily be followed in a second one.

As the crowd began to thin out, Leeming got a better view of his quarry. He saw him go to the front of the queue and talk to a cab driver. Before Fido got into the vehicle, a young woman in a light-blue silk dress and straw hat approached him. From the effusive welcome she was given, he surmised that she must be Kitty Lavender. He was thrilled with his discovery but his pursuit came to an abrupt end. Intent on trailing someone else, he did not realise that he had also been followed. Leeming's hat was knocked off from behind and he felt a sharp blow on the back of his skull. At the moment that the cab was drawing away, Leeming was plunging into unconsciousness.

'What is it like? Did you see any races? Was there anybody famous there today? What time do we leave tomorrow? From where will we watch the Derby?'

Robert Colbeck was met with such a battery of questions that it was minutes before he was able to claim a kiss of welcome. When he got to the house late that evening, Madeleine Andrews was in a state of anticipatory delight. The joy of being able to see the Derby was compounded by the pleasure of being at the racecourse with Colbeck. As the questions continued to come, he held up a hand.

'That's enough, Madeleine,' he said. 'When you get to Epsom tomorrow, you'll be able to see for yourself what it's like. But you must bear in mind that it's not merely an excursion for me. While you are watching the races, I'll still be looking for John Feeny's killer.'

'Will he be there?'

'Oh, I think so. The Derby was supposed to be the culmination of his criminal acts. Even though some of those acts were frustrated, I don't believe he'd dare to miss the event.' He was saddened. 'I see that Bonny Rimmer did not, after all, turn up.'

'Oh, but she did,' said Madeleine. 'How silly of me! All I could think about was myself. Yes, she did come, Robert.'

'Did she tell you anything of interest?'

'I think so.'

'Did she bring anything? The girl talked about keepsakes.'

'Those were gifts that John Feeny bought her and the wedding ring that had belonged to his mother. Apart from that, all she had were a few letters from that friend of Feeny's in Ireland.'

'Jerry Doyle?'

'Yes,' said Madeleine, opening the drawer of the sideboard. 'I asked if I could show them to you but they won't be of any real use. The writing is spidery and there's just gossip about the stables.' She took out the items and handed them over. 'See for yourself, Robert.'

'Thank you,' he said. He read the note. 'What's this?'

'Something that Mr Dowd gave to him when he started there,' she replied. 'It was proof that he'd worked at one of the leading Irish stables and he wanted to hang on to that. It was a form of certificate.'

Colbeck scrutinised the note. 'Dowd wrote this himself?'

'Yes, Robert.'

'Are you certain of that?'

'That's what Bonny told me,' she said. 'I had such hopes that she might bring something that turned out to be valuable evidence but she didn't – just two badly written letters and that short note.'

'Come here,' he said, taking her in his arms.

'Why?'

'Because I want to give you a kiss.'

'Yes, please,' she said, responding warmly then looking up at him in surprise. 'What made you want to do that, Robert?'

'This is much more than mere a note,' he said, waving it triumphantly in the air. 'It's a confession.'

CHAPTER TWELVE

The pilgrimage began at dawn. Derby Day was an unpaid holiday, a joyous release from the workaday world, a national celebration, a glorious opportunity for revelry. People descended on the racecourse from all directions. The road from London to Epsom was a scene of amiable chaos as tens of thousands made the journey on foot, on horseback or seated in an astonishing array of horse-drawn vehicles, ranging from the meanest donkey-cart to the finest carriage. The journey was as much a part of the carnival as the races and it produced all the excesses of which human beings were capable.

There was constant beer-swilling, gourmandising, cheering, jeering, good-humoured fighting, whirlwind flirtation, raucous singing and general ribaldry. The long trek was also punctuated by accidents, arguments and the inevitable collapse of overloaded carts or coaches. Musical instruments of all kinds added to the continuous din and self-appointed entertainers displayed their talents whether invited to do so or not. The endless procession was a thing of wonder in itself, watched by crowds who could not go to the Derby but who nevertheless wanted to be part of an unique annual experience.

On the following day, newspapers would give accounts of the journey to Epsom as well as of the races themselves and reporters were busy collecting anecdotes or noting incidents along the way. In the shared joy of travel, there was enough material for a three-volume novel let alone for a column in a newspaper. Any hideous injuries incurred *en route* were always worth a mention and an overturned carriage would merit a whole paragraph. High drama marked every mile of the excursion. Wherever one looked, raw emotion was on display as racegoers merrily flung off the conventions of civilised behaviour and gave vent to their true feelings. Derby Day was a positive riot of uncontrolled human aspiration.

Edward Tallis was at once shocked and mesmerised by it all, aghast at the air of wild abandon yet unable to take his eyes off it. Seated in a cab beside Victor Leeming, he found new reasons to issue arrest warrants at every turn.

'Look at those delinquents throwing stones at each other,' he said, pointing an index finger. 'They should be taken into custody. So should that woman on top of the beer cart – she's virtually naked! We can't have females disporting themselves in public like that.'

'Everything is tolerated on Derby Day, sir,' said Leeming.

'Not by me.'

'People want some fun.'

'That's permissible,' said Tallis, 'as long as it stays within the bounds of decency and the embrace of the law.'

From the moment they set out from London, the superintendent had regretted his decision to travel by cab. He had simply not realised how slow their progress would be or how beset by what he saw as rampant criminality. When a fat old lady hopped nimbly off a cart, lifting her skirt and spreading her legs to urinate, Tallis winced in disgust. Leeming, however, was savouring it all. Though he was obliged to travel with his superior and endure his ceaseless moaning, he was in relative comfort and spared a journey by rail that he would have hated. A bandage encircled his head but it was hidden beneath his hat. The cab came to a sudden halt.

'What's happening now?' asked Tallis.

'There's a toll-gate ahead, sir,' said Leeming.

'We are from Scotland Yard – we should be waved through.'

'We'd have to get there first and, as you see, we're hemmed in on all sides. We just have to wait in the queue.'

'I want to get to Epsom.'

'Be patient, sir. They sometimes have a brawl or two at toll-gates and that always holds us up.'

'Brawling in public? That must be stopped.'

'Then you'll need to speak to the owners of the toll roads,' said Leeming, 'for that's the root of the problem. Whenever Derby Week comes round, they always put up the prices to make large profits. Somebody refuses to pay and a scuffle takes place.' The cab jerked forward. 'Ah, we're on the move again.'

They soon drew level with members of a brass band, marching in ragged formation and playing ear-splitting melodies that were hopelessly out of tune. The remorseless pounding of the bass drum made Tallis quake.

'How long will the pandemonium last?' he cried.

'You may find it's even noisier when we get there, sir.'

'Nothing can be worse than this!'

'They say there'll be upwards of sixty thousand people on the Downs this afternoon. That means a real uproar. Don't worry, sir. You'll get used to it after a while.'

'Never – this is purgatory!'

Edward Tallis was not all bluster and protest. When Leeming had reported the attack on him at the racecourse, the superintendent had been sympathetic and suggested that they travel to Epsom together so that Leeming would be spared the violent jostling at the railway station. Tallis shot his companion a look of concern.

'How does your head feel now, Sergeant?'

'It still aches a bit,' admitted Leeming, removing his hat to put a tender hand to the back of his skull. 'Yesterday it was agony.'

'I can well believe that.'

'When I regained consciousness, I thought at first I'd been the victim of a robbery but nothing had been stolen. I was knocked out to stop me following Hamilton Fido.'

'We'll have that rogue behind bars before the day is out.'

'It will be very difficult to prove, sir,' said Leeming. 'There were plenty of witnesses and they gave me a description of my attacker before he vanished into the crowd. All in vain, I fear. He'll probably never be seen on the course again so there's no way to link him to Mr Fido.'

'We'll find a way,' said Tallis dourly. 'I'm not having my men assaulted in broad daylight. Besides, the bookmaker lied to you and to Inspector Colbeck. Misleading the police is something of which I take a very dim view. Fido swore that he had no communication with Kitty Lavender yet you saw them embracing.'

'I saw a woman I *assumed* was Miss Lavender, sir, but I could be wrong. Mr Fido is on familiar terms with many young ladies. We'll have to ask him who that particular one was.'

'Do you believe that he'll give us a truthful answer?'

'No, Superintendent.'

'Nor me – an honest bookmaker is a contradiction in terms. But we won't be deterred by that fact,' said Tallis. 'We'll demand answers.'

'What about Inspector Colbeck, sir?'

'The inspector has another quarry in sight. He left a note on my desk to that effect because he knew that I would call in at my office before I set out this morning. He claims to have made a significant advance,' he went on. 'I look forward to hearing what it is.'

Special trains were intended to relieve the congestion on the road and get large numbers of people from London to Epsom much faster than any horse-drawn transport. Accordingly, thousands flocked to the railway station and boarded the succession of trains. Robert Colbeck and Madeleine Andrews were on one of the earliest to depart. Squashed together in a first-class carriage, both of them enjoyed the close proximity and thought how privileged they were compared to the masses in third class who were crammed into open-topped carriages.

Not that anyone complained about the crush. A festive spirit informed the whole journey. As well as singing, storytelling and jollity, there was feverish speculation about the result of the Derby. The train sped through the morning sunshine with a cargo of happiness and high expectation. Colbeck and Madeleine were caught up in the general exhilaration, their pleasure heightened by the fact that they were seated deliciously close to each other. It was easy to forget that they were in pursuit of a callous murderer.

When they reached Epsom Station, a human wave burst out of the train and swept across the platform. Borne along by the surge, Colbeck and Madeleine gradually eased their way to the back. It was almost possible to talk at last without having to shout above the continuous hullabaloo.

'Are you sorry that you came?' asked Colbeck.

'No,' she replied. 'It's wonderful!'

'So you didn't mind having to get up so early?'

'I'm used to that, Robert.'

'When we get to the racecourse,' he warned, 'I'll have to leave you for a while. As you know, this is not only a social event for me.'

'I can look after myself,' she said.

'You deserve to enjoy the fun of the fair, Madeleine. What you did has been of immense value to me.'

'Talking to Bonny Rimmer was no effort.'

'By winning her confidence, you gained information that would always have been beyond me.

I now have a truer picture of the relationship between John Feeny and his former employer. You helped the girl cope in her bereavement as well,' he said, 'and that was important. You provided succour.'

'I wish I could have done more, Robert. When she came to the house yesterday, she looked so lonely and pitiful. The effort of getting to London had really taxed her.'

'It was kind of you to take her back to the station.'

'I'm glad she didn't have to catch a special train like the one we just travelled on,' said Madeleine with a smile. 'Bonny would never have survived that. She was too fragile.'

'Her journey was not in vain. That may give her consolation.'

'Do you really think you can make an arrest today?'

'I'm certain of it,' he said confidently. 'In fact, I intend to make more than one arrest. I just hope that I can do it before the Derby is run. Having been so close to the race and to some of the people involved in it, I'd hate to miss seeing it.'

'I did warn you that Inspector Colbeck would never give up,' said Hamilton Fido. 'You saw what happened yesterday.'

'We were not seen together,' said Kitty Lavender.

'We might have been. If I had not had a bodyguard in the right place, we could have been followed all the way back here.'

'But we weren't, Hamilton.'

'Only because my man knew what to do,' he said. 'Assaulting a policeman is a dangerous game, Kitty. It's like poking a stick in a beehive – there'll be a whole swarm of them buzzing around Epsom today as a result. Why don't you stop hiding?'

Dressed to leave, they were in the bedroom that they were sharing during Derby Week. Kitty was wearing more jewellery than she had done on previous visits to the course and she stopped to examine her diamond necklace in the mirror. Fido grinned.

'That's the difference between Lord Hendry and me,' he said, kissing the nape of the neck. 'He buys you a hat and a hatbox – I give you jewellery.'

'In fairness to George, he did promise to buy me a diamond brooch when his horse won the Derby.'

'When or if?'

'There was no doubt in his mind.'

'How much money has he laid out on the race?'

'A lot, Hamilton,' she said. 'He's risking everything on it.'

'Then he's a bigger fool than I thought.'

'His wife has money but she won't lend him any to fritter away on what she considers to be a pointless sport. It always maddened George that she would make large donations to worthy causes while ignoring him. He's had to raise funds from elsewhere.'

'Loans from friends?'

'He's been forced to mortgage some of his property.'

'What happens if Odysseus loses?'

'George will be finished,' she said with satisfaction.

'In that case, I'll be doing him a favour by killing him in a duel. It will put him out of his misery.'

'Must you go ahead with it, Hamilton?'

'I can't pull out of it now,' he said. 'That would be cowardice.'

'I still feel that George may resort to a trick of some kind.'

'I'll be ready for him, Kitty.'

'I don't want you harmed in any way,' she said, stroking his cheek. 'I couldn't bear to lose you.'

'Lord Hendry poses no danger to me,' he said smugly. 'I'm a bookmaker, remember, and I create enemies without even trying. Over the years, disaffected customers have threatened me with all manner of gruesome deaths. Yet I'm still here,' he boasted. 'Doesn't that tell you something?'

'Yes – you take wise precautions.'

'I also have a sixth sense. I knew that Sergeant Leeming was going to trail me. He came into the betting room once too often and kept glancing in my direction. That's why I gave the signal to one of my bodyguards. Of course,' he went on, 'none of this would have been necessary if you had spoken to Inspector Colbeck. Because of you, his sergeant ended up with a throbbing headache.'

'I don't like getting involved with the police, Hamilton.'

'You have no choice.'

'Marcus warned me against it.'

'It's your decision, Kitty – not his.'

'I know.'

'How much longer do you want to hold back?'

She turned away and walked to the window, gazing sightlessly through the glass. Deep in thought, she stood there for minutes and wrestled with the competing arguments. Fido waited patiently. At length, she turned back to him with a resigned smile.

'I'll speak to Inspector Colbeck today,' she said.

'Thank goodness for that!'

'But only *after* the race,' she stipulated. 'I'll not let anyone distract me from that. It's the reason I got up so early. I want to enjoy every minute of Derby Day and watch Odysseus getting beaten by Merry Legs. Then – and only then – I'll be ready for Inspector Colbeck.'

Although he knew how capable and independent she was, Robert Colbeck did not want Madeleine Andrews to wander about the Downs on her own. There were too many thieves, confidence tricksters and drunken men about, ready to pounce on an unaccompanied female. Since she was keen to see the acrobats performing, Colbeck assigned a uniformed policeman to be her guide. While she set out with the burly constable, Colbeck went off in search of Brian Dowd.

To get to the stables where Limerick Lad was being kept, he had to find his way through a labyrinth. Broughams, barouches, carts, gigs, four-wheeled chaises, traps, cabs, covered vans and phaetons were parked close together in positions of vantage. As he passed a stagecoach, Colbeck counted no fewer than eight people perched on its roof as they consumed their picnic. When the races began, the vehicles would form their own grandstand and those still sober enough to see would have an excellent view of one part of the course.

It took him some time to reach the stables but he was rewarded with a sight of Brian Dowd. The trainer was walking across the yard. Seeing his visitor, the Irishman gave him a broad smile.

'Top of the morning to you, Inspector!' he said.

'And to you, sir.'

'Isn't it just a grand day for a Derby?'

'That depends,' said Colbeck.

'More rain last night and a clear sky today,' said Dowd happily. 'Limerick Lad couldn't ask for better conditions. The going will be soft and he'll have the sun on his back.'

'I thought he'd have Tim Maguire on his back – unless, that is, he's been tempted away from you by anonymous offers.'

Dowd frowned. 'Do I hear a cynical note in your voice?'

'You were responsible for putting it there, sir,' said Colbeck. 'When you showed me that letter sent to your jockey, I believed that one of your rivals really was trying to steal him from you. Then this happened to fall into my hands,' he continued, pulling out the note that had been belonged to John Feeny and thrusting it at Dowd. 'The handwriting bears a strange resemblance to that in the letter, as you'll see.' Extracting the missive addressed to Tim Maguire, he handed it over. 'Don't you agree, Mr Dowd?'

Face motionless, the Irishmen compared the

two items. A flicker of irritation showed before he burst into laughter. He reached forward to slap Colbeck companionably on the shoulder.

'You found me out, Inspector. I wrote both of these.'

'In other words, you reported a crime that never existed.'

'But it did exist,' said Dowd. 'You can ask Tim about it. The only difference is that it was made verbally. I thought that if I put it down in writing, you'd take it more seriously.'

'You deliberately misled me, sir,' said Colbeck icily, 'and I take exception to that. You also gave me an incorrect version of what happened when you and John Feeny parted company.'

'It's my word against that of an ignorant barmaid.'

'The girl can read, write and tell the truth.'

'All she's told you are the lies that Feeny spread about me,' said Dowd, spitting out the words. 'Frankly, I'm insulted that you should believe for a moment anything she said.'

'It accords with my own observations, Mr Dowd.'

'Are you questioning my honesty?'

'I'm saying that you're very parsimonious with the truth, sir.'

'I resent that strongly, Inspector!'

'Your resentment is duly noted,' said Colbeck smoothly, 'but it pales beside my own. You wrote a letter purporting to come from an anonymous rival. That was gross deception.'

'I explained that. I needed to secure your attention.'

'You've certainly secured it now.'

'It was done with the best of intentions.'

'What about that story of two men who tried to cudgel Tim Maguire? Did you invent *that* with the best of intentions as well?'

'It was no invention.'

Colbeck raised a sceptical eyebrow. 'Really?'

'Yes,' retorted Dowd. 'And before you accuse me of lying to you, let me remind you that I didn't report that incident to the police. We dealt with it ourselves as we've done with many similar incidents. If you look at my record as a trainer over the past five years, you'll see how successful I've been. That annoys people, especially members of the English aristocracy who can't bear the thought of an upstart Irishman like me beating their expensive racehorses time and again. At Doncaster last year, someone tied a silk handkerchief around the leg of my colt, Dungannon, then hit it with a stick. It's a miracle the leg was not broken. And you don't have to believe me,' he went on, working himself up into a fury. 'The incident was reported in the newspapers. It happens every time we come to England, you see. We're always under siege over here. Well, look at the evidence. If one of the bastards can send me the severed head of a lad I once employed, you can see what I'm against.'

'Other owners have their afflictions as well, Mr Dowd.'

'Who cares about that?'

'Merry Legs might well have been poisoned,' said Colbeck. 'Can't you find an ounce of sympathy for the horse?'

'I've sympathy for every horse, Inspector, especially one that's owned by Hamilton Fido. Anyone who tries to kill an animal that way deserves to have the poison poured down his own throat. I hope you catch the man soon.'

'Can you suggest where I might start looking?'

'You do your job and I'll do mine.'

'Unhappily,' said Colbeck, 'the two overlap so we're sure to see more of each other before the day is out. As for what was, in essence, a forged letter written to deceive the police, I'll have to consult my superintendent about the appropriate action to take. Since he's coming to Epsom today, he may well want to speak to you himself.'

'I'll speak to the whole of the Metropolitan Police Force, if you wish,' volunteered Dowd, 'and you're welcome to issue a fine or lock me up, if need be. I ask only one favour, Inspector – please don't do it before the Derby.'

Having complained bitterly throughout the entire journey, Edward Tallis reserved his severest remonstrations for Epsom itself. The sight of so many people enjoying themselves on the Downs was anathema to him. He viewed the vast panorama of tents, marquees, booths, stalls and handcarts as if they were a communal entrance to Hell.

'Have you ever beheld such sin and degradation?' he said.

'They always have a fairground here, sir,' replied Leeming. 'On a day like this, people expect entertainment.'

'Entertainment! Is that what you call it, Sergeant?'

'Most of it is quite harmless. Who could object to acrobats and fire-eaters and fortune-tellers? And there are dozens of amazing freaks to see, not to mention jugglers, musicians and ballad singers. I know there are pickpockets, thimble-riggers and swindlers here as well,' he conceded, 'but the majority of people are very law-abiding.'

'At the moment, perhaps,' said Tallis darkly, 'but anything can happen when drink is taken. We saw that on the way here. The most upright citizen can be reduced to a babbling imbecile after six pints of beer. By evening, this place will be like Sodom and Gomorrah.'

Leeming stifled a laugh. 'Yes, Superintendent.'

They alighted from the cab and elbowed their way towards the grandstand. All around them, people from every class of society were eating, drinking, smoking, laughing, playing games or engaging in lively banter. They went past mechanics and members of the nobility, trades-men in their best suits, urchins in their rags, noisy shop-boys, boisterous apprentices, wander-ing foreigners, red-cheeked country folk, orange sellers, minstrels, maidservants, baked-potato vendors, porters, dockworkers, watermen, lav-ender girls, gypsies, soldiers, sailors and everyone else who had been drawn to the jamboree.

Victor Leeming thought that the crowd was remarkably even-tempered but Tallis predicted trouble. The superintendent was pleased to see a number of police uniforms dotted around the scene.

'Let's hope our men can enforce a measure of control,' he said.

'They'll make all the difference,' said Leeming.
'What's that?'
'There were no policemen in Sodom and Gomorrah.'
'I can do without your comments, Sergeant.'
'I was simply trying to make a point, sir.'
'Make it elsewhere.'

The curt rebuff reduced Leeming to silence until they reached the betting room. After Tallis had been introduced to Hamilton Fido, they adjourned to the nearby storeroom with the bookmaker.

'I'd appreciate it if this discussion was brief,' said Fido. 'As you know, I'm needed to take bets. My presence is critical.'

'This is not a discussion, sir,' said Tallis, 'but part of a police investigation. I set no time limit on that.' He nudged Leeming who removed his hat to reveal the bandaging. 'Yesterday evening the sergeant was clubbed to the ground while in the act of following you.'

Fido feigned surprise. 'Why should he follow me?'

'I thought you'd lead me to Kitty Lavender,' said Leeming.

'I told you – I've no idea where she is.'

'We didn't accept your assurance, sir.'

'In other words,' said Tallis, resuming control, 'one of my officers was assaulted while in pursuit of you, Mr Fido. We are bound to suspect that the ruffian involved was in your employ.'

'I deny that wholeheartedly!' exclaimed Fido.

'We had a feeling that you would.'

'I had no idea that I was being shadowed by

321

Sergeant Leeming and, if I had, I would certainly not have set someone on to him. I'd have stopped and asked him exactly what it was that he wanted. My policy is to assist the guardians of law and order as much as I can.'

'That statement flies in the face of your reputation.'

'The only reputation I have,' said the book-maker, 'is for honest dealing. That's why I've lasted so long while others have gone to the wall.' He studied Leeming's bandage. 'I'm very sorry that the sergeant was wounded but I must protest at the allegation that I somehow prompted the attack.'

'I know that you employ some pugs, sir,' said Leeming.

'Only as bodyguards.'

'We have a good description of the man who hit me. He was big, brawny and had a broken nose. Two or three witnesses said that he looked like an old boxer.'

'There are plenty of retired boxers roaming the Downs today.'

'We're only concerned with one individual,' said Tallis.

'Do you have him in custody?'

'Not yet.'

'Do you have any idea who he might be?'

'One of your henchmen, Mr Fido.'

'You're welcome to have a list of my employees,' said the other blithely, 'so that you can talk to each of them in turn. I can guarantee you will not find the man you are after because he has no connection whatsoever with me. Sergeant Leeming's injury was caused by a complete stranger.' He flashed a defiant smile. 'Will that be all?'

'No, it will not be all,' said the superintendent tartly.

'I'm required elsewhere, Mr Tallis.'

'You're required here at the moment, sir. I'm not letting you go until we clear up this nonsense about Miss Kitty Lavender. We must see her immediately. Inspector Colbeck believes that she can throw light on the murder that occurred,' he continued, 'and he's tired of your refusal to bring her forward.'

'I've encouraged her to speak to you.'

'Yet she remains inaccessible. Part of the blame for that should lie with you, Mr Fido, which means that you are hindering a murder investigation and are therefore liable to arrest.'

'Your wait is over, Superintendent,' said Fido, holding up both hands to pacify him. 'I give you my solemn word on that. Kitty has finally accepted the wisdom of my advice and consented to speak to the police.'

'Then where is she?'

'And how do you know she's changed her mind,' added Leeming, 'when you claim to be out of touch with her?'

'I'll take those questions in order. Where is she?' he asked. 'I don't rightly know but Kitty is here somewhere and promises faithfully that she will talk to Inspector Colbeck once the Derby is over. How do I know all this?' said Fido. 'I was informed of her change of heart by Marcus Johnson, her half-brother. He, too, is here today.' He pulled out a gold watch and consulted it.

'Time races on, gentlemen,' he noted. 'May I have your permission to leave?'

'No,' said Tallis.

'You're preventing the legitimate exercise of my business.'

'There's nothing legitimate about bookmaking, sir, so let's not pretend there is. What I want to know is this, Mr Fido.' Tallis thrust is face close to him. 'How will Inspector Colbeck be able to find this woman?'

'Kitty will come to me after the race to celebrate.'

'Ah,' Leeming blurted out. 'That's another way of saying that Merry Legs is destined to win. Thank you, Mr Fido. You've given me the hint I was after.' He saw the reproach in the super-intendent's gleaming eyes. 'Not that I'd ever think of betting on the race, of course,' he said sheepishly. 'That would be quite wrong.'

There was only one place where Lord Hendry would be that morning and that is where Robert Colbeck went to find him. The beleaguered owner of Odysseus had called at the stables to see his horse and to be told by the trainer that the acknowledged favourite would win the Derby comfortably. Emotionally and financially, Lord Hendry had invested so much in the race that he dare not even think about the consequences of failure.

Colbeck had seen the portrait of Odysseus and he was thrilled to view him in the flesh as the horse was walked around the yard. The colt looked magnificent. His coat was glistening, his movement fluid and his fitness self-evident. Knowing that his big moment was near, Odysseus pranced eagerly and tossed his head with equine pride. He was ready for action.

'He looks to be in superb condition,' remarked Colbeck as he came to stand beside Lord Hendry. 'You must be delighted.'

'He's the best colt I've ever owned, Inspector,' said the other fondly. 'I bought him as a yearling for two hundred guineas with a Derby contingency of five hundred. Odysseus's first race was at Goodwood where he won the Ham Stakes. A fortnight later, he won a £100 Plate at Brighton and never looked back. What you see before you are fifteen hands, two inches of pure magic.'

'I can see why you wanted to capture him on canvas.'

Lord Hendry gulped. 'Don't remind me,' he said. 'The loss of that painting was like a knife through the heart. You were right, Inspector.'

'About what?'

'I've been given the chance to buy it back,' said the older man, extracting the letter from his pocket. 'For £3000.'

Colbeck examined the note. 'When did you receive this?'

'Yesterday. It was left at the offices of the Jockey Club for me.'

'By whom?'

'Nobody knows – it was slipped under the door.'

'The thief didn't waste much time,' said Colbeck, returning the note. 'He'll probably make contact again very soon, Lord Hendry, and tell you where to deliver the money. That's when you call me in. Our best chance of catching him is when the painting is handed over.'

'I don't *have* £3000, Inspector.'

'But you have the appearance of a man who does and that's all that matters. Besides, your horse is the Derby favourite. You're seen as a person with excellent prospects.'

'Whatever happened to them?' Lord Hendry murmured.

'When we discussed the matter before,' recalled Colbeck, 'you felt that Miss Lavender might be party to the theft. Do you still believe that or have you thought of any other possible suspects?'

'Kitty Lavender and Hamilton Fido are the obvious ones.'

'What about the less obvious?'

'Such as?'

'You must tell me, Lord Hendry. How many people, outside your immediate family, knew of the existence of that painting?'

'Very few,' came the reply. 'I wanted to guard against derision. If certain people were aware that I had had the portrait of Odysseus painted before the Derby had even taken place, they would have mocked and sniggered. To obviate that, I swore the artist to silence and told only my most trusted friends.'

'Including Miss Lavender.'

'She was a friend at the time, alas.'

'I'm very anxious to meet the lady,' said Colbeck, 'but she's proving reluctant to come forward. When someone does that, it usually means they have something to hide.'

'Kitty is here, Inspector.'

'Do you know where I could find her?'

'Close to that unspeakable bookmaker.'

'Mr Fido is also a racehorse owner.'

'Not in my opinion,' rejoined Lord Hendry. 'His stables were bought with the fruits of illegal gambling and extortion. Talk to anyone of distinction on the Turf and they'll tell you that Hamilton Fido has lied and cheated his way to the position he now holds. I've seen him at racecourses all over the country,' he continued. 'He practises the black arts of bookmaking and travels with a group of ruffians he describes as his bodyguards. I can't think what Kitty sees in such a deplorable character but that's where she'll be, Inspector – in the vicinity of Hamilton Fido.'

It had been Marcus Johnson's idea to visit the Judge and Jury Show. It was held in a marquee and was a grotesque parody of the judicial system. Presided over by a self-styled Lord Chief Baron, it consisted of the mock trial of a man for seduction and criminal conspiracy. Witnesses were called and Kitty Lavender saw immediately that the females who gave evidence were all men in women's clothing. It was lively drama. The unholy trinity of comedy, obscenity and blasphemy made the audience roar with laughter and Marcus Johnson relished every moment. Kitty found it crude and distasteful. When the first trial was over, she was eager to leave but Johnson detained her.

'Watch what happens next,' he said, nudging her.

'I've seen enough, Marcus.'

'This is the bit I really like.'

Through a gauze curtain, they saw a group of shapely young women in flesh-coloured tights, forming a tableau before bursting into song. At the height of their rendition, the curtain was drawn back to expose the elegant attitudes in which they were standing. Kitty was dismayed at the way the male spectators hooted and clapped but she was even more upset to hear some of the foul language coming from the lips of women in the audience. Marcus Johnson had joined in the chorus of vulgar approval and was disappointed when his half-sister got up the leave. He followed her out of the marquee.

'I thought you might enjoy it,' he said. 'A little decadence helps to brighten anyone's day.'

'What offended me was the sight of those girls, being made to pose like that to arouse the audience. There was a time,' she admitted with a shiver, 'when *I* might have ended up in that kind of situation.'

'No – you were always too clever to let men exploit you, Kitty. You learnt how to exploit them instead.'

'It was a struggle at the start, Marcus.'

'But look where you are now – adored by a wealthy man.'

'How long will it last? That's what troubles me.'

'Hamilton is completely bewitched.'

'At the moment,' she said, 'but I'd be foolish to think that my hold over him will last for ever. London is full of gorgeous women. It's only a question of time before he replaces me with one of them.'

'He *loves* you, Kitty.'

'Love can easily cool.'

'You know how to maintain his interest. I've seen you do it with other men. When I met you again after a long absence, you were doing it to Lord Hendry. You led the old libertine by his pizzle.'

She was rueful. 'And what thanks did I get?'

'A blow across the face with his cane,' he said angrily. 'He won't ever do that again, Kitty. I snapped his cane in two. Besides, by the end of the week, he'll be dead.' His braying laugh had a cruel edge. 'What better proof could you have of Hamilton's devotion to you than that he's prepared to fight a duel on your behalf?'

'Yes,' she said, 'that cheered me.'

They were standing in front of a garish poster advertising the Judge and Jury Show and they moved away so that passers-by could see it. Johnson unfolded the newspaper that was under his arm.

'Haven't you seen that enough times, Marcus?' she asked.

'No,' he replied. 'I still haven't made up my mind.'

'But you know the names of the horses off by heart.'

'I'd rather study them in print.'

'I've put money on Merry Legs,' she said.

'A filly hasn't won the Derby for over fifty years.'

'One is due to break that sequence.'

'I'd never risk a bet on Hamilton's horse.'

'Then which one will you pick?'

'The race has to be between these six runners,'

he said, pointing to the paper. 'The rest of the field will simply make up the numbers. Somewhere in that sextet is my chance to make a fortune.'

Kitty looked over his shoulder at the list of betting odds.

7–2 against	*– Lord Hendry's Odysseus*
6–1	*– Mr Dowd's Limerick Lad*
9–1	*– Mr Fido's Merry Legs*
10–1	*– Duke of Sefton's Aleppo*
12–1	*– Sir J Mallen's Gladiator*
12–1	*– Hon E Petre's Royal Realm*

'You can't shilly-shally any longer, Marcus,' she said.

'I'll not be rushed. It's the biggest bet I've ever made.'

'Odysseus is the clear favourite.'

'I'd never waste my money on anything belonging to Lord Hendry,' he said, folding the newspaper up again. 'Favourite or not, Odysseus can and will be beaten.'

'By whom?'

'Limerick Lad,' he decided. 'I'll entrust my future to Ireland.'

Epsom racecourse was shaped like a horseshoe but it would not bring luck to all of the runners in the Derby. Only one could win and, years after the race, that was the name that would be remembered. No matter how close they had been to success, second- and third-placed horses would be consigned to obscurity. Everything depended on a fierce gallop that lasted less than three minutes. No horse could have a second chance to win the fabled race.

Robert Colbeck had been reunited with Madeleine Andrews in time to share a light repast with her and his colleagues. She had met Victor Leeming before but now had the ambiguous pleasure of being introduced to Edward Tallis. Notwithstanding his trenchant views on the distraction caused to his officers by wives and female friends, the superintendent was uniformly charming to Madeleine and showed a side to his character that the other men had never seen before.

The whole day had been built around the Derby and when the starting time drew closer, the excitement reached a new and more strident pitch. Much to his frustration, Leeming was ordered to take a seat beside Tallis in the grandstand. He would have preferred to accompany Colbeck and Madeleine to the paddock but was given no choice in the matter. The sergeant had managed to place a surreptitious bet but he would have liked to see his chosen horse at close quarters before the race.

'Mr Tallis is not the ogre you described,' observed Madeleine.

'You caught him on one of his milder days,' said Colbeck.

'I thought that he disliked women.'

'Only if they take the minds of his officers off their work.'

She giggled. 'Is that what I do, Robert?'

'From time to time,' he replied, squeezing her arm, 'and I'm grateful for it. But you've also been able to assist me, as you've done in the present investigation.'

331

'What does that make me?'

'I suppose that I'd call you a useful diversion.'

'Is that good or bad?'

'You won't ever hear me complaining, Madeleine.'

The paddock was near the finish and a sizeable throng had gathered to watch the horses being paraded. Owners were having last-minute conversations with their trainers and jockeys. Lord Hendry was there, patting Odysseus nervously as a groom led him past. It was Madeleine's first sight of the favourite and she marvelled at his lean head, longish neck and solid shoulders. She also took note of his massive ribs and powerful quarters. Merry Legs, though neat and beautifully proportioned, looked slight beside the favourite.

'Father was going to bet on Aleppo,' she confided.

Colbeck pointed. 'Here he comes,' he said, 'and he may yet cause an upset. So might Sir James Mallen's Gladiator. I've been hearing good things about him all morning.'

'It's so confusing, Robert. How can anyone choose a winner?'

'By a combination of luck and judgement.'

'What's your feeling?'

'I'm just relieved that the Derby is about to be run without any horses having been eliminated unfairly. It's not too late for any foul play at this stage, of course,' he said. 'To guard against that, I've placed some of my officers in strategic positions so that the horses will be watched all the way to the start.'

'You didn't answer my question.'

'No, I didn't.'

'Have you or have you not placed a bet?'

Colbeck smiled. 'It would be absurd not to, Madeleine.'

There was mild commotion as Princess of Fire had a tantrum, bucking half a dozen times and scattering those who had got too near. The groom and the jockey soon calmed the filly. It was time for the horses to go to the starting post. Jockeys were helped up into the saddle and fitted their feet into the stirrups. Racing caps were adjusted. Silk tunics, bearing the owner's colours, flapped in the breeze. Tensions that had built steadily up over months of preparation were finally on the point of release. There was no turning back now.

When they saw the runners heading for the start, the spectators went into a frenzy of anticipation. Lining the course and covering the Downs like a vast human carpet, they roared and cheered and clapped. Six years earlier, the starting point had been altered so that it was more easily visible from the towering, three-tiered grandstand. That was the best place from which to watch the race and Colbeck conducted Madeleine there. While he was very interested in the outcome of the Derby, part of his mind was still concentrated firmly on the murder investigation. Leeming had told him that Kitty Lavender had agreed to meet him soon after the race. Colbeck looked forward to the encounter with her.

They were all there. Lord Hendry was seated among his cronies, hiding his deep fears beneath friendly badinage. Brian Dowd sat nearer the front, dressed in his finery and using a telescope to get a better view. Hamilton Fido had vacated the betting room and stood at the rear of the grandstand, framed in a doorway and watching it all with wry amusement. He had taken an immense amount of money in bets. Whatever the result, he stood to reap a huge profit. He was already considering what he would buy Kitty Lavender by way of celebration.

With the vast crowd baying for the race to start, there was a delay as three of the jockeys were unable to bring their horses in line. In spite of repeated warnings from the starter, it was minutes before the mettlesome thoroughbreds were brought under enough control. Twenty runners were eventually strung out in something resembling a line. The flag came down and the horses plunged forward on their dash into racing history. They were off.

Royal Realm and Princess of Fire were the early leaders with the rest of the field fanned out behind them. They made the running all the way to Tattenham Corner, with over half the race behind them. As soon as they entered the straight, however, they fell back and it was a quartet of horses who surged to the front. Below the distance, with just over a furlong to go, they split into two groups. Limerick Lad and Aleppo were involved in a ferocious battle on the rails while Odysseus and Merry Legs fought for supremacy on the stand side. There was little to choose between any of them.

The Irish horse seemed to be pulling slowly away, then it was the favourite who put in a finishing spurt. Aleppo stayed in touch with both of them but Merry Legs began to falter and lose ground. The race was only between three horses now. Using their whips and yelling their commands, the jockeys sought to pull every last ounce of speed out of their mounts. As they thundered towards the post, Odysseus made a supreme effort and Limerick Lad strained to match it.

The noise reached the level of hysteria and the whole of the stand was on its feet to cheer the horses home. With Limerick Lad and Odysseus riding neck and neck, it looked as if it might be a dead heat. Then Aleppo showed perfect racing temperament by saving his spurt until the critical moment, edging past the others over the last twenty yards to win by a half a length. Another Derby had delivered a shock. In the massive explosion of sound that followed, it was minutes before most people were aware of the full result.

Aleppo was the winner, Limerick Lad was second and the favourite was pushed into third place. Gladiator had stolen up to take fourth place from Merry Legs but that did not appease those who had backed him. The Derby was over for another year and the murder investigation could be resumed.

When the hordes descended on the bookmakers, it was difficult for the detectives to reach Hamilton Fido. They had to force a way through the crowd. Madeleine Andrews had been left with the superintendent so that Colbeck and Leeming could go about their work. In the sustained clamour, they could hardly make themselves heard.

When they finally got to the betting room, they caught a glimpse of Hamilton Fido over the heads of the people in front of them. Beside the bookmaker was a beautiful young woman. Certain that it was Kitty Lavender, Colbeck redoubled his efforts to move through the crowd.

But he was not the only person eager to get close to the woman. Lord Hendry had an even more urgent appointment with her. Crazed by the failure of Odysseus, knowing that he faced financial ruin and enraged by the sight of Kitty Lavender and Fido together, he rushed towards them, using his cane indiscriminately to beat a way through. Panting for breath, he confronted them.

'You're a harlot, Kitty Lavender!' he shouted. 'I won't fight a duel over you because you have no honour to defend.'

'That's enough!' yelled Fido, stepping between the two of them. 'I've told you before, Hendry. If you dare to insult Kitty, you answer to me.'

'This is all I have to say to you!'

Pulling out a pistol from beneath his coat, he fired at point-blank range and sent a bullet burrowing into Fido's forehead. There was a moment of abrupt silence and everyone instinctively drew back. The whole atmosphere in the room had changed in a flash. Then the bookmaker fell backwards into Kitty's arms and she let out a scream of absolute terror. The detectives were the first to recover. All decorum was abandoned now as they shoved people aside to get to the killer.

Lord Hendry did not wait for them. Flinging his pistol aside, he twisted the handle of his cane, drew out the sword that was concealed inside it and used it to create a space for his escape. He went swiftly through the door at the rear of the room and slammed it behind him. Colbeck and Leeming were the only men brave enough to follow him. When they finally reached the door and opened it, a horrifying scene greeted them. Having lost his money, his property and his reputation, Lord Hendry had decided that he had nothing left to keep him alive with any dignity. Falling forward on to the point of the weapon, he had pierced his heart and was writhing in a pool of blood.

Colbeck thought of all the classical texts in the man's library.

'It was a Roman death,' he said. 'He fell on his sword.'

It took a long time to calm everyone down and to have the two dead bodies removed by policemen. A pall of sadness now hung over the room. Devastated at the death of her lover, Kitty Lavender was also tortured by the realisation that she was indirectly responsible for it. In becoming, in turn, the mistress of two men, she had ensured a violent end for both of them. She was anguished.

Colbeck had to be extremely patient with her. Having escorted her to a private room, he waited until the immediate shock had passed. It was followed by a wide-eyed bewilderment.

'Why did George do it?' she wailed. 'Why?'

'I think he was pushed to the brink of despair,' said Colbeck.

'He didn't have to *kill* Hamilton.'

'He felt that he did, Miss Lavender.'

'It was madness – George has ruined everything.'

'This crime is rooted firmly in another one,' said Colbeck quietly, 'and you are the only person who can help me to solve it. A hatbox bought for you by Lord Hendry was stolen from the Wyvern Hotel. Do you remember that?'

'How could I ever forget, Inspector?'

'You were staying there with Mr Fido at the time.'

'Yes, I was.'

'My belief is that the theft was deliberate. There were items of far greater value left in your hotel room but the thief only took the hatbox. Can you follow what I'm saying, Miss Lavender?'

'No,' she said, tears running freely.

'Someone came to that hotel with the express purpose of stealing your property. No other guest was robbed – only you. The thief must therefore have known where you were and that you would have your hatbox with you.'

'*Nobody* knew, Inspector,' she said. 'Hamilton and I wanted to be alone together. That's not the kind of thing that I'd advertise.'

'A casual word to a female friend, perhaps?'

'No.'

'A hint to someone close to you?'

'I talked to nobody.'

'Then we must be looking for a mind-reader,' concluded Colbeck. 'Someone who knew you well enough to guess where you would stay with Mr Hamilton because the Wyvern Hotel might have a particular significance for you.'

Kitty Lavender almost choked and Colbeck

had to support her while she coughed violently. When she had recovered, her face was ashen and she was trembling all over.

'Marcus,' she said in a hoarse whisper.

'Who?'

'Marcus Johnson, my half-brother. I believe you met him.'

'Did you tell him where you'd be staying?'

'Not exactly,' she recalled, 'but he knew that Hamilton and I were going to spend the night together. He'd introduced us. Without him, I'd never have got to know Hamilton.'

'Was he aware of your relationship with Lord Hendry?'

'Yes – Marcus helped me to escape from it.'

'So he might know where that hatbox came from.'

'Of course, Inspector.'

'And might even have *followed* you to the hotel.'

A tremor passed through her. 'I've just remembered something else,' she said, eyes filling with dread. 'Hamilton and George both urged me to speak to you but my step-brother stopped me from doing so. Marcus said that I should avoid the police at all costs.'

'Why do you think he told you that?'

'I'm beginning to wonder.'

'It was because he was afraid, Miss Lavender,' said Colbeck. 'He was afraid that his name would be mentioned and a new line of inquiry would be opened up. He was not thinking of you – he was protecting himself.'

'If Marcus stole the hatbox...' her voice trailed away.

'Then he also murdered the lad whose head was put in it.'

'He'd never do anything like that!' she protested.

'An hour ago you'd have sworn that Lord Hendry would never shoot someone in cold blood then commit suicide. Yet that's exactly what happened, Miss Lavender. In extreme situations, people will do anything. You say that your half-brother introduced you to Mr Fido?'

'That's right.'

'Did it ever cross your mind that he did so on purpose?'

'Not until now,' she said, reeling from the thought. 'Marcus said that he had my best interests at heart but, all the time, he was just *using* me. He wanted someone close to Hamilton so that he was aware of his movements. He even stole my hatbox.'

'I need to speak to Mr Johnson immediately.'

'Yes, yes, you must.'

'Then where is he?'

'Marcus went off to see a friend. He didn't give me his name.'

'Not to worry,' said Colbeck. 'I believe that I know it.'

The argument took place in an empty stall. Aware that they might be overheard by someone in the yard outside, both men kept their voices down but there was no diminution in their intensity of feeling. Marcus Johnson gesticulated with both hands while Brian Dowd kept his fists bunched as if ready to throw a punch at any moment.

340

'Give me my money!' demanded Johnson.

'You'll not get a penny from me,' said the other.

'We had an agreement, Brian.'

'The agreement was for you to make sure that Odysseus and Merry Legs didn't run. I wanted Lord Hendry and Hamilton Fido out of the race but not at the cost of killing their horses.'

'I tried to disable them and failed.'

'That didn't mean you had to cripple one horse and poison another. You went too far, Marcus, and that meant the police were alerted. I don't hold with harming racehorses. There were easier ways of taking them out of the race. I told you what to do.'

'Your methods didn't work,' said Johnson.

'Neither did yours – and that's why I'm not paying you.'

'I was *depending* on that money, Brian.'

'Then you should have done as you were told.'

'I used my own initiative. The irony is that you didn't need to get your rivals out of the race. Limerick Lad beat both of them, as it was. Unfortunately, Aleppo sneaked a win at the post.'

'Years of hard work came to nothing,' said Dowd sourly. 'It was the best chance I had to win the Derby and cock a snook at both Fido and Lord Hendry. Instead of which, I get nothing.'

'Limerick Lad was an honourable second.'

'I only settle for first place. I've lost thousands on this race.'

'You're not the only one,' said Johnson. 'After listening to your boasts about how Tim Maguire would ride your horse to victory, I put every penny I had on Limerick Lad winning. In return,

I got nothing.' He took a menacing step forward. 'So I need the money that was promised to me at the start.'

'I don't have it,' said Dowd, 'and even if I did I wouldn't give it to you. Get out of here and never let me see your face again.'

'I won't take orders from you.'

'You're asking for trouble, aren't you?'

'I'm asking you to remember that we're in this together,' said Johnson, voice rising out of control. 'On your orders, I killed John Feeny. On your orders, I tried to bring his head to you in Ireland. On your orders, I caused mayhem at the stables belonging to Lord Hendry and Hamilton Fido. You can't get rid of me that easily. We're partners in crime, Brian. We're accomplices.'

'Not any more!' said Dowd, flinging himself at Johnson.

They grappled in the middle of the stall and flailed around in the straw. The fight was short-lived. Before either of them could land a telling blow, the stable door was flung open and Colbeck came in with Leeming at his shoulder. The combatants stood back from each other.

'I've never heard such a frank confession before,' said Colbeck. 'The sergeant and I are very grateful to Mr Johnson for clarifying the details. We were standing outside while he did so. There's one more crime to add to the list,' he added, waving a letter in the air. 'I'm talking about the theft of a painting from Lord Hendry's house.'

'That was nothing to do with me,' protested Dowd.

'I'm not accusing you, sir. Mr Johnson is the

culprit. This letter was found in Lord Hendry's pocket. It gives instructions about where he can leave £3000 to buy the portrait back. That money will never be paid or collected. Lord Hendry is dead.'

Johnson and Dowd traded a look of utter amazement.

'He committed suicide,' explained Leeming, 'immediately after he had shot Hamilton Fido. Both of your rivals have perished, Mr Dowd.'

'Is this true?' gasped the Irishman.

'We were witnesses to the shooting, sir.'

'When I searched Lord Hendry's pockets,' said Colbeck, 'I found this second demand. I showed it to your half-sister, Mr Johnson, and she was kind enough to identify the handwriting as yours.'

'Kitty must be mistaken,' said Johnson.

'No, sir – she won't ever make a mistake about you again. Now that she sees you in your true light, she knows you for what you are.'

'Brian is to blame – he put me up to it.'

'Shut your bleeding gob!' yelled Dowd.

Johnson laughed. 'Compliments pass when the quality meet.'

'This is all your fault.'

'You are just as guilty, Mr Dowd,' said Colbeck. 'This whole business sprang out of your hatred of John Feeny. You never forgave him for standing up to you. When you heard that he was working at the stables owned by Hamilton Fido, you saw a chance to get your revenge on the lad and cause some embarrassment for one of your rivals at the same time. It was a clever ruse.'

'Getting that hatbox delivered to you,' said

Leeming, 'made it seem as if you were the victim and not the man who instigated the crime in the first place. You fooled us at first. What let you down was that you tried to do it again.'

'Yes,' said Colbeck. 'When I discovered that you had forged the letter supposedly sent to your jockey, I became very suspicious. I was convinced that you lied to me about John Feeny.'

'Feeny was a vile little bugger!' roared Dowd. 'When I threw him out of my stables, he went round telling everyone that I was a cheat and a bully. If he hadn't fled to England, I'd have strangled him with my bare hands.'

'So you had no compunction about ordering his murder?'

'None at all, Inspector – it was what he deserved.'

'The severed head was my suggestion,' said Johnson airily. 'I thought it would add a suitably macabre touch. When Kitty told me about the hatbox that Lord Hendry had bought her, I couldn't resist stealing it. At one brilliant stroke, I linked Lord Hendry and Hamilton Fido with the death of Brian's former groom. There was an almost poetic roundness to it all.'

'It's not one that I appreciate, sir,' said Leeming.

'Nor me,' added Colbeck. 'Let's take these gentlemen into custody, Victor. I'm sure that Superintendent Tallis will be delighted to meet both of them – on their way to the gallows.'

Leeming produced a pair of handcuffs to put on Dowd but the Irishman tried to buffet him aside and escape. The sergeant had arrested far too many men to be brushed aside. Sticking out a leg, he tripped Dowd up then sat astride him and pulled his arms behind him so that he could put on the handcuffs. He then got up, grabbed the prisoner by the collar of his frock coat and hoisted him to his feet. Dowd was still swearing violently as he was pushed unceremoniously out of the stall. Colbeck was left alone with Marcus Johnson.

'You seem remarkably unperturbed, sir,' said Colbeck, taking out a pair of handcuffs.

'I backed the wrong horse in every sense, Inspector.'

'How did you get involved with Brian Dowd?'

'I spent some months in Ireland,' replied Johnson, 'sponging off friends. I met Brian at a race meeting there and we hit it off at once. I admired his determination to win the Derby at all costs and he was grateful to meet someone who would do anything for money and, moreover, do it in great style.'

'There's nothing stylish about murdering an innocent lad.'

Johnson brayed. 'You were not there at the time.'

'You won't laugh quite so loud on the scaffold,' warned Colbeck. 'Turn around, please, and put your hands behind your back.'

'Your wish is my command, Inspector.'

Johnson turned round obligingly but, instead of putting his hands behind his back, he pulled out a small pistol from under his coat and swung round to point the weapon at Colbeck.

'The tables are turned,' he said, grinning in triumph.

'I dispute that,' said Colbeck, showing no fear. 'As well as Sergeant Leeming, there are four uniformed policemen outside. You can't kill six of us with one bullet, Mr Johnson.'

'I won't need to kill anybody now that I have a hostage. *You* are my passport out of here, Inspector. Nobody would dare to stop me when I'm holding a gun to the head of the much-vaunted Railway Detective. And the beauty of it is,' he went on, 'that you'll be wearing your own handcuffs.' He levelled the pistol at Colbeck's head and his voice became a snarl. 'Give them to me and turn round.'

'As you wish, sir.'

'And no tricks.'

'You have the advantage over me, Mr Johnson.'

'I'm glad that you appreciate that.'

Colbeck held out the handcuffs but, when Johnson tried to take them, they were suddenly thrown into his face. In the momentary distraction, Colbeck grabbed the wrist of the hand that held the weapon and forced it upwards. The pistol went off with a loud bang and the bullet embedded itself harmlessly in a wooden beam. Colbeck, meanwhile, was hurling Johnson against the wall to make him drop the weapon. He then hit him with a succession of punches to the face and body. Johnson put his arms up to defend himself but the attack was far too strong. A vicious right hook finally sent him to the floor. Blood streaming from his nose, Johnson lay huddled in the straw.

Having heard the shot, Leeming came running back to the stall.

'What happened, Inspector?' he asked.

'Fortunately,' said Colbeck, 'he decided to resist arrest.'

It was dark by the time their train steamed into the station. Robert Colbeck first supervised the transfer of the two prisoners into custody before taking Madeleine Andrews home in a cab. An eventful day was finally drawing to an end.

'Thank you, Robert,' she said. 'It was a marvellous experience!'

'That's what I felt when I arrested Marcus Johnson.'

'I'm sorry that you weren't able to enjoy the Derby itself.'

'But I was,' said Colbeck. 'Once I knew that I'd be speaking to Kitty Lavender after the race, I could watch it without any distraction. I was as enthralled as you, Madeleine – enthralled but disappointed.'

'How could you be disappointed with such an exciting race?'

'I bet on Merry Legs,' he confessed.

She giggled. 'You should have followed Father's advice.'

'I'm sure that Mr Andrews will point that out to me.'

'Time and time again.'

They snuggled against each other in the cab and watched the gas lamps shoot past on both sides of the street. It had been a most satisfying Derby Day. Madeleine had been able to wallow in the multiple pleasures of the occasion and Colbeck had solved a whole series of related crimes. Though it had given intense delight to untold thousands, the Derby had also claimed its victims. Hamilton Fido had been shot dead and his killer had taken his own life. Colbeck had little sympathy for the bookmaker but he felt sorry for Lord Hendry.

'He could simply not face it,' he said.

'Who?'

'Lord Hendry,' he explained. 'He gambled and lost. He could simply not face turning up at Tattersalls on Monday and admitting that he was unable to settle his debts. The ignominy was too much for him. At least, that's what I assumed at first.'

'What other explanation is there?'

'He'd been challenged to a duel by Hamilton Fido.'

'A duel?'

'It was another instance of Marcus Johnson's cunning,' said Colbeck. 'It seems that Lord Hendry struck out at Kitty Lavender with his cane. She confided in her half-brother but asked him to say nothing about it. What do you imagine he did?'

'He went straight to Mr Fido.'

'Exactly,' he replied. 'He knew that he could provoke a duel between the two men he was being paid to incommode by Brian Dowd. Had the duel taken place before the Derby, the likelihood is that one of the horses would have been withdrawn from the race out of respect to its dead owner – Lord Hendry, most probably.'

'Marcus Johnson was malevolent.'

'His half-sister realises that now. Miss Lavender

348

thought him a lovable rogue but he was far more sinister than that. He also had a weird sense of humour. Do you remember the name on that hatbox?'

'Yes,' said Madeleine. 'It was Mr D Key, wasn't it?'

'Kitty Lavender told me why he chose it. In his younger days, her half-brother had a nickname. Because of his long face, prominent teeth and braying laugh, he was known as Donkey Johnson.'

'So D Key stood for Donkey.'

'When he put that severed head in the hatbox,' said Colbeck, 'he thought he was starting a process that would help Limerick Lad to win the Derby. It would turn Brian Dowd into an apparent victim and send us after his two deadly rivals. In short, an Irish horse would owe its success in the most famous race in the world to a donkey. That was Johnson's idea of a joke. When I pointed that it to Mr Tallis,' he went on, 'he was far from amused.'

'Is he going to pay your expenses now?'

'Yes – he finally agreed that my visit to Dublin was necessary.'

'He must be thrilled with what happened today,' she said. 'You solved the murder and made two arrests. Superintendent Tallis ought to be eternally grateful to you and Sergeant Leeming.'

'He will be when he finishes wrestling with a personal problem.'

'Personal problem?'

'Mr Tallis thinks that Derby Day is an abomination. But Victor was right next to him when the

349

race was run and the superintendent cheered as loud as anyone. He's lapsed into a period of repentance now,' said Colbeck. 'He can't forgive himself for having enjoyed the occasion.' He slipped an arm around her. 'I hope that you feel no guilt at having had so much pleasure at Epsom.'

'It was an unforgettable experience, Robert.'

'I was afraid that you might be bored,' he teased.

'Bored?' she repeated. 'How could anyone be bored? The Derby was the most exciting thing I've ever seen in my whole life.'

'Really?'

'I loved every second of it.'

'In that case,' he said, tightening his hold, 'you might want to come with me to Epsom again next year.'

'Yes, *please*,' said Madeleine, laughing with delight.

'That's settled, then.'

'Thank you, Robert.'

He pulled her close. 'Though I'm sure that we can find some other excitements for you in the interim,' he said fondly. 'Twelve whole months of them.'

This Large Print Book for the partially sighted, who cannot read normal print, is published under the auspices of

THE ULVERSCROFT FOUNDATION

THE REPAIR SHOP

A make do and mend guide to caring for the things you love

Foreword by **JAY BLADES**

BOOKS

CONTENTS

FOREWORD

BY JAY BLADES

'Everybody has something that means too much to be thrown away. That's where we come in.'

In the modern era it has too often been a case of 'Out with the old, in with the new.' As life moves fast, so do broken objects in this throwaway society – directly to recycling centres – as it seems easier to toss them out rather than resurrect or rejuvenate them. The days of tinkering with things that are failing or fractured are long gone.

People are daunted, probably feeling that they don't have the necessary know-how these days as old-style crafts, once handed down the generations, are being lost for the sake of hectic diaries and cheap retail.

That's where The Repair Shop comes in, with its resident experts ready and willing to take on the heavy lifting.

Behind the closed doors of The Repair Shop the rapid pace of today's living is forgotten as conservators and restorers become absorbed in their tasks, happy to spend hours and days questing for a flawless outcome on a single item.

Furniture restorer William Kirk calls it 'the workshop of dreams,' and not just because people who visit see hoped-for transformations in well-loved belongings. He and the rest of the experts are also living the dream, fixing a vast range of artefacts that might not otherwise come to their work benches.

As soon as their eyes lock on to a new project, their minds start racing about how best to achieve the right results. It turns out their single-minded attentiveness and nimble fingers are spellbinding for viewers, who are gripped by techniques and tips.

And the tale behind each item is just as compelling as the conservation or restoration process. Every story takes us at *The Repair Shop* on a sentimental journey so engrossing we forget the presence of nearby cameras and crew as it unfolds.

Critically, the team aren't refurbishing antique investments so the owners can cash in, but are putting a piece of family history back into place, priceless in a different way and making an emotional return rather than a financial one.

Although they are all masters at their chosen skill, everyone is keen to consult and collaborate on projects, to embrace new or adapted methods that will work with old items. Every day is an education and, as I tell them, if you aren't learning anything, well, what are you doing? You may as well be pushing up the daisies.

This book is designed for people who don't have years of experience behind them like *The Repair Shop* experts, but might share some of the same goals: to retrieve objects from dusty boxes, restore them to a former glory and safeguard them as a legacy to pass on to future generations. For those who want to step off the treadmill for a moment and spend a few hours of tranquillity with some much-loved ancestral item, this is the handbook that can make it happen.

Jay

INTRODUCTION

In our youth we take evidence of the quirky and the classical parked on the landing or lining the shelves very much for granted. But by degrees we lose sight of an aged desk that we knew from childhood, and the worn chair that once stood plush and proud by the door.

Computers have usurped typewriters, which themselves replaced fountain pens and the writing slopes that used to accompany them. Gramophones, radios and even jukeboxes have surrendered to mobile phones. Metal and wooden toys have long since made way for plastic counterparts. Clocks have gone digital.

It's impossible to halt progress and no one wants to stop innovation. But while shiny, modern objects churned out in distant factories by the thousand have their place in today's homes, they don't command the same deep-seated affection as something once cradled by a grandparent, evoking as that does a misty memory of childhood. Years later those once familiar items provide a bridge between generations now gone and those still unborn, who will one day inherit this family's mantelpiece treasure.

Happily, we are a nation of hoarders. Rather than ditching chipped china, perforated pictures or stopped clocks, we tend to stash them in our lofts, with every good intention to one day bring those articles that mean so much back to their former glory.

Inside the open doors of The Repair Shop the air is filled with a symphony of hammering, drilling and the clatter of tools. Here's where experts with those bygone talents in crafts and conservation have gathered to fix neglected heirlooms so that they might be saved for future generations.

There's rarely an idle moment as exceptional craftspeople pore over items that haven't been at their best for decades. Their aim is not to spruce up an object so it gets the best price at auction, as no monetary value can be put upon the sentimental journey that the sight, sound or smell of a cherished possession will induce. Everyone's focus is to get it back in pride of place in a family home. It's a place where nostalgia never gets old.

Between them The Repair Shop experts took widower Albert Thompson on a poignant trip down memory lane when they repaired his GEC portable transistor radio, bought for 50 shillings, when he was aged just 22, with his wife-to-be Eileen in the fifties. Afterwards, the radio went everywhere with them before it became a fixture of family life. When it stopped working for the first time, a repairer replaced the faulty buttons with the rounded ends of toothbrushes. This time it stopped on the second anniversary of Eileen's death – and the problems were far more technical. Nonetheless, Albert insisted he didn't want to discard the radio, despite a range of replacements now available, but needed it back in his greenhouse for peace of mind. After spending some time locating what turned out to be several major faults, radio expert Mark Stuckey sorted out the circuitry. Suzie Fletcher fitted a new handle around the old one, Jay Blades helped her clean the case while Steve Fletcher made a new dial from a clear plastic lid, a spare brass component and the bottom of a lamp stand. Albert returned to hear music beaming from the radio, the soft serenade at a pitch evocating all the best memories of his life and love.

Other items brought into The Repair Shop have a role to play in international history as well as being a pivotal part of a family story. Natalie Cummings brought along a violin in pieces, bearing a crude repair on one shoulder. The instrument had belong to an aunt, Rosa Levinsky who took it with her when she left her home in Leeds in the mid-thirties after she was invited to play in the Berlin Philharmonic. However, Russian-born Rosa was soon swept up in the turmoil of the times. As a Jew, she was first sent to Mauthausen concentration, then to Auschwitz. She spent the rest of the Second World War in the notorious death camp as part of the women's orchestra, playing to entertain guards and to distract doomed arrivals. Although orchestra members like herself escaped the gas chambers she was nonetheless kept short of food and clothing.

The emotional stress must have been phenomenal. Finally, when hostilities ceased, she returned home to Yorkshire and died in 1947. The violin went to her brother Sydney, Natalie's father, also a musician. But it had been stored in the loft for years; the finger board was detached and without strings.

Violin restorer John Dilworth eased the front face of the violin off to find a signature and a date for its manufacture: it was made in 1883 in Dresden, Germany. His approach was so considered he even included the unsightly repair that was almost certainly done at Auschwitz.

There are no challenges that aren't embraced by a team that relishes the old, the unusual and the downright obscure. It takes hours spent at the workbench to accrue the kind of experience that can breathe life into something that is at best tired, at worst entirely wrecked. Crucial among the considerations facing the team are how age and authenticity will be retained. Each expert uses tools and techniques tried and tested throughout their career.

Although much of what they accomplish is the preserve of the professionals, they also provide an antidote to today's throwaway society. The experts are keen to take the mystique out of basic care and considered restoration, to help retain as much of our social history as possible in the best order. That's where this book comes in, as it contains the combined wisdom of *The Repair Shop* experts across all their specialities. Find out how to clean, carry, care for and repair the articles that mean most to you, to safeguard your sentimental legacy for generations to come.

Conservation or Restoration?

When leather expert and saddlemaker Suzie Fletcher was confronted by a decrepit leather patterned pouffe she drew up a detailed plan for its repair. Each tessellated piece was unpicked, numbered, dabbed with saddle soap, lined with fine pig skin and sewn back together again.

The original thread was rotten and was discreetly renewed. New piping was included on the top and 300 hand stitched seams later, with the pouffe standing at twice its previous height, it was ready for return. But although the majority of the 113 decorative pieces were saved, some sections of the Egyptian pouffe were beyond repair and needed replacing. While new thread went unseen, each bit of modern leather would stand out from its age-weathered neighbour. Yet it's unlikely previously used leather taken from a 'donor' item which might have blended would have added the necessary durability.

It's a dilemma that faces master craftspeople like Suzie and the rest of The Repair Shop team on a daily basis.

There's a natural tension between conservation – preserving an item for future generations – and restoration, giving it a sense of newness. On this occasion Suzie opted to include new leather that was instantly apparent, something she felt was an honest repair that gave life to otherwise defunct furniture.

With every artefact that comes through the doors the team must plot a sympathetic treatment that doesn't offend accepted conservation ethics but does make an item serviceable once more. Always, the starting point is consolidation, to ensure nothing further is lost. Then the experts must decide how best to honour an object's authenticity and veracity. Their duty to cultural heritage is one that's keenly felt.

For art conservator Lucia Scalisi, it's a case of combining the ethics of conservation with practicalities, for example, a ripped canvas. Above all, her aim is to impact as little as possible on an artefact, in order to preserve its integrity. No one wants their 92-year-old grandmother to have a face lift, she explains, nor do they want an eighteenth century portrait to look as if it was painted last year.

Julie Tatchell and Amanda Middleditch, the bear repairers, share those guiding principles and focus on fending off further deterioration while hoping everything they do can be undone if necessary. While they will clean a soft toy and restore missing elements, it's imperative any work they do doesn't change its personality and character. Owners want to collect the toy they have always adored, rather than a new version of it.

The Repair Shop team is united in trying to keep the patination – a top layer that forms on wood, metals and leather naturally or unavoidably over time – intact, as with it comes a sideways glance at history.

When clockwork expert Steve Fletcher set about mending a French-built steam-operated toy boat recovered years before from a sea shore, he had no qualms about ensuring the machinery inside worked safely and straightened the hull so the prop shaft would operate again. He replaced two missing masts and even added a French flag.

But although he cleaned verdigris from the 125 year old brass cannon he didn't polish them, nor did he re-paint the boat's battered bodywork so it still had the appearance of an historic object.

A moving story attached to a project tackled by carpenter Will Kirk illustrates his cautious and thoughtful approach. He was presented with a hand-carved wooden Spitfire, made by a Lancaster bomber's crewman during World War II between operations and intended for his much younger brother. When the airman was shot down and killed in 1943, on his 19th mission, the toy was finally delivered to a child and his family, now filled with heartache.

The present owner, that grieving boy's son, was himself distraught after he dropped it within days of his father's death, breaking a wing. Will immediately reassured him that both wing and tail had previously broken and he painstaking scraped away old glue before using a two-part adhesive on the repair. He cut and shaped a tiny metal fragment to replace a missing propeller shaft. But although he added paint to disguise the bonded edges of wing and tail, he left the vast majority of brushstrokes made by the ill-fated wartime airman alone, so it looked just as it would have done 75 years ago. He did however make a stand for it so it would be forever in flight and the chances of future crashes were much reduced.

Sometimes two worlds collide, however, and the experts must undertake wholesale repairs so its very survival is assured.

Brenton West is not only a silversmith but an expert in cameras and projectors. When a machine for 8mm film arrived at the workshop he put in a new bulb and drive belt. This was an occasion when restoration work went beyond a thorough clean, so a family could re-live memories captured on celluloid back in the sixties. Without his work, the projector amounted to so much metalwork. After it was completed, the machine was working as its manufacturers – and owners – intended.

One abiding guideline is that whatever is added can be taken away again, without damage. Yet metalworker Dominic Chinea's considered approach, always item-specific, might also involve safety as well as aesthetics, for example, with a toy pedal car when new pedals to replace worn ones are vital.

Whatever the challenge on the work bench, for the team of experts it's a privilege for their work to become part of an article's unfolding story and to give good order to its prolonged existence.

WOOD

Every artefact that comes into The Repair Shop has a compelling history behind it. But one object stands out for carpenter Will Kirk, for the way it dramatically changed its owner's life.

When Alan Thompson brought in a battered writing slope for renovation, there was little that highlighted its personal significance. He'd discovered it after the death of a sister, tucked under the eaves in her attic. The box was in such disrepair it almost went unnoticed.

It turned out it wasn't the box that was pivotal, but the papers Alan found inside it. Here was the official documentation that divulged that the people he knew as mum and dad were in fact his grandparents. His real mother was the woman he'd always thought of as his oldest sister.

For the first time he had evidence in his hands that laid bare a long-hidden family secret, with everyone involved apart from himself now dead. For Alan, the slope symbolised information buried and relationships unrecognised. Now Will wanted to transform the writing slope into the most beautiful, tactile treasure chest, to store those vital papers and photographs that disclosed Alan's true identity.

Although Alan had no idea about the history of his writing slope, it was certainly in a sorry state. It looked as if it had been in either a fire or a flood, with the lid charred and its veneer either missing or badly fractured.

Usually Will opts for the least abrasive cleaner, or even plain water, to remove dirt, in the hope of saving layers of polish built up over the years. In this instance it was far too late to rescue that lustre. So armed with a cotton wool bud charged with methylated spirits, he gently cleaned a corner of the box unsure of its effect. Happily, it soon revealed glossy grain and a brass inlay, which was appearing for the first time in years.

His next step was to reach for a household electric iron. After placing a cotton cloth over the lid of the box, he ironed it to both flatten down the surviving veneer and revive the original glue. That achieved better results on some parts of the lid than others, possibly because glue wasn't uniformly applied all over the lid surface in the first place. He stabilised the rest with cautiously applied wood glue, tucking it under raised veneer using a thin brush.

Then it was time to replace the missing patches of veneer. He chose cedar veneer as it acts like a blank canvas. Although it was much paler than the rest, it's far easier to make wood darker than to lighten it up.

There were two brass plates on the writing slope: one on the top and the other surrounding the lock. Both were badly tarnished, but using a cleaner with a soft cloth quickly returned them to their former glory. As well as commercially made brass cleaners, there are some tried-and-tested home-made alternatives using pantry staples that will do the job, including ketchup, yoghurt, lemon juice and bicarbonate of soda or vinegar with flour.

The leather inside the slope was beyond repair and had to be replaced with new. With tasks like these, when measurements have to be exact, Will falls back on an old Russian proverb: 'Measure seven times, cut once.' It means that extra preparation will help prevent an error and it is advice that rarely lets craftspeople down. Despite this prudent approach, he still chose PVA glue to fix it in place, as it is low-cost, strong and safe, but also gives a few moments of mobility to freely slide the surfaces into alignment before firmly clamping.

Finally, it was time to return the writing slope to Alan, the sole link he had with his newly discovered past and now a suitably significant and stylish home for mementoes of such magnitude.

Types of Wood

There are two broad categories: softwoods and hardwoods.

Not necessarily more yielding than the rest, **softwoods** are from trees that bear cones and tend to be swift growing, less dense and inexpensive.

Pine: Plantations of planted pines, with trees that reach arrow-straight for the sky, mean that it is an abundant resource. Turpentine is made from the distilled resin of some pine varieties.

Fir: An inexpensive wood that's quick to stain, fir is often used in building projects for reasons of economy.

Cedar: A reddish wood with a straight grain, cedar has a natural aroma that deters moths, making it ideal for bedroom furniture.

Versatile **hardwoods**, from broad-leaved deciduous trees, are highly prized by woodworkers for their creative potential in turning and carving. Those from warmer climates tend to emit more toxic chemicals as a defence from rampaging micro organisms.

Oak: With two recognisable hues – white and red – oak was used on Viking long ships and Britain's earliest navy vessels as it is naturally resistant to moisture and insect or fungal attack. It is characterised by its open grain.

Ash: Both resilient and bendy, this light-coloured wood has a multitude of uses, including for tool handles, baseball bats, electric guitars and even the frames of Morgan cars.

Beech: Light but rarely decorative, beech is used to make furniture carcasses, flooring and plywood. Writing in the first century AD, Roman naturalist Pliny the Elder observed, 'The wood of beech is easily worked – cut into thin layers of veneers, it is very flexible, but is only used for the construction of boxes and desks.'

Elm: A fine choice for chair seats and coffins because it's unlikely to split.

Mahogany: Its warm, reddish brown can be enhanced by either a stain or oil, but mahogany trees are now considered 'at risk' in the wild.

Rosewood: An umbrella term for a family of trees that are typified by a dark-veined, rich wood. Considered the world's most trafficked wild product, there are now international trade restrictions in place.

Teak: Naturally pest resistant, straight-grained, yellowy teak from India sometimes smells like leather and is popular among house builders as well as furniture makers as it doesn't warp.

Walnut: With its rich brown colour and tantalising grain patterns, it's often chosen for veneer.

Maple: Pale but extremely durable, this is an ideal wood to withstand wear and tear. It was another recommendation for veneer by Pliny the Elder, along with box, palm, holly and poplar.

Ebony: A favourite wood among eighteenth century French cabinet makers, its density makes it suitable for creating musical instruments as it gives good clarity.

A Selection of Will's Woodwork Tools

Few craftspeople will match the number of tools in the woodworker's workshop. Some stand like soldiers at attention in floor-to-ceiling racks, while others lie snug in a roll-up bag. Inevitably, some come to hand more than others.

1. **'Antique' screwdriver:** Old-style screws are often wider than run-of-the-mill new screwdrivers. If they are rusted into position, then only a wide, meaty screwdriver will do the job of loosening them adequately.

2. **Chisel with a maple handle:** This is ideal for jobs where the chisel is going to be struck by a hammer to shear one piece of wood away from the next, as the close-knit grain gives it strength.

3. **Chisel for wood-carving:** Choose a tool with a more ergonomically designed handle for comfort and effectiveness.

4. **Oilstone:** Craftspeople need to have the sharpest tools in the box at their disposal. With razor-edged implements the user has better control and, with the chances of slipping radically reduced, is actually less likely to cut themselves. The process of sharpening tools also helps to battle rust. Oilstones are traditionally the cheapest method and are durable.

5. **Waterstone:** Using a waterstone is usually faster for sharpening than an oilstone, with higher grades available to get sharper results.

6. **Diamond stone:** The most expensive way to sharpen your tools is to purchase a diamond stone, which, as the name implies, has industrial-strength diamonds installed in a sharpening strip.

7. **Leather strop:** Finish all blade-sharpening processes by using a leather strop to rub off minute metal filings and buff up the blade metal.

8. **Veneer hammer:** Not a hitting hammer, but a tool to smooth down veneer sheets so that excess glue is pushed to the sides.

My Favourite Tools

For some people, chisels are merely a blade on a stick. Not for Will, who bought a substantial wooden-handled, bevel edge chisel in a second-hand market in Bath recently for a tenner – but says that for him it's probably worth at least ten times that.

It has a blade made from Sheffield steel, dubbed 'rustless steel' when it was invented just prior to the First World War. While cheaper or newer chisels will quickly become blunt, this one stays sharp for the duration of a task. Lying heavy in the hand, the blade is so wide it can be used like a plane.

Of course, it's only one of many chisels in his workshop, some of which have been bought from high street chains. Cheaper tools can be used for knocking into wood that's full of nails or screws, to avoid the risk of damaging a favourite tool.

Inherited tools are the best kind, insists Will, and not just because they are free. These are tools that have already stood the test of time. Without them there are jobs that can't be done quite so well, or even at all.

PROJECTS

Like all crafts, there's a mystique surrounding woodwork that keeps even enthusiastic amateurs at bay. But Will encourages everyone to tackle projects if they feel interested and able. His advice is to spend plenty of time researching any proposed project in books and online, as there are volumes of information about woodworking available now that offer the necessary strategies.

Bear in mind that many restorers spend hours undoing work that's been badly executed, so be realistic about how much patience and application you possess.

The accessibility of the right tools and a well-lit, uncluttered workspace might also be a consideration. But the satisfaction in finishing achievable projects is immense.

If you are new to woodwork but want to get a feel for the craft, then start small. Here are some tasks that everyone can try, which will not only give the satisfaction of achievement, but could improve some of your favourite items of furniture too.

HOW TO FIX A SCRATCH ON POLISHED WOODEN FURNITURE

1. Take an unshelled walnut and, with moderate pressure, rub it in circular motions over the scratch.

2. Rub the same area with your fingers afterwards, to warm the nut oil that's been left on the furniture's surface.

3. Wait for a few moments for the oil to seep in.

4. Buff with a soft cloth. Having been filled and coloured, the scratched area will no longer be visible.

HOW TO REMEDY A WHITE MARK LEFT ON FURNITURE

1. A white mark means there's moisture trapped in the wood. Apply mayonnaise to the affected area and leave overnight so the vinegar-based dressing can draw the offending water out.

2. Clean with a cloth and buff. This will work for surface marks. Any indentation can only be fixed by re-polishing.

3. Invest in some coasters as they are the single best way to protect furniture from ring marks. And avoid putting plant pots at the centre of an antique table.

HOW TO MEND WOODEN LEGS

When chair legs buckle or table legs shear away, there's a bigger job in prospect, but not one that's necessarily out of reach. Here Will offers advice on how to effect a strong repair on broken wooden furniture.

1. Make sure the facing sides of the item being glued are clean and dust free.

2. Apply the glue so there's enough to cover the surface and sufficient even to soak into the wood. However, ensure it doesn't form a gluey wedge, as this will stop the wood holding together after it has adhered and will become a weakness.

3. Remember that glue has an 'open' time, when it is liquid and workable, so be prepared to work in a timely manner before it turns to gel.

4. Clamp the repair as effectively as possible. That means applying firm pressure on the repaired area so that the glue can dry with everything locked into the proper place.

5. Leave for 12 hours or in line with the glue manufacturer's recommendations.

HOW TO REPAIR RAISED VENEER

In an arid land where trees were a rarity, the Ancient Egyptians began using veneer to make the most of a scarce resource. Those limited amounts of timber available to them were cut into wafer-thin sheets and fixed to other, less precious surfaces to give the illusion of solid wood. The same principles have been applied for centuries afterwards, with inexpensive furniture carcasses expertly hidden behind a glossy and luxuriant veneer exterior. To get a satisfactory result using veneer over a large area almost certainly means employing a hydraulic press or a vacuum bag to apply the necessary pressure while the glue is drying. However, as veneer quickly dries out, with rosewood being amongst the driest, it can raise over time and look unsightly. And this is a repair that can be carried out without specialist tools.

1. To achieve the best finish, clear away any traces of old glue on both surfaces.

2. Glue made from the collagen of animals, found in bones and hide, is the best for the job. Professional restorers use hot animal glue, which must be mixed with care, responds to temperature and comes in different strengths. Instead, choose a liquid hide glue, which comes ready-made and can be applied with relative ease by a paintbrush.

3. Press down the stray veneer and wipe away any excess glue.

4. Clamp the repaired area while the glue is setting. Use masking tape to hold the veneer in place in areas that are too tricky to clamp.

HOW TO FRENCH POLISH

French polishing is the process by which a distinctive gloss is applied to wooden furniture, using numerous coats of shellac mixed with methylated spirits. Despite years of experience in French polishing, Will still considers his biggest workshop challenge is to accurately reproduce the patination – the shine and the antique depth – that distinguishes this furniture. It's something that may take a hundred years to form, and it is gone in an instant if an uninformed restorer makes the wrong choices.

French polishing isn't necessarily the preserve of professionals, but given that getting the right colour and shine by mixing wax and polish to the existing pigments in the wood is a real test even for the experts, this is an art that needs to be well practiced. If you have a piece of unloved furniture and want to give French polishing a try, you can mirror Will's steps.

1. Before applying the polish there's preparation to be done, which involves stripping off the old varnish or wax and rubbing down with fine abrasive paper. It's a time-consuming job, but a necessary one to offer a blank, smooth, blemish-free canvas for the polish.

2. To fill in any open grain, Will rubs chalk dust into the surface (although grainy marks will fade more with every coat of polish).

3. Mix commercially made shellac polish with methylated spirits – using about a kilo of polish to five litres of spirit – before applying it with something called a French polishing rubber or fad. In fact it's not a rubber, so much as a material bung.

Make your own by taking a square of lint-free scrap cotton and choosing some cheesecloth or fine-grade waste cotton for the centre. Soak the cheesecloth cotton in polish before pulling up the corners of its material hammock and twisting, ensuring there are no creases on the bottom, to make a pear-shaped pad. Now it should move freely on the surface, with the polish oozing gently through the outer cotton cover to leave a thin and even coat along the grain of the wood in its wake. It's important to squeeze any excess polish out before starting.

4. Work from one side of an object to the next to avoid making an initial landing mark, which will be difficult to remove. In further applications, when a coating has been established, use multiple figure-of-eight motions. When the surface feels sticky and drags on the rubber, it's time to leave the article to dry. It takes at least a week for it to dry before work can begin again.

5. To achieve the smoothness and shine associated with French polishing, the final layers are built up with shellac thinned further still with methylated spirits. This needs to be applied in quick motion across the surface, in a process known as flashing off. In effect, this melts the polish to create a reflective shine.

HALLMARKS OF THE ERA

Through the ages wooden furniture has reflected much more than merely domestic style. It's a fusion of international history and technological advance that mirrors society's evolution. While it's not possible to investigate it thoroughly here, there are clues incorporated in this flying visit around furniture history that might help you date an old family favourite.

16TH AND 17TH CENTURIES

Rudimentary furniture existed in Britain before Tudor times but it was then that chunky, carved pieces came to prominence. Dubbed the age of oak, it began in about 1500 and lasted a century, although surviving pieces like four-poster beds and throne-style chairs were originally the preserve of nobility.

It encompassed the Jacobean period, defined by backed armchairs, hall cupboards, settles and framed chests. The most opulent of these had mother of pearl inlays, which all became more abundant.

The era gave way to the age of walnut, reflecting an advance in sawing techniques that permitted thinner planking, yielding a better return on wood. In turn the science of fitted drawers took a leap forward.

By the middle of the eighteenth century the most fashionable new furniture was made of mahogany and satinwood. Following European expansion into the New World, the rich depth of newly discovered mahogany and honey tones of satinwood were soon in high demand. Early in the century, the taste had been elegantly simple furniture thanks to the high cost of the wood and overarching Puritan ethics. But transport innovation increased the opportunities for import and in 1788 alone 30,000 tons of satinwood was brought into England and Wales from the West Indies.

Before his death in 1779, Yorkshire-born Thomas Chippendale had set a benchmark for carpenters everywhere, reflecting Gothic, Chinese and French rococo styles popular at the time in his widely distributed pattern book The Gentleman and Cabinet Maker's Director.

The increase in ornamentation is bracketed as the Baroque period, a response by the Catholic church to the Protestant Reformation which included the use of extravagant inlays and extensive gilding. It came to Britain with an influx of craftspeople when travelling around Europe became more commonplace.

By 1800, decoration was richer and more imaginative even for workaday furniture including, for example, cabriole legs curved outwards at the shoulder and inwards at the feet. A plain pad was replaced by hooves, ball and claw and then scroll designs.

In the Regency period, prior to Queen Victoria taking the throne, the popularity of rosewood grew. And as education began to shine a light on greater numbers of the population, the demand for desks and especially writing slopes rose. Also called lap desks, they were personal possessions rather than furniture that were taken on military campaigns or overseas tours and used to write novels, letters, contracts and postcards.

They could store the fundamentals of old-style communication. Some have glass inkwells or secret drawers and may have once housed gentlemen's shaving or women's sewing kits alongside pens and paper. These small, shiny chests are frequently decorated with brass, mother of pearl or marquetry.

Bamboo furniture appeared for the first time in the 1740s but enjoyed peak popularity in Victorian times. The same applies to caned chairs.

It was during the latter half of the nineteenth century that furniture styles turned and turned again. For the first time painted furniture began to appeal to home-owners, either to disguise an inexpensive wood or mimic a rare one.

Plywood, formed from gluing thin sheets of wood together, came to the fore in the 1860s not as board but moulded, in furniture. Not only was it cheaper than forest-hewn wood but it could be used in mass produced items.

In the distant past, castors had been made of wood and then leather but finally brass castors made bulky furniture easy to manoeuvre. Now mass production associated with the Industrial Revolution made items much cheaper and easier to obtain. With manufacturers striving to gain prominence in a competitive market, there was a perpetual cycle of revivals of previous fashions, making it difficult for a lay person to distinguish an original Queen Anne piece from a Victorian imitation.

20TH CENTURY

The Arts and Crafts movement, in full flight by the turn of the twentieth century, was a response to this, emphasising the need for integrity, beauty and craftsmanship.

During the twentieth century there were a range of furniture designs queuing to take a bow centre stage, including Edwardian style, more compact than previously to fit into the rafts of new homes built for the burgeoning middle classes, and Art Deco, with its simplified forms. Mid-century it was modernism that was popular: striking yet functional. In Britain downbeat utility furniture was the order of the day as far as the government was concerned, to help manage a wartime shortage in timber. And it was these inexpensive pieces that became familiar to many as they grew up, earning a place in their hearts that no showstopper piece could rival.

MEMORABLE MOMENTS

Will: 'Every piece has its own story. It is amazing to think that some of my work becomes part of that story.'

The oldest piece of furniture to have come through The Repair Shop doors is a Georgian knee-hole desk that had been in the same family from new and was handed down through the female line.

It fell to Will Kirk to return this 'cherished old lady' to tip-top condition before it went on to the next generation. He identified it as an early Georgian piece of furniture, approximately dating from the reign of George I, between 1714 and 1727. Soon afterwards, furniture fashion came under the broad influence of interior designer Thomas Chippendale, and walnut gave way to mahogany while ball and claw feet replaced traditional squared ones.

Although its top featured ink stains, coffee cup rings and veneer chips and there was evidence of a previous wood worm infestation, the desk still stood firmly on its own four feet. So it was rejuvenating care that was required rather than anything structural.

Perhaps the most challenging task for Will was to replace a top corner of the desk devoured long ago by wood-worm. The tell-tale pattern of tiny holes in a patch of wood left spongy by the attack meant it would be impossible to satisfactorily mask the area with a 'sticking plaster' approach. The corner would have to be removed and replaced. After cutting away the damaged section Will found a piece of solid walnut that he could glue into place. Much later, when the glue was dry, he used chisels to carve it into an exact match for the opposite corner.

Missing veneer doesn't usually present a difficulty. This time, though, the historic veneer was cut much thicker than its modern equivalents and Will initially struggled to find a match with sufficient depth to create a smooth finish. When that hurdle was overcome, the carefully selected veneer was held in place by masking tape while the glue dried. Only then could he file it to fit, then colour match it.

Like all furniture, the desk had attracted its fair share of dirt down the centuries. Repeated polishing can trap the gathered grime under a sheen but Will was determined to refresh its appearance, so its colours would be richer and deeper. Using a rag armed with a mild mix of white spirit and turpentine the muck of ages was slowly stripped away before its final polish. In doing so he retained ingrained marks that added to its character while giving it a lustre worthy of its historic status.

* * *

Still, there's no set pattern to the way Will works. When another wooden heirloom came his way he began, rather than ended, his work with a deep clean. This three-legged table had a triangular top which was transformed into a circle when three curved, hinged flaps were lifted into position. The flaps, all in excellent condition, were decorated with inlay. But the top had a central section of veneer missing, probably lifted by the dampness of a plant pot placed there at some stage in its 200-year history.

Immediately Will identified it as a rosewood table, which presented a difficulty. It's a wood that becomes lighter with age and the dark replacement veneer would not sit well among the more aged blond wood surrounding it. Reluctantly, Will decided on a two-stage process bleaching for the strips of veneer he had chosen, something he only uses as a last resort as it's such a caustic and powerful substance. However, once the treated wood was neutralised with a mix of water and white spirit the effect was everything he'd hoped for: smooth, pale and beautifully patterned. Still, he had yet to tackle the challenge of making a seamless repair at the table's heart.

On closer inspection he discovered that the veneer surround the missing patch was mottled and grey – and he called in ceramics expert Kirsten Ramsey for a second opinion. Should he continue with the difficult-to-manage repair or take a bolder route, replacing all the veneer on the table top that was encased in a thread of decorative inlay? After scrutinising the existing veneer, Kirsten appreciated why he was having second thoughts about a small-scale repair. Scalpel in hand, Will began the slow task of removing it all.

Happily, he knew one effective short cut to lift the thin wood from strong, stable adhesive that had endured for decades. With a damp cloth on the table he brandished a warm iron to ease off each section, careful not to impinge on the inlay.

Soon the exposed base wood was re-covered with the treated strips of veneer, cut after being measured – and re-measured – to ensure it was correctly placed. After each side of the triangle was glued, a plank of wood was clamped across it to ensure it dried flat.

The result was impressive, but Will was quickly distracted by a different issue. One of the side flaps stood proud of the table, creating a ridge. When he investigated he realised the some of the hinges were bent with age so these too were clamped to make them straight again.

With a final polish the table was revived to its pre-Victorian splendour, in a condition that the owner's great grandmother would recognise and one that his descendants would appreciate.

* * *

Sometimes it's experience that brings about the right results, at other times, plain instinct. But as with the table, occasionally Will has to rely on the expertise of others to guide him.

That's what happened when he was presented with a broken spinning wheel, once used for tourist displays on the Shetland Islands. When he surveyed the treadle-powered device he admitted he was 'on the ropes' as he had no idea what a working model looked like.

As part of his research he consulted with Joan and Clive Jones, who have been restoring spinning wheels for more than 20 years. Joan explained the spinning wheels from Shetland comprised various woods. As there were no trees on Shetland, makers were historically dependent on what washed up on the shores.

She explained the broken 'flyer', a U-shaped part with a metal shaft which holds the bobbin and helps wind the yarn, would need to be refashioned rather than repaired as the centrifugal force it created would defy any adhesive.

Copying the intact side of the flyer on to graph paper and flipping it to draw its second, broken arm, Will then cut out a replacement and shaped it on a lathe. With the wobbly base below, he pulled out each leg with ease, the connecting adhesive having crumbled. After cleaning out the dried glue he stuck it together again, ensuring the base was horizontal and stable this time. Always appreciative of team work, Will welcomed Joan and Clive back to The Repair Shop to ensure the spinning wheel was working well before it was returned to its owners.

USEFUL TERMS

Flitch: A log that has been made into veneer sheets, which are bundled together and ready to use in the order they were cut. It's a good idea to number these sheets, to ensure they stay in their running order.

Clipped: Sheets of veneer where the defects have been removed.

Intarsia: Italian Renaissance technique by which sawn veneers were laid into solid wood. Today, it equates to marquetry.

Cross banding: A wide strip of straight-grained veneer, used as a frame for veneer panels, sometimes edged with decorative bandings.

Feather matching: Using straight-grained veneer in a chevron shape.

Ormolu: Also known as firegilding, ormolu refers to the metallic mounts that were hallmarks of French cabinet makers in the eighteenth and nineteenth century. Originally, ormolu was a gold and mercury amalgam applied to bronze. However, the mercury component meant gilders rarely survived into their middle years, so the original materials were sidelined in favour of less-harmful copper and zinc.

Rotary cut veneer: Once veneer was hand-sawn, but technology meant that veneer factories appeared from the middle of the nineteenth century. Soon mahogany nut and rosewood veneers, with their rich colours and complex grains, became affordable and desirable. Today the thickness of veneer can be as thin as a flimsy 0.5mm by rotary cutting the tree trunk using a modern machine as if it were a pencil being sharpened.

Shellac: Collected from the bark of trees in India and Thailand after being secreted by a bug, shellac comes in dried flakes and is mixed into polish.

Will's List of Do's and Don'ts

- *Don't put wooden furniture in windows, where it's in the path of direct sunlight, or next to radiators. The heat will shrink wood and warp veneer. Even in an old piece of furniture, the wood is still living. The contraction of wooden furniture is also a hazard with underfloor heating.*

- *Do dust wooden furniture often, but don't use aerosol furniture polish that contains silicone as this may burn through the top layer of polish and create a hazing effect.*

- *Do apply a beeswax polish with a soft cloth every six months.*

- *Do pick up chairs from under the seat, rather than the back, so there's no undue pressure put on the joints.*

- *Don't lift a table from the top surface in case that loosens its fixings to the base. Choose the legs instead.*

- *Don't pull a drawer open with one handle as this will open it at an angle and can harm the runners and joints.*

SILVERWARE

dmired for centuries, lustrous silver is still highly sought
after for making jewellery and other decorative objects.
A collection belonging to one household was deemed so desirable
a burglar put almost all of it into his swag bag, leaving a family
devastated. The sole remaining item of the inherited silver was a
mirror with a blue velvet border smothered in shiny decor, with
one top corner on its ornate border damaged – which is perhaps
why the thief left it behind.

No one knows the age of the silverware or how the mirror frame
was broken but, with the rest of the collection gone, its sentimental
value was vastly enhanced. Carol New bought it into The Repair
Shop to see if the small but significant section of missing silver
could be recreated.

For silversmith Brenton West it was a challenging prospect, but
one for which he had special empathy. In 1980, items he fashioned
during a three year silversmithing course in Kent were stolen while
they were on display in the foyer of a top London hotel, so he
recognised the sense of loss this family felt.

Still, it wasn't a case of merely mimicking another corner as the intricate pattern surrounding the mirror rendered a different formation on each one. He had noticed it was at least a repeating pattern, so with careful observation he could deduce what was missing. Now he combined the ancient craft of silversmithing with some new technology to achieve the results he needed. After photographing the section of pattern he wanted to recreate, he used computer software to put it into the shape of a corner. For the first time he saw the proper formation of the missing link.

After tracing the computer-made pattern he could lay it directly on to a piece of silver. Decorations like this are made by a process called chasing, using punches with shaped ends. Chasing tools come in various sizes and designs and if Brenton doesn't have the one he needs to hand, he will make one that's right for the job. By tapping on the punch Brenton could mould the metal and create raised reliefs. The sliver of silver needs to be held firm while that's being done, however, so Brenton reached for some specialist kit, a cast-iron pot filled with malleable pitch. Heated until it's molten, the pitch holds the silver like glue while work is being done, but doesn't hinder the pattern-making process.

Approaching from the top, he sank small sections of the metal, leaving a protruding pattern. When a similar procedure is carried out on the reverse side of the silver, it is known as repousse. It's time-consuming but, with limited changes since the third century BC when the first evidence of the craft appeared, it's a living link with all the great civilisations of the past in which decorative metalwork was prized, including the Egyptians and the Incas.

To liberate the elaborate outline he'd forged from its original silver rectangle, he chose a jeweller's piercing saw with a blade little wider than a single hair. Exerting only mild pressure, he cut downwards to create the spaces that would reveal glimpses of the blue velvet behind the silver border. Inevitably tiny slithers of silver were lost to the floor. Brenton collects these for a scrap pot, the contents of which are recycled annually.

The sight of the fixed and freshly polished looking glass stirred powerful emotions, this time not for the loss the family had suffered, but sheer joy that this splendid memento would be saved for future generations.

Hallmarks

A set of symbols on precious metals that guarantee its purity. They include marks that denote the Assay Office where the article was tested, the name of the maker and the date it was made. Additional marks might also reveal if it was a commemorative item, whether it was imported and if duty has been paid. The system of publishing the provenance of the silver to safeguard the metal's value has been in existence for more than 700 years.

A Selection of Brenton's Workshop Tools

Silver is soft and pliable, which dictates some of the more unusual articles in his collection.

1. **Leather sandbag:** A firm cushion against which Brenton can mould silver.

2. **Pitch bowl:** To hold silver while work is carried out.

3. **Ring mandrel:** A round form used for making rings.

4. **Files:** To smooth imperfections from the metal before polishing.

5. **Punches:** An array, all of which he has made.

6. **Soldering equipment:** Silver is notoriously difficult to solder, but some repairs dictate it must be done. For example, old silver spoons that may fracture can have the split sawn out, hammered down and soldered to effect an invisible repair.

7. **Piercing saw:** Rather than large wood saws, Brenton's tend to have delicate frames and minute blades.

My Favourite Tools

Not just one but three tools are rated as essentials by Brenton when he's in his workshop. First of the trio is a doming hammer, which he would use to make a pot or vase out of a flat silver sheet in a bowl-shaped indent formed in the cross-section of a tree trunk.

Next is the raising hammer, used to 'raise' the metal by hammering on cast-iron stakes.

Finally, there's the planishing hammer, used to smooth a surface by lightly tapping so that each hammer mark overlaps the last.

Projects

HOW TO POLISH SILVER

1. Don't use the wrong polish on silver as those made for brass or other metals are too abrasive. Specially designated silver polish is less so.

2. Use a soft cloth and a small amount of polish.

3. Rub the cloth in an up-and-down motion, rather than a circular one, which risks abrasion.

4. Turn the cloth frequently so there's no chance of putting back the tarnish taken from one item on to another.

5. Be careful polishing around the silver hallmark. A sustained campaign of vigorous polishing could render the mark illegible.

6. Rinse and buff.

7. There are numerous suggestions for cleaning silver using household goods. However, the advantage with polish is that it guards against tarnish and slows its encroachment.

HOW TO REPAIR A SCRATCH
IN A SILVER ITEM*

1. Only use this technique on everyday silver items. Seek professional help regarding valuable pieces.

2. Soak some very fine wet and dry sandpaper (2,000 grade) and work it gently over the scratch.

3. When the scratch has disappeared from view, use even finer wet and dry sandpaper (4,000) and repeat the process to rid the item of any residual marks.

4. Next, take some brass or chrome cleaner and use vigorously on the area.

5. Finally, use dedicated silver polish to refine the finish.

* Do not use on silver-plated items

HOW TO REFURBISH BRASS DOOR KNOBS

Brass door furnishings are found in houses old and new. In Victorian times, unlacquered brass was relentlessly polished to keep it shiny, although today a degree of natural tarnish is sometimes seen as lending character. Modern equivalents are usually lacquered, eliminating the need for regular maintenance.

1. Lacquered brass has a clear protective sheen. Dust with a soft cloth and do not use polish.

2. If black spots have started appearing on a lacquered item it indicates the lacquer is breaking down. The same is true if dull patches are evolving.

3. To remove failing lacquer, Brenton uses acetone or alcohol and works in a well-ventilated room, wearing goggles. In addition to commercially-made solutions, bicarbonate of soda and boiling water will also strip it back. Use a stiff brush – not one with metal bristles that could leave scratch marks – to remove stubborn stains.

4. You can then choose to leave the door knobs unlacquered and commit to a regular polishing regime. This will be especially necessary if the brassware is exposed to weather and body oils from skin.

5. Or you might prefer to re-lacquer, either immediately or later after ensuring the surface is clean so a new layer will properly adhere.

6. There's a chance your door handle isn't solid brass. Test with a magnet. If it sticks to the handle then it's a ferrous metal underneath with a brass finish, which could be rubbed away by over-polishing. If the magnet doesn't stick, double check by making a small scratch in a hidden area. Should the scratch mark show up a silvery colour, then it indicates the item is also brass-plated. In both instances, a lacquered finish is probably the better option.

MEMORABLE MOMENTS

Brenton: 'In these days of efficient manufacturing processes our thoughts have been drawn away from the skill of the craftsman. My job is to entice people back into appreciating the dexterity of the hands and the efforts of minds that created items that I repair.'

In Wales a love of poetry, prose and music is celebrated in Eisteddfod festivals across the country in a tradition that dates back to the Middle Ages.

One 15-year-old was proud to win the silver crown adorned with a red velvet cap for her poetry recitation in 1937. Eventually she passed both the silver-plated diadem and a love of performance art to her daughter. But the engraved crown came off second best as it got dented and bent when it was stored in a box. The task of reviving the tarnished prize fell to silversmith Brenton West who started by giving it a thorough clean. His next move was to pass the velvet insert, now parted from the crown, to the bear repair duo Julie and Amanda for cleaning and renovation.

The crown was a compressed oval instead of being head-shaped. Rather than squeeze the crown this way and that, Brenton cut a strip of brass and formed it into a pattern that would fit his head, to use as a guide. As he discovered, the crown with its nickel base was tough to manipulate. He pressed it against his leather sandbag, constantly checking it against the brass ring until the shape was properly refined.

Then he cleaned the crown again, this time using a finely textured Water of Ayr Stone. Also known as a Tam O'Shanter hone, Scotch or snakestone, it was first quarried north of the border, and then mined. Always used in conjunction with water to stop it scratching, the hone stone is used for both polishing and sharpening. Afterwards he could clearly see where the silver plate had worn away and the nickel beneath was showing through.

To rectify that Brenton used silver plating solution, with an electric charge running through the crown to make it adhere.

As for the red velvet cap, it was now itself in two parts. Amanda washed the lush material in mild suds while Julie reinforced the separated band with a strip of felt, that was then covered by the original satin. The two parts were then sewn together and returned to Brenton so he could glue it into the crown, where it once again stood proud of the rim.

The crown was now gleaming and plush, a regal addition to Welsh cultural history.

* * *

The small silver purse, used to hold mementos of a mum long gone and barely known, had seen better days. It was discoloured by time, and pock-marked by dings, with a leather inset that was frail and flapping.

Crumpled and dulled, it sat in the palm of Brenton's hand while he considered how to tackle a project that held special significance for a woman who was 22 when her mother died, as the deep-rooted maternal bond was poised to bloom into a loving, giving friendship.

None of his plans could materialise, though, until Susie stepped in to remove the leather purse sections which were so finely folded they looked like origami. She gently levered the leatherwork off its thin cardboard backing to give herself a pattern to follow while making a replacement.

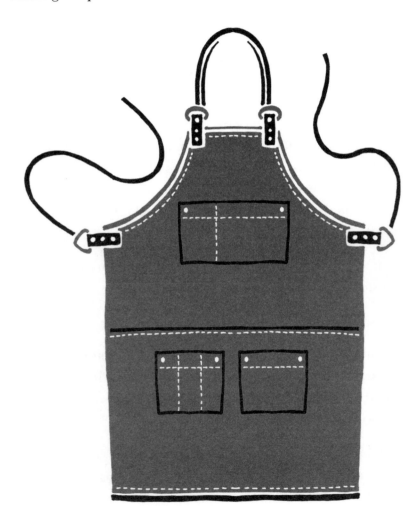

Back in Brenton's hands the lightweight purse had its small chain handle removed as well as the pin hinge. With each separated side he now embarked on the process of annealing, heating and cooling the silver to make it more malleable. In turn he warmed the tree resin in his pitch pot, which acted like a supportive hand beneath each curved side as he tapped out the lumps and bumps of the thin and brittle silver. It was a painstaking process. Working on the inside of the purse, he used a hammer and a chasing tool, striking it gently to achieve minute movements in the metal. Inevitably, that caused tiny ripples on its outside, visible despite the lined pattern. To counter those Brenton turned the purse sides over and used smaller taps still, working between the lines for a smooth finish. Then it came to polishing which finally revealed the evenness in the shaped halves that he had been working towards.

He poked the hinge pin back into place using parallel pliers before returning it to Susie so she could reunite it with the leather insert. She had recreated the three internal compartments after grasping the way it was folded and stitched, and now carefully glued it back into place. When the chain was attached it looked just as it did when its first owner saw it. Soon the family treasures were nestling inside once more: a Victorian crown said to be an unknown grandfather's first week's wages and a mother's wedding ring.

USEFUL TERMS

EPNS: Stands for Electro Plated Nickel Silver and refers to the base metal of an item, which might have been silver plated. The name is misleading as there's no silver involved, rather an alloy of nickel, zinc and copper.

Annealing: Heating and quenching metal to make it more malleable.

Bezel: A grooved ring that holds the cover of a watch face, photograph or a locket in place.

Lemel: Scraps of silver.

Chasing: A metalwork technique in which soft metal is gently hammered to create patterns.

Repousse or repoussage: A metalwork technique in which the metal is gently hammered from its underside into a pattern.

Brenton's List of Do's and Don'ts

- *Don't put valuable or old silver in the dishwasher. This is particularly true of antique dinner service knives, which have handles filled with pitch resin that melts at high temperatures. In modern silver knives that's been replaced by epoxy resin.*

- *Do put cleaned silver that's not destined for a shelf in an airtight container to help maintain its lustre.*

- *Don't attempt to fix silver with lead solder. Lead quickly corrodes silver.*

- *Don't eat eggs with silver cutlery as the sulphur in them turns silverware black.*

LEATHER

I n 1967 a suspended chair went on sale that seemed to characterise both easy living and the ethos of the decade. Instantly it became a design icon. Called the Leaf Chair, for the shape of the seat that dangled in a white, powder-coated steel frame, its designer was Rupert Oliver, the pioneer of soft play equipment.

So perhaps it was fitting that the chair, which became a fixture of Carl Sebastian's childhood, was not so much high fashion furniture as a rocking boat that he sailed with his sisters and cousins when he visited his Italian grandmother's flat, where the chair was hung in reach of the record player. Eventually Carl was given it when his *nonna* downsized.

But, as the years passed, the chair became less of a boat and more like a leaky tub. The leather turned increasingly brittle until it was finally reduced to chunky shreds, flapping from leather lacing that held them fast to the frame.

The Repair Shop's leather expert, Suzie Fletcher, was left scratching her head about the best way to make this exemplar piece of furniture shipshape again without sacrificing one iota of its comfort. Usually, craftspeople prefer to maintain the original materials in a restoration project, but this time the buffalo hide was beyond repair so an all-new seat had to be fashioned. However, the original design was far from straightforward, using three seamed sections to create a clever bowl shape that cradled the body. Now the challenge was to ensure a seat replacement didn't ride too high on the frame, nor was slung too low. Fortunately, upholstery guru Sonaaz Nooronvary was on hand with feedback and ideas.

The way forward, Sonaaz felt, was to make a pattern from calico and tape it to the frame so they could use nips and tucks to test width and depth, and see just how the three-section seat would look before making any inroads into a costly leather hide. It was time well-spent as the pattern seemed to be a perfect replica. Immediately, the margin for error was substantially reduced and Suzie could cut out the shapes with certainty – although not before she triple-checked measurements for this monumental project.

Suzie realised she would have to use a piece of full grain leather, the tough top layer of a hide, to ensure the seat stood up to wear and tear. Folding, sewing and trimming the seams on each of the three sections was a relatively straightforward task for a seasoned stitcher like Suzie, but when she joined them together, the animal skins became bulky and difficult to manoeuvre, especially as they were being machine-sewn. The seams would be the backbone of the new seat, taking all the strain, so even and strong stitching was essential. With Sonaaz at her side, she wrestled the leather through the sewing machine at a snail's pace.

As a master saddler, Suzie is used to heavy work, which was fortunate as the onerous job of punching 100 holes around the edges of the new seat and securing brass eyelets in them still lay ahead. It was a time-consuming process. Only then could she finish the job, threading yards of leather thonging between seat and frame to hold it secure.

Carl and his Italian *nonna* were delighted with the chair, while for Suzie there was a different satisfaction. She had not only tested her craftsmanship, but also learned something new, having collaborated with Sonaaz. For her, it's not the amount of certificates she keeps in a drawer that pay tribute to her ability and professionalism, but the excellence of the last job she did.

TANNING

Tanning is the process that turns animal hides into leather. Without it the skin would putrefy, and historically tanners were relegated to the outskirts of villages and towns because of the noxious smells associated with their craft. Although it's a far less malodorous job today, the necessary steps to turn skin to supple material are much the same.

1. The first step is to cure the hide, by salting or chilling, which not only arrests further deterioration but also removes water content. This can take anything from hours to days.

2. The hide is then soaked in water to rehydrate and clean it.

3. Liming then takes place, to remove the outer layer of skin and hair. It also helps to eliminate grease and fat while conditioning the skin. Any remaining hair is taken off either by machine or by hand using a knife, in a process known as scudding.

4. Afterwards the hide goes through a machine to remove any remaining fleshy tissue.

5. Now the alkalines are neutralised to stabilise the skin's tissues, in what's known as deliming.

6. That's followed by bating, a softening process once carried out with animal dung, but now with the use of enzymes.

7. Then it's time to pickle the hide, first using a salt solution, then a weak acid, to bring down its pH.

8. Degreasing using solvents takes out the last of the excess fat prior to tanning.

9. There are several different processes when it comes to tanning. Mostly chromium salts are used to make stretchy leather suitable for clothes or handbags. However, tanning with different chemicals or even plant extracts also takes place. In all cases the hides are neutralised afterwards to remove any remaining chemicals.

10. At this point the leather might be dyed.

11. Afterwards comes fatliquoring, that is, applying oils to lubricate the fibres and keep the leather supple.

12. Samming is the process of putting the hide through a large mangle-style machine to remove water.

13. Setting out means the leather is stretched and smoothed. Together with the next process of final drying, the water content is further reduced.

14. A staking machine massages the leather to make it softer. It might even be subjected to dry drumming, being tumbled in a rotating drum, for the same purpose. Now the surface is reading for mechanical abrasion if it is destined to be suede, or buffing, to produce a fine nap. All leather is graded before it is despatched.

A SELECTION OF
SUZIE'S HAND TOOLS

1. **Knives:** Suzie uses round, head, straight and French knives.

2. **Plough gauge:** This cuts strips of leather to a specific width.

3. **Awls:** These come in various sizes and are used for making holes.

4. **Pricking iron:** In hand-sewing, this is used to mark stitch length and size.

5. **Crew punches:** These come in various sizes, to make rectangular holes for buckle tongues.

6. **Edge tool:** This removes the sharp edges of recently cut leather.

7. **Edge creaser:** A heated iron used to put a line on leather, either for decoration or as a guide for stitching.

8. **Splitting machine:** Also known as a skiving machine, it slices thick leather to create two layers.

9. **Flocking iron:** Once used to position specially tufted wool in saddle panels and seats. Today, wool has been largely replaced by foam.

10. **Smasher:** This is used to flatten the wool going into the saddle.

The tool kit also includes assorted hammers, mallets, rulers, needles, punches and a staple gun.

My Favourite Tools

As a teenager, Suzie had a workshop in her grandparents' house, in a room that had once belonged to her father. One of the first tools she used there was a pair of pliers with red plastic handles and a narrow head. At the time they belonged her grandfather – the clock repairer who inspired her brother Steve – but they soon became part of her tool kit and are still in regular use today. Although part of the plastic handle has come away, the tool's head remains shiny and its ridged teeth are intact. For Suzie, having them is like maintaining a tangible connection with him.

She also feels that craftspeople are so at one with their tools that they can identify each by feel. Every awl, knife and pricking iron has its place on her workshop walls. She has even been known to cry when an often-used and much-loved one breaks.

1. 'The Beast' is the name of Suzie's heavy-duty sewing machine, a German-made Adler, which can stitch through tough and thick leather 'as if it were butter'.

2. By contrast, 'Edith' is a medium-weight machine for less robust projects, once again made in Germany.

3. Her third machine is called 'Pearl', a 29K Singer treadle machine, made for industrial use and with a revolving foot so it can sew in any direction. Her serial number reveals that 'Pearl' was one of 2,000 machines of this type that were made in 1951. Suzie admits it is sometimes difficult to work with the historic machine, but respects Pearl because of her great age.

4. Suzie has a cobblers' 'last' called 'James', with three arms that are shaped like human feet, used for shoemaking.

5. Emptying her father's workshop after his death, Suzie picked up more small pliers and nippers, which she didn't know she would need, but would be lost without today.

Since being part of The Repair Shop team, Suzie has learned hot foil embossing in order to decorate a rocking horse's reins. She taught herself the skill after the rocking horse was bought in for renovation by a woman whose husband, like Suzie's, had died from cancer. Now she has a number of embossing wheels in her tool collection, which she uses to imprint gold or coloured foils on to leather.

PROJECTS

Few craftspeople will have as many tools in their locker as leather workers like Suzie. Since learning her skills at a seven year apprenticeship after school, she has gathered an array of tools to cover every eventuality. Still, there are maintenance routines and small repair jobs that are within everyone's grasp thanks to Suzie's guidance.

HOW TO CLEAN AND 'FEED' LEATHER

When leather loses all its natural oils, there's a risk it will crack. When leather becomes riven with cracks that are deep and well-established, it could break. Using a conditioner will help replenish it with appropriate grease, to make it supple again and add resilience. A good leather conditioner will also provide a stain repellent barrier, brings out the natural shine rather than changing the colour of the leather and won't feel sticky. Depending on the item, it might be best to look for a conditioner that offers UV protection.

1. Dip a clean, soft cloth in tepid water and squeeze to remove excess moisture.

2. Wipe it over the leather in broad sweeps, gradually turning the cloth so it picks up all the surface dust, mud, sweat and grease. If you are cleaning shoes, be sure all the dirt is gone from seams and beneath laces because the sand and grit embedded in there act like sandpaper.

3. If there's a stain, wipe over a larger area instead of concentrating on one spot, to avoid soaking the patch with water or marking the surface by rubbing too vigorously.

4. Don't use harsh cleaners or abrasive tools, even if that seems right for the job. There's a risk the leather will be scratched, discoloured or frayed.

5. When it's clean, let the item air-dry. Don't be tempted to put it by a radiator or in the sun to quicken the process as that may compromise the leather.

6. For saddlery, solid cases and harnesses, Suzie recommends bar saddle soap. Once again, wring out a clean cloth, rub it on the bar and then apply to the leather. It both feeds and protects the leather, leaving it supple and glossy.

7. Now it's time to finish the job with a coat of conditioner. If the item comes into contact with clothing – like belts, furniture seats, car interiors or handbags – make sure the formula you use won't come off on your clothes. Suitable products usually come as a cream that's wiped on, left to dry and wiped over again afterwards. Test creams on a small and unseen patch before use. Don't overdo it when you apply conditioner though. If the fibres of the leather become saturated they become prone to overstretching and disfigurement. Overstretched leather cannot be restored to full health.

8. Let a thin layer of purpose-made conditioner sit on shoes until it is absorbed. Afterwards, use shoe polish, which will help seal in the newly added oil, then buff to a shine.

HOW TO MAKE AN EXTRA HOLE IN YOUR BELT

Losing weight, or gaining it, could render a well-loved belt unusable. Add an extra hole to give it a new lease of life by following these simple steps.

1. To avoid injury, use the right tool for the job. You need a rotary hole punch, available from tack shops, shoe shops or online for as little as £10. Its wheel will have six different sizes of hole punch.

2. Mark the belt where you need a new hole and choose the appropriate size hole punch to create it.

3. Line up the hole punch and squeeze its pliers-style handles. Some effort will be needed, depending on the thickness of the belt. It might be helpful to pull the leather around the punch to be sure it cuts cleanly through.

HOW TO MEND A HANDBAG

With bags and briefcases, a timely stitch will either effect a temporary repair – to stop it getting worse before you get a professional's help – or mend it so it is ready for use again.

1. Assemble everything you need. The problem has started with worn thread, so the first thing to locate is a heavy-duty one, which you will find on sale in tack shops or at shoe repairers. In addition, you will need a blunt end needle – which is typically stubby with a large eye – a piece of beeswax and a pair of scissors.

2. Pull out all the loose thread and, if it's possible, knot it with the thread ends still attached to the bag to stop it unravelling further.

3. Cut a piece of thread long enough to go two and a half times the gap that needs sewing.

4. Run the thread through a piece of beeswax so it's better protected as it is pulled through the leather.

5. Using holes that already exist, thread up the needle and start by pulling the thread through the first hole for half of its length.

6. Start sewing using each hole, with this half of the thread, in a running stitch, pulling the thread tight.

7. At the end of the line of stitches, unthread the needle and return to the unused half-length of thread. Now use this to stitch in reverse. When it's complete there should running stitches between holes on both sides of the seam and loose thread on each side.

8. To finish, stitch one hole backwards so the threads are the same side. Sew one of the threads back one hole and the other back two holes to lock the stitches in place so you don't have to made a knot, and trim the threads.

MEMORABLE MOMENTS

Susie: 'I just take my time, You never want to rush it. You never want to feel the pressure of time.'

One man who fought in two world wars left a remarkable legacy, including a helmet, a pair of stirrups and a war diary outlining his exploits at the front.

Inevitably, time and active service had taken their toll. The worn steel helmet was missing a chin strap and one of the leather fastenings on the stirrups had snapped. However, even if the cover of the diary was now fragile, his spidery handwriting was still clear. For leather expert Suzie it was an opportunity to pay a personal tribute to a brave soldier whose voice could still be heard, by replacing and rejuvenating helmet and stirrups so they lasted another century at least.

Initially First World War soldiers fought in cloth caps, until the introduction of the bowl-shaped steel helmet in 1915, designed by John L Brodie and officially called Helmet, Steel, Mark I. Helmets weren't universally welcomed in the army until statistics proved their worth in protecting wearers from head injuries.

Given the dent in the top of the helmet, it seems fortunate this soldier had worn one. The treasured items were brought in by his grandson who explained that their owner had joined the army as a teenager in the First World War and seen action at Gallipoli, the Somme and then finally at Ypres.

One diary entry might explain how a ding occurred. 'On Friday we got very close to the firing line. Shells seemed to whizz a few inches above us and shrapnel burst close to where we were several times. One hit my helmet. A fellow said: "Are you all right?"'

After the conflict he was in the Territorial Army as a cavalryman and was pictured in the spurs as part of the official parade at the coronation of George VI. Two years later he was called up for service in the Second World War, surviving the carnage of Dunkirk.

The patina on the outside of the helmet was testament to the action it had seen so there were no plans to change it. But Suzie set about making a chin strap by cutting a strip of new leather of an appropriate length. To soften its sharpness she used an edging tool to pare down the angle. After staining the new leather to give it uniformity she ran it through cloth held in gloved hands, gradually introducing a new softness. Before threading it through the buckles on the helmet she heated a creasing iron to add a decorative trim. Inside the helmet, the lining of Rexine leather cloth was subjected to a careful clean using pipe cleaners to draw off the gathered dirt.

Suzie was determined to keep the same leather on the stirrups because, although it was dry and brittle, she could still sense some strength in it. Carefully she applied oils and grease until a little suppleness returned, then she could attach a backing.

To splice together the split in one of the straps she cut both sides into wedges, so one would slide alongside the next, and used adhesive to fix them. Although the repair would always represent a weakness, it meant the original leather could be preserved.

As she used fine wire wool to clean up the stirrups she discovered the name of the manufacturer, Moss Bros of Covent Garden, London. The extraordinary heirlooms that transformed one man into his grandson's boyhood hero were ready to inspire generations to come.

* * *

Once, a travelling man relied on a sturdy leather trunk to keep his possessions intact – and the most fortunate chose one made by Louis Vuitton.

So it was for one Victorian agricultural expert who travelled the globe with just such a trunk which, according to publicity, had 'unpickable locks' to help keep goods and clothing safe.

When his great grandson brought the trunk into The Repair Shop it was for leather expert Suzie to rejuvenate the dry, biscuity leather and undertake several repairs.

Trunks like this had wooden frames covered in 3mm-thick leather and were lined inside. Some were custom made, and travellers flung back the lids to reveal cupboards, cabinets or even an ironing board. Box maker Louis Vuitton began his company in Paris in 1854, with the first London branch opening some 30 years later.

There was no doubt about this case's provenance, with the prestigious name appearing on studs holding the leather in place. But when Suzie tried to free the stubs of a broken handle from the case she discovered the stud stalks were bent back and so impossible to move. Determined to re-use the monographed studs she was compelled to peel back a section of the linen lining to straighten them before they could be lifted out. It all created considerably more work but, as she observed, as someone had made the case in the first place so it could always be re-made. It was the order in which tasks were undertaken that was key.

The hinge that held the heavy lid in place had split so Suzie made another from new leather. She also cut a replacement over-strap, treading it into the gravel path outside before fixing it to the trunk to age it so it would better blend in. To feed the leather she used saddle soap, creating a lustre without masking any of the marks that were a memory of ships and trains during voyages of a bygone age.

USEFUL TERMS

Tensile strength: Each piece of leather has a tensile strength, the strain that can be applied to it before breaking.

Splitting: The hide is split into layers, with the top being a fine, smooth grain leather and the underside used for suede.

TEDDIES
AND TOYS

Toys are made to be treasured by their young owners, but sometimes they end up bearing the scars of being loved too much. Coupled with great age, the consequences of abundant affection bestowed over years can turn a once proud figure into something weary and worn.

This was the case with the elephant on wheels bought for Pam Edwards by her father when she was a toddler. Every Thursday afternoon the elephant went on parade, being ridden or dragged across the small Welsh town where she grew up to have tea with an auntie.

When it was presented to her, Pam – who had never seen an elephant before – cried: 'What a big mouse.' And after the elephant arrived at The Repair Shop it was promptly named Mouse by Amanda Middleditch and Julie Tatchell, known as 'The Bear Ladies' for their expertise in repairing vintage teddies and toys.

They had their work cut out with Mouse, who had no eyes or tusks and whose detached ears arrived separately in a bag. His accessories were frayed, his wheels were wobbly and there were bald patches starting to appear on his body. Constructed on a metal frame, they estimated that the toy was at least second-hand when it came to Pam as it was made in about 1910. The wood wool stuffing inside was disintegrating, causing the body and the legs to sag.

The first task was to painstakingly remove the accessories that had been glued to the toy's body years before. Not wanting to further damage the ageing fabric, it was a case of removing threads from the glue film one at a time. In doing so, they noticed different threads on the headdress, which once held bells in place, and the stubby felt foundations of the missing tusks.

Crude stitching attached the elephant's tail to its body. Often, Julie and Amanda choose to leave previous repairs in place as they form part of the toy's heritage. However, on this occasion the stitches had created a weak point on the elephant's backside that needed reinforcing if his tail was to be attached correctly.

With all the accessories and body parts removed, Mouse was vacuumed and gently washed to revive the flagging fur. Only when it was completely dry did they begin carefully reconstructing the toy. Its ears were added after being lined in red felt. Two vintage eyes taken from their collection helped to transform Mouse's hitherto blank expression and his trunk end was artfully renewed, not only lined with matching red felt but now clutching a hand-sewn peanut. After being lined with felt, worn patches on his body were darned so as to strengthen the vintage fabric.

Pure wool felt for the new saddle and headdress was chosen carefully in a muted scarlet, so as not to look too new and out of place, and sewn to the felt-lined back. Julie mimicked the decorative stitches that had graced the originals and two shiny bells were attached.

The job wasn't complete, though, until two other Repair Shop experts had played their part. Steve attached one of the rudimentary wooden wheels that had come loose, while Will waxed them, bringing up a protective shine that would ensure they kept rolling for many years to come.

Mouse was once again a picture of dignity and elegance and Pam was overwhelmed by his appearance. Although his fading glory was rejuvenated, he was instantly recognisable as the toy she knew and loved.

How to Age Your Bear

Since 1902, when American President Theodore Roosevelt lent his nickname, Teddy, to jointed toys made in the image of a bear, their popularity has never been dented. Today, they are made in quantity all over the world. But if you have kept a bear from childhood or are a keen collector, there are signs that point to which decade it was made in.

1900–1910

Morris Michtom created a soft toy in honour of the US President who, as a hunter, had become famous for refusing to shoot a tethered bear. Sales led to the launch of the Ideal Novelty & Toy Company in America. At the same time, the Steiff family in Germany were making long-limbed, slightly humped-back bears, with stringed joints quickly replaced by metal. From 1904, Steiff bears were distinctive for having a button sewn into an ear, a trademark that goes on until the present day. Buttons on vintage toys are often long gone, but check to see if there is a hole where one previously existed. Steiff toys, along with others, also bore chest and ear tags. The bodies of early bears were made from mohair and were stuffed with wood wool, which feels crunchy when it's squeezed. Black boot buttons or wooden buttons were used as eyes, while noses were sewn on. The pads of the bears were usually made out of felt.

1910–1920

Glass eyes were now the norm, while kapok, a natural fibre from the seed pod of a tropical tree, began to replace wood wool inside stuffed toys. Sometimes both substances were used. As a result, teddies were firmer and heavier. German makers Bing produced the first wind-up teddy bear in 1910. An all-black bear, representing national mourning, was sold in the aftermath of the *Titanic* disaster in 1912. Other toys also distinguished the era, with many being made from First World War coats, shirts or army blankets. German bears, distinctive for having long arms and snouts, were not imported into the UK during the conflict.

1920–1930

Artificial silk plush was now the fabric of choice for teddy bear makers and cotton was a popular fabric for paws. In 1921, author A. A. Milne bought a bear made by toy firm J. K. Farnell, which became the inspiration for Winnie-the-Pooh. Merrythought, a Shropshire-based company, began manufacturing a distinctive broad-headed, wide-eared bear.

1930–1940

Manufacturers developed unofficial trademarks, like sewing noses in a particular shape or colour. Nylon silk plush was invented in 1938 and the bears being made from it generally had flatter faces and shorter limbs.

1940–1950

An alternative toy filling used by makers during the Second World War was dubbed 'sub', effectively the sweepings from the mill floor. It feels denser and heavier that other stuffings. In 1945, Wendy Boston began making the first non-jointed bears. Three years later she included the earliest lock-in eyes to reflect increasing concerns about child safety. Koala bears made from kangaroo skin started appearing in homes, sent as gifts by distant relatives.

Foam rubber was now being used to fill an acrylic plush body, and by 1954, the first fully washable bear was produced, delighting housewives who could now regularly put washed and sodden toys through the mangle. Wendy Boston even ensured both ears and head were made from a single piece of material, so one wouldn't be lost when it was pegged on the line. Plastic became a mainstay of teddy bear features. Stitched noses were replaced with moulded plastic ones and glass eyes were likewise dispatched to history. Screw-in plastic eyes closely resembled their glass counterparts though. One way to distinguish which your bear has is to hold the eye to your lip. If it feels abnormally cold, it is glass, while if it is room temperature, it is made from plastic.

1960–1970

Teddy bears became ubiquitous, usually filled with polyester wadding. But there was a rival for the affections of the latest generation of children with the popularity of pandas, in the wake of Chi Chi the giant panda's arrival at London Zoo. If a bear or panda had joints, they were by now made from plastic. But safety laws were being tightened to stop them being removable or a choking hazard.

A Selection of Julie and Amanda's Workshop Tools

Working from a studio, Julie and Amanda have numerous crafting tools that assure them of professional results. However, perhaps the most valuable items, packed safely in plastic tubs, are the collection of vintage eyes gathered down the years that can restore the kindly character of an ancient teddy.

1. **Needles of all sizes:** From 25cm (10 inch) doll needles, long enough to pass through a doll's head when fixing eyes, all the way down to small needles with impossibly small eyes to thread.

2. **Needle-nose pliers**: Also known as pointy-nose, long-nose or snipe-nose pliers, these are needed to curl the pointed ends of the cotter pin joints, which are used to give soft toys moveable joints.

3. **Wooden handled stuffing sticks:** In various sizes, these are wielded through small seam openings to pack soft toy stuffing into bodies and limbs. Stuffing is wound around the prongs like candy floss and pressed in to achieve a firm finish.

4. **Brushes:** These help to care for the fur coats of much-loved toys. Julie and Amanda have a variety, including slicker brushes, like those used for pets, through to wire brushes. The choice of brush depends on the frailty of the material.

5. **Large headed pins:** These are used in toy-making so there's no danger of one getting left behind. Julie and Amanda have found rusty short pins inside soft toys left over from previous repair work.

6. **Good light:** Needed for close work like stitching and darning.

7. **Thread:** The correct thread helps to disguise a repair. Julie and Amanda use strong thread with a matt finish rather than a shiny alternative.

Our Favourite Tools

Every working day, no matter what job is in hand, Julie and Amanda reach for their small, sharp embroidery scissors to snip stitches or thread or even make small holes. Easily lost during busy days, scissors like this are vital for tackling delicate or fiddly tasks.

PROJECTS

HOW TO WASH YOUR BEAR

No matter how clean a home, bears kept on shelves and beds may well pick up dust or even acidic grit, which will penetrate the fur pile causing damage. Jointed or aged bears and toys can be washed, but it needs to be a careful operation.

1. Lightly brush and vacuum the bear.

2. Using a mild detergent, like baby shampoo, whip up suds and put only the bubbles on the bear.

3. Wring out a flannel and use it to remove the soap. Avoid scrubbing, wringing and rubbing.

4. Dry naturally, by sitting the bear on a towel in the airing cupboard. If the job has been done properly it should not be that wet.

5. If the toy is two-tone, like a panda, consider taking it apart for washing to avoid the risk of dyes bleeding from one area to the next.

6. Consider using insect-repelling cedar wood balls and lavender bags within your bear collection.

HOW TO MEND YOUR BEAR

Using skills they picked up at their grandmothers' knees, Julie and Amanda have made a thriving business out of bear repair. Just by looking at a beloved toy they can tell how it has been carried: by an ear if it's missing, by a limb if the stuffing is crushed, in the crook of an arm if the head has been pushed sideways. When paw pads are threadbare and noses have been kissed away, the pair pool their knowledge and skills and aim to restore a bear, or any other cuddly toy for that matter, so it can be handed to the next generation looking just as it always has. When it's a toy that has accompanied someone through childhood illness, wartime evacuation or any other given trauma, then repairs need the utmost care and, Julie and Amanda say, it's a privilege to undertake work on items of such great sentimental value. It's estimated a quarter of people keep their childhood companion into adulthood, although time inevitably takes its toll. Julie and Amanda happily tackle the tricky task of re-lining toys to help preserve vintage outer fabrics, using techniques honed through their careers. On particularly frail areas, they choose conservation netting to cover holes before darning. But some refurbishment is within many people's skill set. Here's their advice for anyone embarking on a bear repair.

1. First, buy a jointed soft toy from a charity shop and dismantle it, to better understand some of the pitfalls ahead. Or purchase a bear-making kit.

2. Before starting on your chosen toy, photograph it from all angles, so you have evidence of what it looked like before the repair process started.

3. Do some historical research to help preserve the toy's authenticity. Different manufacturers had hallmark habits, like the shapes of paws, the length of arm or the angle at which ears were attached, and these should be faithfully replicated.

4. Don't do anything you can't reverse. The aim is to ensure the bear resembles its original self.

5. Make sure all improvements are in keeping with the bear's character. For example, don't put a furry or new fabric arm on a balding body. That might mean reversing a piece of loom state mohair and pulling threads through from the back to make the new limb indistinguishable from the old.

6. Carefully colour-match new material with vintage. Julie and Amanda tone down the colours of modern fabrics by using mild dyes made from, amongst other things, diluted tea, coffee, turmeric and soot.

HOW TO STUFF A TEDDY BEAR
(OR OTHER SOFT TOY)

Keeping a favourite soft toy at its right weight regarding maintains its familiar expression and helps to preserve ageing fabric.

1. First locate the closing seam, which is usually stitched in a different way to the rest. In vintage bears it's likely to be hand-sewn and found along the back seam. On more modern soft toys the stitching will be overlocked and discreetly placed, for example, between the legs or on the back of the neck.

2. Carefully undo the closing seam using sharp embroidery scissors, without damaging the fabric.

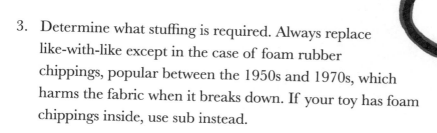

3. Determine what stuffing is required. Always replace like-with-like except in the case of foam rubber chippings, popular between the 1950s and 1970s, which harms the fabric when it breaks down. If your toy has foam chippings inside, use sub instead.

4. Always begin the process by stuffing the outer parts of the body, like the toes or muzzle.

5. Stuffing like sub or polyester should be 'fluffed' before being used. Julie and Amanda use a stuffing stick to pull it apart but a chopstick or spoon handle are also options.

6. Take small pieces of stuffing and place them inside the toy firmly and evenly, to avoid creating lumps.

7. Vintage fabrics are supported by appropriate depth of stuffing. Under-stuffing causes creases which stress the fibres and over stuffing generates unnecessary tension. Both could cause damage. Using memory and common sense, decide how firm your toy needs to be before neatly closing the seam once more.

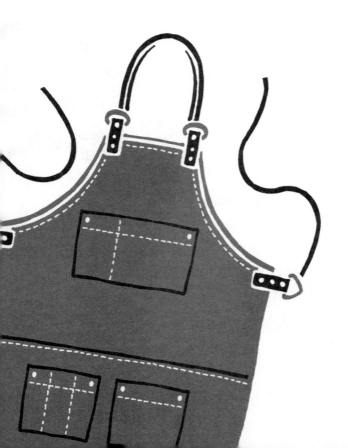

HOW TO RE-ATTACH A GLASS EYE

Bears of a certain age are distinguished by having glass eyes, attached in pairs. If time has taken its toll with one eye, it's likely the other will be failing soon, so take it off and fix both at the same time.

1. The glass eyes used with vintage or mohair bears have a wire loop in the back. Locate the original eye 'sockets', which will have flattened fur and a hole in the centre.

2. Pull a generous length of extra strong thread through the loop on the back of the replacement eye and double knot it so that the eye is held firmly in the centre of the thread.

3. Thread a long needle – known as a doll needle – with both ends of the thread and push the needle out towards the back of the head, so it emerges at the nape of the neck. (The needle needs to be longer than the depth of the head.)

4. Repeat steps 3–5 with the second eye, so the thread emerges at the same point.

5. Tie the eye threads firmly together at the back of the head, ensuring the tension is similar on each side.

6. Pass the remaining loose threads back through the bear's head and snip off any loose ends.

MEMORABLE MOMENTS

Julie: 'I get anxious before I reveal the item even though I know I have done my best. The relief I feel when I see the delight on the owner's face makes it all worthwhile.'

Amanda: 'I love working on the features of a bear, the face especially, all the things that give it character. I just love seeing them come back to life.'

Pink Teddy had an inspiring history. Bought for its owner during the Second World War from prestigious department store Harrods, it accompanied her when she was evacuated to Scotland and later, to boarding school. It was her companion during childhood illnesses and survived being played with by her children and grandchildren. Sadly, it didn't survive the attentions of a puppy.

Now minus one arm and half an ear, it arrived at The Repair Shop with an owner concerned that any repair work didn't bring about any loss in the dignity that befitted his senior years.

Rather than being made of mohair, this was a sheepskin bear, with mohair supplies at the time Pink Teddy was made being directed towards soldier's uniforms and blankets. But that meant the body was less durable than other bears. Julie and Amanda took enormous care as they snipped open a stomach seam and removed all the 'sub' used as stuffing.

To recreate the missing ear they took off Pink Teddy's remaining good one and split it. The original material then became the front of both ears while replacement fabric was put on the back.

When it came to disguising the new material on the back of the ears and the replacement arm Julie and Amanda had to recreate the pink tinge that the teddy's fur now bore. It turned out the best option in this case was hair dye, which was carefully applied to blend in with the rest of the body.

Although Pink Teddy looked just the same, it was benefitting from being lined which offered new resilience for future play. The owner didn't mind some distinguished bald patches. However, the repairers put on some almost invisible patches to ensure the body remained robust.

* * *

Beloved bears that suffer with the ravages of time are often subject to home repairs. George was one such bear, bought for the eldest of six daughters when she was born in 1941 and handed down through them all until being lovingly stitched by the youngest sister in a bid to stem damage.

The moment they saw George, Julie and Amanda recognised elements of his history. He was an Irish-made bear, common in Britain during the Second World War when the import of the more-ubiquitous German bears was halted. Typically Irish bears like George had ears riding high on heads which tended to be sharply triangular in shape and long limbs with pointy paws.

For now George's paws looked more stubby, after being turned over and sewed to stop stuffing leaking from worn-out pads. But the somewhat unsightly repair was welcomed by Julie and Amanda as it kept the original fabric intact.

Their first job was to empty George of stuffing. He was filled with wood wool, which gives a dry crunch when stuffed toys are squeezed. Using pliers the chest was emptied until they found the long-dead growler, once a memorable sound for its succession of owners.

With the paw pad beyond repair Julie and Amanda reversed all the limbs to sew in new felts ones from the inside. There was another new addition too, to make before the bear was re-assembled. The old growler couldn't be saved so it was replaced with a new one. Although it sounded more farmyard than wilderness, it was in fact a sound rooted in the noise a baby bear makes when calling for its mum.

After a missing eye was replaced, the last job of a pamper session fell to Julie. She massaged only the bubbles yielded by mild soap into his body before the foam was removed with a flannel. Afterwards he was dried and brushed, leaving him a smart ted ready to celebrate a fresh start as an octogenarian.

* * *

Throughout her childhood and beyond one woman held fast to her toy panda. It was a gift from her father who died when she was nine and afterwards, by her own admission, life went from colour to black and white. The loss haunted her for years during which time Panda become her only confidante and friend.

Fifty years later the English-made bear was suffering from bald patches, weak seams and missing facial features. The black fur was particularly worn, a problem Julie and Amanda have seen before and assume the dyeing process to be responsible.

First task for team was to remove the head, one small stitch at a time. Only then could the foam rubber stuffing be removed and the body parts separated before being cleaned, to avoid any risk of the dark colour leaching into the pale.

Each bit was then lined to give the ageing fabric new strength. When it came to sewing them back together Julie and Amanda were careful to follow pre-existing stitch lines. Fabric that had been hidden behind the seams for decades had vibrant colouring compared to the rest. But to give panda stripes to mark his age like this would mar his appearance. His label, originally sewn in upside down by the manufacturers, was also stitched back in exactly the same way.

Once the head was firm with new stuffing Amanda sewed on a new nose and replacement red tongue. She also had the tricky job of stitching the head back into place. Vintage fabrics are prone to stretching which could leave the bear with a drooping head or a cricked neck if the seams are inexpertly joined. Lining the fabric lends stability and that's how Julie and Amanda sidestepped the pitfall.

When he was returned to the owner, ready for a second lease of life, she felt the final piece in the bereavement puzzle had slotted into place.

USEFUL TERMS

Plush: A rich fabric of silk, cotton, wool or alpaca with a long, soft nap.

Mohair: The silky wool of an angora goat.

Squidge test: Not a textbook term, but one used by Julie and Amanda as they determine what the stuffing inside a bear is made from and whether it is disintegrating.

Arctophile: A teddy bear collector.

A hug of bears: The collective name for teddy bears.

Julie and Amanda's List of Do's and Don'ts

- Do cuddle them regularly and, while doing so, check for signs of moth or carpet beetle damage. Both insects lay eggs inside toys and have larvae that feed on fabric, leaving bald patches and holes.

- Don't ignore early warning signs. If you suspect there are insects at large in your soft toy collection, put affected articles into a sealed plastic bag and pop them in a domestic freezer for two weeks. That's how long it will take to kill dormant eggs.

- Do take the vacuum on a low or upholstery setting to your soft toy to help deter infestations. Also, regular use of an appropriate brush is at the heart of a good maintenance routine.

- Don't keep soft toys in direct sunlight or next to radiators as heat may cause fabric deterioration.

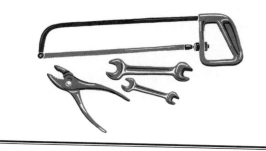

METALWORK

On Christmas morning in 1959, Mervyn Bell awoke to find a gleaming red go-kart waiting for him under the tree. Nearly sixty years later, the go-kart had wobbly wheels, a holed seat and its paintwork bore multiple scars. All the signs were that the low-slung vehicle had been ridden exhaustively by Mervyn and, much later, his children. Now it was time for grandchildren to enjoy this much-loved machine – but not before The Repair Shop's resident metalworker Dominic Chinea made it roadworthy once more.

Made by toy company Tri-ang, the design of this three-wheeled go-kart was striking. Riders pulled two upright handles forwards and backwards to operate cranks that turned the wheels, so heading up hill needed strong arms rather than legs. Their feet rested on a bar that linked the two front wheels and steered by pushing one foot or the other forward.

Tri-ang – part of the world's biggest toy company in the middle of the twentieth century – also made bicycles and pedal cars, marketing their products as 'the toys for happy and healthy recreation'.

Metalworker Dom's first task was to take the go-kart apart and give it a thorough clean, assessing each piece individually before deciding on his next move. With the original red paint hidden by a coat of black, he was at first reluctantly resigned to a re-spray. But now some vigorous rubbing removed the black, so Dom re-evaluated. After some considered touching up with carefully matched paint, the metalwork matched the fifties finish once more, although selected dings and dents gathered over the years were deliberately left in evidence, as reminders of Mervyn's childhood scrapes.

Although the larger rear wheel was original, the two front ones had already been replaced by smaller versions of those initially used, making the front dip and posing a problem that even the power of the internet couldn't solve. While Tri-ang was a well-known toy manufacturer, this particular go-kart model was unusual and *The Repair Shop* research team, along with Dom, struggled to find any original images for comparison purposes. Finally, he settled on a pair of wheels from a similarly aged Triang pram. At the time manufacturers used the same fittings across different ranges, so there was no need to modify the go-kart to fit the new wheels. At the back the wheel was in poor condition, with loose spokes in danger of buckling. Bicycle expert Tim Gunn, working alongside Dom at The Repair Shop, replaced the spokes and put on a new solid rubber tyre.

To make the seat serviceable again, the rusted hole in the metal saddle was cut out and patched up, and a new mounting point for it was welded in too. Once again, when thoroughly cleaned the saddle had ample amounts of the original green paint, which Dom was able to colour-match so it was fully refurbished.

There was evidence that the manufacturer's sticker had once been on the framework, but sourcing an authentic replacement proved impossible. Instead, Dom took a digital copy of a time-appropriate sticker and made one himself, even fashioning some symptoms of wear and tear.

With the go-kart in bits on his work bench, Dom likened it to a giant Meccano set. When it was back in one piece again, after some careful handling to avoid scratching the paintwork, Mervyn was transported back to his childhood, while his grandchildren were transported up some nearby Tarmac, after seizing the chance to try it out.

Types of Metal

When he works with metal, Dominic is continuing a tradition forged in ancient times, when the earliest chemists experimented with ores found in the Earth's crust.

Smelting copper with tin created bronze, a more durable metal than anything else available at the time. This distanced civilisations in command of bronze-making technology from their Stone Age predecessors, giving them stronger tools and weapons, and a desirable commodity to trade.

The Bronze Age, which lasted for centuries, was itself superseded by an age when iron predominated. Both are broad-brushstroke terms, as their dates were dictated as much by geographic location as the calendar. Iron had a much higher melting point than either copper or tin. A shortage of tin in about 1,300 BC prompted a leap forward in iron smelting, which produced cheaper, more durable ironware. Other metals known in antiquity were gold, silver, lead and mercury. Nickel and chromium were discovered in the eighteenth century, aluminium in the nineteenth century, while plutonium was among 20 metals found in the twentieth century.

Today, there are more than 80 metals recorded on the periodic table, the names of most being unfamiliar to us. However, they share a few common properties with the metals and alloys we know well. Metals are shiny, good conductors of heat and electricity, and have a high melting point. They are ductile or pliable when put under stress, hence their use in cabling, and sonorous or resonant when they are struck, thus are made into church bells.

Here's a quick guide to common metals:

Aluminium: Soft, lightweight and fireproof, it brings these qualities to any alloy. In a raw state, it is found in the ground as abundant bauxite.

Iron: Pure iron is silvery-white in colour and almost soft enough to cut with a knife. To become a functional metal it is treated in a blast furnace and adopts numerous forms, including cast iron, when molten iron is poured into a mould and allowed to cool, and wrought iron, when liquid iron is mixed with some of the waste products in production. Basic raw iron is called pig iron.

Steel: Pig iron is the major component of steel, which is then mixed with other metals to form a broad range, each with particular strengths. For example, pig iron blended with chromium and nickel creates stainless steel, famously resistant to corrosion, while pig iron with tungsten and nickel makes tool steel, which is then toughened by a tempering process. Although there are scores of different steels, the greatest made by volume is carbon steel.

Chromium: Best known as a shiny car part, chromium is tough and lustrous. As an alloy with cobalt and tungsten it makes Stellite, which is used for cutting tools.

Copper: Versatile copper, mined throughout the world, can be found in anything from cooking pans to the Statue of Liberty. Copper and zinc together produce brass.

Tin: A silvery-white metal produced by smelting the ore cassiterite. Food tins are coated with tin to stop the steel beneath from rusting or reacting with the contents.

A Selection of Dom's Workshop Tools

As a professional metalworker – as well as restoration projects he's also a set designer – Dom has machinery at hand that most people wouldn't recognise, let alone use. But he also owns a large range of tools that are more familiar, which he's been collecting since the age of 14.

1. **Large collection of hammers with heads bearing different contours:** Dom uses these for panel beating.

2. **Clamps:** These lend a firm grip when items are being welded together.

3. **Shaped dollies, spanners, pliers and metal saws:** All these feature in his range of hand tools.

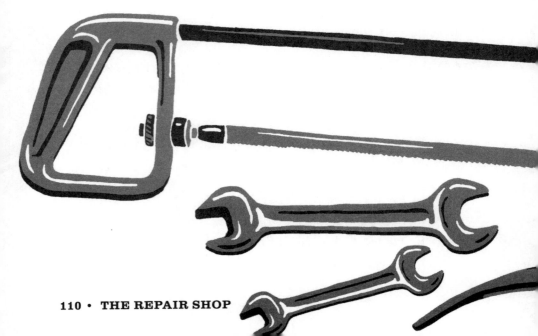

4. **Angle grinder:** With its various attachments, it can be a cleaner or a cutter.

5. **Welders:** Dom has two: a Mig welder, used to weld steel, and a Tig welder, a much more adaptable machine used for aluminium, stainless steel, even brass or copper.

My Favourite Tools

A collection of metal engineering set squares take pride of place in Dom's workshop. Ranging in size from 2cm (³⁄₄ inch) to 62cm (24½ inches), he uses them to mark straight lines and accurate angles.

Projects

HOW TO DEAL WITH RUST

1. If an old tool hasn't been used for a long time and has seized up, soak it in a mix of acetone and automatic transmission fluid for a few days to free up the internal mechanism.

2. With a small rusty item, like a tool, leave it to soak in white vinegar to kick-start the de-rusting process.

3. Afterwards, use a pad of wire wool in conjunction with a lubricating oil to tackle the rust that's still clinging to it. Wire wool comes in numerous different grades, with 4 being coarse and 0000 super fine. It's advisable to start with a fine mesh and graduate upwards.

4. If the rust remains stubborn, there are further options, ranging from a nylon-bristled toothbrush, through brass and steel brushes to an angle-grinder attachment.

5. With chrome, use one of the least abrasive wire wools with lubricating oil. The presence of rust indicates the chrome plating has broken down, revealing the steel below. In order to stem rust for good it needs to be professionally re-plated, but you can delay that by putting on a protective coat of wax.

HOW TO ELIMINATE A MARK
ON NEWLY PAINTED METAL

A fly corpse or a running drip ruins an otherwise unbroken sheen on a recently painted metal item, but the problem is soon remedied.

1. Use a face mask to protect against dust.

2. Take what's known as wet and dry sandpaper, that is, very fine sandpaper. To work out what you need, look for the number on the label. The lower the number, the rougher the grit. So 30 grit is very coarse, 100 grit is medium and 320 grit is fine. But this is a job for a sandpaper classified as more than 2,000 grit.

3. Use the sandpaper with a bucket of water containing a few drops of washing-up liquid, washing the sandpaper out frequently in the water.

4. Using a sanding block to keep everything flat, rub over the imperfections. That should be sufficient to take off the top layer of paint without leaving scratch marks.

5. Polish to perfect the finish.

MEMORABLE MOMENTS

Dom: 'There are so many things going on inside my head when I see a new project; the thought process begins immediately, starting with what's needed, drawing up a plan of attack and the end goal that I'm trying to achieve. And also, I must make sure it is safe.'

In the 1930s Manchester and nearby towns were criss-crossed with 470 km (292 miles) of tramlines and 953 trams trundled along 46 different routes daily. Among the 328 million passengers each year was a schoolgirl who saved up her pocket money for the sheer joy of riding the number 81 service between Salford and Deansgate.

But after operating costs soared and tracks were ripped up for the war effort, its days were numbered. The trams were shut down in 1947 and a vast number of carriages were dispatched into a mammoth bonfire. Although she was devastated by the closure, the schoolgirl who loved riding the trams enjoyed a stroke of luck as her parents' neighbour brought back a tram seat which took pride of place in the family's front garden. Later her widowed mum sat in it, chatting to neighbours and passers-by.

Wooden tram seats sat in an iron framework and were distinguished from others by a slot on the seat side that enabled the back rest to be pushed to and fro, so passengers could face the direction of travel.

Seventy years, on the seat had suffered in the face of British weather, and parts of it had already been inexpertly renewed.

Now aged 93, that schoolgirl was concerned her little piece of history was crumbling.

At The Repair Shop, Dom quickly realised it wasn't a case of rubbing down flaking paint and rust to secure this restoration. Much of the wood was rotting and the metalwork rusty. To make it structurally solid again would be a big task.

He began by dismantling the seat, making a careful plan of it as he went, and sending the metalwork off to be sandblasted. Before it was whisked away he spotted a tiny section bearing the original red coachwork, which he could then duplicate. With sections of wood shearing away, he decided to replace all the planks that formed the seat, together with the tricky-to-mimic curved side slots, using a chunky length of slow-growing American pitch pine, something similar to the material that would have been used for the original seats. Careful measuring meant he got all the necessary lengths from just one piece.

When he had the gentle lines of the new wooden seat in front of him, the sandblasted metalwork arrived back, giving him a new, unscheduled task. The process had been so robust it had stripped back more crumbling metal than expected. For safety reasons, he would have to copy its outline and cut a replica. Originally the frames would have been made in vast numbers, in a factory. Dom sought to imitate the curved feet by making relief cuts in the end metal section, and heat-treating it before bending it into shape. As a nostalgic reminder of the long lost travel system he painted the number 81 on the back rest, the last remaining piece of original wood. When it was re-assembled it looked just as it had when it was new, probably around the turn of the twentieth century. On this occasion it wasn't the attention to detail that gave Dom most job satisfaction but the elation of the owner, transported back to her youth thanks to his expertise.

* * *

Years before the advent of the internet, towns relied on signage to promote themselves and their wares, and a museum in Polperro, south east Cornwall, boasted an eye-catching board to attract visitors. It not only had large lettering and jangling bells but stood on a pole attached to a wheeled stand so it could be pushed around the thronging harbourside.

The fishing and smuggling museum was 'the place to see' in Polperro, it promised, although the sign itself had been smuggled out of the town at some stage. After being reclaimed from an antiques centre in Wales by a resident, the community now needed this uncommon placard, set in its wrought iron frame, future-proofed so it could rally tourists once more around the town's narrow streets.

Fortunately, metalworker Dom was given a decades-old postcard featuring the curiosity in its prime before damp sea air had beckoned in the rust.

To rid the sign of rust – essential if it was to survive for further decades – he had to rub down both the sign and the frame. It meant erasing the remainder of the lettering but Dom set about tracing what was left to preserve the size and style beforehand. With a clean slate he could re-paint the white background and re-draw the black lettering in durable sign-writing paint in the same style as the original.

The links that held the bells in place were worn thin and needed replacing while the bells themselves were tarnished. At this point Steve Fletcher offered to dip the brass bells in clock cleaning fluid to help bring back their shine.

Jay was also recruited onto the project, to replace long colourful tassles that had once hung down the sides of the frame. Making the most of the internet himself, he took tuition tips from a nine-year-old before setting about making them himself.

After replacing frail and eroded metal curls, Dom cleaned, primed and painted the framework in red, yellow and blue. The two dozen bells were re-attached along with the tassels and it was ready to face time and tide in the Cornish fishing village once again.

USEFUL TERMS

Coated abrasives: The proper name for sandpaper.

Oily rag restoration: A term used when restoring an item, but preserving as much of the original patina as possible. Rubbing a lightly oiled cloth over the metal item helps protect it from further encroachment by rust.

Steel wool: Another term for wire wool.

Dom's List of Do's and Don'ts

Although the specialist equipment necessary for major metalwork projects is beyond ordinary householders, some items can still be stripped down at home. Here Dom signposts the best way forward.

- *Do take photographs, measurements and even drawings of your item before you begin a refurbishment project. Document everything that might help when it comes to re-assembly.*

- *Don't forget to use protective gear and clothing.*

- *Do label everything as you take items apart. Put screws in named bags, for example, and use paper tags on larger items to avoid confusion in the future.*

- *Don't use the wrong type of paint. For example, restored items staying outdoors need the protection of exterior paint and will deteriorate without it.*

- Do think outside the box when you undertake repairs and use different component parts, if necessary. When Dom fixed a spinning barber's pole, he discovered the manufacturers used a motor from a gramophone.

- Don't skimp on preparation. Procedures like cleaning and sanding down may seem tediously repetitive, but any compromises taken here will be visible in the end result.

- Don't use excess paint in the hope of hiding areas that haven't been properly prepared. Layers of shiny paint will only amplify any outstanding issues.

- Do create a template out of cardboard or even wood if you are making or designing a new part for an item, to be sure your planned addition will fit.

- Don't strive for perfection at all costs. The quest for a flawless replica is daunting and deters many from starting a project.

- Do become a hoarder. Dom buys inexpensive broken items at sales to liberate unusual nuts and bolts and other mechanical debris that he may well need for future restorations.

- Do use the correct drill bits for the job as those designed for masonry will make a mess of metal. Everything is easier with the right tool!

UPHOLSTERY

After it opened in 1914, Derby Hippodrome was an elegant variety theatre, packed to capacity each week as it hosted the nation's best-loved acts. Later it became a cinema and its final incarnation before closure in 2006 was as a bingo hall.

Seat number 11 from the now defunct building found its way to The Repair Shop after Jamie Woods liberated it from his parents' attic. It had long been a fixture there after plans to renovate it were shelved, with bingo cards lying unnoticed in the wooden pocket on the chair back. The well-worn flip-up seat chair, had only one arm rest and arrived in pieces, with the metal framework that formed its sides also missing the base necessary for it to be freestanding.

It was the first time upholstery expert Sonnaz Nooranvary had renovated a folding theatre chair and she began by stripping back the threadbare green velvet that gave a nod to its former glory, levering out traditional pins that clung stubbornly to the frame.

Inside she found the coiled springs that gave the seat its bounce in such good condition that they could be re-used. Nestling among them she found a tell-tale label, revealing the seat was originally the work of the Elson & Robbins Company, experts in sprung units, based in Long Eaton, Nottinghamshire, which was the heart of the UK's furniture industry in the early twentieth century.

Carefully poking the label back into place, she replaced the ageing hessian that covered the springs with new, stapling it into place around the wooden seat base. Then she stitched the springs firmly to the hessian across the seat to stop them slipping out of position. On the top she added two layers of foam to create extra comfort, using contact adhesive to bond them all into a single unit.

As she turned her attention to the seat covering, metalworker Dom Chinea was rubbing down and re-painting the metal frame in a warm gold and fashioning a replacement arm rest, as well as new 'feet' that would make it a stand-alone item at last. Sonnaz had identified a richly textured green velvet as a replacement fabric, slightly brighter than the original, but in a tone reminiscent of its theatre heyday.

Before measuring, she checked the direction of the fabric pile so that when fixed into place, it ran from top to bottom and from back to front. That meant sitting in the chair wouldn't entail an uncomfortable conflict between clothes and pile.

On the domed seat base she used staples to secure the plush material into position, while on the back she chose more traditional tacks around the edges, for aesthetic purposes, trapping a shallow piece of foam into place. Once that was completed, she could re-assemble the chair in preparation for Jamie's arrival. While to him it appeared almost new, the marks on the surviving arm rest told a different story, scored or scuffed by countless thousands of snugly seated theatre-goers, as they cheered and chortled down the decades.

Hallmarks of the Era

The craft of upholstery in Britain dates back at least to the fifteenth century, when a guild began. But upholders, as they were called, didn't make squashy sofas and soft chairs; rather they created curtains, drapes, tapestries – all vital for insulation – and lined coffins.

At that time furniture was rigidly unforgiving as bare wood was the sole option, with the only relief for the numb backsides sitting on them coming in the form of an animal skin. Only when cushions started being made in the Middle Ages – from leather and stuffed with dried palm leaves – was there some respite.

By the time Queen Elizabeth I was on the throne, padded chairs began to proliferate, partly because the art of stitched edging was developed. For the first time, furniture makers could stuff sawdust, grass, feathers or deer, goat and horse hair into a chair cover to create a luxury seat, albeit still hard.

After the influence of the Puritans ebbed away, the first daybeds were designed, the ancestors of today's sofas, and makers began to decorate exposed parts of the wooden frames. Still, furniture like this really was the preserve of the very rich until Victorian times, when there were two important innovations. Firstly, there was the helical or coiled steel spring, invented just before Victoria arrived on the throne, that kept its shape in a seat pad providing it was adequately lashed into place to control the way it compressed. Then came an abundant supply of fabric being produced in the factories spawned by the Industrial Revolution. Cotton wastage from the burgeoning factories, dubbed mill puff, was used for stuffing.

With a soft furnishings industry in full swing, there were initially chairs stuffed with coir, taken from coconuts, and alva marina, a seaweed found in France and on the Baltic Coast. But after the Germans pioneered the use of curled horse hair – the tail and mane of the animal – its popularity put other choices in the shade and it endured throughout Europe. At the time it was far cheaper to come by as horses were used for transport. Now a more expensive option, it is nonetheless a matter of etiquette to replace horse hair stuffing when older items are re-upholstered today. As manufacturers competed in the comfort stakes, sofas and chairs became increasingly plump, until buttoning and deep buttoning became fashionable.

Duck, goose and swan feathers provided another source of stuffing, especially for cushions and top-of-the-range furniture. Milled or chopped feathers were a lesser product.

Foam rubber, first developed in the twenties, became widely used in upholstery after the Second World War.

A SELECTION OF SONNAZ'S UPHOLSTERY TOOLS

Sonnaz is another of The Repair Shop experts who generally favour second-hand tools for the workshop above new, in terms of quality and longevity.

1. **Regulator:** With two ends – one pointed and the other flat – the regulator is essential when it comes to renovation. The pointed end is designed to tease out horse-hair stuffing, bringing about a smoother finish in old-style seating, while the flat end is useful in pleating when buttons are added.

2. **Tack hammer:** To knock in the pins that hold material in place.

3. **Staple gun:** Staples are used in quantity to secure hessians and fabrics to seat frames.

4. **Rulers:** Essential for measuring out material.

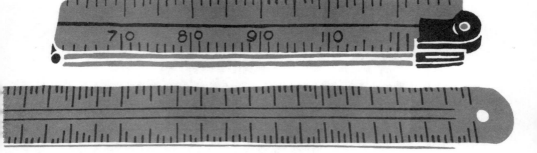

5. **Bull-nosed pliers:** For gripping and pulling out staples.

6. **Tack lifters:** Used to remove historic upholstery pins.

7. **Chalk or wax:** Both are used to mark up material before cutting.

8. **Hot melt glue gun:** Electrically powered so the glue – inserted in stick form – is heated as it comes out of a nozzle, to allow maximum dexterity in tasks like attaching braid.

My Favourite Tools

With cutting material a key part of her job, Sonnaz values above all a pair of shears that are sharp from hilt to tip. Although sometimes the term is interchangeable with scissors, shears are typically longer and heavier in the hand and leave a crisp edge.

PROJECTS

HOW TO REPLACE DECORATIVE BRAID THAT'S PEELING OFF

Sometimes it's the little things that need fixing. Replacing the decorative edge on an ageing chair is often sufficient to give it a fresh look.

1. Measure the length of braid already in position before buying its replacement.

2. Gently remove the failing braid.

3. Fold the new braid's raw end under and track a hot melt glue gun along the line left by the previous one. With careful manipulation you should be able to achieve a perfect curve, but there are obviously perils to using a glue gun like this without considerable practice.

4. For beginners, try instead folding the end over and use coloured tacks to fix the braid in place. After putting the first tack in place, put some tension into the braid by pulling it before inserting the next tack some 10cm (4 inches) from the first. It's likely this will result in a '50 pence piece' effect around the top of a chair.

5. Finish by folding over the fraying edge of the braid back beneath itself and fix it in place with a tack.

HOW TO REPLACE THE COVER OF A DROP IN DINING CHAIR SEAT

The patina gathered on wooden tables and chairs are attractive signs of age and the joys of meals past. But the material covers on seats are prone to altogether less appealing bald patches. Happily, these can be swiftly rejuvenated by anyone confident in cutting material and using a staple gun.

1. Take the seat out of the dining chair and carefully remove all the staples holding the fabric in place.

2. Take off the 'bottom cloth', the mono-coloured material beneath the seat that hides the chair seat's insides.

3. Using the old cover as a template, mark out a replacement for both from new material using chalk or wax.

4. Check that you have the measurements right.

5. Using sharp shears, cut out the new material.

6. Lay the seat material centrally on the pad, then flip it over so the bottom of the seat is facing you.

7. Find the centre of one of the sides and staple the material in place. Repeat for the other three sides, being careful to maintain a tension in the fabric as you do so.

8. Now staple along the remainder of the sides to the corners. Be sure the fabric remains stretched or there's a risk that the seat will look saggy.

9. Fold the corners into a neat pleat and staple. There should be evidence on the original piece of material about how this was first done, which might help.

10. Take the replacement bottom cloth – usually hessian or black Diprol – and fold over the raw edges before stapling it into position.

HOW TO MAKE SCATTER CUSHIONS

Cushions can add opulence, colour and comfort to any space, no matter how small, and they are simple to make, especially if you have access to a sewing machine.

1. If you plan to make 45cm (18 inch) cushions, cut out two 50cm (20 inch) squares with careful use of a rule and chalk.

2. Turn the right sides of the material to face each other.

3. Choose a point about 15 cm (6 inches) from a corner to anchor your thread and sew towards the nearest corner.

4. Sew around the three other sides and about 15cm (6 inches) of the first side, leaving a gap of some 20cm (8 inches) in the centre.

5. Turn the cushion cover the right way around.

6. Choose your cushion filler. If you are using a hollowfibre pad, make sure it measures about 5cm (2 inches) more than the cushion cover. If it's feather, look for a cushion that's 10cm (4 inches) bigger, as these will compress more quickly over time.

7. Using a neat slip stitch, sew up the opening.

HOW TO REPLENISH THE STUFFING IN A SOFA SEAT CUSHION

Over time, sofas start to sag as the stuffing inside is pummelled flat. This is a quick way to breathe new life into an old suite.

1. Buy some hollowfibre stuffing from a craft store – you may well use more than you think.

2. Take the cushion cover off.

3. Inside there will be another cover, this time made of calico or another utilitarian fabric that holds the stuffing in place. Unpick a portion of one of the back seams.

4. Push the stuffing into the cushion, taking care to space it evenly across the seat. Some cushions will have channels running down the seats that can be filled.

5. When the cushions look plump, sew up the opening with blanket stitch and replace the cover.

MEMORABLE MOMENTS

Sonnaz: 'I get real sense of freedom when I'm working with my hands and I love seeing things come together in front of my eyes. There is a magic that happens, especially when you are doing something for someone who you know will appreciate every detail you consider for them. It is amazing to think that many a craftsperson before me has stood at their bench doing what I am doing. It is fabulous to carry those skills forward.'

A sturdy chair was already a half century old when it was transported to Britain from Germany as a Jewish family fled from Nazi persecution. It was a chair associated with a beloved matriarch who saw her life turned upside-down after political upheaval in Europe.

As a child her great grand daughter plaited the fringe that encased its bottom edge and bounced on its broad seat. Now there was wear on the arms, a split in the seat and springs that were skew. Yet the chair's dark blue fabric was reinforced with squares of carpet, an upholstery technique that expert Sonnaz had never seen before. When she began stripping back the faded material, it seemed they were used as part of a repair. In any event, both colourful carpet sections were part of the furniture's familiarity and the owner wanted to keep them.

Wearing a mask to defend herself against a century and a half of gathered dust, she removed the old upholstery, revealing the original colour of the chair fabric as she did so. Jay used it to match some new material for the covers while Sonnaz retrieved the best preserved portion to make a scatter cushion.

Her first job on the chair was installing the webbing, the strips that support the body weight, which she stapled into place to get a firm grip in the ageing chair frame. Then she put in new springs which she lashed to keep them in place. After putting a layer of cotton felt on the seat for comfort she covered everything in a tight layer of calico, to hold everything firmly.

Still, Sonnaz was pondering the real purpose of the carpet pieces. She spent some of her childhood in Iran, the home of Persian rugs, and still had never seen a soft furnishings configuration like this one. As it happened, art conservator Lucia Scalisi, who had been observing the project from across The Repair Shop, had the answer.

The carpeting was in fact the split sides of a saddlebag, once used on a horse or camel and would have been decorated with the fringe that bedecked the bottom of the chair which colour-matched the squares perfectly. From clues in the pattern, it seemed the saddlebag was made in the second half of the nineteenth century in Shiraz, Iran. After Sonnaz stitched the saddlebag bag into place she shared her information with the owner, who had no idea of its provenance.

Clearly, the forced move from Germany was only half of the chair's story while its link to Iran would likely never be known.

* * *

The torn baize of a collapsible card table dating from the 1940s was marked with teacup rings and the imprint of a Worcestershire sauce bottle. If the table was to come into use again, the material would have to be replaced.

Yet Sonnaz and Will Kirk, who paired up to fix the table, were reluctant to bin the baize as it was a tangible link for one man to his grandfather. Not only did the older man used to eat at the table but he had his grandsons gather around it as together they worked out forthcoming match results in the hope of winning big on the weekly football pools. A family man, he didn't necessarily have money to spend on the youngsters but devoted ample amounts of time to them.

Biaze is a woollen fabric that's been made in England since 1783, making it one of the country's oldest fabrics. Apart from card tables it's been used for soundproofing, altar cloths and monks' habits.

The baize-covered section of the table could be liberated from the frame. One side of it was green, the other red. Sonnaz used shears to cut out the baize that remained, exposing the bare wood beneath. After stapling new fabric to the insert top and bottom, Sonnaz turned her talents to making coasters and a mat out of the redundant sections.

Will cleaned the corners of the table out before gluing and clamping them, to stop a previously persistent wobble. He also polished up the wooden legs. Now it was a table the owner hoped would become a living room memory for his own grandchildren.

USEFUL TERMS

Lashing springs: Tying springs into place so the load is equally spread.

Gimp pins: Fine, coloured tacks.

Webbing: Closely woven fabric strips for supporting the seats of upholstered chairs.

Deck: The flat platform under a seat cushion but above the springs, usually in plain material.

Ragtacker: The colloquial name for a journeyman upholsterer.

Sonnaz's List of Do's and Don'ts

- *Do measure twice or three times before cutting material, to help eliminate costly errors.*

- *Don't use blunt shears to cut material.*

- *Do take time. If something isn't going right, walk away and come back the next day when the answer to the problem will probably fall into place.*

- *Don't skimp on quality. From springs to stuffing, buy the best on offer in order to get great results. For example, hessian comes in two weights: 10oz (283g) and 12oz (340g). Always use the heavy weight option for upholstery.*

- *Do go the extra mile with fine detail.*

- *Don't assume you know everything. Always be open to learning new things, especially from people who've mastered the craft over decades.*

- *Do think about customising cushions, curtains or duvet covers by adding fringes, pompoms, braid or tassels.*

CERAMICS

In a fleeting moment, family heirlooms that have been cherished over several lifetimes can be reduced to shards. Many of us know that sinking feeling, as a sickening crash fills our ears, while cold dread clasps our hearts.

So it was for Norman Jenner, whose misplaced foot descending a ladder in his lounge started a domino effect that ended with a nineteenth century blue-and-white pitcher lying in pieces on the floor.

The statuesque ceramic once belonged to wife Brenda's grandmother. An impressive nineteenth century commemorative piece, its sides were busy with depictions of warriors in battle and were a source of endless fascination for Brenda as a child. She didn't know it then, but these were scenes from an historic massacre at Teutoburg Forest in Germany in 9 AD, when Roman soldiers were defeated by Germanic fighters and 35,000 legionnaires died.

Brenda finally inherited it after the death of her mother and it took pride of place in a bay window of her home before it toppled . After keeping the body of the pitcher and assorted remnants in a box for 15 years, the couple visited The Repair Shop to seek help from ceramics expert Kirsten Ramsay.

For her, commonplace domestic disasters like this one are meat and drink. Her first concern is always that as many broken pieces as possible are collected up and kept before they disappear up a vacuum. Happily, the Jenners had collected all the large pieces and many of the smaller ones. Then she must assess what she has – and what is missing – by fitting the fragments together like a 3-D jigsaw puzzle, feeling for that perfect fit to indicate the piece has found its proper home. Using tape to keep the pieces in place, she can start to picture an end result.

As she looked over the pitcher pieces, she discovered that Norman's mishap was not the first it had suffered. Yellowing glue clearly visible on the inside betrayed a previous breakage with a less-than-professional repair. It meant Kirsten had to remove all the old adhesive, by wielding a sharp scalpel, creating for herself several more pieces to fix.

Her next job was to remove dust and grime gathered on the glaze of the 120cm (47 inch) tall pitcher using a steam cleaner. It's a satisfying job, and also an ideal opportunity to put the item under close scrutiny, getting acquainted with its smallest details. In the frantic action played out on the pitcher, she saw raised swords, rearing horses and numerous silent screams in addition to the flowing scrollwork that bordered the terrifying tableau. And then she noticed a further crack in the body of the jug, caused during the firing process at the time it was made. It was a raised ridge rather than a rupture and had previously been filled with a rudimentary substance like plaster.

Before tackling that, she did a second dummy run with the broken pieces, this time scheduling the order in which she would glue them. There's no room for guesswork at this point. Without a system it's easy to bond four pieces in place and consequently find a fifth locked out. Using epoxy resin, she finally secured the pieces, once again using tape to hold them in position while the adhesive cured.

The job was far from complete, however. Often Kirsten would not repair a firing crack as it forms part of an item's heritage. But this was a large crack down the side of a big ceramic, so she chose to work on it to improve its stability. After removing the material that had been used previously to fill the firing crack, she mixed a two-part adhesive with various pigments to recreate the blue colour and unobtrusively pack the hairline fracture that remained. To plug gaps created by missing pieces, she used modelling clay mimicking the raised patterns evident on the original.

At last it was time to put the finishing touches to the pitcher and return it to its former glory. This entailed artful use of carefully mixed paints. The electric lights of The Repair Shop barn reflecting against the pitcher's shiny glaze made colour matching difficult, so Kirsten took the jug outside to complete the work in daylight.

When Brenda and Norman returned, they were stunned by the seamless repair, with the pitcher looking just as it had years before in Brenda's childhood. For them, it was like bringing a member of the family home. Through her painstaking observation, detailed attention and patience, Kirsten liberated this crushed pot from the attic and readied it for the next three generations.

TYPES OF CERAMICS

Ceramics is an umbrella term that covers a multitude of pieces that are shaped, decorated, glazed and fired. Remnants from ancient times reveal that ceramics have been part of human existence across the globe for millennia. In the earliest examples, clay was baked on a bonfire or left to dry in the sun. However, clay artefacts remained porous until the use of protective glaze spread from Egypt from the first century BC. Although terms related to ceramic items are commonly used interchangeably, there are defining traits to each.

Porcelain: This was first developed in China in about AD 600, when white kaolin clay was mixed with the mineral feldspar and quartz and fired at a high temperature. Its surface was translucent and smooth and it became the envy of trading nations everywhere. Inferior imitations of porcelain were made in Europe prior to the first decade of the eighteenth century, but lacked its hardness, translucency and colour. It was in Meissen, Germany, that the first proper European porcelain was then made, with French and British manufacturers soon adapting the recipe for themselves. Today, porcelain is fired at about 1,455 degrees Celsius (2,650 degrees Fahrenheit).

Fine china: The name given to European-made porcelain-style items, by way of recognition of the country where the porcelain tradition began. It's fired at 1,200 degrees Celsius (2,200 degrees Fahrenheit), making it softer than porcelain and more suitable for plates and cups.

Bone china: This is made with powdered bone ash mixed with ball clay and kaolin, in a process developed by Josiah Spode and his son, also called Josiah, in the nineteenth century. Again, the kiln temperature is not as high as that used in making porcelain.

Pottery: A catch-all term that usually refers to functional clay objects.

Earthenware: This term applies to the earliest pottery found, usually made from red clay and fired at a low temperature, and it is still available today. Earthenware is naturally porous and needs to be glazed before it is water-resistant.

Stoneware: Made from clay feldspar and silica, stoneware is more durable than earthenware and it is also non-porous.

A Selection of Kirsten's Studio Tools

With vast technical expertise at her disposal, Kirsten has numerous textbook ways of approaching a restoration. But sometimes she goes off grid, for example, using paint stripper rather than steam or a scalpel to take previously glued ceramics apart. To each project she brings a clear eye and fresh judgement, but these are her most frequently used items.

1. **Sharp scalpel:**
   To remove aged adhesive used
   in previous restoration work and also to cut back
   filling material.

2. **Steam cleaner:** To effectively clean items, a steam cleaner is useful because steam doesn't make anything too wet. Preparation is key and that means removing all dirt and dust, not just for aesthetics, but also to ensure the adhesives bond properly. Conservation is a niche area, so Kirsten's steam cleaner, with its narrow nozzle and jet of steam, was in fact made for companies constructing dentures.

3. **Specially manufactured adhesives:** The kind conservators like Kirsten use will stay stable for 50 or even 100 years in the correct conditions, which avoids sagging yellow glue appearing around repairs in the future .

4. **Magic tape:** Used for ceramics repair as it is clear and stretchy.

5. **Paint brushes:** These are necessary to complete the decorative pattern that's been disrupted by a breakage. For delicate patterns she uses the finest available.

6. **Specialist water-based acrylics:** She uses these for re-touching. Her aim with artwork is not only accuracy, but also to recreate the tone and ambience, sympathetically blending the restoration to the style of the piece.

7. **Sandpaper and polishing fabrics:** Repairs are made smooth with the use of fine glass paper and cloths.

My Favourite Tools

Kirsten's go-to tool is a flexible steel spatula (size no. 47) that she's used since she was a student. With it she delves into hidden crevices and prods at previous restorations, applies filler to cracks and mixes pigments for painting. At work it's like an extension of her hand. When one breaks, she buys a replacement from a specialist British company established 125 years ago to provide tools for sculptors.

HALLMARKS OF THE ERA

Ceramics have existed alongside mankind since the start of the earliest civilisation, when pliable riverside mud was sun-dried to form plates or vessels.

There's a rich history associated with it but few people today will have a Ming vase, made during the rule of a Chinese dynasty which ended in the mid-seventeenth century, or even a piece of English Delftware, tin glazed pottery made between 1550 and the late eighteenth century. But there is an opportunity here to define some of the major movements that frame ceramic history.

18TH CENTURY

For the enthusiastic amateur a tour of china likely to be found at the back of the cupboard probably starts in the era of Josiah Wedgwood. He went into business in Burslem, Stoke-on-Trent, amid a highly competitive market, and instituted all the principles of industrialisation.

A stickler for high standards, Wedgwood was also fascinated by scientific advances. He is credited with perfecting transfer printing on to pieces, to replace the labourious hand-painting process, as well as pioneering marketing techniques which saw his pottery sold across the globe. One of his great commercial successes was branded 'Queensware' after Queen Charlotte commissioned a tea service in his cream-coloured china in 1765. Afterwards he trumpeted the royal link at every opportunity.

His great rival, Josiah Spode, is credited with advances in transfer printing in underglaze and raising the quality of bone china. Both men dominated the pottery industry that was flourishing in the eighteenth century and more people had the chance to own their own dinner services than ever before.

19TH CENTURY

All the well-defined cultural movements that swept through British society after this point had a marked influence on ceramics. The Arts and Crafts movement, in which William Morris was a leading figure, fell back on simple design, luxuriant glaze and assured quality as a protest against industrialization. It was hotly followed by Art Nouveau, recognizable for its sinuous curves, flowing lines and using nature as its major inspiration.

EARLY 20TH CENTURY

Following the First World War, Art Deco prevailed, with startling geometric shapes, bold colours and innovative design. Clarice Cliff and Susie Cooper were amongst its most famous designers. Then came the decorative modernism of the jazz age.

But it was practicalities that were to make a bigger mark on the ceramics industry in the twentieth century than design. Decoration by coloured lithography first appeared late in then. In short, it's a printing process rooted in the solid chemical principle that grease and water don't mix, thus limiting the absorption of ink, but blips in its results had British potters quickly returning to more conventional options. After the First World War it was still considered expensive despite its extensive use in Europe, but by the 1950s the process dominated, widening the range of decorative pottery.

POST-WAR

Its contribution was especially noticeable as manufacturers responded to the austerity of the war years with richer and more ornate designs.

There were strong colours and a sense of confidence in 1960s design as British style proliferated. Although it didn't last, there were ceramic success stories, including the soaring popularity of Scandanavian design.

It's also worth noting that for every modern pattern there were large numbers of traditional ones throughout the twentieth century that remained family favourites, with Royal Albert's old country roses being prominent among them.

Technological changes in the kitchen called for a new dynamism and saw British designers and producers respond with improved clay and glazes so that pots could tolerate the microwave, a freezer and dishwashers, and could be transferred effortlessly to the dinner table. Despite astonishing progress, crazing, the spider's web of fracture lines that appear when a glaze is under duress, still torments less experienced ceramicists today.

PROJECTS

HOW TO FIX A BROKEN ARM OR HEAD
ON A PORCELAIN FIGURINE

Frequently broken, and hardest to mend, is a plate or platter, when even experts like Kirsten are challenged. When it is created, a plate is charged with an inner tension during manufacture in the kiln. The breakage means that tautness is gone, and recreating it so that the plate properly aligns is problematic. Handles are likewise difficult, with gravity working against repairs in progress. But there are easier tasks to undertake, like attaching an arm or head detached from a figurine.

1. Firstly, thoroughly clean all the pieces involved. Wash and thoroughly air dry them – Kirsten leaves them for several days before starting work.

2. Before starting the repair, wipe exposed edges with acetone to make sure they are grease and grime free.

3. On a clean surface, lay out the bits that are being reassembled to get some idea of how to rebuild and to see if any of the pieces are missing.

4. With some previously cut thin strips of magic tape at hand, do a trial run to establish in which order the pieces should be put in place.

5. Try not to scrape fragments together as that risks losing the sharp connections that exist between pieces.

6. Number the pieces so you know that you won't miss out part of the puzzle.

7. Choose an adhesive that's suitable for the material, ideally one that's softer than the item so any errors are reversible.

8. Don't use too much of it.

9. As you work, use tape again to hold the pieces in place like an extra pair of hands while the adhesive cures.

10. Wipe away excess adhesive with acetone on cotton wool swabs.

11. Stand the item safely while it dries, putting the least pressure possible on the repaired area. If gravity is likely to draw the newly attached limb down, then consider using a sand box to support it while the adhesive cures.

12. Remove the tape when the adhesive is dried, or cured, and remove any further protruding excess with a scalpel.

13. Cracks and small areas of loss can be filled using fine surface Polyfilla. If necessary, rub back carefully using fine sandpaper.

14. Study the item carefully to work out how best to re-touch the repair, if necessary. This can be done with specialist ceramic restoration acrylic glaze and colours. You don't have to necessarily ape the work of the original artist as creating an overall impression may be sufficient.

MEMORABLE MOMENTS

Kirsten Ramsay: 'There is nothing I like more than sitting, cleaning objects. It's an opportunity to look at how they are made. You get to see amazing details that normally would be missed.'

Heirlooms aren't necessarily items of high value or fine art. It's the things that have sentimental significance or longevity that gladden the heart. For one family, its treasured memento was a large, brash barge-wear teapot passed down through the female line, representing the contribution of generations past and the hopes that lay wrapped up in those yet to come.

Sadly, the passage of the teapot was going to be interrupted after the untimely death of a 28-year-old mum. It meant the next recipient would be her 16-month-old daughter and her grandparents were determined the youngster should receive it in the best possible shape.

Barge-wear is distinctive for its chocolate brown glaze, usually described as treacle, and its bulging hand colour motifs. It was made in and around Burton-on-Trent between about 1860 until 1914 and often bought as a gift to mark a birth, anniversary or a marriage. Sometimes the banner on the side of barge-wear has a less personal motto, like 'Remember Me'. Commonly called Measham china, it was named for a town lying on the Ashby canal where the pottery was sold.

This time Kirsten was presented with something that had a number of cracks and chips – but those were not her biggest challenge. Missing from the top of the lid was a finial in the shape of a tiny teapot that had to be made from scratch.

Still, her first priority was to consolidate a crack running down the side of the teapot which rendered the pear-shaped body at risk of breaking into fragments. When that was done she put a putty base on the lid where the new teapot finial would be attached.

Then it was time to hand-sculpt the new baby teapot that mimicked the larger model, in pliable clay. Having mirrored the details on the body of the Victorian pot, she let the new addition dry, rubbed it down and finally painted it in a treacly brown, carefully manoeuvring the teapot lid from workbench to teapot by holding its base.

Finally, it was in pristine condition and ready for the family to collect, hoping to one day tell the story of a mother's love through an item lovingly maintained.

* * *

Gifts personalised by a photograph have always been popular – although decades ago they were not as ubiquitous as today.

When one Irishman brought a soft heart-shaped china plate bearing a hand-coloured picture of his wife, it became a symbol of enduring love. It accompanied them when they emigrated to London and took pride of place in the family home for years.

But while marriage and family life stayed strong, the plate was altogether less resilient. At one point it was accidentally shattered and no amount of glue could disguise the damage.

Five weeks after the woman in the photo died, it was brought into The Repair Shop by her daughter, now more attached to the cracked keepsake than ever before.

For Kirsten it was a daunting task, with fractures clearly evident across the transposed photograph and bits of the decorative plate edge missing. Her first job was to thoroughly clean it and remove the adhesive built up around the well-meaning repairs that had already taken place. She paid special attention to the break edges to ensure they were free of old glue and grime.

In a dry run, before fixing the plate, she put the shards together using her fingertips to sense a bite, which happens when broken edges properly lock into place. While most did, there was one section that didn't produce that connection she expected. For a second time she cleaned the edges and came across a scintilla of old adhesive that had been missed. When all the pieces were bonded into place the plate once again regained some of the structural strength it would have had as new.

To recreate the missing decoration surrounding the plate she pressed moulding material firmly into some that remained intact. She then moved this newly created mould to the missing section and filled it with epoxy resin, forming a new frill. Although the plate and the new section were both white, Kirsten knew from years of experience that not all whites are equal. So when the resin was dry she had to carefully colour match the paint, adding minute amounts of different hues to get the right result.

The last stage was the most difficult, to disguise the repaired lines that seared across the photograph. Dark colours would have left the picture looking sinister so Kirsten chose minimal intervention that would nonetheless mask the intrusive lines. For a grieving daughter, it was a poignant reminder of a woman who remained at the heart of her family.

* * *

There are a lucky few that do possess work by acknowledged artists, although that didn't end well for one woman whose stunning terracotta jug made by Frenchman Jean Lurçat ended up in pieces on her floor. It danced off the window sill thanks to heavy duty drilling going on in the road outside.

Born in 1892, Lurcat studied alongside Matisse, Cezanne and Renoir. He is best remembered for exquisite tapestries – as well as his work for the French Resistance during the Second World War. This jug was reminiscent of the ceramics produced by Picasso, who Lurcat also knew.

The base of the white jug with a bold black design was largely unscathed but its top section and handle were shattered. The owner scooped up all the fragments, even brushing its dust into an envelope – a move that Kirsten advocates for all breakages. At her workbench Kirsten then laid all the pieces, from large chunks to slithers, as she tried to work out where each belonged.

Even the smallest shred was replaced where possible, to reduce the amount of time spent filling, sanding and re-painting. Still, it didn't look like a new model based on the original, as some of the scars still showed.

It was, said Kirsten, a sympathetic restoration, meaning that it wasn't perfect but nor was the integrity of the item substantially altered. When the three-dimensional puzzle was completed she decided not to smother it in paint to disguise the repair lines but leave them visible although not eye-catchingly apparent. The jug's unexpected fall – and ensuing repair – had been absorbed into its story.

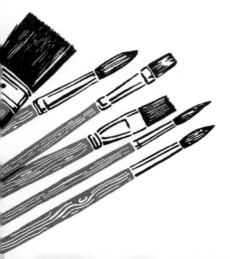

Useful Terms

Adhesive: The conservator's term for glue.

Bond: The conservator's term for sticking.

Abrade: To wear away by friction.

Sprung: A tension introduced in production into bowls, platters and big dishes and released when it's broken.

Shards: Pieces of broken ceramic.

Sherds: Fragments of historic pottery, also called potsherd.

On glaze: Decoration on top of the glaze, like gilding.

Underglaze: Decoration beneath the glaze, like painting.

Micro-mesh: A mildly abrasive fabric, which helps to smooth down ceramic surfaces after repairs or prior to polishing.

Plastic polish: Originally designed for cleaning the canopies of Spitfires and still used to clean aircraft windscreens today, plastic polish is used in ceramics restoration to add shine.

Renaissance wax: Developed by the British Museum in the fifties, this is another way of providing a protective coat to some items.

Kirsten's List of Do's and Don'ts

- Do clean decorative ceramics if they are not broken. The first step is to determine whether the item is glazed, that is, whether its surface has a glass-like coating. This is protective, so it's fine to wash ceramics in a washing-up bowl with mild, soapy water. But don't treat broken or unglazed items the same way as this can lead to damage and staining.

- Don't use superglue in a ceramics repair. Ideally, it should be possible to take a repaired item apart again at some point, particularly if the glue has aged and discoloured.

- Do try the tap test to work out if your item has unseen cracks. Using your knuckle, gently knock its body and listen. There's a ringing sound if it's intact, but if a dull thud sounds, it means there's a flaw to be found.

- Don't be tempted to fix a handle on a teacup in case the repair gives way and you end up with hot liquid in your lap. Only mend it if it's to become a decorative item.

PAINTINGS

When his favourite painting was holed during a house move, Terry Courtley considered mending it with a patch and some paints. It's a quick-fix, low-cost solution that no doubt lures many into the treacherous territory of DIY art repairs, blind to the pitfalls.

Fortunately he decided against this initial instinct and brought it instead to The Repair Shop so conservator Lucia Scalisi could unleash her expertise – and reveal just what it takes to patch up a painting so you can't see the joins.

As a young man who had just started a small business, Terry bought the painting having been attracted by the tree-lined avenue depicted in it. He had grown up on the south coast and, with its oak trees and parkland, the picture reminded him of the Ilex Way at Goring-by-Sea in West Sussex.

In the bottom left-hand corner was the monogram JWM and a date, 1887. Not only did it now have a gap in the canvas, its finer detail was obscured by years of gathered dust. Altogether, it was a complex repair of a canvas made brittle by age.

Lucia's first task was cleaning the tabby weave canvas, a satisfying if slow process. At the start of it she carried out a 'spit' cleaning test, with saliva-soaked cotton wool rolled gently over a small section of the canvas. Enzymes in the saliva help to remove the loose surface dirt and give telling results. An oily film reveals the picture has likely been hung in a city, yellow brown marks indicate it belonged to a smoker, waxy residues probably point to a church setting where candles have frequently been lit, while smoke ash signposts that it's fire-affected. No one has enough spit to tackle a major item, so surface cleaning is carried out with a solution tailor-made for each task.

Lucia can discern as much from the wall-facing back of a painting as the front. Flipped over, she sees how well it fits the frame and whether it's previously been lined or cut down. She may well catch a glimpse of a hitherto hidden corner that will reveal how just dirty it has become.

When she lifted this 130-year-old painting out of its frame she was greeted with the expected level of dust and fly carcasses – previously she has found the skeleton of a bird tucked away here. Even glass-covered paintings can become grime traps if the paper on the back is torn. This time the detritus was swiftly dealt with by her professional museum vacuum, specifically made for delicate objects. Carefully, she removed the tacks that attached the painting to its wooden stretcher.

At the margins of the painting there was ample canvas to snip out a small section that would patch the holes. The next job was to line the back of the canvas, to give it additional strength and stability and to hold these sections of infilling firmly in place.

She rolled out a heat-seal adhesive film on the back of the canvas and then pressed on to it some polyester sail cloth, using a specially made iron set at a specific temperature to activate the bonding process. Although the nap bond that she created was strong it was also reversible so, if it was heated again, the sail cloth could have been removed.

After cutting away the excess lining fabric she placed the painting back on its stretcher, using original tack holes to avoid making extra perforations, and precisely folded the corners as if she was making a hospital bed. Looked at from the front the surface was now uneven, dipping where the patches had been laid, so she used filler to raise the level, 'Like plastering on a micro-scale,' she explained. When all exposed areas of canvas were covered and smooth, Lucia could finally open her box of paints.

Oil paints are not an option in any of Lucia's projects. The drying process takes months and by the end of it, the colours have changed from the original.

Lucia works with dry pigments that she mixes with a medium. She not only has to match the colours, but she must emulate the techniques used by this unknown artist to blend her modern brushstrokes with those applied during the nineteenth century. The meticulous work paid off, however, as when Terry came to collect his painting it looked pristine once more.

Pigments and Paint

In simple terms, paint is two materials mixed together: a pigment – which used alone won't stay where it's put – and a medium to bind it so it becomes serviceable. In Lucia's studio dry pigments are stored in glass jars, while the medium she uses is a synthetic resin, chosen for its robust anti-ageing quality.

It's not the only option, though, as numerous mediums can be used with pigments, including glue, casein, waxes, clay and oils. Painters then need a diluent – solvents for synthetic resin, for example, and turpentine for oils – to make the colour flow from the brush.

Earth pigments are long-held palette staples, but that's not to say that there haven't been some changes to the colours used by present-day artists. Lead white was present in most paintings – and household paint – until the twentieth century, when its toxic qualities were finally acknowledged. Titanium white is today's safe alternative.

As well as the six earth pigments Lucia uses daily, there are organic pigments from plants and chemistry set colours too, comprising a palette of 15 dependable colours that she can blend to produce many more. Although the pigments are costly, she uses only tiny amounts with each project, decanting them individually into small glass vials to contain colour pollution.

Conservators are few in number and must pass a colour blindness test before qualifying. With colour blindness affecting an estimated one in 12 men, as compared to one in 200 women, it means there are a more limited number of male candidates for a world where discerning minutely different shades is a prerequisite for the job.

A Selection of Lucia's Workshop Tools

Lucia needs a surprisingly limited selection of tools to salvage or save art of the past.

1. **Fine blade scalpel:** A scalpel like this is usually used for surgery and she is as cautious as any doctor when she wields it on a canvas.

2. **Easel:** The ratchet-operated double easel at her London studio once belonged to Victorian painter George Watts.

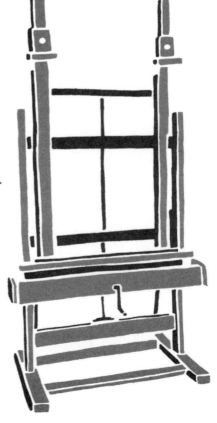

3. **Table:** Lucia needs an uncluttered horizontal space to investigate paintings.

4. **Paint brushes:** Lucia uses expertly made brushes that control the flow of paint.

5. **Heated spatula:** This is used for re-attaching paint flakes.

6. **Lining iron:** This iron secures new canvas to the back of an historic painting.

7. **Cotton wool and bamboo sticks:** These are used to make cleaning swabs.

8. **Chemicals:** As part of more heavy-duty cleaning processes or to remove obstinate layers of varnish, Lucia uses a range of chemicals that she needs a licence to buy.

My Favourite Tools

Conservators like Lucia must borrow from other professions to assemble their equipment. As a consequence, her favourite tool is one usually used in dentistry to mix fillings. She bought two as a student from a dentists' practice, but only uses one, which nestles comfortably in the crook of her hand.

How to Wrap Paintings for Transport

For years Lucia worked at the Victoria and Albert Museum in London, helping to maintain a vast art collection. When it comes to moving pictures, institutions use tailor-made packing cases lined with Plastazote, inert foam that will safely cradle precious cargo until it reaches its destination. Then it's left for days to acclimatise in new surroundings before being opened. That's not an option available to most of us, but there's plenty of scope for paintings to be damaged in transit, as Terry has illustrated. Here Lucia advises on the best way to package pictures.

1. First protect the vulnerable corners by taking a sheet of acid-free tissue paper and folding it into a chunky strip.

2. About two-thirds of the way along, fold the strip 90 degrees, creating a thick right-angled triangle at its heart, compared to two thinner end pieces, which all together look like a pair of wings.

3. Put the midpoint of the triangle's longest edge diagonally across the face of the picture so it touches one corner.

4. Fold both edges of the strip behind the picture so a well-fitting pointed cap is created.

5. Fix in place, using masking tape rather than Sellotape.

6. Make a similar tissue paper cap for the other three corners.

7. Repeat the steps above using bubble wrap to consolidate protection.

8. Take two lengths of cotton tape, one to encircle the height and the second the width of the picture. Lay them across the front of the picture and tape the ends to the back of the picture if it is covered. Tie them if not.

9. After that, the paining is ready to be wrapped in tissue paper and, for a limited time, in bubble wrap to add further protection.

MEMORABLE MOMENTS

Lucia: 'Everything we do there is a story to it in one way or the other. I just love this workshop because of that.'

Children playing hide-and-seek at home sank gratefully into an obscured spot beneath a desk and behind a painting being stored on the floor during house decoration. Naturally, they wanted to gain an advantage on the seeker so they used a pencil to poke several spy-holes through the canvas that blocked them from view.

At the time they didn't realise the painting, done by a distant family member, was worth thousands of pounds. Worse still, when art conservator Lucia saw it she not only recognised it as the work of Fred Appleyard (1874–1963), whose paintings hang in the Tate art gallery today, but suspected the damage might be beyond repair.

The owner – the artist was his grandmother's uncle – wasn't surprised to hear her sober verdict, given the extent of the holes and the tears that now peppered the country cottage scene.

Lucia's first challenge was to release the canvas from its frame. Immediately she passed the wooden surround to Will to enlarge its window by 4mm on each side, so the picture could be replaced rather than rammed in after the repair.

As always, her overarching aim was to keep the artwork as close to its original condition as possible. For this she has an array of specialist equipment and professional techniques that would leave even the most enthusiastic amateur floundering.

Aiming to preserve as much of the existing paint as possible she fixed the perforated edges around the rips using tape, so nothing more could flake off and be lost. When that was in place she flipped the painting over to work on the back of the canvas, initially using a process of carefully applied moisture in minute quantities and blotting paper to shrink the stretched fibres back to something like their proper length before placing nylon gossamer patches over the holes.

Back on the front side she carefully filled the crevices left by the healed rips using an acrylic filler, that was both soft and plasticised. This has to be gently smoothed to make an even surface before the paint can be applied. Then it was a case not only of colour matching but of being faithful to the integrity of the artist. The reward for patient hours spent poring over the artwork was that Lucia exceeded her own expectations, producing a canvas where outward signs of her work were all-but invisible.

* * *

At the start of the twentieth century living in a rambling country home with extensive gardens wasn't solely the preserve of the rich.

There were staff who kept the house in order and gardeners who saw to the luxuriant plot surrounding it.

During the Second World War a housekeeper ended up living at Ickneild House in Tring, Hertfordshire, with her daughter and granddaughter, a young girl who spent her courting days in the garden of the house and finally left there as a bride.

Today one of her prized possessions is a canvas of that same house painted by its owner, Violet Mcdougall, in the early part of the twentieth century and presented to her grandmother. Unfortunately, it was extensively damaged by fire 40 years ago and had been stowed in the attic since.

Some of its problems were starkly apparent, like a broken frame and substantial white marks where the paint had been burnt. Only on closer inspection did Lucia notice a vast array of small spots that were tiny but deep so would catch the light if they were left untended.

But her first task was to consolidate the lumps of paint that were in danger of lifting, using a heated spatula to activate adhesive which were in turn sealed by small sections of acid-free tissue paper. Then it was time to carefully clean the canvas, removing the tissue as she progressed. Beneath there were blazes of bright colour along flower beds that had been dulled by accrued dirt.

Lucia then had to fill an estimated one thousand spots of paint loss, ranging from small to minute, to ensure every semblance of damage was eradicated. To do this she put on an illuminated magnifying head-band, so she could see almost every original brush stroke. For Lucia, getting as close to a work of art as the creator is one of the privileges of the her job as conservator.

Using colour-matched tones she finally covered the filler she'd put on without having to encroach on the artist's work. The aim was that no one would be to see her contribution while the vast majority of the original paint was still intact.

For the owners the revived painting, now a sentimental symbol of a love story that lasted a lifetime, made them feel young once more.

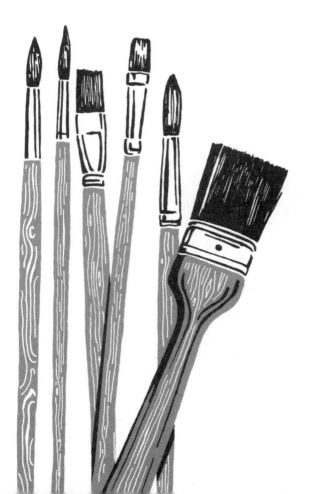

USEFUL TERMS

Stretcher: The wooden framework around which a painting is mounted.

Diluent: A substance that dilutes.

Winchester bottles: Narrow-necked 2.5 litre glass bottles that contain the costly chemicals Lucia uses in her work.

Tabby weave: Also known as plain weave, this is the most commonly occurring canvas with a warp and weft threads simply interwoven.

Polyurethene varnish: A mid-twentieth century invention that's particularly difficult to remove from paintings because it's insoluble and goes grey with age.

Lucia's List of Do's and Don'ts

Lucia's love of art was sparked when she was a schoolgirl, and fanned by Sheffield's museum service picture lending scheme. Having been loaned a picture, she took it home on the bus, which would probably be top on her list of 'don'ts' today. Here's her guide to best domestic practice when it comes to art.

- *Do hang pictures on the wall. It's the safest place for them to be.*

- *Don't touch the surface of a painting.*

- *Don't wipe the frame or any other part of the picture with a wet cloth. If you don't clean a painting, it probably won't fall apart, but should you wash it, it might.*

- *Don't used bubble wrap as a long-term solution for storing pictures. It releases a gas that may harm the picture and could also pockmark its surface.*

CLOCKS

E ffortlessly, an assortment of cogs and wheels spinning this way and that ensures the hands of a mechanical clock move forwards and at the right frequency. Skeleton clocks, so called for having no body, are enchanting showpieces for revealing the exquisite harmony of every tiny motion. First seen in France at the end of the eighteenth century, the popularity of English-made ones chimed with a Gothic revival in Victorian times and modern versions are still sought after today.

Nigel and Viv Burge had inherited a prized skeleton clock, which once belonged to Nigel's soldier grandfather. After a First World War shell rendered his left arm useless, he took up running to keep fit and won the clock in an athletics competition. The tone of its tick was a cherished childhood memory for Nigel.

Still in pride of place on the mantelpiece, the clock had in truth become neither used nor ornament, as it looked jaded and no longer worked.

Poignantly, the couple brought the clock to The Repair Shop after their son Peter also suffered a catastrophic injury to his left arm following a motorcycle accident. He too had his sights set on competition, for him the Tokyo Paralympics, and they hoped the clock could once again be a shining symbol of courage in adversity.

Clock restorer Steve Fletcher was bowled over by it, not least because the original glass dome that shielded the clock from dust and damage was still intact. His first job was to dismantle the scores of parts, large and small, and to carry out his first, but by no means his only, assessment of what had gone wrong.

Embarking on every project Steve is filled with anticipation, not knowing what he might find. Although decades separate himself and the manufacturer, he feels an affinity as they are treading the same path. In this case the original craftsman was Charles Wieland, one of 35 clockmakers listed in Norwich in 1854.

Almost immediately Steve discovered major problems. One of the pivots responsible for bearing a main wheel was worn to almost nothing, while another cog had a section of teeth bent over so badly they were no longer capable of the slick operation working clocks require.

The pivot was beyond redemption, but forging its replacement was an especially tricky task. In substituting new for old he snipped off the damaged pivot end, drilled the rest out and forged a replacement using specialist equipment. Then he reached for a broken watch-repairers' tool that he'd kept for the useful size of its blunt and tapered blade. Clasping it firmly in one hand, with the damaged cog in the other, he set about manually levering back the bent teeth to an upright position.

Steve transformed the tarnished cogs and wheels by dipping each one into ammonia-based clock cleaning fluid and then scrubbing them with various brushes, so they appeared as new. But this was a project he could not finish alone. This skeleton clock was mounted on a rosewood base decorated with an inlaid metal pattern – and both were in dire need of refurbishment. Happily, The Repair Shop experts are always keen to work as a team.

Will Kirk, the woodwork expert, replaced missing veneer with a matching grain. The new patch was lighter than the rest, but he used pigment and polish to conceal that. As he by turns polished and sanded the base to bring out a long-lost lustre, silversmith Brenton West recreated the intricate metal inlay. Having photocopied the original, Brenton painstakingly cut out a pattern from the paper picture, stuck it on a piece of brass and sawed out a replica.

Then Steve was ready to re-assemble the clock and its many components. Blessed with a brain that sees things in three dimensions and with years of experience behind him, he deftly orchestrated its reconstruction. Sometimes, despite his best efforts, a repaired clock fails to work and he's always prepared to start from scratch, carrying out more assessments as he goes on to find any obscure problem he has missed. This time, however, the mechanism settled back into working life immediately. After the glass was cleaned and a replacement red braid was put on to mask the seam between dome and clock base, it was ready for collection by the Burges. For Nigel it was an emotional moment, made more so when he immediately presented the clock to son Peter.

SERVICING A CLOCK

A ticking clock marks the daily rhythm of a household, with everyone growing accustomed to its calm heartbeat. But there's a risk people take this soothing sound for granted. Inside, the movement of a clock may beat tens of millions of times a year. During a lifetime, the number runs into the billions.

So, it probably shouldn't be a surprise to know that clocks, both large and small, need regular servicing. When owners neglect to put a care plan in place for their timepiece, they put its longevity at risk.

The aim is not just to keep the innards of the clock clean and shiny, but to preserve them by reducing wear and tear. For the purposes of both conservation and maintaining value, it's preferable, but not always possible, to rejuvenate existing parts.

Small clocks need more regular servicing, with carriage clocks benefitting from an overhaul about every eight years. Every dozen years a grandfather clock needs attention. Most clocks run for eight days after being wound and if they begin to falter on that timescale, it's probably a sign they are in need of a service.

In between times, clocks may well need lubrication to keep their movements silky smooth. Without oil, a clock – like a car – may well seize up.

Although this is basic maintenance, both are jobs for an expert clockmaker as tinkering with the inner workings has all kinds of pitfalls, according to Steve. It's essential, for example, to put oil only into the correct places. And it's a specialist clock oil that's called for, rather than multipurpose varieties. Steve's attended to numerous clocks that have come to a shuddering halt after being subjected to a lubricating spray, usually one that gets its best results on car engines.

Clockwork Toys

With his mechanical dexterity, Steve can turn his talents not only to clocks, but also to clockwork toys.

Although Leonardo da Vinci is credited with making a clockwork toy in the early sixteenth century, a golden age occured three centuries after that, when moving tin toys were in vogue. At The Repair Shop, Steve fixed a wind-up Alfa Romeo toy racing car, dating from 1925, repairing its rack and pinion steering system as well as its internal mechanism. The decline in the popularity of mechanical toys corresponds with a rise in the number of battery-powered toys at the end of the twentieth century.

With all their internal joints rivetted into place, clockwork toys were not made to be repaired and, once again, it's unlikely an inexperienced hand or eye could successfully overhaul one. It means breaking into the clockwork mechanism's housing, so there are two repairs to be done instead of one.

A Selection of Steve's Clockmaker Tools

Like most craftsmen, the walls of Steve's workshop are lined with tools, typically with the fine proportions necessary for working with the small parts of a clock. If he doesn't have the right tool for the job, he's likely to design and make one.

1. **Screwdrivers:** Steve bought his first screwdriver when he was aged ten. Since then, his collection has expanded somewhat. In addition to using a screwdriver belonging to his grandfather, Steve inherited tools from his father, also a clock and watch repairer.

2. **Pliers:** Steve has in excess of 50 pliers, each designed slightly differently and appropriate for job-specific tasks.

3. **Tweezers:** These are used for picking up and locating the small parts of clocks and watches.

4. **Lathe:** This is used for a multitude of tasks, for example, turning a new pivot for a clock.

5. **Glasses:** Steve is often filmed wearing two or even three glasses at the same time, to get the maximum magnification necessary for the job in hand.

My Favourite Tools

Steve's favourite tool is a 6 inch (15cm) long ratchet screwdriver, with the shiny maroon of its handle now mostly worn down to wood, hinting at its great age. It's something that belonged to his grandfather, Fred, also a clock and watch repairer. After Fred joined the army in the First World War and was dispatched to the Middle East, his skills were spotted by an officer who sent him back to the comparative safety of the support lines to mend watches and military instruments. As a consequence, he survived the conflict and came home to Witney in Oxfordshire to resume his trade.

It's not known when Fred bought this screwdriver, but in his later years he used it every day, even after his retirement in 1964. After Steve set up a workshop, Fred was a daily visitor and dispensed plenty of advice. Steve was keen to plot his own path, but down the years he has discovered the wisdom of his grandfather's words – and also found he inherited the older man's infinite patience. Now when Steve wields the screwdriver, he feels as if he is holding hands with Fred across the decades. Fortunately, the balance of the tool and the quality of its blade have not been diminished by the passing years.

MEMORABLE MOMENTS

Steve: 'It really gives me great satisfaction to take a clock or watch that is important to somebody and keep it alive for future generations. It is a passion.'

To clockmaker Steve all timepieces are things of beauty. Yet even after years in the business he sometimes encounters examples that even to his experienced eye are little short of stunning. One Victorian clock brought into The Repair Shop captivated him for its sturdy mechanism and eye-catching decoration.

The clock was built in extravagant Louis XIV style, with its pendulum in the shape of the sun. But it was the case with its breath-taking brass and tortoiseshell inlayed patterns that elevated this model above some others of a similar age.

Called Boulle work, the marquetry technique was named for its pioneer, Frenchman Andre-Charles Boulle, who came to prominence when Louis XIV was on the French throne. During the era an obsession for ornate design spread across the continent, not least because Louis XIV, known as 'the Sun King', suddenly withdrew freedom of worship in France, forcing 200,000 Protestant Huguenots to leave for Holland and Britain, many of them accomplished craftsmen.

Steve immediately identified the clock in hand as a Victorian replica built with outstanding craftsmanship. The job naturally fell into two distinct parts: the clock mechanism and the case.

Once it was unscrewed and removed from its housing the heavy clock mechanism was taken to pieces. As he examined each component, Steve found one bent tooth on a single cog capable of seizing up the strike mechanism. All the parts were cleaned before then being re-built by Steve with gloved hands, so there was no risk of human sweat tarnishing the brass workings.

With the case empty he used cotton wool charged with brass cleaning fluid to rejuvenate the Boulle work. That in turn left the mounts decorating the clock face looking dull so these were duly dipped in clock cleaning fluid so they matched the gleam on the rest of the clock. To complete it, he coated both with a Shellac-based lacquer to lock in the glossy finish.

When the two elements of the clock were re-united it was time to see if the chime was sounding sweetly. In fact, it was dull and echoed, until Steve adjusted the gong block. After that it was back in tune and sounded every bit as splendid as it now appeared.

* * *

An elderly 'grandfather' clock arrived for a check-up at The Repair Shop in the nick of time. Although problems weren't evident at first glance, it was dangerously wobbly on its feet. On closer investigation, Steve and woodwork expert Will discovered the wooden plinth at the base of the clock had been made so brittle with the dryness of age it had broken. The elegant timepiece, which towered above them both, was close to toppling over.

Although an engraved plaque on the clock face dated it to 1712 Steve estimated it was probably made in about 1750. The maker

was William Robb, a long-case clock specialist mostly based in Montrose, Scotland, who produced handsome French-style specimens throughout the last half of the eighteenth century.

Even Will didn't realise the extent of the problem when he first inspected the clock case, marking missing corners and other areas scheduled for repair with small swabs of blue tape. Only when the mechanism was removed and he could heave the wooden case on to a work bench did the age-related problems fully reveal themselves. He set about bonding together wood that had sheared off and nourishing the upright panels to re-create a stable case.

Steve had problems of his own to contend with, as the workings of the clock were black with age. It had been at least 20 years since it last worked and, prior to that, Steve estimated it had ticked some seven and a half billion times in its life before its enforced retirement.

Unsurprisingly, some components were worn, although he managed to made minute critical adjustments with careful use of a scalpel rather than having to find replacement parts. There was one new introduction, though: a hammer that would sound the chime every hour.

When it arrived, the ornately engraved clock face was entirely brass. However, originally it would have had a silver-coloured centre and it seemed appropriate to mimic that oft-seen style. Steve worked silver powder gently into this section to give the clock a face lift that would make it look the same as it did in its youth and complete its transformation from a jaded and distant echo of former glory into a show-stopper for a semi.

* * *

A broken pocket watch was the sole link for one Dutchman to his family's history. Given its traumatic journey, it was fortunate to survive at all.

His grandparents lived in Indonesia when they were forced to flee in the face of the Japanese invasion in 1942. Leaving all their possessions, his grandmother only had time to save the watch, which had an Albert chain and a fob bearing her photo.

The couple were separated, with his grandfather sent to work on the Burma railway while his grandmother was dispatched to a camp in Sumatra. As soon as she could, she stitched the watch into the hem of her dress, hiding it from not only guards but other hungry prisoners who would have traded it for food.

Happily both survived the war and returned home to Holland with the watch, their only possession from the era and a symbol of their courage in adversity. But the watch, a Swiss-made Invicta model, hadn't worked for decades before arriving at The Repair Shop.

The moving story resonated with Steve who, after inspecting it with a magnifying eyeglass, was hopeful it would be back ticking after a rigorous clean. But this wasn't something that could be carried out beneath the thatched roof of The Repair Shop barn. He removed it to a more sterile atmosphere as the workings were so fine that any descending dust would only add to the issue.

Both hour and minute hands needs straightening and an additional one had to be found to mark the seconds, which recorded on a small dial on the watch face. A specialist dial restorer helped Steve clean the face and restore the delicately drawn roman numerals on it.

After it was put back together, the watch began to work once more, proving Steve's theory that prison camp grime was the cause of its problems. As the watch once gave reassurance to a hungry internee, its restoration was a comfort to her surviving relatives.

Useful Terms

Movement: The clock's mechanism.

Clock gears: These make the hands of the clock work, comprising larger wheels and smaller pinions.

Balance wheel: A weighted wheel that rotates back and forth to regulate time.

Pendulum: Another method of regulating the speeds at which a clock will run.

Escapement: The mechanical link that releases the power to a balance wheel or pendulum.

Mainspring: The power source for mechanical clocks and watches, with energy stored in it after being wound.

Hairspring: This controls the running speed for a clock or watch with a balance wheel.

Weights: Another power source for differently designed clocks.

Stoppers: A term used by Steve's grandfather Fred and other clockmakers to describe clocks that have an intermittent problem. Despite a repairer's best efforts, they can randomly stop, causing frustration for craftsman and customer alike.

Steve's List of Do's and Don'ts

Stripping down a clock or watch is not for the faint-hearted. There are many parts inside a clock: they may be tiny, fragile and/or have three or four different functions. Ambition is all very well, but without previous experience, there's a risk the components will end up as so much scrap on the workbench. But still, there is much you can do to help preserve the life of your clock.

- *Don't put a clock on the mantelpiece of a working fire, or above or near a radiator. The heat will adversely affect its mechanism. Keep it out of direct sunlight too, for the same reason.*

- *Do make sure your clock is level and stable, whether it's on four feet or hung on a wall, to aid its internal balance. Grandfather clocks – properly called longcase clocks – should stand squarely on the floor or be attached at the back to the wall, to stop the case rocking in sympathy with the pendulum.*

- *Don't carry a clock with its pendulum still attached as that may damage its suspension or skew the clock's balance. Unhook it from the clock casing and carefully lift it out.*

- *Do use a soft cloth or fine paint brush to clean clock cases.*

- *Don't use liquid polish on brass cases in case it seeps into the mechanism.*

- *Do use wax polish rather than silicone sprays when attending to wooden clock cases, to feed the wood.*

- *Don't leave a pendulum clock ticking when you go away. If you let it run down, there's a chance of throwing the clock out of whack or damaging its internal ticker. Stop the pendulum by holding it still for a moment and re-start it when you return.*

- *Do wind a clock fully, but don't try to force those last few clicks of rotation in the hope it will run for longer, as that risks snapping the mainspring.*

- *Don't push clock hands backwards when setting the time. Guide them gently forward around the clock face, pausing if necessary for the clock to strike each hour and half hour.*

- *Do seek advice from a clockmaker about the care of your clock and its internal workings. After the fifteenth century, when weight and spring-driven clocks became increasingly abundant, clocks have been made in all shapes and sizes with different refinements inside, so it's specialist knowledge accrued over years that's needed rather than raw enthusiasm.*

With special thanks to *The Repair Shop* experts
for their contributions to this book.

9 10

BBC Books, an imprint of Ebury Publishing
20 Vauxhall Bridge Road,
London SW1V 2SA

BBC Books is part of the Penguin Random House group of companies
whose addresses can be found at global.penguinrandomhouse.com

Copyright © Woodland Books 2019

Main text by Karen Farrington

This book is published to accompany the television series entitled
The Repair Shop, first broadcast on BBC Two in 2017

First published by BBC Books in 2019

www.penguin.co.uk

A CIP catalogue record for this book is available from the British Library

ISBN 9781785944604

Printed and bound in Great Britain by Clays Ltd, Elcograf S.p.A.

Penguin Random House is committed to a sustainable future for
our business, our readers and our planet. This book is made
from Forest Stewardship Council® certified paper.